I0770194

SON OF SHATTERED SOULS

BOOK TWO IN THE SHATTERED TRILOGY

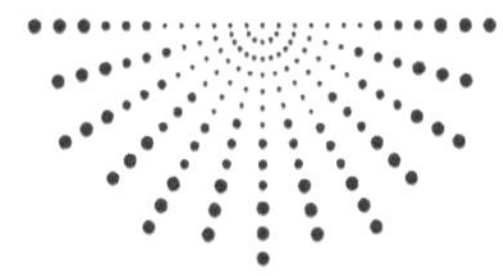

SARA DELAVERGNE

Son of Shattered Souls is a work of fiction. Names, characters, places, and incidents either are the product of the author's imagination, or are used fictitiously. Any resemblance to actual persons, living or dead, events, or locales is entirely coincidental.

© 2024 Sara DeLaVergne

All rights reserved.

ISBN / 979-8-9897129-3-9 / ePub

ISBN / 979-8-9897129-4-6 / Paperback

ISBN / 979-8-9897129-5-3 / Hardcover

No part of this book may be reproduced in any form or by any electronic or mechanical means, including information storage and retrieval systems, without written permission from the author, except for the use of brief quotations in a book review.

For every reader with a story in their heart,

And for every soul with a war in their mind.

PRONUNCIATIONS & DEFINITIONS

A GLOSSARY OF KEY CHARACTERS AND LOCATIONS

ELLORHYS - *(EL-OR-IS)*

The collective name for the known continents of the planet.

The Mythos
> **Aurelia** - *(Or-el-ee-uh)*
> The Primordial Mythos of Light - *deceased*
> **Obsidia** - *(Ub-sid-ee-ah)*
> The Primordial Mythos of Darkness - *deceased*
> **Baelfor** - *(Bail-for)* - Terran Mythos
> **Naia** - *(Nigh-ah)* - Water Mythos
> **Tarlix** - *(Tar-licks)* - Fire Mythos
> **Zephyrus** - *(Ze-fear-us)* - Storm Mythos

ESPERA - *(ES-PEAR-UH)*

Capitol city of Ellorhys, the seat of Imperial power.

ISSARIA ELYSITAO - *(IS-SARI-UH EL-EE-SIT-OW)*
Imperial Princess of Espera, last Imperial of the Elysitao line.

HECATE MESSOREM - *(HECK-ATE MEZ-OR-HEM)*
Empress Regent of Espera, Issaria's aunt, and eldest daughter of Primordial Mythos Obsidia. Wields powerful elemental magic, primarily shadows.

ELON SAINTHART - *(EE-LON SAINT-HEART)*
Captain of Princess Issaria's guard, and oldest childhood friend of the princess. Terran alchemist.

NOTABLE MEMBERS OF ELON'S REBELLION
    RHORI GALERYDER - *(ROAR-EE GALE-RIDER)*
    XENVEIRA LIGHTIZNER - *(ZEN-VEER-UH LIGHT-IS-NER)*
    ROANE WETHERWOOD - *(ROW-N WEATHER-WOOD)*
    CALTAC KHOLOZZO *(KAL-TACK COAL-OS-SO)*
    SAFAIA CARDINALÉ - *(SA-FY-AH CARD-IN-ALL-AY)*
    MAIYRA CARDINALÉ - *(MY-RUH CARD-IN-ALL-AY)*

HINHALLOW - *(HEE-N-HOLLOW)*

The western most city on the Southern Continent. Ruled by the Ballentine family for generations.

CALIX BALLENTINE - *(KAY-LICKS BAIL-EN-TINE)*
Crown Prince of Hinhallow, a powerful fire magician with armament magic.

AKINTUNDE BALLENTINE - (*AH-KIN-TOON-DAY BAIL-EN-TINE*)

King of Hinhallow, known as the Warlord of the West. A fire magician with armament magic.

EMMALEIGH BALLENTINE - (*EMMA-LAY BAIL-EN-TINE*)

Queen of Hinhallow, mother of Calix, Bexalynn, and Darres. Terran magician of unknown talent.

BEXALYNN BALLENTINE - (*BECKS-UH-LIN BAIL-EN-TINE*)

Princess of Hinhallow. Calix's younger sister. A fire magician of unknown talent.

DARRES BALLENTINE - (*DARE-ES BAIL-EN-TINE*)

Infant brother of Calix and Bexalynn. His magic has not manifested yet.

SHAIRI CHRYSANTHOS - (*SHY-REE CHRIS-AN-THOSE*)

Princess of Ares, ward of King Akintunde since before the Eventide divided the land. A Terran magician with a poison immunity.

ISSARIA'S HANDMAIDS
    RHAMINTA - (*RA-MINT-UH*)
    EIREN - (*EYE-REN*)
    CIZABET - (*SEES-AH-BET*)
    ASMY - (*AS-ME*)
    CYLISE - (*SIGH-LEASE*)

CALIX'S GUARD
    RAIF EVANOFF - (*RAY-F EVE-IN-OFF*)
    ZAKARIAN - (*ZACH-AIR-E-EN*)
    ALANDER - (*ALL-AND-ER*)

RHUNMESC - *(RUNE-MESS-K)*

The only citadel on the northern continent. This frosty stronghold has long been held by the Wintersea family.

SHURA WINTERSEA - *(SURE-UH WINTER-SEA)*
Prince of Rhunmesc.

RISA AMORELLE - *(REESE-AH AH-MORE-EL)*
Commander of Prince Shura's forces.

PHELIX STORMGREN - *(FEE-LICKS STORM-GREN)*
Captain of Prince Shura's guard.

OTHER

JALLAH COPPERKNOLL - *(JA-LA COPPER-NOL)*
A fearsome slave trader of unknown magical talent.

KIDALMA - *(KEY-DOLL-MA)*
Elderly woman on Jallah's crew. She is a Terran oracle and uses paper-folding to divine the future.

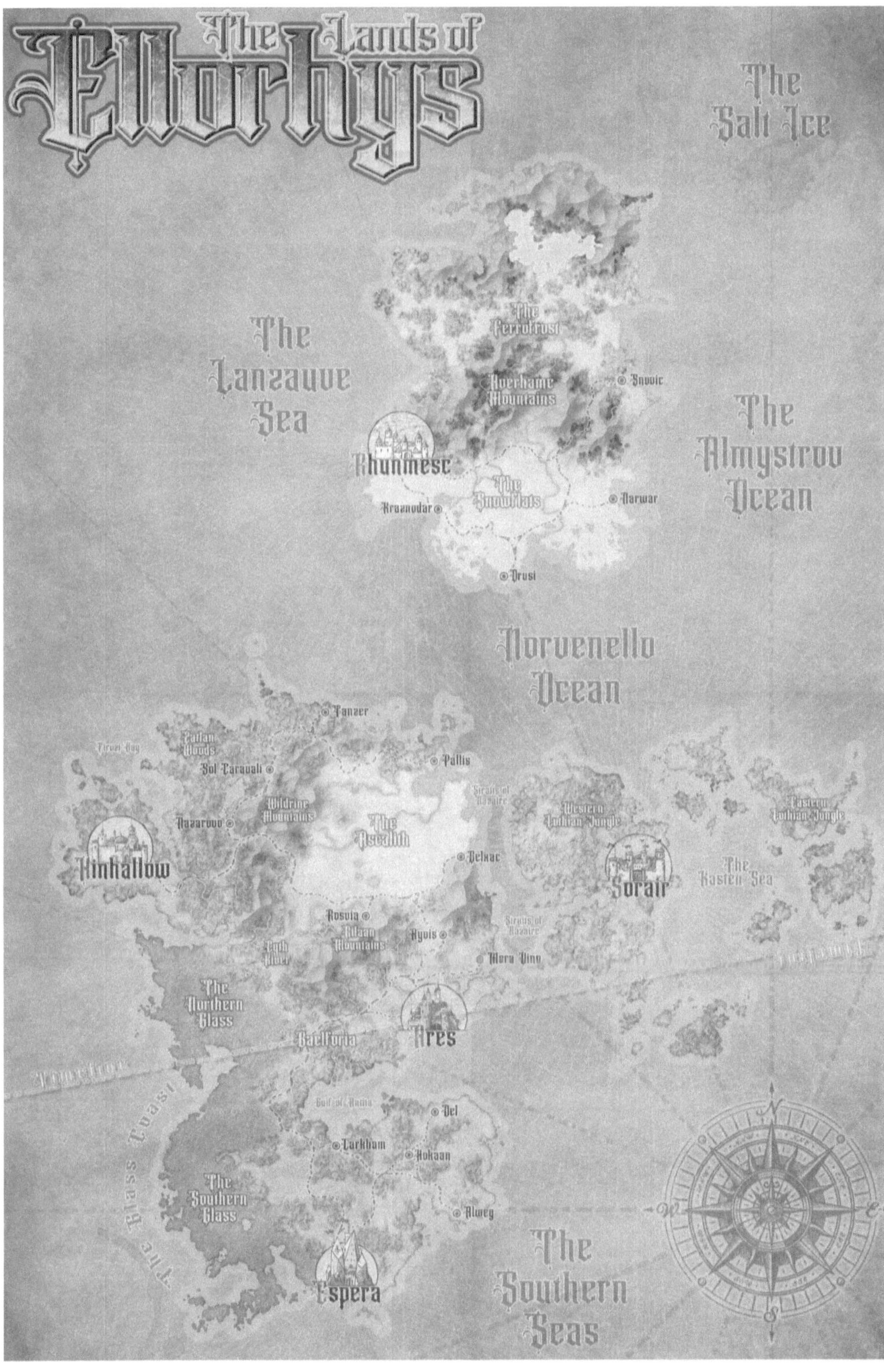

The Lands of Ellorhys
The Salt Ice
The Lanzauve Sea
The Ferrofrost
Averhame Mountains
Snovic
The Almystrov Ocean
Rhunmesc
The Snowflats
Kraanodar
Narwar
Drusi
Norvenello Ocean
Tanzer
Tiruzi-Bay
Taffan Woods
Pallis
Sol Caravali
Strait of Nazaire
Wildrine Mountains
Western Luthian Jungle
Eastern Luthian Jungle
Nazarovo
The Ascalith
Sorair
The Kasten Sea
Ninhallow
Delnac
Rosvia
Ridaan Mountains
Hyvis
Strait of Nazaire
Lyth River
Moru Vinu
The Northern Glass
Ares
Barlforia
Glass Coast
Gulf of Naina
Del
Lurkham
Hokaan
The Southern Glass
Almeg
Espera
The Southern Seas

SHURA

Year 3317
Eight Years Ago

S hura kept his bolt knocked, bowstring drawn only just as he made his way north through the sentry-like pines of the Ferrofrost. Snow crunched underfoot. Sunshine lanced through the verglas-crusted boughs. Pinecones and loosed needles littered the white expanse between trunks. Caribou tracks were easy enough to spot in the knee-deep drifts against the trunks of the coniferous trees. Snowmelt pocked the snow with little holes, disguising the prints in the gulches between trees, but the impression of hooves gave way to a clear trail under the canopy of heavy branches.

Silence was impossible in these conditions; the crust of the snow was enough to betray the hunter's position, but Shura was no stranger to these wild lands. He knew the secret to hunting these woods was not to make oneself invisible to their prey but to mask the noise of his approach among the symphony of forest sounds.

Snow sloughed off a tall pine. A branch popped under the release

1

of weight. Shura took several steps as the snow fell to the forest floor with a hearty *fwump.*

Wind ruffled the fringe of blond hair that had escaped from beneath his fur-lined hat. Sweat beaded his brow, but he knew how dangerous it was to fall victim to the illusion of warmth this far north. To remove his thick cloak, fur-lined hat, or mittens would be to invite the ice-rot. In his eighteen years, he had known many of the rough mountain men in Rhunmesc who had ventured to the Ferrofrost and lost digits, and limbs, and some did not return from the untamed north at all.

They were not true men of the ice.

Not as Shura Wintersea thought of himself.

When he was a boy, his father took him out past the snow flats and the Ferrofrost, past the Averhame Mountains to the northern shore where the Salt Ice breaks across the black sand beaches in frozen shards of sea. King Tayman was never a warm man, but he'd not uttered a single word to his son until they stood side by side in the shade of a solitary pine that stood sentry on the shoreline. Beneath the boughs of the ancient bristlecone, his father shattered his reality so completely that Shura was still processing the weight of the words when the King struck him with a fist that left him dazed and bruised.

Shura, you are broken. The might of your mana is an embarrassment to the Wintersea line. You *are an embarrassment to the Wintersea name.*

"You must take from the world what will not be given," King Tayman instructed as he lashed his son to the tree trunk. "I rue the day your *wretched* mother brought you to me and begged for sanctuary. If you are unable to make your way back to Rhunmesc, you are no son of Wintersea."

After freeing himself from his bindings, Shura began his trek south. He had foraged shriveled crowberries from the exposed grasses on the wind-whipped tundra and dug little burrows underneath carpets of moss to keep himself warm at night. He trapped and killed and dined on bloody rabbit for weeks as he journeyed south. Hundreds of miles. He had crossed hundreds of miles at eight years old to prove to the magician he called Father that he was enough.

That his weakness would not define him.

Shura still recalled the numbing bite of winter, and the deep purple-black of his fingers and toes when he managed to navigate his way back to the Keep. Happy to be warm and safe, Shura had popped doughy chunks of sweet surrepan into his mouth to fill the void inside him as the healers worked to push back the start of the ice rot. If they sensed the emptiness of his mana within him, the absence of its presence, they said nothing.

His father, Shura had thought, would have been relieved to see him return. Instead, when King Tayman came into the study that evening and found him recovering by the fire, Shura was certain he had seen disappointment fall upon his father's weathered face.

He resolved to make sure that his father never looked upon him with that expression again. He would earn his name if it was the last thing he did.

In the years after, Shura returned to the mountains, the tundra, the forests, and seas. He learned the trails of the mountain goats, climbed the jagged cliffs of the Averhame, and found that he knew where to find hand and footholds as easily as he knew how to adjust his breath in the thin mountain air. He learned to wield weapons of alloy instead of magic and mastered the sword and bow before he had hair on his chest. He learned to track the stars across the Cosmos, to fish the seas and the rivers, and to stalk the trees as hunter instead of hunted. He was attuned to the land in a way no other magician was.

Shura believed he belonged out here: In the wilderness, beyond the gentleness of men. There was something freeing about being out past the rule of the city, a crown. Out here, beyond the realm of magicians...no one cared if he was broken, if his magic was not whole.

Ten years of cartography expeditions across the furthest reaches of the northern continent had taught him that. He mapped the coasts of the Northern continent, traced tree lines across the parchment, and presented his findings to his father at each return to Rhunmesc. All a pretty ruse to keep his father pleased where he would otherwise find only disappointment.

Perhaps King Tayman would have allowed the excursions no

matter the reason Shura provided if only to excuse him from his sight. Even his mother seemed to treat him with unfathomed disdain. He had not seen her since before his childhood excursion across the continent. It seemed she was always taken ill when he returned to the Keep of Rhunmesc. Knowing what little he did of the Queen and her hammered gold bowl, Shura feared she had Seen something in his future that had turned his own mother against him, but could never muster the courage to ask.

It was no matter. Even if he did not know the cause, he knew that King Tayman and Queen Lyranna held no love for him, their only son, in their hearts.

Now, Shura stalked the frost-gilt trees imagining himself a king of the feral wood. A wild prince of the North, beholden to no crown, no law, and no magic. No prey evaded the swift arrows he loosed. No predator was foolish enough to hunt him in return.

So when the small hairs on the back of his sweat-drenched neck stood on end, Shura Wintersea knew that something was very, very wrong in the Ferrofrost.

Moments later, the incessant cawing of crows erupted from the pines as a frenzied flock took wing into the thick grey of the winter sky.

The blizzard was upon him before he even knew it was coming.

Snow blinded him as it cascaded from the storm-bright sky. Tall pines of the Ferrofrost barely buffeted the howling north wind—Zephyrus was angry today, it seemed, as the great Storm Mythos had risen from the grave just to make him slog through a snowstorm. Shura's mink mittens were hot and damp with the sweat from his labored trek as snow squalls washed over him in furious waves. It was almost like drowning, the surf racing over him in cold spray. He stumbled forward and dropped his bow into a snowdrift as the storm swallowed him with unnatural force.

At last, he managed to make his way to the base of a massive pine and took shelter against its trunk. He shivered as snow piled up around him, encasing him first in flakes and powder, then inches of bitter cold.

For hours the storm raged. Night would have fallen beyond the covering of cloak and snow. His teeth rattled in his skull as he shivered into his furs and the dark thought edged into his mind.

Perhaps King Tayman would finally smile when his son never returned home.

Why suffer under the thumb of a usurper when you could be remarkable?

A cold voice bit into the back of his mind and Shura shivered.

That voice was not his own. It spoke to him from… within.

You know it to be true, Prince. Long have you suffered at the hand of falsities when you should have been guided to greatness.

"Greatness?" Shura whispered, the moisture of his breath forming ice crystals on his lips and around his nostrils. The unnatural freeze had seeped in through his cloak. "I am nothing great," he confessed to the voice.

Not yet, no. The voice sounded almost sad at that. *But you will be,* it assured him.

Silence became deafening. The forest creaked with the storm's force, but it sounded so far away now as if he had found another world beneath his cocoon beneath the drifts. The chill set into his bones. His muscles contracted until his spine ached.

I can help you survive, and more.

"How?" Shura croaked in disbelief.

Let the truth set you free. The voice echoed in his skull, pressing against his senses with obliterating force. All but the voice, as cold as the void of a collapsed star, vanished into the pressure of the darkness in his heart. *You are no son of storms but born by the radiance of the stars. Your path is that of Cosmic legacy, it cannot be undone.*

The words were the answer to the question that ate away at him like some parasite, feeding on his shame. "Queen Lyranna? King Tayman?"

*False are the crowns they wear. It is upon **your** throne they sit. You were not birthed by the weak flesh of magicians but of carnal union with an Imperial. A son of Darkness, heir of Khaos.*

Yes.

The word had only surfaced in his mind, but the roots of desire ran deep into his soul, claws hooked deep into the darkness of his heart. The sky overhead flashed with threatening promise. Filament jumped between thunderheads, igniting the sky. The very fabric of reality seemed to shatter with a deafening pop as violet lightning crackled from the sky and struck true, filling Shura's veins with dark power.

Paralyzed with electricity, Shura lost his vision to the Sight. Long-forgotten memories washed over his mind and he collapsed to his knees. A woman and her lover trapped in the Ferrofrost, far from home and reeking of desperation. A babe born in the eye of a blizzard, power sealed with a kiss to his bloodied brow alongside a sacred promise for revenge.

Within him, a curse unlocked after eighteen wretched orbits of feeling worthless and broken, to knowing he held within him a deeper purpose.

Shura felt his breathing hitch as he regained his body. He had crumpled to his knees with his hands fisted into the frozen earth. The sharpness of the frigid air burned his lungs even as his breath fogged in the air. Sweat trembled on his lip as gained knowledge settled into his bones.

Rise. We do not kneel, for we are the last of an ancient power. You are your mother's heir, to be crowned in the true dark.

Shura trembled with the static of the lightning strike. He felt the current of it in his bones, in his veins. The sensation of it consumed him. His skin was alight with power, he felt it burning inside him like the white-hot heart of a star. He staggered to his feet, knees buckling under his own weight, but he managed to keep his balance as he blinked into bright beams of daylight piercing the clouds. Golden rays embraced him, welcoming him back from the brink of an abyss the likes of which Shura was certain no magician had ever seen. He let the moment sink in.

Shura had not just a future, like some mundane magician trudging across the continent, but so much more. Shura wore the noose of fate around his neck—the mark of a true king: a summons of destiny from the Cosmos.

How Tayman would tremble at his might now.

It was then that the wrongness of the day enveloped him like a second skin. He could sense the change in Ellorhys as if a new season had been born upon them. He turned north and saw a smudge of twilight staining the sky from beyond the Salt Ice. "What have you done?" he asked aloud, not certain if the voice still existed within him now that he had opened the door to free it. Or if he was now the voice. "What have I done?"

You have done nothing. It is this which you must undo to earn your true crown and unite all of Ellorhys.

"And what is *this?* I must change the very stars?"

Only a curse, invoked with Imperial blood. It will be no small thing to break. There is another whose fate is bound to yours. She will be the light that will cast your shadow. She will rise and the Mythos will awaken, drawn like moths to the flame. Gather them, like so many fragments of power to fill your mana before they are able to yield to the Maiden of Light. Only then will you be able to rule a unified Ellorhys and spread the message of true dark.

"How will I know her? She who will awaken, your Maiden of Light?"

Like calls to like. It is fated, woven into the Cosmos. Bide your time well, Shura Khaoson. You will know when she draws near.

And as quick as it had come, the storm dissipated, rolling back into the mountains and melting to mist among the frosted peaks.

Shura stood in the Ferrofrost, allowing the changes of destiny to wash over him. He felt purified from the storm. Awakened. Enlightened. His skin was no longer cold as he stood bare-chested in the forest. The chasm of his magic within him, for the first time, did not feel broken.

Deep at the bottom of the canyon of his mana… it was no longer empty. Power bubbled up like a spring. He could hear the echo of its trickle. It was weak, shallow like a puddle, but he had only now accessed the river of shadows. It would grow until the roar of his power rivaled that of his primordial ancestors.

Until his name would disquiet the Ethereals in the Cosmos.

He vowed to cultivate that fragment of shadow within him. When the Maiden of Light awakened as the voice of his ancestors foretold, he would be ready to take what had not been given, as his false father had instilled within him.

Perhaps the only lesson the king bestowed upon him worth remembering.

With his oath fresh on his mind, he set off south toward the Keep of Rhunmesc and the false parents that dwelled within high stone walls, for he had a reckoning to deliver, and he no longer felt shame.

PART I
RETURN OF THE HEIR

1

SHURA

Year 3326

Braced against the flagship's gunwale, Shura extended his brass spyglass and peered out across the night-black sea toward the glittering trove of lights on the distant shore.

Espera.

He'd never seen such a beautiful city before. Rumors of the elegance of the capitol, how happier people were not to be found, had reached him in the north but nothing prepared the forsaken prince for the sheer magnitude of it all. It dwarfed anything he'd seen in the north. Domed roofs capped every structure and shone like a rainbow of pearls in the moonlight. Jagged crystal pillars of the palace blotted out swaths of starry sky. The crystal shifted light from the city with unearthly grace across mirrored panels of iridescent black and reflective white. Shura knew then why it was the first people who bowed to the Imperials had believed them to be *other*.

Magnificent didn't cover it. The sprawling seaside city tucked under its shadow like a mother's wing shimmered with the light of a thousand gems. Rhunmesc, the winter-weathered citadel of the north, was drab ruins compared to the jewel-laden city nestled between the Glass and the sea. Bay of Prisms surely earned its name.

11

And it was all his for the taking.

A few leagues off the shore, veiled behind thick fog and thunderheads the armada lay in wait.

One-hundred and fifty ships strong, it had taken them nearly three weeks of sailing south on the Lanzauve to cross the Timeline. Employing a regiment or two of storm magi, the ships brought with them squalls and rough seas to deter ships from leaving port down the entire western coastline of the southern continent. Lamps doused and crew silent, the serene city slumbered on as the jaws of true darkness readied to swallow it whole.

"Prince Shura," Phelix Stormgren, Captain of Shura's guard, said from the pitch behind him. "I've received word from the last fleet. They're days past Hinhallow and will be joining us shortly. Hinhallow will be active in the waters again within hours, I'm sure."

"And there's been no suspicion from old Akin?" He asked without taking his eye off the spyglass. He knew there would not be. He'd planned this for too long. The old warlord thought himself the mastermind of the continents still, but Akintunde Ballentine had yet to match his wits to Shura.

Phelix shook his head. "No, sire. All their ships stayed in port as we passed. Our storm magi kept the seas high and the winds wild."

"And the Titans?"

"Each regiment's lodestones are with their commanders. Orders have been issued. We only await your command."

Shura collapsed the spyglass and stowed it in the inner pocket of his military coat as he turned at last from the bounty of his conquest, eyes alight. "Risa and her command flank the eastern ports. Timbrel can hold the Spires and the West, make sure my dear sister doesn't escape."

Phelix turned his head to the side and raised his hands to his mouth. A series of birdcalls, trills, and tweets like the signal for a coming dawn lifted on the breeze. The wind picked up, whipped up the whitecaps, and tossed sea spray into the night like a handful of stars. Phelix's long black ponytail snapped like a pennant as winds tore across the deck. He turned back to Shura, dark eyes like flint in the night. "It shall be done."

A weight on the wind shifted and like wraiths on the black Southern Sea, the ships began to move. Dark sails puffed out while storm magi manned the rigging, guiding each ship into position as envisioned.

"I want the false heir for myself."

"No one would dare touch the Empress Regent, sire." Phelix was silent for a moment before he said, tentative as his breath fogged the air between them, "And the Maiden you seek?"

Shura looked back toward Espera and sunk inside himself to meet the dark fire that burned bright as a void. It reached up to meet him like an old friend. A velvet soft touch on his shoulder, a guiding hand more constant than a star. "She's no longer here. That's not why we've come."

"Then… we came here for naught?"

"Never for naught, my friend." Shura closed his eyes and breathed deeply. He brought himself back to that moment when he knew the time had come at last, that she was here and ready for him. He'd felt the echo of her power. Scented her in the wind and on the sea. As familiar a sensation as observing his reflection. There was no mistaking that cosmic power. "The maiden is… elsewhere. She will call to me again. And now I am here to answer when she does." He opened his eyes and looked back to Phelix. "Like calls to like. Our little dance has only just begun, I'd be disappointed if victory came so easily. She and I are the shadow and the flame, as our ancestors before us. " A cruel smile carved his face as he added, "And we all know the darkness existed long before the light. It is time to return us to our humble beginnings."

In his pocket, idle fingers turned a lodestone over and over. The stone grew hot against his palm as he gripped it tight. Behind him on the deck, the titans created by his Opifex team began to wake. A low hum accompanied a hiss of steam as alloy eye sockets filled with yellow light. Like in the demonstration in the cavern beneath Rhunmesc, light seemed to leak from the geometric eyes like tears, following intricate paths to illuminate runes etched into the gold-colored alloy armor of the monstrosities.

"Take the city."

2

ELON

Rebels arrived at the encampments deep within the ancient wood in varied degrees of anger and weariness. Farmers brought with them skinny cows and wiry goats with nub horns and strange pupils. Their wives and elder children carried meager belongings, smaller siblings, and woven baskets with chickens inside. Occasionally, and it was only due to the unlikelihood that a child would be able to navigate so deep into the Baelforia unaided, children wandered in alone; dirty and weak, with tear tracks in the grime on their sallow cheeks as they collapsed at the sight of others.

But whoever arrived, they all had one thing in common. First-timers arrived at camp with an escort. The Silent Patrol.

One wouldn't see them as they approached the boundary for the land they'd staked out. But the Silent Patrol saw them.

Guards for the rebellion, they stalked the woods relentlessly, ushering in those who wished to fight against the Empress, and disposing of those who sought to thwart their efforts. After Elon escaped the Crystal Palace, Hecate, and Commander Acontium sent troves of soldiers after him. So far, only a handful made it back to Espera alive, telling tales of beasts in the Baelforia. Creatures long since believed to be dead returned to the trees.

Shadows from the campfires danced around the edges of the camp like specters as rebels mulled around. Some transported goods from one tent to another, boxes laden with blackpowder, shrapnel, and noxious shatterspheres; baskets of vegetables and hard breads; women with laundry on their hips. Others tended fires and stirred cauldrons of stews that scented the forest with roasted garlic and savory herbs, ready to serve bowls to hungry bellies after their tasks. More magicians laid out by the various fires, curled on bedrolls trying to rest between patrol shifts and training schedules.

The camp, bustling with refugees and rebels all setting about their assignments, was looking more like a shanty tent town amongst the trees than the barren campsite it had started as.

Elon found himself at the back of the encampment, where they'd begun fashioning a makeshift stable for the horses they'd acquired. It had started with just a few mounts, tied to a low tree branch but as the rebellion grew, bringing in farmers from the moorlands between Larkham and Del, more animals had been brought on pilgrimage with their masters.

Chickens roamed wild between the trees, the error of a broken cage that freed several winged beasts into the Baelforia. It wasn't uncommon to find eggs in the oddest of places, or while out for a stroll in the wood. They'd already erected a pen for the nine goats and a few sheep, useful for their milk, cheese, and wool, but the pigs had been slaughtered for their meat, and they'd traded the rams to a farmer in Rosvia in exchange for barrels of grains and rice.

Now it was time for the horses to be given a space.

Thwack! He swung his hammer overhead again, shoulders groaning from the continued effort as he brought it down upon the fencepost. *Thwack!* The post drove deep into the dirt.

Many of the horses were accustomed to working the fields. As Elon brought his hammer down on the post again, he realized almost *all* the horses they had, just over a dozen in total, were older farm horses. Except, of course, Dandelion. Elon's mount and inherited steed from his adoptive father, Soren Sainthart. Beside the weary and wary animals, the black warhorse looked to be a wolf amongst the sheep.

Dandelion wickered haughtily at him from nearby, ears pinned back as he eyed the gleaming alloy hammer in Elon's hands.

"It's all right, you big baby," he teased as he leaned his tool against a thick oak. "I'm nearly finished." Elon hefted a long pine beam up between the last post he'd driven in and the previous one, fitting the shaved ends into slots on the posts. He bent to lift the next beam and set it into place between the posts, the top railing of an enclosure fence, when Dandelion brayed and turned his head, ears swiveling atop his head toward the darkened forest.

Elon, not one to discredit the superior senses of animals, dropped the beam. "What is it?" He asked in a whisper as he craned his neck and squinted into the dark.

And then he heard it.

Brush breaking. Branches snapping. Bodies crash through the underbrush.

Where was the Silent Patrol?

Elon grabbed the hammer from where it rested against the oak tree. A tool, and not a weapon, but his sword was in his tent and his Terran magic was only good for alchemy. He'd never wanted to be an armament magician more than in that moment as he brought the hammer's thick alloy head to sit on his shoulder.

"ATTACK!" A familiar voice shouted from beyond the tree line.

The cry roused the encampment.

At once, there were no sleeping men, no cooks at the fire. Magicians summoned weapons, blades of fire, ice, and wind. Even those without battle magic brandished their element as fiercely as they were able: A tailor who'd been mending trousers brandished her scissors like a dagger, a shimmer of green magic glimmering along the sharpened edges; a laundress, apron soaked with soapy water raised bubbles like globes above her head, hands trembling with blue light as she struggled to hold their shape.

"Espera is under attack!" Xenviera Lightizner burst into a swath of shifting firelight, sweat-slicked and dirty from running through the trees. One of the founders of the rebellion, Elon's grip on the hammer loosened as he absorbed her distress. Black hair matted to her neck and shoulders as she sagged against a tree. "Elon there's--"

"Hundreds of ships," Rhori Galeryder finished for her as he stumbled through a thorny bush to Xenviera's left.

"Is it Hinhallow? Have they come?" Elon asked, heart full of hope. Had Issaria done it so quickly? Was she on the shore, looking for him as she brought down the gates?

Xenviera and Rhori exchanged skeptical glances. "They fly no banners."

"The city is on fire, Commander Sainthart. I don't believe Princess Issaria would return with an army just to destroy the city," Rhori added.

Those closest to the pair of Silent Patrol scouts passed the information through the camp in whispers. Murmurs eddied like mist over water as the dissent began to rise among them. "Let the witch burn."

"Whoever it is did us a favor."

"Let's see how *she* likes burning for a change."

"Even the Evernight Witch has her enemies."

"How can you all say such horrid things?" Safaia Cardinalè's voice trembled with rage as she strode through the camp, elbowing her way toward Elon and the others. "That is our home! Our *friends!*"

"They stayed behind. They're no friends of ours."

"You would stay idle and let innocents burn because they did not have the spine to leave their homes and livelihoods?" Elon challenged. "Or is it only the overtaxed farmers deserve to be free of tyranny?"

The man who'd spoken out, an older, grisly-looking fellow with wrinkles on his wrinkles, seemed aghast to be addressed. He flushed crimson and averted his beady eyes as he stammered, "Well, I... I didn't mean it like that. Only that they made their choice."

"And I have made mine," Elon said as he stalked into the crowd of rebels and met Safaia near the largest fire, at the camps center.

He snarled as he neared those who'd wanted to hide in the woods. "This rebellion was formed to protect the city from Hecate. If Hecate has brought enemies down upon our people, we *will* protect them."

Cheers rose from armament magicians, those thirsty for battle. "Ready yourselves. We go to defend Espera as soon as the regiments are formed up."

A brown-haired boy ran up through the gathered rebels. "Commander! Elon!"

Elon recognized Basl Koellewyn immediately. He'd not changed much, but his face no longer had the soft lines of a city boy. Basl had spent his time in Del with Rhori's parents well. "What is it, Basl?"

The boy's chest puffed up. "I'm coming with you."

"Can you fight?" Elon asked and Basl nodded vigorously.

"I've been training since I got here. I'm not great, but I've always been fast, and I know the city well. Messenger and all. I can help, Commander."

Elon bit his tongue. The boy was more likely to be a liability than an asset, but there was something about the defiance in Basl's eyes that made him waver. It reminded him of a young Issaria, ready to find a way to accomplish her goal without him if need be.

"She killed my father, Commander. I never got to see him here. He never got to see this. He was supposed to arrive days after I did. And he never came." Basl's eyes hardened like jasper stones. "I'm coming with you."

"This isn't Hecate we war with. She may be there, but this is no revenge mission, Basl."

He steeled his jaw. "If this army took my revenge from me, my quarrel would only shift from her to them."

Elon nodded once and patted the kid's shoulder. "All right. Arm yourself, Basl Koellewyn. Espera needs us."

3

ISSARIA

I ssaria jolted awake. Nightmare still sour under her tongue, she gasped, freeing her lungs from the phantom scent of woodsmoke, night, and salt sea air. A cold sweat gleamed on her clammy skin in the candlelight—

With the back of her hand to her lips, Issaria froze.

Every candle on every surface of her bed chamber flickered with golden light. Dozens of them. No sputtering flames she'd grown accustomed to, but perfect silent pillars of light when not a single wick should have been lit.

Wary, she slipped from beneath her bedcovers and started toward the nearest candelabra upon her vanity. Behind the triple flames in the mirror, her reflection approached the glass: One vibrant violet iris, shifting hues of amethyst and plum in the light; the other pearl-grey, blind and useless. A price paid to the ancestor lurking within Issaria's mana for protection the last time an assassin very nearly ended her. She swallowed hard at the memory of coming to just after the attack as gooseflesh prickled her skin.

Suddenly half-blind and frightened beyond belief, she'd turned to find Prince Calix and....*it*. A pile of pinkish-red mush, and the twisted spine and ribs that had been left as evidence of what happens when

20

someone threatens Aurelia's vessel. The *benevolent* Mythos of Light, Issaria's ancestor, had invited herself into Issaria's magic with a bloodline curse and sought revenge for her murder. Balance, she called it. But Issaria was not so blind as to see that dark thirst in her divine relative.

Issaria wanted to laugh at the very idea of the woman who *stole her eye* as being benevolent. Vengeful? Yes. Selfish? *Absolutely.* Naive? Well…Aurelia *had* thought that she could just step into Issaria's body on her eighteenth birthday and do away with all of Ellorhys, so yes. Check on naive and double-check on unhinged.

And impatient, too, if the candles were intended as a reminder that she's still there.

"I'm going as fast as I can," she hissed to her reflection, to Aurelia, watching and waiting from behind Issaria's dead eye. Issaria rolled her eyes. Lurking was more like it.

"Issa!"

Issaria jumped, startled by the interruption.

"Are you up yet?" Rhaminta called from the other side of her bedroom door, rapping knuckles solidly against it to rouse her. She tried the knob, but it only jiggled in place. "We don't need *another* reason for the queen to snub you!"

The very thought of Queen Emmaleigh's dismissals made Issaria grimace as she crossed the room to let her friends in.

"Shouldn't we at least call her princess or something?" Asmy's soft voice countered Mint's candor.

"I'll call her princess when she's not late," Mint replied. "Emphasis on *late*, Issa!" she shouted through the door.

"No need to shout, I'm right here," she said as she unlocked the door, pulled it inward, and stepped aside. "Good morning to you, too, Mint. Asmy."

Asmy dipped into a low curtsey and murmured, "Thank you, Princess," before dipping into the room and beginning her chores. Still skittish from her time at the brothel, Asmy was dutiful to her tasks as one of Issaria's handmaidens and bustled about the room.

Rhaminta glanced between Issaria and the bed chamber behind

her, dozens of candles lit and twinkling in the darkened room. Thick, dark eyebrows raised in silent question as she said, "You know, opening the curtains is easier than lighting all those candles."

Heat crept up Issaria's neck as she crossed her arms over her chest. "I happen to like candles. They're...very old-world. It's quaint these chambers haven't been updated with solarium," she lied smoothly. Making them worry about Aurelia when they were already coddling her was the last thing she wanted.

Mint snorted as she swept past Issaria, one arm poised before her with a scarlet swath of fabric draped over it. "Quaint is one way to put it. Insulting is another. Antiquated living quarters," Mint muttered as she thrust the silk at her. "Here. Put this on. I'll find a pair of sandals and some jewelry for you."

"Red again?"

"Yes, red! What *is* your aversion to red?" she asked over her shoulder as she opened Issaria's wardrobe and began rifling through it.

"Nothing!"

Rhaminta looked back at Issaria, skepticism on her face before she resumed rifling through the wardrobe. It took all of Issaria's willpower not to look at the folded paper cow on her nightstand.

"I just...don't think I look good in red."

"It looks better on you than yellow does, and those are Ballentine colors. Oh, *these* are nice. Who gifted these to the new *Crown Princess*?" She grinned and held up a pair of gold sandals with long beaded ties that would lace up her around calves.

Issaria frowned first at the red dress, and then at the sandals. "I'm not the crown anything yet, Mint. A lot of gifts were already stored away in drawers when Prince Calix brought me here. I'm sure they weren't even meant for me. Just whomever ended up with the prince."

"All the more reason to act like you already are." Mint shrugged and dropped the sandals next to the vanity. "These are perfect. Red silk, gold sandals." She ushered Issaria behind a carved, ivory changing partition. "You should seek to display your alliance at all times now. It's imperative the people see you as being on our side after living so long in the Eventide."

Issaria slipped out of her nightgown and tossed it over the top of the partition for Asmy to collect with the other laundry. Thinking of the menial chore made her miss Liara, one of her friends and a laundress in the Crystal Palace in Espera. The memory of her old life was enough of a sting to remind her how high the stakes were in this alliance, and that Rhaminta wasn't wrong to advise her to tread carefully.

But it sounded crazy to tell her that Issaria didn't want anything red anywhere near her, lest the color become a signal-fire to whatever moment lay attached to the paper cow. Issaria wasn't even sure why she felt that way. Kidalma had said that whatever the cow was meant to be…when she got to the moment she'd know it. She stepped into the dress, slid it up over her hips, and knotted the ribbon at the back of her neck in a bow.

The Hallowvanian-style dress, sheer and form-fitting exposed much more bare skin than she was comfortable with. But no matter how daring, it wasn't her paper-cow-moment. For all the red dresses Rhaminta had stuffed her into over the past few weeks, nothing significant had happened. Or perhaps she was a fool for believing an old slavewoman with stars in her eyes, and the stupid folded paper cow she often used as a bookmark meant nothing at all.

"I am not wearing this," Issaria said flatly from behind the partition.

"You already are, and you're late so you can't change now." Mint came around the divider and seized Issaria's wrist, dragging her out to the vanity. "Asmy, get those sandals on her feet. I'll work on her hair."

"But *Mint!*" Issaria protested, "You can see my entire back! It's hardly appropriate—"

"Red for the Ballentines, to show you belong to them," Mint said as she took a brush to Issaria's inky curls. *"Backless,"* she emphasized, brandishing the brush at Issaria's reflection, "for the prince because now you have to make *him* belong to you."

Heat rushed up Issaria's neck. The memory of being tangled with

Calix in a kiss that had her whole being coming undone wended through her mind. She hadn't spoken to the girls of the *enthusiastic* reply he'd given to her acceptance of their marriage alliance. "I umm… I don't think that will be a problem."

"No? Last we spoke about him you were still pining over your soldier back in Espera."

At her feet, with one sandal laced up to Issaria's knee, Asmy said, "But what about Prince Calix?" Asmy's mossy eyes went wide as she looked up between the two older girls. "He's so handsome and kind, and you know he's really powerful. You can't possibly—"

"Asmy."

Issaria's smile softened, her sadness tangible only by the pain reflected in her remaining violet eye. "It's okay, Mint." She folded her hands in her lap and looked back to the mirror before adding, "He's dead. He gave everything for me, and I had only begun to acknowledge my feelings and then we were forced apart." Her smile wavered and she added, probably more for her own benefit than Asmy's, "We probably never could have been together…but I would have tried. For Elon, I would have tried."

Asmy fell silent and slipped the remaining sandal onto Issaria's foot and began lacing again before she said, "You're heartbroken right now, but just wait, Princess." She tied a bow on the outside of Issaria's knee and looked up at her. "You and Prince Calix will be so happy together."

Issaria gritted her teeth against Rhaminta raking a brush through her hair but smiled down at Asmy. "What makes you say that?"

Asmy rose and dusted off her dress and said, "You didn't see him run into the pavilion for you when you screamed."

Issaria looked up to Rhaminta, the question on her face. "Don't look at me. Eiren told me to keep my mouth shut and my nose out of it." She looked pointedly at Asmy. "And you should too, or I'll tell your sister you're causing trouble."

Asmy stuck out her tongue before collecting the tea cups and saucers from the previous night. "Cizabet wants to see them together as much as I do! She even caught them kissing that night!"

Asmy's hands flew to cover her mouth, but it was too late.

Issaria's face flushed redder than her dress.

Rhaminta's jaw dropped. Then melted into an I-told-you-so smirk as she laid the hairbrush on the vanity. "I can't pretend to know what's going through your head with all this, Issa. I know you've got a lot on your shoulders, and you probably didn't tell us about that night for a lot of reasons." She took Issaria's hair in her hands and began braiding strands in the same way she had the night Mint revealed she knew who Issaria really was. Warrior's braids, an earned tradition in her people's tribe going back to ancient times. "I want to tell you why *I* know that you and the Prince will be happy together, kiss or not."

ISSARIA COULD HEAR THE CROWD AS SHE RUSHED UP THE SPIRALING tower steps. A dull roar like ocean waves pummeling the shore. Her heart fluttered in her chest like a caged bird at the noise. She had to still herself on the stairs, just before the landing. Pressed against the cool stone, her skin suddenly felt on fire as she listened to the pulse of excitement and joy that reverberated through the very stones of the White Palace.

Never had the people of Espera cheered for her aunt like this. Her memory from before her parent's assassination recalled flower petal showers over them as the Imperial Emperor and Empress rode horses through the city. A young Issaria, too young for her own mount, sat between her father and the pommel of his saddle. The people had cheered then, hands outstretched to touch her father's radiance, tears in their eyes as Issaria looked upon them. It wasn't joy though, that bent heads and had prayers whispered from lips when the Elysitao family passed.

It had been reverence.

And after? Issaria fought back a scoff at the very idea. *After* there was no joy. Not until she thought, perhaps, with the crown that *she* could make a difference. One wrong step later and her last shred of family set a sleeper assassin on her and forced her...here. To Hinhallow, another struggling empire, to a people in need, and to a prince she was being forced to marry.

But was it forced, anymore?

She looked up to the doorway at the top of the stairs. Rhaminta's confession of what happened when she'd been poisoned set her heart aflame as she recalled waking and finding Prince Calix asleep at her bedside.

"Prince Calix didn't leave your side for more than a few minutes the entire time you were afflicted. He was the one the healers spoke to about your progress. He was the one who lifted you so we could change your linens. He prayed to the Mythos and the Cosmos to save you. Begged them to bring you back to him so he could tell you—"

"Stop."

Rhaminta paused but shook her head. "Issaria, you don't under—"

"Mint," she'd cautioned with a firm tone. "Whatever he wished to tell me is his alone to tell."

She knew what he would say to her, but she wasn't able to return that feeling. Not now. Not yet. It was all too much, too fast. A few weeks ago she'd nearly died. *Twice.* Before that were weeks of slavery and abuse, and there were nights she dreamed she was *still* walking across the Glass with no end in sight.

Right now, all she could do was brace herself for the next task at hand and try to maintain some semblance of control over the alliance that was about to take over her life even more than the Mythos inside her.

"That girl better not back out," a familiar voice reached Issaria's ears from beyond the doorway at the top of the landing. "She's late, again!" Queen Emmaleigh sighed in irritation as Issaria took a bracing breath. "Well? What are you waiting for? Go fetch her!"

Sucking down a calming breath, Issaria gathered her dress in her hands and sang out, "No need!" as she pranced up the remaining steps with a serene smile plastered on her face.

The soldier who'd been ordered to retrieve her melted in relief at her arrival before he shored up and regained his stoic posture, more fixture than person until called upon again by his monarchs. Queen

Emmaleigh, resplendent in a brassy, yellow gown that seemed to accentuate her goldenness appeared demure with a high collar and capped sleeves. In comparison to her own dress, Issaria noted as she sent vile thoughts at Rhaminta, the queen looked a vision of grace and poise, while Issaria was shimmering, seductive and sleek. At Queen Emmaleigh's elbow stood a younger, more summery version of herself. In a powder blue dress with white bows and lace that enhanced her youthful appearance, was Princess Bexalynn.

"So sorry, your Grace, for the delay. My girls couldn't decide if I should wear my hair up or down." She dipped into a quick curtsey, giving deference to the golden queen, and again to the young princess, lest Emmaleigh find another reason to be a thorn in Issaria's side. Lifting a hand to pat the ornate poof of braids and ringlets of curls that brushed across the tops of her shoulders when she turned her head, she finished, "I thought Prince Calix would like it best up."

Her smile hurt her jaw with how much she hated this charade of theirs, but the blush on her cheeks was genuine as she spied her betrothed across the veranda with his father and council, looking severe in charcoal, crimson, and gold. Several medals decorated his chest, and his golden crown weighed his crow-feather hair into submission. His strong jawline was prickled with stubble, he hadn't shaved today, but the dark shadow of a beard looked good against his defined face, a dark golden brown from so many years under the sun. The Ballentine men, side by side, looked almost as similar as the women, Issaria noted. As willowy and golden as the women, the men were all dark hair and corded muscle beneath their sharp military coats.

Queen Emmaleigh did nothing to hide the roll of her eyes, as Issaria did nothing to hide her appreciative gaze. "Well, if you couldn't be entirely proper, at least you're wearing a gown and not that horrid dancer-girl costume." She scoffed and stared down the length of her nose at Issaria. "The Crown Princess of Hinhallow garbed as a slave-girl. In front of the whole court. Disgraceful. I'll never live it down."

Issaria bit her tongue and smiled at the woman. It was clear she wasn't Queen Emmaleigh's first choice for her son's bride, but it was neither *her* choice nor the queen's. *Better to fight that losing battle another day,* she thought as she turned her attention to Bexalynn, and her smile faltered only for a moment at the callous reproach behind the girl's eyes. "Princess Bexalynn," Issaria said, "Lovely to see you again. I tried calling on you earlier in the week for a garden stroll, and again for tea in the afternoon and evening, but you are quite popular!" She forced an airy giggle, but Issaria was not familiar with these coy, courtly games. In Espera, she had been kept from court. "Even Princess Shairi was unavailable."

"I was avoiding you," Princess Bexalynn replied. For one so young, her pale gaze was cutting. "Everyone says you're so smart since you walked the Glass, I thought you would have figured it out the first time I turned you away."

"Bexalynn, manners." But Queen Emmaleigh's lips pursed to hide a smile as she brought an ivory-gloved hand to her mouth. "Your brother is quite enamored with his bride-to-be. We should be wishing them both happiness."

She huffed and rolled her eyes, looking so much like her mother that Issaria had to suppress a shiver. "Yes, Mother." Princess Bexalynn turned back to Issaria and frowned. "Forgive my impropriety on such a *joyous* occasion, but I don't much like that you stole my brother from Princess Shairi. *She* was supposed to be my sister. Not you." She wrinkled her nose and shook her head. "I don't even *know* you."

Princess Bexalynn looked to her mother for a steeling moment, as if weighing options, then she rounded on Issaria and blurted out, "Calix only likes you because you have big boobs. You're not even pretty enough to be his type, dead-eye!" She stuck out her tongue before seizing her skirts and storming down the stairs. "I don't have to be here for this!" she shrieked from beyond the doorway.

Issaria bleated out a nervous laugh, too baffled to be offended, before covering her mouth with her hands. She'd known she didn't have the queen's favor, but she hadn't even *considered* that the young princess would have an opinion on the matter. But of course, she did. Shairi told her on several occasions how close they were. *Like sisters,* she recalled.

"Bexalynn!" Queen Emmaleigh half-scolded and half-called after her daughter before turning on Issaria, effectively silencing her anxious giggles. "While there is no excuse for Bexalynn's behavior, her feelings are sound and heard." She pursed her lips, deliberating for a beat before she finished, "Princess Shairi may have taken the slight with grace, but I too thought I had been grooming a daughter in her for years before *you* arrived and so thoroughly turned my son's head."

Her eyelashes fluttered, her simpering smile grew, and like watching an actor take the stage, Queen Emmaleigh's disparaging comments melted into a sweetness akin to something Issaria had heard from Aunt Cate's lying lips. "Calix, *darling*, are you certain you want to make these announcements so soon? There's still time to consider your options, you know. Bexalynn is very upset."

4

CALIX

Even if he hadn't been watching Issaria like a hawk since the moment she arrived, he would have to be blind—he winced at the callous reference and made a mental note to say no such thing aloud *ever*, let alone in her presence—not to see that his mother and sister were rabid jackals ganging up on her. Issaria had confided in him that his mother had been bitter about their abrupt engagement, but he hadn't taken her complaints seriously until now.

Bexalynn's tantrum was far too much, and his mother did nothing to hide the disparaging looks she saved for Issaria, sneering down the end of her nose at her as if she were a bug that needed to be squashed *immediately.* He'd talk to his sister, but they were both going to have to accept it.

Mythos willing, Issaria was going to be his bride, his wife, and *their* queen. Every quivering mote of his being was ecstatic to know she'd chosen him of her own accord, despite their albeit *straining* circumstances. These slights had to end if there was ever to be a moment of peace in the palace again. Calix had to prove he was serious about this. About her.

"I am entirely certain, Mother, that if I had all the *options* in the world laid before me, I would still choose Issaria," Calix replied as he approached from across the veranda. "How fortuitous that you and father had attempted to arrange it so long ago." His words were for his mother, but he only had eyes for Issaria. He devoured her with his gaze: each dip and curve accentuated by the crimson silk of her dress.

Cosmos above, it was as if she *wanted* him to conspire to sneak her off to some hidden corner where he'd find out just what she tasted like—Issaria turned to him, relief washing over her at his arrival, and he banished his thoughts lest he sweep her away this instant and demonstrate just how serious he was.

"Princess," he said as he dipped into a bow and brought her fingers, so soft in his *fervent*-mauled hand, to his lips. Her cheeks flushed as he looked up through the fringe of his hair to meet her eye. "You're absolutely stunning, Issaria. I now have a profound weakness for red dresses."

She flicked her wary gaze to his mother before replying in a breathy whisper that made him again wish they were alone. They'd spent so little time together. "I had my girls choose my outfit with you in mind. Had I known it would weaken you so…" A dreamy smile twisted her lips and he got this distinct feeling that she enjoyed needling his mother as much as he enjoyed the opportunity to shamelessly flirt.

"Is that so?" Prince Calix arched an eyebrow in challenge and smirked. "Let's see then. Give me a twirl." Calix lifted her hand above her head and she spun slow, a music box dancer on her last notes, allowing him a lengthy view of the pale expanse of her spine before it vanished into scarlet silk. Mythos above, if the back of that dress went any lower—he had to drag his eyes back to her face. "Compliments to your ladies. I sense Mint behind this one?" Issaria nodded confirmation of his suspicions. "I quite like it. It's a shame I'll have to order all the red dresses in Hinhallow burned to prevent this weakness from being used against me."

Issaria giggled, the blush tinting her cheeks genuine.

His mother tutted, tongue clicking against her teeth in consternation. "Honestly, Calix. A bit excessive, don't you think?"

As Issaria completed the small pirouette Calix brought her in close, wrapping strong arms around her petite frame. It was delicious to feel how tiny she was compared to himself. With his face against her midnight hair, Calix was brought back to a distant memory. A night-blooming meadow where he, Raif, Zak, and a much more adventurous Shairi ran wild, kicking up fireflies around their heels on a moonless summer night. In eternal Day, that scent had long faded to legend, and it reminded Calix that he would never be able to mistake her for a citizen of Hinhallow or any other Daylight city. Her scent betrayed her as something else. Issaria smelled like those stalks of purple-blue flowers and an endless sea of stars for a sky.

Calix twirled a loose curl from her hair, tucked it back behind her ear, and pressed a chaste kiss to her exposed throat, feeling her pulse gallop beneath his lips. Resisting the urge to taste her here and now, he whispered none-too-quietly against the shell of her ear, "Despite Bexalynn's observations about your ample and dare I say, entrancing bosom, the dress is nothing without you to fill it."

Issaria snickered, and his mother's fuse ignited. "Calix!" Queen Emmaleigh shrieked as she stalked away. "Is this how you act in front of your mother? Have some dignity!"

Raucous laughter had them all turning to face the assembled courtiers. "The boy is besotted, Emma!" King Akintunde boomed from where Calix had left him in conference with the councilors. "Leave them be. Soon enough she'll be with child and Espera will be ever closer to being a seat of Ballentine power." As Emmaleigh joined him across the veranda, Akintunde looked to Issaria and winked. "I knew my boy would win you over, girl." His storm-cloud beard streaked wild with white trembled with his triumphant laugh. "Daughter soon though, eh? I knew you'd come around and see reason." He harrumphed and shook his head. "Undecided indeed."

Issaria tensed in his arms and Calix nestled his face into her hair, soaking up as much of her intoxicating scent as he could. "Easy, now," he murmured to her, lest she try to go toe-to-toe with his father. *Again.* The very thought had him smirking as he reassured her that this union had *nothing* to do with his father's demands of them. "He's thinking of himself, but you *know* I am only thinking of you. Of us. I'd give you and Espera our armies without all of this if I could."

She stilled against him and he couldn't help but want to discuss the most obvious obstacle before them. He may have been downright jubilant about their agreement, but she had once loved another. Truly loved the man with all her heart, and he in turn had loved her. The idea that Calix could be overstepping into territory he had no business staking a claim on unless she invited him left him unsettled, to say the least. He'd never had a rival before, let alone a dead one with as much honor as her Esperian solider. As much as he had enjoyed taunting his mother with his open affections for the daring princess, there was much left unsaid between them on that matter.

He swallowed and pulled back, turning her so that she could face him. "Issaria, I won't force you to do anything, but we *will* have to put on a unified front if we hope to take control of this alliance instead of being pushed across the board like pawns. And that may mean we will have to be...*familiar* in public. Convincingly so. The people aren't stupid and neither are my parents, but if we can put on a good enough show..." Even suggesting this sounded foul.

"Mr. Assassin." At the mention of the first name she'd given him, he stopped speaking, even as she pressed two fingertips to his lips to silence him. Issaria's smirk was flippant and familiar of the overconfident princess he'd discovered in the Baelforia months ago. Calix loved catching glimpses of Issaria unrestrained, as he came to call it, the fierce woman he'd likely become infatuated with from the very moment she challenged him in the woods. "Be realistic. If I can *walk* across the Glass, become a slave for weeks, and then dance as one well enough to fool your entire court? Face it, Blaze." A sardonic smile twisted his lips at his own idiotic pseudonym. "It's not me we have to worry about keeping up appearances." She patted his chest confidently. "Besides, your mother and I have been playing this game since I arrived. She's not my fondest advocate, in case you haven't noticed."

Calix sighed and pinched the bridge of his nose. "She's just upset I'm not marrying Princess Shairi. I'll speak with her. I'll speak with them both."

"And are you?"

He raised his eyebrows. "Am I, what?"

Issaria pointedly looked away and bit her lower lip. Nervous hands fidgeted with a gauzy layer of her gown. "Upset that you're not marrying Princess Shairi."

He cracked a smile. "I promise you, I am not the least bit upset that I am not marrying her. Even with my mother pushing her at me at every opportunity, I have *never* turned my attention on her until my Father commanded I do so." She released a tiny sigh and Calix's smile grew wolfish. He leaned down to level himself with her gaze as he asked expectantly, "Are you concerned? Maybe just a little jealous?"

"No!" Issaria exclaimed, and his grin grew downright malevolent. She *was* jealous. How ironic. Maybe he had nothing to fear when it came to her affections either. "I was...only concerned that I'd forced your hand as much as your father forced mine."

Calix barked out a laugh. "I thought I had made my intentions clear when you so graciously accepted my proposal." Her nervousness was palatable. A tentative, but good sign if he was reading her apprehension correctly. He cupped her cheek beneath her milky-white iris as he had the night they'd agreed to marry. Again, she pressed her face into his blackened palm, embers shifting like stars beneath his charred flesh. He resisted the urge to kiss her as he had when she turned her wanting stare upon him.

"As long as you'll have me, Issaria, I am yours."

A wave of emotions broke across her face and she jerked back as if she'd been burned. Was it something he said? Was that not the type of thing she wanted to hear from him? Wasn't that what all women wanted to hear from their lover?

"Oh, Prince Calix," she began, voice tight with remorse.

"Please, Issaria. Whatever it is, we are to be equals in this. We don't need to use titles."

"Prince Calix," she began again, wringing her hands together as she looked down at her sandals. "I am—I am *so* grateful that you and I have been able to unify our goals and you are *absolutely* the only—"

"Quickly now!" Queen Emmaleigh hissed, jolting them apart. Her impatience radiated across the veranda from where she stood just behind her husband, gesturing for them to join them. "He's to announce you both any moment. I want you *presentable*."

"Sorry, Mother," he murmured, looking not-at-all-sorry as he ushered Issaria alongside him, a hand on the small of her back as they crossed the veranda to where his father was already mid-speech, his tattooed skull gleaming in the sunlight as he spread his arms wide enough to embrace his whole kingdom.

Queen Emmaleigh pushed them beside each other, Issaria on his left, and arranged their hands so that Issaria was politely holding his elbow. As soon as Emmaleigh released her and turned her attention to straightening Calix's collar one final time, Issaria's fingers began to tighten on his sleeve. His mother tucked a stray lock behind his ear then turned a final appraising eye on his bride for whom she reserved judgment with another sour-puckered face before she sighed. "At least you won't be a *total* embarrassment to the dynasty," she quipped as she turned and joined her husband before the gathered crowd.

"Mother!" Calix admonished.

Issaria clenched her jaw and gripped his elbow fiercely, but held her tongue and whatever whiplash retort lingered behind that fierce scowl.

King Akintunde, his voice amplified by some Storm Magician manipulating air currents so that he resonated over the crowd, "It is with great hope for our future that I have blessed the union of not only two great houses but of two worlds unified against a great evil! Queen Emmaleigh and I are pleased to present to all of Ellorhys, but to you bold Hallowvanians *first*, Crown Prince Calix and his betrothed, Imperial Princess Issaria Elysitao!"

At first, he thought it was his mother, but Issaria's hand was fisted in his sleeve and she kept trying to subtly turn her head to look about the veranda behind her as they listened for their queue. At the last moment, he stepped quickly behind Issaria switching her from his left to his right so that he lingered just beyond her line of vision.

Shocked, she turned to him, and Calix gave her his best reassuring smile before they emerged into the sunlight as an official pair for the first time. "If it is a comfort to you, I'll try to stay on your left."

She snapped her attention back to the front, but her blush was red enough to match her dress. It was adorable how easily she was flustered. She gave a barely noticeable nod. "It is. You're the only person I'd trust to stand where I can't see them."

He fought to keep control of his expression to keep from grinning like a fool. Mythos be damned, his father was right. He *was* besotted. "It is an honor," he murmured as they stepped up to the balustrade.

Beneath the white-stone balcony that protruded from the castle's southeastern tower, it seemed the whole of Hinhallow's population had gathered for the presentation of the new royal couple. It had been blessedly overcast the past few days, but the storms had stayed out to sea, and today bright sunlight warmed the gathering, making the people glad for distraction. Bright bursts of magic sparked in vermillion arcs and spirals before glittering motes of light evaporated. Pennants snapped in the wind, and colored bits of paper accompanied flower petals, spiraling madly through magicked air like birds in flight. People leaned out of windows and waved crimson flags and yellow scarves in the air. Cheers loud enough to rattle the sky erupted in waves from the crowded streets below. Music cued up from within the crowd.

Calix squeezed her hand for only a moment before he nodded encouragement and raised his hand to acknowledge the cheers. Issaria followed suit, and the crowd grew louder.

"Mythos above," Issaria breathed, awe brightening her eyes as she looked out across Hinhallow, unable to fight the smile overtaking her face.

"Didn't you do this in Espera? Speak to the people?" Calix asked, glancing down at her as she shook her head. "Father says it's important for a people to know their King. When something happens, the people need to know they can trust their leaders to tell them the truth. I've been doing this since I was a boy. Small announcements, seasonal blessings on Sacred Rites of the year, anything that they needed to know, they found out from us. Bexalynn started a few summers ago, and Darres, my younger brother, should start appearing with my parents in a year or two if we haven't been officially appointed by then."

"Your father is uncharacteristically wise."

Calix laughed and slipped his hand from hers to the small of her back, an endearing posture for a newly betrothed couple. Familiar, but he could feel her tense beneath his touch and it felt a bit like icicles in his veins. He was surprised his hands weren't steaming. He cleared his throat before saying, "Shocking, I know, to find the Warlord of the West to be a mighty philosopher as well."

"Not as shocking as you would think," she replied. And then, with all the city watching, Issaria leaned into him, easing the line of their bodies together as she smiled up at him. "As it turns out, your father might be one of my favorite philosophers."

A thrill went through him as his hand on her back became the hand that held her against him, thumb stroking her hip through silk. "Is that so?"

"Oh for certain, Blaze. After all, one of King Akintunde's teachings is fast becoming my mantra."

"And which wise teaching did my father bestow upon you?" he asked as he tore his gaze from the city and looked down at her. His grin was wide and he felt almost as coy as she looked. It was the same smirk he gave her at their first encounter—surprisingly less than a full season ago, though it seemed a lifetime had passed since he happened upon her in the Baelforia that day.

They both knew the phrase. It was one of the first things he told her when she had no idea who he was. Just Blaze and a renegade princess in the woods.

Be afraid, but then you must do it anyway.

"It reminds me that there is often great reward bestowed on those who go to great personal risk." Fast as an adder, Issaria twisted and brought herself up on tip-toe to press her lips against his jaw.

Beneath her kiss, Calix stilled, shocked she'd conceded such an intimate gesture when she'd been about to tell him something before they'd been called upon. Issaria pulled back, blushing brightly as she laughed, exhilarated by her daring.

Issaria looked pleased with herself as she said, "Wipe that grin off your face or they'll think it's the first time. I *told* you it wasn't me we've got to worry about." She tried to go back to waving but must have felt his attention. Finally, she turned back to him. "What? You said—"

"You missed is all," Calix murmured as he captured her face and tilted her mouth to meet his. Sweetness and liquid gold pooled in his stomach, his craving for Issaria insatiable, but he kept the kiss tame, knowing he'd likely overstepped. He still wasn't sure how real this marriage was for her, but there was no doubt left in him as the citizens of Hinhallow erupted with applause and delighted sighs at the sight of their crown prince in love.

They parted, both with delirious smiles and eager eyes. Calix met her amorous gaze and realized what he'd been denying since he met her. Real for her or not, he was in love with Issaria. Radiant and fierce, the woman who walked across the continent for her city, and her people. The irrefutable Empress of Ellorhys who'd taken one too many wrong turns in a moonlit forest and still had the brass to stick him in the chest. It didn't matter that his father orchestrated this marriage, forced both their hands like a hot brand held to their flesh. It didn't matter that Issaria was harboring a vengeful deity inside her mana. It didn't matter that they were likely fated for something far beyond their control.

All that mattered was that Calix would choose her in this lifetime, and in the next when his soul returned from the Cosmos, he would remember this kiss. This woman. These moments. And he would find her again.

This was real for Calix. It was always real for him.

Now he just had to make Issaria love him in return.

5

ELON

With only one real warhorse for their ragged regiment, Elon opted to leave Dandelion behind in the encampment with the other farm horses, and those who could not fight: the elderly, young, and those responsible for them. The rebel army traveled in one long line through the Baelforia. Though the forest was quiet as they hurried, the trees themselves seemed to sense their urgency. Elon, at the head of the rebellion, was able to pick a clear trail between gullies and drop-offs that would have cost them hours of maneuvering their numbers had they approached from any other angle. They wended through the brush toward Larkham, now a shell of a town with only a few loyalists remaining.

They could smell the smoke, thick on the night air, before they'd even cleared the tree line. Larkham was a small, backwater village nestled in a valley at the edge of the Baleforia, but the village marked that they were only a few hour's march away from Espera. Had they been a cavalry unit, or charioteers like Ares boasted, they could have cut the time in half. It was not the first time Elon cursed being so ill-prepared for this.

The carnage was still miles away, but Elon knew in his bones that their forces were too late.

Too late to save the city.

But maybe they could save some of her people.

Though their silent march toward Espera continued, their pace quickened. Desperation was one hell of a motivator. Soon, they reached the final rise before they would look down upon the northern hillside of Espera. They halted the rebels, and Elon pointed to his team and motioned for them to join him at the top. They needed some reconnaissance. Charging in blind would do them no favors against an unknown enemy.

"The air reeks of death, Commander," Xenviera said as she joined him. "Zephyrus has been busy today." She didn't sound afraid, but rather, eager to join her Mythos in his honorable work. Storm Magi were strange folk when it came to death and its commander, Zephyrus.

Elon said nothing. He could already taste blood in the air, and feel the trembling of the earth beneath his feet. He closed his eyes and was instantly reminded of his home village, the very same Larkham they'd passed through earlier, burned to cinders from a careless fire when he was a boy. It was a small disaster that claimed his whole family. Those that hadn't been affected had been Mythos blessed. Everyone else…

He opened his eyes and shook the memory away. Espera would not be like Larkham. He was not a boy anymore. Now he could *do* something.

At the top of the rise, it took him a moment to understand what he was seeing.

It was madness.

Espera was red. So bright it looked as though it had found a way to break the Eventide, if only over the city itself. Fires blazed so rampantly that he was unsure how this *wouldn't* spread to the countryside, maybe even to the Baelforia beyond, and snuff out the survivors they'd left behind. Smoke churned into the sky from dozens of infernos. Neighborhoods, shops, the bazaar where he and Issaria had escaped almost certain death as children—he sucked in a stabilizing breath to find the air seared with heat and dust, with pain and death.

Elon's home was burning. Again.

Flashes of magic blasted out with massive force from a wide constellation of points across the city: lightning crackled from near the Temple, a spiral of fire ignited the fish market by the docks and almost immediately there was a series of explosions popped off in succession, igniting the block surrounding it. Black smoke billowed into the sky, blotting out the remaining stars. His eyes kept darting to identify black pockets where he knew buildings were missing from the skyline. The city shook, and he watched the House of Healing collapse, likely with people inside, and release a cloud of dust and debris like a tsunami in its wake.

"Cosmos above," Rhori whispered. "What *are* those things? That's not a magician, is it?" Half wonder, half awe, all revulsion.

Gold…creatures wielding magic had infested the city. There were no words for what he saw. Dozens of them that he could see, were peppered among the wider streets, offering him glimpses of a fire blast from one's barrel-like arm; a magician-crushing…could he call it a leg? Whatever it was, it flatted a man easily, before expelling what he had to guess was some type of Terran magic by the green glow that obliterated the alley like a hammer strike from below.

It was worse than Larkham. The village by the wood had burned by careless accident. It haunted him, but this? *This?* He couldn't even name this.

Attack. Invasion. Infestation.

None of it sounded right for what he was bearing witness to. He rested his hands on his belt, fingering the release for blackpowder shatterspheres, for a new composition he called a lightning rod, and another for the quick-stick silex he'd created as a boy. Since its first use on assassins in an alley, he had perfected the concoction and now it might be perfect for this type of assault. Stop these abominations in their tracks.

Xenviera's mouth had hardened into a merciless scowl. Her nostrils flared wide, her indigo gaze hyper-focused. Already her fingertips crackled with electricity. She walked into battle prepared and had already donned her silex gloves that would protect her from being electrocuted herself. She might command the storm, but she was not impervious to Zephyrus's might. No one was—that was why he was the master of death. Being his blessed warrior was to master death itself. Her rage had already surpassed typhoon-strong winds to drop the pressure enough for her to harness pure electricity.

On her other side, Roane was staring intently at the ground, his rugged face a mixture of confusion and anger. As if he sensed Elon's gaze, he met his gaze and shook his head. "I feel it in the earth. Something's very, very wrong down there, Commander. Those things aren't natural."

He couldn't unhinge his jaw to reply. He had clenched his teeth together so hard he was sure he was fused that way for life. His fury at the sight of his city—of *Issaria's* city—burning rendered him mute. Elon couldn't look at it any longer and turned his attention to the sea.

The carcass of the city was bleeding into the bay.

At least a hundred ships lay in wait beyond the wreckage of the bay. He counted how many had dropped their boats to disembark soldiers. *Maybe* twelve ships, twelve of hundreds had loosed their horrors, and the battle was already won. The city was as good as sacked. The other ships lay in wait, either as a threat or reinforcements, Elon wasn't sure. Perhaps they had expected to encounter some sort of resistance. Maybe they were lucky and the other ships weren't hauling these unholy beasts, but Elon wasn't willing to make that wager with the lives of his kinsmen.

The enemy had shown in force, and they planned to obliterate anything, any*one* in their path.

He swallowed hard with the knowledge that *he* was supposed to be the resistance. That he had brought all these people here to liberate Espera, and instead he had brought them to their graves. They had deployed ruthlessly and captured Espera between their forces as a scorpion would its prey. Swift and effective, with two pincers and a deadly tail. At the east, assaulting the docks and neighborhoods of lower-class citizens. In the west, preventing escape across the Glass, which Elon now knew was a completely viable option, since Issaria had managed to make it to Hinhallow. And a forward assault right into the Bay of Prisms.

"Mythos be damned," Xenviera cursed as she gesture with a sparkling hand to the ruin of Espera. "Zephyrus is down there taking life from my kinsmen, and I will be *damned* myself if I let him go uncontested." Filament crackled from her silex-gloved hand, curving into a sizzling arc of lighting. "I'm ready with the first assault when you give the word, Commander Sainthart." Elon met the warrior's fierce gaze. A thunderhead brewed behind indigo eyes as she said, "I can keep them busy while you get as many as you can out."

Roane caught her wrist. "Xen, don't. That's reckless."

She wrenched her hand out of his grasp. "It's not reckless, Roane," she replied as her other hand summoned an actual bolt of lightning and knocked it against the bow. "It's smart and I'm the only one who can do it. I'm fast. Faster alone." She cut him a withering gaze. "And with the size of the volleys of bolts I'm going to launch at them? They'll think we have twice as many storm magicians."

Elon managed to unclench his jaw long enough to say in a rough voice, "You know it could be suicide."

Xenviera didn't balk as she shot back, "This whole mission is suicide, in case you haven't noticed. But I'm not pulling back when there are people down there who need to know there is someplace they can go. That they don't have to just…die."

She looked back at the small army gathered at the base of the hill, shifting uneasily in the dark, unseeing but *knowing* that devastation lay beyond the next hillside. Their friends and family, neighbors and shopkeepers, Cosmos, even the strangers they'd once passed on tidy cobblestone streets, were being slaughtered. "I'm not pulling back. But maybe some of them should. Elon…evacuate the forest. This is…this will hunt us until we are dead. I would if I brought a force this massive and something tried to stop me."

Elon had furrowed his brow. She was talking about retreating. She was talking about sending in just a few soldiers to *maybe* save a few civilians. Xen held his gaze. "You know it to be true, Commander.

Whoever this is, they did not bring this *army* to sit in one city. We need to evacuate as many as we can into Ares, warn the King there, send a message to Fraxinus, and warn him both of this adversary and our impending arrival. He will likely send correspondence to Hinhallow if his alliance holds true, or if he rightfully fears this foe. If Issaria is wise she will stay far from this. This is not the city she should come back to."

Rhori laid a hand on his shoulder. "She's right. Elon…these soldiers aren't ready for this. It will be a slaughter if we bring them all down there."

"Elon, let me help," Xen said.

Elon was struck with the thought that this might be very close to pleading for her. The vengeance promised in her eyes made him nod once as he said, "Strike fierce, Reaper. If Zephyrus is indeed down there, I hope you give him something to fear."

Roane's stone-scale fist snagged Xen again, and Elon blinked in surprise as he kissed her fiercely then murmured, "You're crazy, Xen."

A faint smile tugged the storm magi's lips and she replied, "You love it, rock-boy."

"I do. I love you Xenveira. Don't do anything stupid."

At that she pulled away, casting a glance back at Elon before nodding. "Do I ever do anything stupid?" And then she was dashing down the hill, using whatever trees she could for cover as she descended into the outer edges of Espera.

When she was gone from sight, Elon coughed and nodded to the troops. "Rhori, I'm going to need you to take the ones who turn back to the forest, gather up the camp, and head for Ares. When we gather as many civilians as we can, we will follow."

"Elon, I can't leave you alone here."

"I'm not alone. Xen is here. Roane…" One look and they both knew he wasn't leaving Xenviera here on her own. Elon was surprised he'd let her go just now, but she was a fierce woman, and Roane must have known there was no way he could cage her. How he'd ever managed to capture her heart was a mystery to him in and of itself.

"I'm not alone Rhori. And those people will need you more than I will."

"You say it like you're not going to come back, Sainthart."

Elon gave him a grim smile and clapped him on the shoulder. "I knew you'd be the man for the job."

Three instead of four descended the hillside, and the rebellion fell silent as they approached. "It's not good," Elon announced. No amount of fancy wording could mask that. Whoever crested that rise would see it in an instant. "It's not good, and there are people down there who need help. But there are people we left behind who will also need help. Espera…" Elon choked back his words. "Espera cannot be liberated from a force this massive. Not by us."

"What will we do, Commander?" Basl asked from where he stood in the front row, eager eyes confused by Elon's resignation.

Beyond the ridge behind them, the sky cracked open and hundreds of lightning bolts rained down into the harbor. The roar of thunder echoed from a storm-dark sky and ships ignited in violent pops and sparks as the barrage of lighting bolts struck true. Some of the rebels gasped and stepped back in fear.

"We're going to do what we can, and that means that most of you need to go back and help the rest of the camp get to Ares. This force will not stop at borders, and we *must* warn the realm of these horrors."

"And those of us who wish to stay?" Maiyra questioned. Her arms were crossed over her leather-armored chest in defiance. "I hear the winds Elon, though I need not with the stench so ripe. Something unholy is ravaging our home and you mean us to turn tail?"

There were murmurs of agreement, silenced by another sizzling rain of lightning from the sky from beyond. Roane wrenched his head around and stared over the rise. "Sainthart."

"I know, Roane." Elon looked to Rhori, who stepped forward.

"All who wish to help our comrades and deliver this warning across the border, come with me." And with one final glance, his face solemn as he turned, Rhori began to walk through the crowd.

"And those who wish to descend into the city with me," Elon said.

The group began to divide. Like a mother goose with her ducklings, Rhori began to trail people behind him. In the end, Elon and Roane were left with Issaria's old tutor, Magi Caltac Kholozzo, the former Captain of the archers Gilben Hamm, Maiyra, and Basl among less than twenty-five other faces, most of them on a first-name basis with Elon. Hundreds cut down to a familiar few dozen.

It would have to do.

6

ELON

Though they knew the battle raged only streets away, it was quiet on the outskirts of Espera.

Too quiet.

Elon and Roane led staggered lines of soldiers between houses as they continued toward the heart of the city. Teams of magicians broke off, knocking gently on doors and whispering warnings to those who were keen to listen. Now that they were in the city, they could see the sky alight with Xenviera's power. One bolt pierced the dark clouds overhead, Xen's lightning arrow, the cloud rumbled as it swallowed the filament, then like a petulant child, showered the arena beneath with a volley of lightning that cared not if it stuck ship, water, or abomination in the street. Screams and moans of pain echoed from buildings and the remains.

Some, Elon thought with dismay, could not be helped.

When Elon looked again for Roane among their ranks, he was nowhere to be found, but he could have expected as much. Xenviera was deep in the city, fighting alone. She was right about the damage she could cause, but with that much power, they would want to eliminate her once they discovered the pattern of her attack. Elon was glad

47

Roane would find her. They would be stronger together. At his side instead, was Basl, and behind him was Maiyra.

It started slowly, but then they started to see them—the citizens they were here to help. They came out of their homes, satchels on their backs and arms full of possessions. A family, crying babe in its mother's arms, scrambling through the brush with a rebel guarding their retreat, stone sword at the ready. A man carrying his two children, both almost too big to be held, led the way for Daphnica, who held a pale, bleeding woman in her arms. Her left leg was gone below the knee.

The cut was not clean, but the wound had cauterized. Daphnica had likely removed the limb herself with her fire mana. Elon steeled his spine against the horrors, knowing more awaited them the further they went into the city.

At the next corner, Maiyra flung out her arm, her face pale in the darkness. "It's just there."

Using the flat of his sword Elon peered around the corner. Indeed, one of the...things was stationed on the next street over. The golden-colored casing sparkled scarlet in the light of a nearby fire. Across the street, a large group of refugees led by Magi Caltac approached, unaware they would cross paths with...whatever those were.

It all happened so fast. So out of his control. One moment he was peering at the creature's reflection, wondering which of his shatter-spheres would incapacitate such a monstrosity, and the next Maiyra was barreling past him, hands alight with silver wind magic as she blasted Magi Caltac and his band of refugees backward from the intersection.

A maelstrom of spinning fire engulfed the street.

Elon flung his arm out, pushing a curious Basl behind him as he too, pressed against the building they crouched beside. Searing heat rushed past sucking oxygen with it as it ravaged the street, igniting trees and homes alike. Across the street, singed but alive and well, Maiyra was already moving the group and Magi Caltac back the way they'd come.

He fisted a blackpowder shattersphere in one hand, his sword in another, though what a blade could do against such unholy magic, he was not sure. Surely to brace for combat against one of these things was to kiss the Cosmos at last. "Ready, Basl? We hold the line here. Nothing gets past us while our people get away."

The ground shook as the creature advanced. The familiar spark and crackle of a storm pressurizing textured the air. The hair on the back of his neck stood on end. Truly, they faced Zephyrus the storm reaper this day.

Pale as death, Basl swallowed hard and nodded. He brandished a terramond-studded hilt and summoned a blade of black crystal. Elon raised his eyebrows in surprise. "An armament magician, Basl?" The boy only nodded, too nervous to speak. Elon nodded his praise and understanding. "What a waste you'd been as a mere messenger. You should've been my squire."

He watched the boy's face alight with pride, then he was running across the cobblestone street to where Maiyra was vanishing into an alley with the last of the group she'd saved. Elon launched the black-powder shattersphere against the chest of the beast. It exploded, engulfing the thing in flames that charred its casing black. Steam poured out of the cavities between its plating. Fire blazed in an unholy halo that made its golden gaze seem as though this *thing*, merely one of many that they'd seen, seemed born of the Cosmos to smite them from the world.

And still, it advanced, barrel-like arm raised to attack with a crackling white light akin to Xen's ferocious mana. Without thinking, Elon heaved another sphere which shattered atop the thing's arm. The silex compound expanded, pillowy foam that hardened to a rock-like grey substance. It swallowed the opening and silenced the storm.

Elon glanced back to where Basl still braced himself where he'd left him, frozen in fear as he looked on.

As if it sensed his distraction, or could understand that Elon's attention was divided, the creature tried again to fire its weapon. This time, at Basl.

"No!" Elon cried, much too far away now to save the lad.

White hot light poured from the clogged arm. Steam screamed out of the gaps between its joints as lighting shattered the weapon from within. The guttural groan of alloy twisting and tearing wrenched through the alley as the blast of magic detonated inside the creature, shredding alloy to shrapnel in seconds.

The golden light that filled its eye-casings dimmed, then flickered out. Its head sagged against its chest, and the only life left in it was the fire that smoldered at its neck and shoulders.

Elon didn't wait. "Basl! Move!"

And Cosmos above, he did. Scampered out into the ruined street and to Elon's side like a hound. "I...I..."

"It happens," Elon replied without looking at the boy. "C'mon. Let's make sure they—" Maiyra's scream pierced the night as if she were standing beside him, delivered on silver wind. "Move! Move, move, move!" Elon cried, half dragging the boy down the streets in the direction Maiyra had retreated with the civilians.

Down side streets and between homes, how he knew where he was going, Elon had no idea, but he arrived at his destination all the same.

"Here, you foul creature!" Magi Caltac taunted as he came into view. He wielded a morning star of flame and danced back and forth on surprisingly spry legs as the mace spun like a comet above his head. His eye patch had torn free to reveal the black, shriveled remains of his right eye, taken by the *sanguignis fervent* ages ago. "I'll remind you why they called me the Fist of the Forge!" He loosed his weapon on the golden monstrosities before him, bashing them with the fireball like a meteor strike.

When the smoke cleared, it was apparent the fire Magi had done little damage besides blackening their metal casings.

Three of the abominations had cornered dozens of refugees. Cowed them into a corner behind the old fire magician, where Maiyra lay bleeding from her temple in a sobbing woman's arms.

A soot-smeared child shook her leg pleading with rasping breath, "Wake up, wake up!"

The sight unhinged him.

"They're not alive, Magi!" Elon shouted as he leaped into the fray. "We can disable them!"

"I'd like to see you try!" An unfamiliar voice replied vehemently.

Magi Caltac rounded on Elon, golden eye wide in terror. "Elon, no!" was all he managed as green light filled the narrow alley, and the stones beneath his feet became as pliable as water.

He plunged into the earth so quickly that his arms lifted above his head as it swallowed the fire magician. The ground regained its solidity and all that remained were Magi Caltac Kholozzo's twitching hands, scrabbling for purchase to pull the magician free of his earthen tomb. Basl pushed past Elon and fell to his knees, scratching and clawing at the ground where the fire magi had stood.

Elon only heard the silence in his head as a white-hot bolt of lightning surged past him with frightening nearness that had currents of electricity snapping between himself and the projectile in sizzling arcs. He hadn't dodged, but it had missed.

Basl's spine arched violently in the wrong direction as the bolt slammed into him. The sound that tore itself free from his charred corpse as he fell was no more than the sound of his ghost coming to haunt Elon's dreams for the rest of his days.

"Stupid boy," an enemy voice sneered.

Elon whirled and flung a blackpowder shattersphere at the colossal beast nearest him. He felt the searing heat ripple off of it as fire erupted from the chemical reaction within. Blade drawn, he sliced across the backs of its knees as if it truly were a beast of flesh and blood instead of gears and pistons—mechanical, he realized. This thing wasn't born but *made* by the hands of magicians.

Though it was some machination, his slash was rewarded with the hiss of air from within the leg of the thing. Something gave out inside, and its entire left flank stalled out, sagging several inches lower than its counterpart.

Elon did not linger. To stop would be to die, and he had the debt of lives to repay.

Moving toward his next target with unerring hatred roiling inside, he threw another sphere from his belt—a shrapnelsphere meant to do the most damage as it splintered outward with shards of alloy and stone meant to impale and kill. He heard it strike true against the red-glowing chest cavity of the machine. Heard the scream of his opponent as he dropped to his knees and slid behind the leg of the remaining creation.

Something tore into his thigh. Pain stung in the back of his mind. The warmth of his blood seeping into his lap was secondary as he hauled himself back up and raced toward the fool who had thought to trap them here like wild animals. Elon's vision slicked red as he brought down his sword upon the soldier's outstretched arm. The strange rock held aloft in his palm spiraled into the air with his hand as crimson spurted from the severed limb. He pivoted, swinging his sword again, relishing in the feeling of crunching alloy armor giving way to tender flesh beneath.

The satisfying crunch of bone as his blade severed his spine just inches above his shoulders. The body dropped to the ground and blood pooled, running between the cobblestones like scarlet rain. The head rolled to a stop, and black smoke and fire reflected in lifeless eyes.

Still, Elon advanced. The machines were still active, glowing golden from every inch of polished casing. The impact of the shrapnelsphere left a blackened starburst on the chest of one, but otherwise, both were fully functional, though they had stilled now that the magician was dead. He drove his blade into metal bellies, ripped open their backs, and tore fistfuls of wires from within. Without someone to tell them what to do, the machines only endured the brutality until the golden light faded from their eyes and their inner workings fell silent.

Only then did Elon kneel to retrieve the strange device. A black stone embedded with element crystals and carved with unfamiliar symbols. He was turning it over in his palm when he heard Roane.

"Commander," he rasped, choking on tears or debris, Elon did not want to turn to find out. His soul ached with the knowledge that he'd evaded death for it to find another in his place. Before him, beside limp hands growing out of the dirt like strange trees, was the blackened corpse of Basl Koewellyn, too green for this war though he'd demanded to come anyways.

He turned to face another atrocity.

Roane's dark skin was still stone-scaled in patches, his mana's use of stone manipulation in creating an intricate armor for himself. Xenviera lay prone in his arms, head back, indigo eyes vacant of her vengeful storm. "I couldn't..." He shook his head, unable to say the words.

Three arrows had punctured her armor with deadly accuracy. For all his stone-scales were worth for himself, it offered nothing to another.

Zephyrus took home his reaper at last.

It was too much. He wanted to fall to his knees, scream at the sky, and demand justice from the Cosmos, but there would be time enough for that later. Now, *right* now, he had to honor their sacrifices and get these people to safety.

Xenviera, using herself as a decoy to allow them time, was too much. Caltac, defending dozens of innocents, was too much. Basl, whose death should have been Elon's own, was too much.

He would lose no more. Not today.

"Retreat," he whispered, though the command sounded foreign and wrong on his tongue.

Elon limped toward the back of the alley where the civilians were crouched in terror. The dirty little boy who had been shaking Maiyra backed away as Elon hoisted her limp form into his arms. She was still warm, and that was a good sign, even if her head lolled back and made her look otherwise.

At least he would bring Safaiya's sister back to her.

"Retreat!" His voice cracked and sounded pitiful even to himself as he called out to anyone who could hear. "Retreat! Rebels retreat!"

7

SHURA

The Titans took the harbor with hellfire and hurricanes. Ruthless as always, Risa set the eastern ports aflame. Playing with an element alien to her own seemed to delight her. Ships smoldered as the sea swallowed them at the docks. Bodies littered the bay as gulls and whatever lurked in the sea picked at frosty corpses. From there Risa's regiments took the bazaars and the fountain squares with little resistance and a myriad of destruction. Plumes of smoke towered over the flames like monoliths dedicated to the old Mythos. In the West, Timbrel had secured the spires and whatever ships had docked nearer to the palace. There were fewer flames in his direction, but then Timbrel never was one for fiery theatrics. He would ensure that there were no refugees.

Not from the palace, and not from the city.

Shura's orders had been clear.

Make them fear. Make them hate. And then break them.

The elegance he had admired before shattered like the fragile mirror he'd known it to be. Shura shook his head, tutting under his breath as he mentally scolded the weakness his dear sister had fallen prey to. This *Eventide*, as she called it, was a pathetic and gross abuse of power. He saw no use in it save the fear-mongering she lorded over

54

the poor people of this city and a death sentence to the rest of the world.

When the chaos was at a peak, the screaming a gallant backdrop to smoke and ruin, Shura disembarked his vessel and strode across the last dock with Phelix at his side and a regiment of soldiers at his back. The massive forms of his metallic titans rising from the ashes of a glittering city reduced to cinders brought a cruel smile to his face as he strode through the wreckage. Titans nearest him swiveled to watch him pass: a constant moving guard of unrivaled proportion.

"Magnificent. Look at this mess," he commented as he entered the temple district. A vandalized courtyard, half-flooded from a broken fountain, loomed before them in shadow. Inside, several soldiers were looting, pillaging, ransacking, raping—whatever they pleased really. Shura wasn't one to bind men by trivial things like morals in something as base and hedonistic as war.

He would curb crueler appetites when he was rightfully on the throne. Until then, he was a conqueror, and nothing would be barred. His name would strike fear into the fabled Warlord of the West.

Ellorhys would either fear him or love him. It mattered not which it was.

When he was able, Shura planned to set out and find the fragments before his Maiden could turn the tide of fate against him and sweep him out to sea.

Before them, a lone soldier ran at them through the debris—one of their own. "Sire! Prince Shura, there was great resistance in one of the northern burrows, but we've secured the palace. Commander Amorelle has detained the Empress Regent in the throne room."

Wicked delight ignited a dark fire inside him and the chasm of his mana purred at the perfectly executed conquest. "I'd hate to keep my sister waiting." He looked to his left and found Phelix, a cunning smirk upon his Commander's face like a satisfied jungle cat.

"We can take our time, Prince Shura. Risa knows to make the Evernight Witch comfortable until you arrive."

"Tut, tut, Phelix," he scolded lightly. "Let's not stoop to name-calling, shall we? We've come uninvited to my dear sister's door. Let's at least *try* to be a bit respectful?"

Phelix's tight-lipped smirk pulled into a wide half-moon grin. "Sire, I do believe you've made a joke."

"I can be the joking sort, my friend. When the mood strikes me fit."

Debris clattered, tumbling clumsily down a haphazard pile of ruination. Weapons drawn, elements flared to life in sparks and splashes, and a dozen of his guards rounded on the nearby alley.

"Hold," Shura said.

From the rubble of a collapsed building, still spewing white smoke from embers hot deep inside, a soot-smeared child in a tattered grey chiton dress scurried across the street before him like a cockroach. Fear etched in her ragged face at the sight of him gave Shura a thrill. They feared him now, but they would love him soon. They'll see this show of might was the only way to make his claim. To ensure he was taken seriously, ignored no longer by these southern fools who only knew him as King Tayman's bastard prince.

Once he'd dealt with the little issue of his sister, he would make the citizens of Espera see him with fresh eyes.

As the true king and rightful heir to the Imperial throne.

The path to the palace was cleared by Titans, then monitored by soldiers as he passed through the twisted remains of the alloy gates. There were no soldiers on his walk up to the palace, so he took his time. A leisurely stroll, his hands tucked neatly behind his back as he beheld the sheer elegance of the Crystal Palace up close.

Ornate balconies, terraces, and bridges had been laboriously carved into the blackish-purple crystal. Pillars were decorated with flourishes at their cornices, windows had Mythos guarding their sills. Towers glittered in the starlit night, an endless sea of stars ready to drown them all with purpose. At the base of the palace flanking the front doors, grand mosaics of shell and stone, gem and metal unfurled the sky: Night on the southern side and Day on the north. An uncanny division that had lasted far too long.

Enough of that. It was time for a family reunion.

Shura strode up the stairs and into the wide open doors. Risa knew just how he liked to be welcomed to his new home. Every few feet, a guard in black with a ruthless expression inclined their head in deference as he passed. Portraits illuminated by solarium hung between every other pillar.

Aurelia and Obsidia, side by side. The style was a bit gaudy for his tastes, but perhaps it had been hard to look at the Primordial Mythos. Something about the first portrait was just *off*. The next was Aurelia and her Emperor consort, Endymion Elysitao. Fair-haired and lion-faced, the rugged man still paled in comparison to his beloved. Resplendent in hues of white and purple, Aurelia looked near-metallic next to her spouse.

The place where the next portrait should be was barren. A series of empty brackets lined the wall where the oversized and ornately framed canvases hung. Shura did not need a guide to tell him whose image had hung here.

Like everything bearing his mother's image, he imagined the portrait had been destroyed in the purge of the Black Arts following her death.

Shura moved on to the next portrait, again of the happy Elysitao pair, this time, with a golden-haired toddler cradled lovingly between them. Helios. He passed by the portraits of Helios and Umbriel on their wedding day, and another with a young, dark-haired girl. Shura came to pause in front of the last portrait before the long hall emptied at the base of a grand staircase.

A pair of midnight-haired ladies in silk and sparkling finery. Both wore nearly identical dresses in indigo, violet, and lightest lilac. Pearls and amethyst encrusted each bangle, bauble, and brooch. The eldest held an onyx scepter with a golden sunburst caged around a massive yellow diamond. Her left hand, bejeweled and domineering, rested on the younger's pale, bare shoulder. Curls fell around the young woman's face in delicate spirals. Her mouth was a rosebud, upturned only just, a secret just waiting to bloom.

But those eyes.

The striking violet of her irises appeared to be honed and polished from gemstones themselves—somehow fierce and naive, calculating and kind. Even in paint, her gaze was magnetizing. It was clear the artist was enamored with the princess. It was contagious. Shura wasn't sure if he wanted to devour her or destroy her.

Do not become bewitched. Her allure is only one of balance. You seek her as your opposite, like calls to like. She is your kindred, as once she was mine.

Shura stiffened. He knew this. Lovely though she was, she was nothing more than an obstacle.

A necessary sacrifice.

"The Imperial Princess, Sire?" Phelix asked after they'd lingered much longer than the previous portraits.

He answered without looking away from Princess Issaria's visage. "She is the one I seek. My Maiden of Light." He tore his gaze from the portrait. "Let's see to it that I snuff her light out before she becomes too much of a problem."

"I already dispatched riders to seek the rumors you spoke of. The oddities, the bizarre, and unfounded. If such stories are out there, our soldiers will send word immediately."

"I can ask nothing more, Captain." Shura continued toward the stairs, Phelix Stormgren not a step behind.

"Risa, darling!" He called out lovingly as he ascended a double-sided staircase that framed the receiving hall. "I hope you've been kind to the Empress Regent, my little cobra!" He made a show of sauntering into the Throne Room unabashedly.

He made note of a golden-plated titan lingering in the corner of the room. Its golden-brass plating marked it first, the same one they had tested in the caverns. Risa had become a bit attached after its malevolent display. She'd even nicknamed the Titan *Ra'ak Shar*, old tongue for world-breaker.

Skewered with a jagged icicle against a charred pillar nearest the throne, though the corpse was nothing short of fresh, was a hideously disfigured man. A sparse slice of crimson hair graced one side of his head, but the other was a melted-wax monstrosity. Truly, he was shocked the man had withstood whatever caused *that* long enough to match talents against Risa Amorelle.

Kneeling at the base of the throne—a truly garish thing in itself if he was being honest. The whole thing looked crude compared to the refined artistry of the palace craftsmanship—was a tear-streaked, make-up-smeared, shivering heap of his eldest sister. Silken black hair was in complete disarray, and her tundra-frosted gaze was bloodshot as she met his identical stare.

Frigid, winter solstice eyes. Akin to Obsidia's bloodline.

He held her gaze long enough for recognition to pale her temper before he returned his attention to his Commander. Risa was wearing what he could only assume to be the Imperial crown atop her snow-white coils. The crown was as gaudy as the throne, even from a distance. And she was perched on his throne, degrading Hecate to a footstool beneath her bloody, mud-caked boots. As if sensing how it soured his mood, she removed her feet from his sister's back and stood.

Though Hecate tried to stand, Risa narrowed her golden eyes and tightened her fist and Hecate only whimpered, bending low over her bent knees. "I didn't say you could move!" Risa shrieked before turning to Shura and addressing him with reverence. "Your Eminence."

Walk with graceful death, she had said upon their first encounter. Graceful death was a gift she could but did not often provide as was evident by the dripping corpse of a melted man. Regardless of her methods, she was instrumental and deadly, if not as toxic as a viper and just as temperamental. Given her past, he was inclined to let her have free reign. Her cruelty was fantastic, and he quite enjoyed the little games they played. A bored cat toying with its second lunch.

"I was keeping the seat warm for you, sire," she lied smoothly.

"Thoughtful of you, Risa. I do *detest* a chilly buttocks and it is much cooler here than I anticipated."

"And this..." she said as she gestured vaguely to the obscenely sparkly crown of raw crystals atop her moonbeam hair. "I thought it more suited to my tastes than yours. I thought I'd earned myself a present for taking the palace."

He shook his head as he mounted the dais and tossed his weight onto the throne without an iota of hesitation. He leaned back, thoughtful in his expression as he brought a hand to his chin. "A gift for my most esteemed Commander on a day of undisputed triumph?" His eyes fell upon his groveling sibling. Without looking away from her piteous state, he said flippantly, "It suits you, Risa. Keep it if it pleases you. On that note, take whatever finery you desire. Too long have your skills gone unrewarded, and I dare say I may overtax your talents tonight."

"Nothing is too taxing, Sire," she simpered, sparing a glance at the fallen regent. "You are generous, and I will certainly claim more rewards later. Right now, I am your humble servant." Even in a game, she knew how to stroke his ego.

A wicked, sadistic smile curled his mouth. "Oh. Hello, sister," Shura said as if she'd surprised him for tea without sending a rider in advance. "I didn't see you down there. It's so good of you to come congratulate me on my grand entrance to Imperial Court."

"I am no kin of yours, *conqueror*."

Shura crossed his arms. "Is that any way to speak to your baby brother?" He looked back to Phelix, who stood at attention at the foot of the dais. "And after I defended her to you!" He huffed and shook his head. "Ungrateful family members, I tell you. Well, Captain Storm-gren, you can go right ahead and call her a witch if you like."

"I'd say she very much deserves it after you've so kindly removed responsibility as Empress Regent from her after so many years tormented by murders and tragedy," Phelix replied in a rather rehearsed tone.

"I am no longer the Empress Regent!" Hecate announced with some modicum of dignity. "The Council voted me to ascend the throne!"

Measured and slow, Shura asked, "And...have you ascended the throne?"

"Not officially, no." Shura's gaze narrowed and she became flustered, "But that's only a technicality," she floundered. "The documents are being drawn up, and a ceremony is being planned. We've only just had news—"

"I've heard enough from you." Shura glanced at Risa and shook his head.

Again, she clenched her fist. Hecate cried out as she convulsed, her back arching so far he thought she may break in half. It was as if she were being squeezed by an invisible fist. Bones splintered under the pressure exerted by an unseen force. She coughed, blood bubbled at her lips like dribbled wine.

"I think it's time you listen to *me*, dear sister." Shura folded his hands before him and nodded at Risa.

Beside him, Risa widened her stance and brought her hands up like claws. Razor-sharp nails glinted as she flexed her hands and dragged them through the air. Simultaneously, Hecate's prone body was wrenched upright, and made to curtsey in a series of jerky, disassociated motions that made her look like a marionette.

"Much better." Shura clapped. "You've learned etiquette so quickly! There's hope for you yet, sister."

As if flattered by the compliment Hecate flapped her arm as if she were fanning herself, the movement too wide and slow to appear natural. She looked more mechanical than Ra'ak Shar as he pivoted on pistons in the corner, watching and waiting for Risa's lodestone commands to be violated.

"I'm going to tell you a story, sister. It's a very sad story, about a baby born in secret to a forsaken Queen. Why was his birth a secret, you ask? You should be familiar with this intention. His aunt, the Empress, would have wanted him dead if she knew of his existence. So the Queen fled with her lover where the Empress could not follow, and there she gave birth to a prince.

"And though the queen and her king loved their son very much, they had a duty to uphold and sought to overthrow the tyrant empress who ruled from the south. The time for their ascent to True Darkness was nigh upon them and they had to leave their precious son behind without even a promise to return." Shura sighed and put the back of his hand to his head. "I can't. It's just so tragic. Risa, will you?"

"Overconfidence beckons fate, it would have it. Their plan, though glorious, was flawed, and did not account for two small factors."

Through gritted teeth and compulsion Hecate strained out like a poltergeist, "We know this story, your Grace! Please, tell me what happened to the orphan prince!"

"Oh, all right," Shura replied indulgently. "If you insist."

"The prince was raised crudely. Roughly. The bastard offspring of an aging king in a failing, frozen kingdom. He would have been better off with the wolves." Shura bared his teeth, his eyes predatory. "At least then I'd know something of mercy."

"And then one fated day you slaughtered your cosmic sister, as we Imperials are want to do. Murderous tendencies run in the family, after all. And I was caught in an unnatural blizzard caused by *your* upset of nature. While I was in that blizzard, I almost died. And that unlocked something in me that hadn't been there before." Shura glared at his sister. "Do you know what it was that made the cruel king and his frigid bitch of a wife detest the orphan prince so much?"

Hecate did not respond. In the thrall of Risa's blackwater, there was nothing she could do without being compelled.

"Risa!" Shura barked.

She flexed her hands and grappled claws at the former regent. Hecate squawked not unlike a parrot repeating old bits of conversation, "I do not know!"

"Of course you don't. You've never wondered for a day in your life what it would be like to be powerless."

"Powerless! How could you ever be powerless!"

"I know, sister. It's hard to believe, at this moment, that once I was as sad and manipulated as our sweet niece is sure to be when I locate her. But alas. It's true. It's another thing we share, she and I. We both spent a majority of our lives believing ourselves to be lacking something vital, only to find that not only is that something there, but it is beyond anything I could even attempt to explain to one such as yourself."

"It can't be!" Hecate repeated.

"But it can, big sister. It can."

Shura gloated on his throne as Hecate stood rigid before him. It was a moment he'd imagined a thousand times over as he prepared for the invasion. It was overkill to have Ra'ak Shar present. It almost spoiled the moment. *Almost.*

"She won't help you!" Hecate blurted out in blind rage.

The outburst was so unexpected that Ra'ak Shar rotated, sensors focusing on whether or not it would have to intervene. While there had been no mishaps so far, the Titans were prone to being loose with their firing commands. It brought wary glances from Shura and Phelix as Risa tightened her grip on the Imperial's body lest she get herself incinerated before they were through.

"I don't need her help, darling. I need yours."

Hecate's eyes widened but she was unable to answer. A glance and Risa released her enough for a scathing reply. "You murdered Galen! I will *never* help you!"

Shura rolled his eyes. "I am willing to wager that's an awfully hypocritical statement from you, Hecate."

Risa needed no signal to increase the pressure and pain.

Hecate's screams were unearthly and haunting as they echoed off the throne room ceiling.

"Tell me, sister. The atrocities you have committed in the name of our mother." He clucked his tongue against his teeth. The sigil branded on his chest burned with dissatisfaction and his ice eyes bled into murderous black.

Did you think it was enough to redeem your betrayal, Dark Daughter? Did you think this feeble mimicry of a shattered dynasty would spare you from my wrath now?

Hecate chuckled darkly as she hung her head. "Spill my blood all you want, *brother,*" Hecate spat. Red, blood, and other viscera amid a black tar-like substance splattered on the crystal between them. "The Eventide curse was not sealed in my blood that night." She laughed.

Hecate's cackle echoing off the ceiling was more chilling than her screams.

"No." Shura's icy iris returned like a mirror wiped of ink as he realized whose magic had been gathered like water in a carafe.

"It is bound by hers." Hecate's reaper-moon eyes glinted with malice and cunning as she confirmed it. "As long as that little brat lives, the curse cannot be undone. I had intended to take it into myself with a vial of fresh blood and the original ritual," she taunted. "You can torture me as much as you'd like, *brother*, I'll never tell you how I did it."

Shura furrowed his brow. "And I believe you, dear sister. I would not force your tongue so barbarically! No matter," he said as he clapped his hands together and mimed wiping them clean. "I had hoped to demonstrate benevolence by obliterating your Eventide curse, but all in good time." He scoffed, "You mistake me, sister, I harbor no love for our dear niece. I only need her magic." To Phelix, he said, "Assemble whatever citizens you can find. Bring them where I may speak with them."

Phelix nodded once and was out the doors barking orders, soldiers falling in line in moments.

When Shura looked back to his sister he was shaking his head. "A shame really, sister. Since I can't have a benevolent demonstration, I'm forced to perform a malevolent one. The citizens have to know who I am, and that I *will* free them from your wretched curse."

By now, Hecate was shaking so violently, that her shivering vibrated through Risa's compulsion. "You wouldn't hurt...*family*, would you?" she croaked.

And then Shura's face softened. His eyes thawed and his smile grew wistful and light. "Funny you should ask that, sister, when you failed to ask about the fates of the aging king in the north or his water-seer wife when I was telling you the story of the orphan prince."

It took a long while, but Risa allowed the fallen Queen this one grace. The time it took her a long moment to ask of her own accord, "What happened to the cruel king and his wicked queen?"

"When my Saros Curse broke, and Obsidia was able to reach me, her chosen heir at last, I returned to the Keep in Rhunmesc. My false mother refused to see me as usual, but I had no problem saving her for second."

"Second?" she parroted as her skin turned ashen.

"Well, I killed the king, of course. Don't worry. Your execution will at least have witnesses."

8

CALIX

"And you *really* think Princess Shairi will just go along with it?" Alander asked as he stretched his arms over his head and mussed his tawny hair.

Flanked by Raif and Alander, Calix made his way across the palace yard toward the stables. "She's not going to like it, but it's the only plan I've got," Calix replied. "I'm a little more concerned about telling Issaria the finer details."

"She'd hold a grudge like that?" Alander asked. "Even when it's the *only* option?"

Bright sun lanced through sparse clouds in broad beams that dappled the crisp lawn underfoot. The sweet scent of hay and sun-warmed fur filled his nose as they neared the barn, but it was his ears that picked up on her voice.

"It's *absurd,* Eiren. Four ceremonies. Four!" Princess Issaria, as promised by the guards, had excused herself to the stables after a trying afternoon with his mother and a slew of councilors who were officiating the wedding ceremony, and thus the preparations.

Raif cut Calix an amused look, eyebrows raised high into his mess of blonde hair. "I see someone's already had the liberty of warming her up for us."

66

"Maybe what I've got to say will ease some of the…stress."

Raif laughed and Alander looked perplexed. "Surely the princess will see that Calix only has her best interests at heart?"

"You haven't met the girl yet, have you Alander?" Raif asked.

Again, her frustrated cry echoed from the stables, "They want me to be *naked*, Mint! I don't care if it's tradition! It's barbaric!"

"Perhaps then, we should intervene with our news before your bride's dulcet concerns reach some not-so-sympathetic ears?" Alander suggested.

The trio entered the barn, and relished the brief reprieve of shade and slightly cooler, if not stagnant air, pungent with the scent of animals and sun-ripened fields. Far at the other end of the long stable hall, Eiren siphoned water from the fountain like a river through the air, filling the troughs of the nearby stalls. Rhaminta leaned against an open stall door with a half-full bag of grain feed propped beside her.

Rhaminta straightened at their approach. "Oh, Issaria, the—"

"No, Mint! I won't do it! Not this moon, not the next. How is it even supposed to be a moon? She just wants to humiliate me and if I'm just supposed to lie down and take it, she's got another—" At that moment Princess Issaria stormed out of the open stall, fury on her face and yellow hay sticking out of her hair, despite her attempt to pull her hair back into a tail at the back of her head. Blinking, she turned to take in the newcomers. Delight rippled through his stomach as her violet eye met his and the angry pink tint on the apples of her cheek deepened to cherry, her protests forgotten on her lips. "Oh, Prince Calix," she murmured.

"What did I say about names, Issa?" Her blush crept down her throat and Calix could barely keep the grin off his face. "What are you doing in Arietes' stall?"

"Arietes?" Issaria looked back at the stall and the tawny mare inside.

"She's been my steed and faithful companion since she was a foal." Calix neared the stall and Arietes stuck her muzzle out and lipped at the air. "You know I always bring you a treat," he murmured as he reached into his pocket and offered a pair of sugar cubes.

"She has the kindest eyes," Issaria said from beside him as Arietes lipped at his palm, then finding that he had no further treats, turned to Issaria and nudged her chest.

"She likes you."

"She probably likes everyone."

From behind them, Raif interjected, "Not true, Princess. That horse hates me. Won't get any closer than this."

"Arietes only bit you the one time, and you *were* being a jackass." Calix laughed before refocusing on the matter at hand. "I take it the meetings with my mother did not go well?"

Issaria shrugged nonchalantly and rubbed Arietes' nose, then moved his mane from his eyes. She gave his neck a few pats before she answered, "Let's just say I don't come out to the stables when things go my way. I like to care for them when I'm…"

"Furious?" Calix provided and she laughed, elbowing him in the side. "It's okay, Issa. My mother is incorrigible at times. She was rather meddlesome when she kept hoping I would finally pick Shairi, but shifting that dedication to making you miserable instead isn't going to be tolerated."

"The stables, the work…it helps."

"I told her princesses shouldn't do the stable boy's work but she just wouldn't listen," Rhaminta commented.

"I just needed to vent. The work feels like being at home and needing a moment to scream. Your mother is…well she makes Aunt Cate feel like a loving relative."

"Didn't your Aunt try to kill you? More than once?" Alander asked.

Issaria shot him a look. "Point made. I would rather try to hug Aunt Cate right now than sit in another meeting about my wedding. No one has even asked what I want!"

"Ah, yes. We couldn't help but hear you as we approached," Raif said. "Might want to tone it down a tad." He gave her a knowing smirk. "Always causing trouble, Princess."

"I warned her about that," Eiren said as she returned the water to the fountain and wiped her hands on her cobalt skirts. "Voices carry, Issa."

Issaria cut a glare at Eiren before she folded and said, "I'm sorry about my volume but *you* try being told to purify yourself for marriage in front of dozens of officials. Naked, mind you!" She looked back to Calix, resigned defeat on her face. "I'm certain your mother loathes me more now than she did before we were officially engaged, but I sort of lost it when she insinuated that I'd lost my...my virtue when Jallah transported me here as a slave."

Calix clenched his jaw. "That's quite enough of that. I'll speak with her. I meant to address it after the announcement and got distracted with logistics, and that's my shortcoming." He reached out and plucked a sprig of yellow hay from her hair. "I'm sorry you had to endure that, but I may have a solution to quite a few of our problems." He tried to smirk at her but it just felt vengeful. "And my mother is going to be *furious* when she meets the fake us in Sol Caravali and has no choice but to let them continue without interference, lest she cause a scene and become a *total* embarrassment to the dynasty."

Issaria gave him a wicked smile that sent his blood rushing. "You mean I won't have to be naked, *purifying* myself for you like some fancy desert, in front of dozens of strangers?" Her venom was unmistakable.

"That does sound rather invasive when you put it like that, Princess," Raif said with a dry chuckle.

"The purifying ceremonies would be one of the problems addressed, yes."

"Perhaps we should gather the players, Sire?" Alander suggested.

"Yes, let's. It would be best to coordinate our movements."

"Absolutely *not!*" Princess Shairi shrieked, her voice echoing off the walls in Prince Calix's parlor. "I will not be a *decoy* while you traipse about the continent on some magical quest!"

"It's not a sight-seeing adventure, Shairi!" Calix hollered back, his patience long since dissipated. They'd been arguing tactics for hours. Dinner had been brought up for all of them, but the meal lay cold beneath alloy domes on the table as the argument raged on. "We need a distraction while we make for the Ascalith!"

Issaria laid a gentle hand on his elbow. "I have to agree, Prince Calix, this does sound risky."

"Risky? It's taking *all* of the risk!" The whites around Shairi's emerald eyes were visible as she rounded on Issaria. "I don't even look like you!" She looked back to Calix, the vein in her neck throbbing as she added, "This is cruel, even for you."

"I'm sending Zakarian with you! As me!"

"He's not even a Fire Magician, *Calix!*"

"I *am* a little concerned as to how I'm supposed to impersonate you, Sire," Zak said from where he sat by the hearth. "The only commonality we have is black hair."

"It's all for ceremony! There will be a whole battalion of soldiers with the procession, so there's no need to use magic," Calix explained. "You'll wear gloves, which is not uncommon for me while I travel, and you'll be so far from Hinhallow that no one should know what I look like for certain."

"And how exactly am I supposed to pretend to be as pale and frail as her?" Shairi yowled, then simpered at Issaria unapologetically. "Sorry, dear. But your complexion is so fair. I'd never pass. And not to mention our hair is just…I suppose I could always wear a wig of horse hair or something."

"Horse hair?" Rhaminta scowled from the lounge. "Issaria's hair is lovely!"

"Actually," Raif interjected from beside Mint before the two Aresians could get into it with each other. "Princess Shairi, you're not going to be playing Issaria."

Shairi's tirade died in her throat. "I'm…not? Then why am I here while we talk about decoys and distractions?"

"Because having you along with the decoys would add credibility to the procession," Calix supplied. "No one would doubt that Zak *wasn't* me, and no one this side of the Timeline has ever laid eyes on Issaria up close, so other than her black hair and purple eyes, her appearance is a gamble." He crossed the room and opened an adjoining door to his receiving area. "But I thought we might as well stay as close as possible."

A second Issaria entered the parlor. Wild black curls framed a petite, pale figure. She carried herself with poise as Calix ushered her deeper into the room. Issaria's mouth was open as she stood to meet her false twin. Calix watched as Issaria lifted the girl's thick curls, and circled her for inspection. Issaria was inches shorter than the decoy, and she'd still not gained back all her mass from crossing the Glass, so she was still too thin, but the resemblance chilled him all the same.

"Who are you?"

"My name is Vixenya, Princess." Bright blue eyes, the only startling difference between them, sparkled in the firelight as Issaria examined her. "I'm from Rosvia, but I haven't called any place but the harem my home for a long time."

"Harem?"

"I've long served to please King Akintunde."

At last, Issaria looked over her shoulder at him, blind-eye like a pale full moon on the horizon. "What is this?"

"I saw her leaving his chambers the first morning I went to speak to him about you," Calix explained. "I recently returned to my father and told him how I found it distasteful that he would lay with the likeness of his new daughter…the implication of my words swayed him to gift her to me…and then I gave her a proposition."

"Please, it would be my honor to portray you," Vizenya said as she clasped Issaria's hand.

"So I'm not even really needed?"

"Princess Shairi, you are perhaps the most important player in the decoy party," Alander said from beside the bookcases where he thumbed through a volume before replacing it on the shelf. "As the only genuine identity among the three of you, you'd be the one to lead the envoy. We'd place you as Vixenya's handmaiden, always within reach, and speaking for the princess. Vixenya, as the Princess Issaria, would be the most vulnerable member of the party, as a target for assassins from Hecate."

At the mention of Issaria's recent brushes with death, Princess

Shairi paled, the golden hue of her skin likening to that of the Evernight Princess. "Surely the Evernight Witch will leave Princess Issaria alone now that she's allied with Hinhallow?"

Alander shook his head. "It would be unwise to count her out just because the last two attempts on Issaria's life failed. In fact, with two attempts so close together, we should consider her vendetta against the princess to be a sincere one, and expect that she will make another attempt upon her as soon as the opportunity presents itself."

"And what better place to attack than when we're on the move?" Raif contributed. "Limited resources, a set retinue of soldiers, and the fact that we'll be traversing unfamiliar ground opens up a whole host of possibilities."

"No."

"Well, it's not like we *want* to—"

"I said no!" Issaria, horrified, shook her head and ripped her hands from Vixenya's. "No, no. This is…no. I can't do it like this. There's too much risk!"

"I'll happily take your place, Princess," Vixenya said dutifully.

Issaria's attention snapped back to her decoy as hot tears spilled down her cheeks. "Don't you know you could die?"

Vixenya nodded and gestured to Calix. "The Crown Prince was very forthcoming with the dangers that would be presented to me if I took his proposition. I am not without my own weapons, your Grace."

Issaria shook her head, "Why? You don't even know me, Vixenya! Why would you want to die for me?"

Vizenya's brow furrowed. "I don't want to die, Princess. But I *do* want to see a sunrise again. A sunset. A night sky filled to the brim with stars. I believe that you can make that happen, but only if you're given the chance. And if I can't see it…I want my son to."

Silence swelled in the moments following the concubine's admission, interrupted only by the hiccuping sob caught in Issaria's throat as she fled the tower.

"Issaria! Wait!" Mint rose from her seat, but Raif snagged her wrist and shook his head.

"Let her go. We knew she wouldn't like this."

"That could have gone worse," Alander said. "She could have stayed to hear about the ship."

"Well, if the whore is going," Shairi huffed as she settled on a footstool. "I *guess* I could help."

Vixenya cut a withering glare across the room at the Princess. "This *whore* will remember your insolence when you're waiting on me hand and foot, *Princess*."

Shairi opened her mouth to protest but Calix tuned out their catty argument as he shifted his attention to Eiren, silent by the window. Her disapproving blue eyes bore into his as she solemnly shook her head. She'd told him once of the man who'd sacrificed for Issaria in Espera, but he'd not thought of the moment until he'd seen the tears in her eyes.

This had fallen apart so spectacularly, and yet…it wasn't exactly a failure if everyone else was on board. Issaria was just going to take some convincing.

"Zak, work with Raif on the details. I'm going to…" he threw his hands in the air. "I don't know, I'm just going," he finished as he followed Issaria out of his suites.

At the bottom of the tower, Bhanu, one of the palace guards, pointed across the gardens. "She went that way, Sire."

"To the pavilions?" Calix asked but was already moving across the white gravel, looking for her among the jade-leafed citrus trees and lotus flowers on the pond.

His footsteps crunched as he ducked a low branch and proceeded along the winding path through the garden. The air wavered with heat and insects droned ceaselessly into the azure sky. He found her, seated in the shade beneath a lemon tree bursting with star-shaped white flowers. Issaria pulled her knees to her chest as he settled into the grass beside her, his legs stretched out before him.

Calix looked out over the pond, watching jewel-colored dragonflies darting low over the water. Songbirds trilled from branches and spires. For a long while, neither one of them spoke. Cattails and reeds rustled in the gentle breeze. He wasn't even certain what he would say, or if anything he could say would even make a difference. Ever since she'd been poisoned it felt like destiny was careening off course, following a map of its own making and dragging them along with it.

Beside him, Issaria rested her chin on her knees. He examined her profile, as much as he could without staring at her. Her grey eye was vacant, staring out across the garden. The breeze stirred her hair, teasing loose strands out of place. Sunlight cast indigo highlights in her curls where it siphoned through the foliage.

"I don't want anyone dying for me," she whispered without looking at him.

"I don't think that's for you to decide, Issaria. People are willing to do things that outweigh the risks for even the hope of a better future."

"Who's future? Certainly not theirs!" Issaria snapped before burying her face in her arms. "They do this all for me and they die, and for what, Calix? For what?"

Calix was quiet for a moment before he softly said, "This isn't about Vixenya, is it?" Issaria shook her head. "Is this...about the soldier who helped you escape your aunt?"

She gasped and sat upright. "How did you know about Elon?"

Calix shrugged. "Eiren told me when we went to retrieve Asmy from the brothel. He died so you could try to escape?"

"It's how she found me so quickly. Has to be. He would have *never* betrayed me. She must've done unspeakable things to force his tongue against me."

"I am sorry, Issaria. I can't pretend to know how your heart grieves."

She was quiet a while longer before she wiped her eyes on the back of her hand. "What you said, at the engagement announcement?" He nodded in recognition of the event and she continued, "Elon said nearly the same thing."

"Oh," was all he said. The sudden pain in her eyes, her fumbling apology, it all suddenly made sense. Calix had inadvertently reminded her of the one person she probably didn't want to think of at that moment.

"I'm to be your wife and here I am crying over another." She forced a laugh. "How unbecoming!"

Calix caught her face with a blackened hand and turned her towards him. Wet tracks glistened on her cheeks. "Please don't ever hide your true heart from me, Issa." His thumb caressed the curve of her jaw. "I won't pretend I'm not disappointed I don't have your affections all to myself, but it seems rather naive of me to think you'd be without ties. Besides, I think you'll find I'm rather hard to resist," he finished with a wink.

She leaned into his hand and shook her head as she laughed softly. "I didn't intend for any of this to happen, Prince Calix. I'm sorry you've been dragged into it."

"What did I tell you about names, love?" He dropped his hand from her face and took her hand in his, pressing her open palm to his lips. "I didn't intend for any of this to happen either, but I look at you, Issaria, and I know I wouldn't ask the Cosmos for anything else."

Issaria stared at him with wide eyes and he felt himself growing greedy for more of her. Cinders sparked in his molten stare and he leaned into her. "I should have kissed you in the woods that day. I wanted to. Wild and obstinate, you had no idea who I was and..." he trailed off. As the doe senses the hunt has begun, Issaria stilled beneath his touch. "Issaria, I think I—"

"Please, don't."

The confession died on his lips. "Issa?"

"Please, Calix." She pried herself away from him and stood. "Not yet," she said as she left him alone beneath the lemon tree.

9

ELON

Elon limped into the square outside the palace walls with the remaining citizens of his shattered city. A glorious empire of hundreds of thousands reduced to a mere fraction of their previous numbers. Too many had died in the assault on Espera. Here before the gates, locked out of the place he'd called home for more years than he'd been in Larkham as a boy, he knew it had been a mistake to come back. At first, he thought it clever to infiltrate the city again while Hecate had bigger foes to contend with than himself, now that *whoever* had taken up residence in the palace with her. If she was even alive, that was. He didn't think this was the *friendly* sort of siege.

Not after the battle that had claimed nearly the entire functioning force of the rebellion. Roane. Xenviera. Magi Caltac. Young Basl Koellewyn's death had felt particularly raw. Dozens more had died and he had no more room for names in his heart. Soren Sainthart. His parents and sister were among the first names to be etched into his being. Those that would not be forgotten. He refused to add Issaria's name to that list.

But now he was trapped in Espera with the civilians, and the

76

wound he'd taken to the thigh still hadn't fully healed. He needed to change the bandages and see Safiya's healing hands.

The crowd had been gathered by soldiers belonging to the invading force. Elon had been swept up in the streets with whatever citizens they could find. It had been relatively easy to get them all to comply, as the soldiers had been accompanied by those…those *things*. In the end, being herded into the square had been futile to resist when they were so cosmically overpowered. Now they were corralled like animals and those *mechanisms* stood sentry while a line of soldiers prevented the gathered from breeching the Crystal Palace. If they were hostages or more cannon fodder, he wasn't sure.

Elon could only call them mechanisms. Fascinating to look at, now that they weren't splattered in blood and offal. Ingenious. They didn't house a magician but somehow harnessed the power from the elementia stones enclosed within the chest cavity to replicate a magician's abilities in devastating discharges of power. He wanted to know how they worked, how they'd come to exist. What schematics were available—

Elon cut himself off from that train of thought. They were not impressive. They were horrific and they had claimed the lives of hundreds, if not thousands, of innocents. He did, however, want to know who was behind the monstrosities, though. Only a deranged sort of mind could come up with something this…malevolent.

The dull murmurs of the crowd quieted and Elon turned his attention to the balcony that protruded from the crystalline pillar of the palace wall. Dozens of solarium crystals imbedded in the railing illuminated as a tall, black-haired man with the build of a well-seasoned soldier approached at the railing, awaiting total silence.

When not a soul dared speak, anticipation like a static charge among the crowd, the man announced in a voice projected by storm magic, "Behold, magicians of Espera, a prince born of Imperial blood has found his way home at last! The true heir to the throne has returned to liberate you! Be grateful and bow before your new Imperial Prince Shura, last born son of the fallen Empress Obsidia."

No one breathed as the storm magi stepped back. But gasps and shocked responses peppered the crowd as a tall, blond man with an impeccably straight nose, narrow jaw, and intensely blue eyes stood before them. Eyes like his reminded Elon of a glacial freeze deep in the bowels of a berg on the Salt Ice. Hecate's eyes seemed a watery version of the ice that illuminated this foreign prince's gaze from within. Even if his man had not announced him to be the son of Obsidia, there could be no mistaking the hellfire frosting this man's gaze.

Elon blinked back the recognition between the way Issaria's soft aura felt and the churning maelstrom of this man's presence. They were the same in nature, the way a breeze was kin to the hurricane, but this man's power would drown Issaria in a teacup if they were to face off.

Shura drummed his fingers on the railing, observing the crowd with a pensive expression as if he had to find the words to speak to them. "My forlorn people, too long have you suffered at the hands of a usurper without even knowing to whom you'd pledged your fealty!"

Shura looked over his shoulder, irritation twitching his scowl as there was some scuffle behind him, but regained his composure as he faced the crowd again. And then Hecate Messorem, Empress Regent of Espera, slunk to the railing, urged forward by the storm magician who'd introduced the prince. She recoiled as Shura gestured to acknowledge the pitiful thing that she had become. "Look upon her! Look at the one who betrayed you all!"

Harsh whispers and cruel words led to fingers pointed in accusation at the ruined regent.

"My sister, your Empress Regent Hecate, has carelessly spent the lives of your children, your brothers and sisters, mothers and fathers, like Metals from her treasure troves for her own obsession with power. And worse yet, she turned on her own *family*, and like my dark mother before us, harvested the mana of her sister in order to wield the very Cosmos themselves!"

Ripples of acknowledgment worked their way through the crowd. There had always been rumors, but no one dared to speak it so boldly. Hecate had betrayed them all and her lies had led them here. To this.

Darkness and war. Violence on their very doorstep. Blood in the streets. A harbor blackened and burning.

"We can have our days and our nights! I have no need for the desecration of time and find this division of the world to be an abomination. I will rid us all of this curse." A few people, easily roused by empty promises, cheered before those around them shamed them to silence. "I know your princess to be alive—for as long as she breathes this midnight curse will plague the land. And it is for the good of this world that I will find and *end* the lost princess!"

At that, the crowd erupted. Shouts of protest mingled with calls for the princess's head alongside Hecate's. Soldiers guarding the gate pushed back against the people that surged toward them. Magic flared, razor-sharp winds and searing flames arced over the mob. The scent of metallic blood was fresh in the air as the upheaval grew.

"SILENCE," a bright, feminine voice resounded over the protests.

And there was. Not immediately, but all too suddenly, the voices that had been bold and riotous were plucked away. A phantom hand snuffing out candle flames until there was nothing left but smoke.

Elon felt it first, in his fingertips. Cold static, like hoarfrost coating his veins, crystalizing as it raced up his limbs and flooded the rest of his body. Before him, people began to kneel. One by one, until *rows* of people sank to their knees, some crying out in pain as they tried to fight against…

What manner of black magic was *this?*

Elon's knees buckled beneath him, and instead of fighting it, he let himself collapse to the ground on hands and knees. Even permitting the invasion in his blood, it wasn't a pleasant sensation. As if his very bones had turned to ice and he was being manually repositioned with indelicate claws. He allowed himself to roll upwards on his spine until he sat genuflect before the terrace.

A woman had joined the foreign prince. With hair as white as moonlight and midnight skin to match, she held a wide stance with arms raised beside the invader. Contorted fingers bent at unnatural angles as if they were being broken and re-broken as she moved her arms like a maestro conducting an orchestra. Translucent bubbles of indigo mana oozed from the thick aquathyst bangles on her wrists, amplifying her dark powers.

"There will be *silence* when King Shura is speaking. Am I understood?" Golden eyes glinted like embers in the night as she stared out over the crowd that could do nothing against her. Her satisfied smirk curved upward in a cruel grin as she said, "Don't make me repeat myself. I won't be so gentle next time."

"Risa, dearest, go easy on them." Shura placed a hand on her forearm, and she dropped her hands to her sides. The dark mana that seeped from her evaporated. "They did not ask to be lied to and manipulated like game pieces. I'm sure they'll choose who rules more wisely in the future." He pouted at her. "And you ruined my big announcement."

There was a collective gasp as the frost evaporated from their veins and people's bodies were returned to them. Some scrambled to their feet, frightened or awed, Elon wasn't sure. Like many others, Elon took his time getting to his feet. The beautiful water magician was definitely responsible but...*what* was *that?* How? Elon couldn't wrap his head around it. He'd never even heard of such a thing.

When everyone assembled had risen to their feet again, dignity forgotten as they raised wary eyes back to this would-be-King.

"I only speak for your best interests. All it takes is her life. And I will gladly sacrifice one for the many *devoted* citizens in my empire." Shura's benevolent voice turned to chips of ice as he gripped the railing. "I do, however, require your absolute acceptance of my reign. Nothing less will be tolerated as I shed the name of my false lineage and assume my rightful place in the realm. I do not want to be your Emperor. I want to be your King."

He paused a beat before his smile returned, and his eyes began to emanate a violet darkness. Glowing darkly, he seemed to meet the eye of every citizen. Even the wind was silent as he spoke. Elon froze as he felt his own gaze connect with the dark prince. Magi Caltac, may his soul find peace in the Cosmos, had described Issaria's eyes as holy fire, and almost difficult to gaze upon.

This was entirely the opposite. No longer that clear, deep-berg blue, they seemed to draw you in to gaze upon the abyss of his eyes. An empty sort of black that wanted to consume and devour. As Shura's darkness passed over him, Elon felt himself release a breath he hadn't realized he'd been holding. "Your *only* King. Ellorhys united at last beneath one crown."

"You may find my ways violent. Unnecessary. Cruel." Shura offered a sympathetic smile as he said, "Let me be clear when I say that I do not particularly care for the whims of sheep. When I am done remaking Ellorhys, what the elementals did for humanity will look primitive. You hate me now. So be it. I do this now, so that you may grow to love me as you realize what I do for you. For your children, and your children's children. What I sacrifice so that you may be truly *free.*"

Not a soul spoke. No one moved, save a stray dog weaving through the assembly seeking scraps and affection. Elon wouldn't, *couldn't* look away.

"But now, a demonstration of what will happen should anyone defy me."

An inhuman howl rattled from within her as Hecate was wrenched to her feet and brought to the very edge of the veranda by the black-haired soldier who had announced him.

Hecate kicked and squirmed in the soldier's firm grasp as he held her firm as she changed hands from minion to master. "No, please. Don't!"

When Shura held her firm by the nape of her neck and one wrist—twisted and angled for maximum control—and said with a sinister smile, "Unfortunately dear sister, I am not a very forgiving king."

Shura's eyes began to radiate darkness that devoured Elon's gaze, and a hungry, starless energy crackled off of him like a snake shedding skin. Holding Hecate as close as a lover, he punched a closed fist toward the sky and split a wicked grin that made him look like a void-eyed monster. *"Xellux val Sabahtra."*

Snapping sparks and bolts crackled through the air around them. The air grew thick and hot. Air pressure dropped and Elon's eardrums popped against the sudden change. A sinister spiral of clouds churned in the dark sky. Thunder grumbled awake, made cranky by the summons. Filament danced along the edges of the thunderhead in anticipation, eager to please.

Lightning cracked through the sky, striking Shura's raised fist. A blade of negative energy, crackling like black lightning, formed in his grasp like a weapon delivered by the Cosmos itself.

Elon dared a glance around. The whole crowd was rapt and slack-jawed as this crazed, powerful magician leveled his dark weapon at Hecate's throat. Someone gasped in alarm a moment before the bastard jerked his starless blade across the Empress Regent's throat in a motion that would have sprayed arterial blood across the balustrade like fireworks, but Shura had never been after blood. A precise, thread of black light cut across Hecate's throat and an iridescent mist poured from a razor-thin slice across her neck. It streamed out not like gore and the horrors of bloody death Elon had become accustomed to, but like shimmering ribbons of light that shifted in hues of indigo and violet.

It was mesmerizing and luminous, and then Shura was sucking it into his open mouth like a blackhole swallows the light of everything unfortunate enough to draw too near. Horrified screams went up from the crowd, but no one dared move. The liquid light continued to stream from the slice as if it were pouring through a punctured levee.

And then Hecate seemed to wither, her flesh thin and stretched tight to her skeleton as she desiccated like a withered flower before them.

The sword of black lightning flickered, then faded like an image on the inside of one's eyelids, a bright remnant burned into their retinas.

Shura shoved Hecate's husk over the balcony railing as if he couldn't be bothered with her now that he had taken what he wanted. Her corpse disintegrated on impact, releasing a cloud of dust and ash from her empty sheath of a dress.

A woman in Elon's peripheral collapsed.

Someone not too far behind him whispered, "Mythos, save us all."

Shura sucked his digits as if he could savor the flavor of someone's soul. He licked his lips and smiled. The darkness pulsing from his eyes —unholy light after what he'd just done to Hecate—seemed brighter, stronger. "So now you see, my wayward flock. Not only will I take your mana, but I will also take your life. And it will not be pleasant. Now kneel before the true heir! The True King of Ellorhys, Shura Khaosson!"

Elon hesitated only a fraction of a second as the assembled crowd sank to their knees in a rippled wave. As he knelt in the dirt in the shadow of a crazed tyrant that just *executed* the *last* crazed tyrant, Elon knew he had to help as many as he could and get the hell out of Espera. Issaria was not coming back to this without one Cosmos of an army, and Elon was certain the Warlord of the West would not wildly charge in against unknowable odds.

Help was not coming.

Espera had fallen at last.

10

ISSARIA

The day they were set to depart, Issaria woke early. Soft snores filled her bedroom like the murmur of turning pages in a quiet library. Last night the girls had insisted they spend their last evening together before they parted ways. They hadn't spoken of it in so many words, but when the curtains were drawn and the candles snuffed out, they'd all found a place in her room and settled in to tell stories until they drifted off one by one like fireflies in the forest.

The serene calm of being surrounded by friends enveloped her like a mother's embrace. Tears prickled her eyes. She wouldn't have another morning like this for a long while yet. Maybe ever, she realized, if Aurelia was to have her way.

Beside her in the bed, Rhaminta's warmth saturated her side and Issaria eased herself out from between the sheets. Nestled in an array of thick blankets near the fireplace, Cizabet's poppy-orange hair stuck out like a wiry bird's nest, and beside her, Asmy tucked in tight against her sister's back. Cylise had sprawled out on the chaise beside them, one leg hooked over the back, mouth open and gargling saliva—Issaria chuckled quietly at the sight as she tiptoed around them.

Silently, she extracted a pair of riding pants and an understated linen blouse from her wardrobe and padded over to the carved ivory changing screen in the corner of her room.

"I already laid out clothes for you, Princess." Eiren's whisper made Issaria jump, hand flying to her heart as she whirled around.

Curled up in a chair by the balcony doors, Eiren was nearly impossible to spot beneath a rumpled sage-colored quilt. "You startled me!" Issaria hissed.

Eiren's smile was sad as she rose to her feet and left the blanket in a heap on her abandoned chair. "I couldn't sleep," she said as she stooped to collect a stack of clothing on a table. "Vixenya will be wearing this when she arrives." She pushed the clothes into Issaria's hands. "Are you certain you don't want at least one of us with you?"

Doubt roiled in Issaria's stomach. "Of course, I want you *all* with me. But it's going to be incredibly dangerous—"

"All the more reason for us to be with you!" Rhaminta crowed from the other side of the changing screen. "I hope you didn't think you were going to leave without saying goodbye to us."

"She was going to try," Cizabet huffed. "I told you she was going to."

There was a quiet knock at the door. "Breakfast, your Grace," a familiar voice called.

Eiren pointed at the clothes. "Dress. I'll let Vixenya in. Time grows short."

Issaria shucked her nightgown and dressed quickly. The bright scent of citrus and sugar combatted the stale sorrow of parting that hung between them. Teacups rattled on saucers and spoons clinked as tea was served and scones were buttered. When she emerged from behind the partition, all five women were seated around a low table by the hearth.

Vixenya stood immediately, dropping into a curtsey before her. Issaria's breath caught in her throat as her gaze fell upon her decoy. She knew how this would go, but it was startling to see herself dressed identically to the former concubine. Buckskin-colored riding pants tucked into supple leather boots that laced to her knee. A modest tunic belted at her waist with a thin zoster, and a grey woolen cloak was draped over the back of the settee.

"It will be less…jarring I think, Princess, when I am dressed as you instead of you dressed like me."

Rhaminta sighed. "Well…the disguise isn't going to make itself. Come, Vixenya," she said as she took her tea to the vanity. "I'll fix your hair to look like Issa's."

Nervous energy vibrated within Issaria as Vixenya settled before the mirror and Mint began sectioning out her hair. Asmy and Cylise flit about like birds, bringing jeweled combs and a selection of dresses and shoes to Vixenya, trying the fit and folds to hide the extra inches of height. Issaria watched in silence, keenly aware of the differences between them, height being the least of her worries. Some were subtle to those who would not know her face, but drastic differences, like her newfound blindness, were worrisome enough that one glance from King Akintunde or Queen Emmaleigh, and the plan would dissolve like sugar in water before she'd even left the palace grounds.

Vixenya, seeming to sense Issaria's trepidation, met her gaze in the mirror's reflection. "You still don't agree with this plan?"

Issaria's mouth drew taught across her face. "I don't. I think this is an unnecessary risk for you, and I don't entirely understand why you'd agree to this."

Vixenya offered a small smile, for a moment only, before looking back to her hands, folded neatly in her lap. "I have lived most of my life in one hovel or another until King Akintunde brought me into his harem. I was twenty-one then." She wrung her hands together in her lap. "I'm eighty-seven, Princess," she said, voice strong despite the tremor in her hands. "And since I've been stuck in this," she spat, "*hellhole*, I've had three stillborns and a boy I had to give to my brother when he was still wet with *my* blood." When she looked up again, her deep blue eyes were spangled with unshed tears. "He doesn't even know I'm his mother. He can't." She swallowed hard. "Haven't you ever wanted to be someone else, if only for a little while?"

Vixenya's question seared into her soul like a fire-hot brand.

Issaria hadn't just wanted to be someone else. She'd *become* someone else and was almost swallowed by the desire to leave it all behind and really *be* Kai. When Issaria had first arrived in Hinhallow, she was Kyria. A dancer from Ares, and it had been easy to fall into her story; the fabricated memories were ghosts of her own with different names and places in lieu of her beloved Espera. No expectations, no rules. Just Kai, survival, and whatever coin she could earn from her dance. That selfishness had cost Espera precious time. Time that could have saved Elon's life, had word of her arrival in Hinhallow reached Aunt Cate's ears before she'd put him to the blade. Now, he was gone, and Issaria waged a battle to remain herself.

The vicious circle couldn't be more apparent to her. She couldn't manage words that wouldn't betray the harrowing guilt eating away at her, so she nodded her silent understanding to the woman who looked so much like herself.

"If I'm to be someone else…I may as well be a princess." She lifted her chin and added, "If I'm to risk my life, your Grace, I may as well do it to save all of Ellorhys, not just my son."

She didn't realize she was crying until Eiren blotted her cheeks with a kerchief. "I will do all I can to bring back the stars, Vixenya. Thank you, for seeing clearly when I did not."

Eiren had a hand on her elbow, ready to guide her away when Vixenya's brow furrowed. "Before you go, Princess?" Issaria nodded, and as Mint finished with an elaborate side-sweep of braids kept back with sapphire butterfly combs, Vixenya said, "The ship you're boarding with the Prince? It's a *smart* disguise."

Issaria cocked an eyebrow at her. "Prince Calix would have nothing less," she said cautiously, as she realized at once she had no inclination of the details of this part of their plan. Switch with decoy. Meet Calix. Board ship. Sail to Pallis on said ship, for which passage and secrecy were already bought and paid for. It seemed simple enough she hadn't asked further about it.

"Maybe now isn't the time for this, Vixenya?" Rhaminta said, eyes wide with intention.

"Out with it," Issaria said.

"Should have just let her go, Xen. Can we call you Xen?" Cylise said as she sat back on a footstool. "Xenya? I think I like that, actually," she prattled on, looking warily between Rhaminta and Vixenya. "Of course, once we're part of the Promenade, we'll have to call you things like, 'your Grace,' and 'your Excellency', which if you ask me—"

"Oh, go on and tell her then!" Mint said as she threw her hands in the air and strode away. "Might as well now, she'll never let it go."

"Tell me what?" Issaria asked again. "Mythos above, someone tell me right this instant!"

Eiren stepped forward, clutching the kerchief she'd used to wipe away her tears moments ago. "The ship the prince chartered belongs to Jallah Coppernolle."

A strange ringing sensation echoed between her ears in the moments that followed the utterance of his name. She was certain she'd heard Eiren but was also unsure that what she'd heard was correct. Eyes wide, she blinked vacantly as the realization that she would be on a ship in the middle of the ocean with the man who sold her, sold them *all* as slaves settled upon her like hoarfrost.

Issaria swallowed hard and took a deep breath before she looked about the room. "And it's a smart option? A *safe* option?"

Cizabet rushed up and clasped her hands, nodding eagerly with earnest green eyes. "Princess, it was the *only* option."

"No one else would defy the King so brazenly," Mint said from somewhere behind her. "Prince Calix was hoping to tell you himself," she added with venom. Issaria didn't have to turn to know Rhaminta was glaring at Vixenya.

"Then it will just have to do," she replied with all the practicality she could muster.

Issaria allowed Eiren to lead her away, leaving Vixenya to change with Mint and Cizabet to assist. "We'd go with you if you'd let us," she said as she swept the cloak off the settee and turned to face her. "We know most of us have to go with Vixenya and Princess Shairi." She fastened the cloak around Issaria's shoulders, adjusting it so the furred collar shadowed her eyes. "But I could go with you…"

Too soon, Vixenya emerged from behind the changing partition, a vision in indigo silk and bejeweled ornaments. No one could dispute she didn't *look* the part. But it was the finer details Issaria was inspecting. Her eyes were a dead giveaway, but a memory inside her made her recite her father's words with more confidence than she felt, "You bow to no one, Princess Issaria."

Vixenya's eyes widened at the moniker but she lifted her chin and nodded once. "May the Cosmos favor you on your journey."

"And you on yours."

"There's something, Issaria," Eiren said, her eyes wide with her unfinished statement. "We haven't much time and… "

"And we wanted to say goodbye," Cylise finished as she came up beside her, offering a canvas laundry bag filled with clothing, boots, and other trinkets and trifles to help along the way. She cinched the top and helped her heave it over her shoulder. "It's going to be a while before we see each other again."

"But we will," Rhaminta said as she wrapped strong lean arms around her shoulders, giving an intense squeeze before releasing her. "We *will* see each other again."

"Of course, we will, Mint," Issaria confirmed, a whisper strangled through clenched tears. "You'll *all* help Vixenya through this ruse, help Princess Shairi in any way you can to enforce that *she* is me," she finished pointedly. "I'm so sorry you can't come with me, but I don't know what my journey will bring me…and the less we have to bear, the faster we will move."

Mint grinned, her wide smile taking up her entire face. "Maybe you can get to know your future husband. I see you blushing at him and looking at his mouth when he speaks. It's okay to be excited for yourself." She planted a swift kiss on Issaria's forehead and then smeared a sigil on her forehead.

Such a familiar figure…the same as Kidalma's after the fortune reading that day? Issaria searched her friend's dark eyes for some recognition of the night, but her hopeful face only betrayed sorrow at their parting.

"You're too hard on yourself. Your soldier would want you to be happy, right? So let yourself be happy, Issa."

"She's right, Princess," Asmy said, taking Issaria's hand.

Cizabet came up beside her and took the other. "Go with a free heart, Princess." Her mossy eyes watered, but she swallowed and steeled herself. "You've brought light in the wake of darkness. We all believe in your journey."

"He *is* awfully handsome." Asmy beamed. "And you already kissed—and not that fake one you guys did for the city." If it was possible, the girl's grin grew. "So just let it happen. Anyone with *eyes* can see that he's in love with you."

"Ah, about that." Issaria withdrew her hand and stepped back. "He might have tried to tell me so the other day."

"And?" Eiren asked from the back of the room.

"What did you do, Issaria?" Rhaminta did her best to keep her voice steady, but her pinched forehead and flared nostrils spoke volumes.

She sighed. "I told him not yet."

"Argh!" She threw her hands in the air, paced in a circle then shook her head. "Is it so bad if he does? You've agreed to spend your life allied to him and his people."

"It sounds like a perfect ending for a star tale about a princess who goes to the ends of the world to save her kingdom, Princess," Vixenya interjected from where she'd lingered on the edge of the group. They all turned to her, for she sounded a great deal like the Issaria herself. "It sounds like a story I'd tell my son while he falls asleep at night."

"You can let yourself have that happy ending after everything you've done," Mint confirmed. "After everything you're planning to do."

Solemn, Issaria gave a single nod. "He is a *very* good kisser," she whispered with a coy smile as she looked up at her friends from beneath the shadow of her hood before she pushed it back. "And I guess it *is* my turn to kiss him."

They broke into giggles and laughter, and when they settled, Issaria had already slipped out the door.

They waited, silent, nervous. Exchanging glances between each other and the ajar door.

"It's time," Vixenya said.

"Let's do this."

PART II
BEASTS & SIRENS

11

CALIX

The courtyard outside of the White Palace was a myriad of activities. Men loaded wagons with trunks, barrels, and boxes. Courtiers and chancellors wandered about the staff, ensuring nothing was broken or mishandled. On the palace steps, King Akintunde and Queen Emmaleigh, with young Prince Darres on her lap, sat in the shade of large parasols lifted by servants with shaky arms. Prince Calix conversed with Princess Shairi and his sister, Princess Bexalynn, on the steps. A slew of soldiers milled about. They checked horses and armor, making final preparations for the first league of their escort retinue.

The procession from Princess Issaria's suites on the far side of the palace arrived. Five handmaidens flanked the raven-haired woman from the Eventide.

Princess Shairi smiled and curtsied briefly, before embracing Vixenya enthusiastically. "Princess Issaria! Thank you again for inviting me to attend you! I'm truly honored to be selected. We're going to be such good friends!"

"Oh Princess, it is I who am grateful to have you," Princess Issaria replied.

"My love!" Prince Calix bounded down the stairs and brought her

95

hand to his mouth. "Are you ready? I can hardly wait to leave, for the sooner we return and can be wed!" the Princess nodded. "I brought you a parting gift, of sorts."

"A parting gift? But Prince Calix, you're coming with me, surely?"

"Of course, of course. I meant a parting gift regarding…the discussion we'd had." He stepped back. "A parting gift from Hinhallow."

Golden hair shimmered in the sunlight as Princess Bexalynn approached, a pout on her face. She dropped into a curtsey and recited, "I'm sorry I said such mean things to you the other day." She rose and lifted her gaze to meet Princess Issaria's—and froze. She looked to her brother, who waited eagerly for her to finish. She looked from Prince Calix, to the Princess, then to Princess Shairi.

Somewhere in the crowded courtyard, a palace maid helping to tighten a horse's girth held her breath.

Princess Shairi smiled and urged the young Princess on with a nod. "It is becoming to apologize for one's mistakes, Princess," she chided. "I bear *Princess Issaria* no hard feelings concerning…recent events."

With a swift glance back at the King and Queen, watching idly on the stairs, Princess Bexalynn swallowed and looked back to Princess Issaria, eyes wide. "I look forward to your return from the Rites so we can truly get to know one another as sisters should."

Queen Emmaleigh clapped. "Well done, Bexalynn. Modesty begets dignity, love."

Princess Bexalynn smiled at her mother then turned cold eyes on her brother and hissed, "Whatever is going on here? I want no part of it. Father is going to be *furious*."

"You'll be completely innocent. We'll say we switched her after."

"You'd better, Calix. I don't like being blindsided like that," she said as she swept past him and joined their parents and brother on the steps overlooking the courtyard.

Prince Calix pressed a kiss to his betrothed's head. "Go wait in the carriage, I'll be there in a moment," he said as he made for his family.

Escorted by her handmaidens, Princess Issaria went to an ivory carriage with curtained windows. Once settled, the maids closed the door and went about their own business, securing their belongings and disappearing into their own carriage.

"Mother." Prince Calix embraced the Queen and turned to King Akintunde. "Father."

"Son...you look pleased," he said with a smirk.

"How could I not be? Have you seen her, Father? And all it took was the promise of our armies. I look forward to returning from these tedious rituals so we can honor our alliance and liberate Espera." He grinned as he added, "I'll be happy to prove to my bride that I have the strength to uphold *both* our peoples."

King Akintunde's brow furrowed. "You've not heard the reports?"

"What reports, dear?" Queen Emmaleigh asked.

King Akintunde cast a wary eye around the courtyard, pausing on the carriage containing Princess Issaria, then said in a low voice, "The city was attacked. There have been...many casualties. Too many. A rebel faction tried to resist but..."

Calix's throat was tight as he hung on, waiting for more information. "But what?"

"There were...abominations. Devices. Unholy magics. Details vary from report to report, but one thing is certain. Espera has fallen."

"To whom? We should send our battalions immediately!" Calix exclaimed.

"Quiet!" King Akintunde snapped as he cast a wary eye about the courtyard. "There is *nothing left* to liberate, Calix. We'll have to learn a whole new enemy...I highly doubt the Witch survived whatever calamity befell her accursed city. Your girl is lucky to have escaped. Her charade on the Glass may have saved her life," he commented absently.

"Father, we can't just—"

"Don't tell me what I can and cannot do, *boy*." King Akintunde turned his heated stare upon his eldest son. "You may be my heir, but I am king until Zephyrus comes to take the breath from my lungs himself." He waved him off dismissively. "Bring the girl around the country, make her feel welcome and loved. Put a baby in her belly if it will ease the ache in her heart. The only throne she's sitting on is the one inside these walls."

Turning from his father toward the carriage that contained who they believed was his bride, the Crown Prince felt no remorse for his deceit.

OUTSIDE THE PALACE WALLS, A MAID CROSSED HER ARMS OVER HER chest as she lingered in the shade of a corner tavern. A large canvas sack leaned against her leg, and despite the heat and humidity of the day, her furred hood remained up. She glanced nervously between the palace gates and the back of the alley behind her.

"You look mighty suspicious for someone who says I don't have to worry about her faking anything," a hooded figure said as he approached from the northern street, one that ran alongside the palace walls. He leaned down and took her bag, shouldering the weight.

"There you are *Blaze*," she replied with a smirk. "I was getting worried you wouldn't make it."

Behind them, the palace gates groaned as they opened. Trumpets blasted a fanfare and a procession began to roll through the gates. Soldiers on horseback flanked a caravan of carriages and wagons that rolled through crowded streets. The pair watched as a familiar white carriage disappeared from view, then turned to each other.

He reached out and snagged her hand. He had to tell her, she could see it on his face. But again, she didn't want to hear those words from him. She wasn't ready to let go yet.

"Issa—"

She snatched her hands away and looked aside. "Maybe you shouldn't call me that."

Calix considered, then nodded. "All right. What shall I call you?"

She smirked. "I was Kai before… why not now?" Calix smiled, but it was tense. Issaria placed a hand on his arm. "I mean, I admit it's not as *original* as Blaze but—"

"No, no. It's not that. Kai is fine. It's—I need to tell you something."

"Is it about the boat?" She asked. "I already know it's Jallah's if that's what you're worried about."

Calix blanched. That hadn't been what he was going to tell her, but he was shocked all the same by her admission. "You know about the ship?"

"It's okay. The girls...Vixenya let it slip that we're going with him." Issaria took a bracing breath. "I don't like it, but I understand the need outweighs my personal...grievances."

"Well, I'm glad that you're so open-minded."

She smiled. "Don't look so nervous. The hard part's practically over. Now we just have to get to the ship right?"

Calix forced a smile. She still didn't know about Espera. "Right. Yeah. Okay, let's get going. Jallah is waiting for us and we better be gone by the time anyone figures out that I dropped out the false bottom and Zak's been waiting in the carriage since the stables."

"Raif and Alander?"

"On *The Henrietta* with our gear, making sure Coppernolle doesn't sell us out."

"He's more likely to sail off without us," she replied. They walked for a while, the scent of the ocean growing stronger than the scent of forges, bakeries, and sun-warmed stone. "*The Henrietta?*" Issaria questioned at last.

Calix shrugged. "I didn't ask. I only asked that it not be the ship you were brought in on and that there is as small of a crew as possible."

"So...none of the...slavers will be there?" Her voice was tight in her throat.

He glanced at her as they reached the docks. "He's only bringing as many men as he needs to crew the ship, and will return to the rest of his fleet when he's left us in Pallas."

"That's...that's good."

"I'm sorry," Calix said. "I wasn't left with many choices. Not ones I trusted anyway."

Issaria nodded. "It's all right. I trust your intentions were in the right place," she said patting his arm. "I think I see Sethik!"

"Sethik?"

"He was…kind of a friend," she said as she dashed off toward the ship, leaving him groaning in her wake. He had to tell her about Espera.

Sethik paled as Issaria bounded up to him. "Princess!" He jerked his black hood off and knelt.

"Hush!" She pulled him up and straightened his jacket. "It's Kai. It was always Kai." She smiled up at him. "It's good to see you again, now that the circumstances are different."

"You do seem a lot less…furious than the last time I saw you."

She arched an eyebrow at him. "Was that when you helped to sell me as a slave to that horrid little errand-man, or were you referring to when Jallah brought you to the council chambers with him, and you watched my very existence come into question?"

At last, Sethik grinned. His broad face held it like a half-moon beneath his mop of blond hair. "There's the venom I was expecting. It is good to see you, Kai. If there's anything I can do…Jallah doesn't own me, is what I mean to say."

Issaria nodded as Calix came up beside her at last. "Sethik, this is…"

Calix considered the man and said, "We've met. Not formally but… you were there the day Coppernolle was brought to court."

Sethik stood a little straighter. "I was. And I was changed for it." Spoke a little more sure of himself. "I made sure he remembered which girl was Asmy. Got you the right place the first time instead of the wild boar hunt he wanted to send you on."

Issaria scoffed. "Of course that slime would—" She took a deep breath and shook her head. "No. No. Coppernolle is taking us where we need to go and I will be a delightful guest aboard his…" she swept an arm up toward the prow of the ship and squinted at the faded crimson script adorned with barnacles, "Aboard his lovely *Henrietta*."

From above, came the distinct sound of clapping. "And I'm thankful, *grateful* even, for your forgiveness in regards to my most recent transgressions, my most esteemed patrons." Jallah Coppernolle emerged at the mouth of the gangplank and made his way down the ramp as he spoke. "I was more than happy to offer your husband here a bargain because I feel just *awful* about how we met." Jallah's rust-colored mane had grown a bit since the last they'd seen him. The shaved half of his head looked as though it needed attending, but the long portion was braided tight against his scalp. "I'd be remiss not to do all I can to right my wrongs." Dark eyes roved over them. "Those were such pretty words about my *Henrietta.* And a man loves having his lady complimented," he said with a roguish wink that sent a cruel shiver down Issaria's spine.

"Was she your lover?" Issaria dared to ask.

"Aye. Henrietta was the first love I ever had. And when I lost her, it broke my poor little heart."

Issaria brought a hand to her heart, her face forlorn at the heartbreak that mutated this man's morals. "I'm so sorry."

Jallah's laughter rumbled up from the core of him as he joined them on the docks. "Henrietta was an old milk cow I sold when I was seven."

"Oh, you!" Issaria punched him in the arm. "I thought she was a woman!"

He sniffed and wiped a tear from his eye. "Aye, many do. But no love have I had since that matches that of my love for Henrietta. I vowed I would make myself rich so I would never be forced to part with another friend again." He spreads his arms wide and gestures to his shop. "I do think I've kept my vow, don't you?"

With a vapid smile and a flutter of eyelashes, Issaria said, "Never forced to part with a friend but profiting from stealing girls from taverns and woodland paths, then selling them as whores in a city so massive they cannot possibly regulate all those slaves?" Issaria tilted her head to the side, her dead eye caught the sun like opal fire. "Yes, *quite* the legacy for your poor milk cow. Now that pleasantries are out of the way, I believe we have a schedule to keep, and you've some Metals to earn, right?" She looked over her shoulder at Calix and jerked her head toward the ship. "Shall we, Blaze?" she reached out her hand for him to take.

Calix ignored an indignant Coppernolle as he took her hand and let her lead him toward the ship. "You'll never let that go, will you?"

"If it wasn't so amusing, maybe I would."

"I need to think of something better than Blaze," he groaned.

"An alias?" Sethik asked as he flanked them up the gangplank.

Issaria patted Calix's arm. "We'll think of something, I'm sure."

"Well, *anything* is better than Blaze," Sethik said, "if I'm being honest."

Jallah joined them on the deck and last-minute preparations were made. Before long, *The Henrietta* was hoisting anchor and gliding out of the bay, cobalt sails puffed up against an azure sky.

1 2

CALIX

Afternoon brought wide swaths of blue, both above and below, as the *Henrietta* cut north across the Lanzauve Sea. Gulls that flanked the sails in the harbor had long fallen away and all that lay around them were open skies and tepid seas. The ship pitched on the waves, sea spray lifting off whitecaps in refreshing volleys of mist and breeze. At the prow of the ship, Prince Calix leaned across the gunwale, his face a particular shade of green. Beside him, Raif leaned back on his elbows, face turned toward the sun. He waggled his fingers like a court gossip as Issaria approached.

"There you are," she said as she stepped out of the shadows of the sails and into the sun.

"Prince Calix is not overly fond of ships, Princess," Raif explained as he surrendered his place next to the prince. "I'll leave you two alone."

"You don't have to—"

"Oh no, Princess," Raif objected, his hands in the air as he backed away. "He's all yours. I've heard enough about how horrible the ocean is."

"Give me a horse any day," he moaned. "Arietes *never* made me feel like this."

Issaria stifled a giggle as she rubbed Calix's back between his shoulder blades. "Awww, Mr. Assassin's tummy doesn't like the widdle ol' ocean?"

Calix attempted to glower at her, but seasickness twisted his stomach and he only groaned as he hung his head over the railing. "Mr. Assassin isn't much better than Blaze."

Issaria considered this as she leaned her forearms against the rail. "You're right. It's worse. I can't believe you were going to kill me."

Calix laughed roughly, "I wasn't going to kill you. I knew it as soon as I saw you, there was no way I'd do it. Not in the woods. Not in the city. Not by my hand." Issaria bumped him with her shoulder and he looked up from his nauseated misery, guilt twisting his gut at the hint of color on her cheeks more than any ocean swell ever could. "I didn't even want you to go back to that Mythos-forsaken city that night, Issaria."

Issaria must have seen it then, on his face or in his eyes. She froze against the railing, eyes wide and brow knit with concern. "Prince Calix?"

"I would have taken you with me right then. Never looked back. I should have. Maybe then—"

"Maybe then what, *Calix*?" her plea was thin with desperation as she drew away from him.

"Issa, I'm so sorry. Espera…there was an attack…from the sea." Her hands flew to her mouth. Tears in her eyes, she shook her head as he continued, "The reports are unclear but my father mentioned that…*unholy devices* were unleashed."

"Unholy devices? What does that mean? What about my people? My friends?"

"We're not certain. All we know is… the darkest of the Black Arts swept into the city." He couldn't look at her as he said, "He's refused to send the battalions."

"He can't."

"He won't send the soldiers against an unknown enemy. He says we must learn about them first."

"Unknown enemy? What about Aunt Cate? What about the city?"

He shook his head. "The city has fallen. There was a rebellion against…the assailants but there have been heavy casualties. There's nothing to send aid *to,* save enemies unknown."

Below, a cerulean sea swirled in eddies against the prow of the *Henrietta.* Seafoam churned as the wooden vessel sliced across the Lanzauve. He could no longer stand her silence and turned to her. She wasn't looking at him. Hands clasped against her chest, she was staring at the deck of the ship, discolored eyes darting back and forth as she tried to calculate some retaliation, any rebuttal to hold against the King to force his hand.

"But the treaty! The alliance! He would…he would…" she trailed off as she realized exactly what King Akintunde would do.

Why it was that *Calix* was bringing this news to her, instead of a war council.

"He intends to see it through."

Her face fell. "You knew?"

He straightened, shaking his head as he refuted, "It wasn't like that. I only found out on the steps—"

"And you let me get on this boat?" She shouted, her flushed face reddening as she looked back in the direction the ship had come. "You brought me *further* from my city? Whatever's left of it? Of my *people?*"

Overhead, white stripes of clouds thickened and darkened the sky.

"Issa, I never—"

"Don't call me that!" Tears that had threatened to spill over rolled down her cheeks.

Calix scowled. "Kai? I hardly think this is the moment for us to be coy, Issaria!"

"No. *Issa.* You don't get to call me that," she glowered at him and he felt something in him break at the sight. "Not after this. You're allowing them to be sacrificed!"

He caught her waist in his hands as she reeled back from him, gentle as captured dove, begged her to still so he could explain—

"I did no such thing, Issaria—"

"You knew! Cosmos above, Calix! You knew in the alley when you took my hand and I thought—" she cut herself off and wrenched herself away from him. As Issaria cradled her head in her hand, her brow pinched in annoyance and fury, the ship pitched on the sea, whitecaps forming as strong winds whipped up the swells. "Ugh! I thought you were going to tell me you might love me! How *stupid* of me!"

"Issaria." Her name was a curse on his lips. Each time he said it, she turned on him more enraged and offended than before. "Please, it's not like that. I didn't realize that this would change our plans. If I had thought for a moment that you'd want to—"

"Want to go save whatever's left of my kingdom—the only thing that's mattered to me since Elon died?" Her words stung almost as much as the salt-heavy winds whipped off the whitecaps.

Calix opened his mouth but words failed and instead, he cast his gaze out across the choppy waves. Storm-grey clouds on the horizon approached fast and seemed to match their turbulent relationship. "I had hoped that I had at least started to matter to you. You matter to me, Issaria, more than anyone. I thought that was obvious."

Thunder clapped on the horizon. A flash of lightning lit the sky between them and Issaria looked to the storm clouds gathered overhead as fat drops of rain began to pummel the deck.

"Where did this storm come from so quickly?"

"The weather changes fast on the open sea," Calix replied, vaguely aware that the storm *had* appeared rather suddenly. Maybe *too* suddenly. He made to reach for her, but withdrew his hand and instead stepped aside so she could pass. "Let's get inside."

Jallah's men dashed about the deck. "Secure the rigging men! The Sirens won't have us today!"

Alander rushed toward them, shouting, "Get her inside, Calix! This storm is unnatural!"

"Magicians?" Calix asked over Issaria's head, as he tucked her against him, however resistant she was.

He nodded gravely. "Pirates."

Lighting cracked across the sky. The rain fell fast, soaking through their clothes.

"It'll be the *Siren's Song*, my Lord and Lady," Jallah bellowed from behind the helm. Leaning into the storm he gripped the wheel white-knuckled. "Best secure yourselves and prepare for battle! Siyari is as fierce as they come!"

"We're going to fight, right?" Issaria asked as Calix pushed her along the deck toward the Captain's cabin. "I can help! I don't need to be protected!"

"Princess!" Sethik's voice was sharp steel as he neared, drenched from the storm, silhouette steaming. "Siyari Crowsong is one of the most notorious pirates on sea and she is no friend to Jallah. We've lost more than a few ships to her. She's a Storm Magi, and her crew is full of other dangerous summoners. I don't want to frighten you, but I've lost a lot of friends to her because we're on Jallah's payroll." He scowled. "If she is upon us now, we are not going to escape easily. Her vendetta is strong, and her mana stronger."

Prince Calix nodded and steeled his spine before looking down at Issaria with a sad smile. "Forgive me, love, but if this pirate has been bought by our enemies, known or unknown, you need to stay hidden." Calix gave her a roguish grin. "Don't worry. I'll take care of this." Burning swords erupted from his fire-black palms and cinders spiraled into the downpour before the rain scorched them out. "You keep away from the mess and I'll fetch you when we're clear of danger."

"Fetch me!? I'm not a dog, Calix! No!"

"Issaria." Calix's face was like stone. Water ran rivers down his face, matted dark hair against golden skin. "If you don't go willingly, I will have Sethik lock you in the Captain's quarters. Water beats fire." He lifted his *Fervent* black hands. His flaming swords smoldered, steaming in the rain, looking smaller and more feeble than they had when he first called them forth. "This is going to be hard enough without looking over my shoulder to make sure you're okay." She opened her mouth to object, but he plowed over her, "Don't tell me I don't have to, because I will. You are mine to protect, and I will do so until my dying breath. Are we clear?"

Her mouth fell open and without another word, Sethik hoisted her over his shoulder, kicking and screaming. "She's never going to go willingly, Prince Calix," he announced as he crossed the deck and ascended the stairs to the quarter deck. All the while, Issaria beat her fists against his back and tried to bite his shoulder.

"Who do you think you are? Unhand me!" Issaria screamed as she thrashed about. "Put me down this instant!"

Sethik opened the alloy-braced door and dumped her inside without ceremony. He slammed the door shut and locked it with a key from his pocket before she could recover, but they heard her muffled cries and her fists hammering against the door. "I'm sorry Princess, but this is for your own good," Sethik called through the door. "I'd be a fool to say I wasn't afraid to face Siyari." He slipped the key back into his pocket and turned back to the men on the deck, his face pale as he added a little quieter. "I really hope we don't die."

13

SHAIRI

Nazarovo was a rainbow of color as the royal caravan approached. Even from a distance, they could hear the music and cheering. Sandstone gates opened wide to receive them, and though floral garlands had been hung over streets cobbled with mosaic mandalas made of river stone, the people that lined either side of the wide boulevard were thin as reeds as they called out for blessings.

Inside the ivory carriage at the center of the procession, Shairi handed pouches of metals to Zakarian and Vixenya. "Part of a good ruse is that people are too blind to see what's right in front of their faces," she explained, keenly avoiding making eye contact with Zak, who looked rather shocked to hear her say something so callous with such candor. "By distributing alms you ensure the common folk don't even want to think you aren't who you say you are. When we stop at the temple, stand on the steps and toss these out over the guards."

"You're bribing the people?" Eiren asked baldly.

"I prefer to think of it as investing in a good reputation, but if you *must* phrase it like that…"

"Prince Calix doesn't do this when he's out," Zak commented, his gaze heavy as it met hers.

109

"No, I'm sure he doesn't. He's beloved as the guardian of the White City. His father has crafted his public persona so that Calix doesn't have to. But you're not him, and truly Calix has put himself in a position where he might *need* to buy his people's affections." She turned her sharp gaze to Vixenya and clucked her tongue. "And *you,* well, you're the whole problem, if I'm being truthful." A coy smile tugged her lips as she let the insult fall before continuing, "Issaria spent eight years living under the Evernight Witch's thumb in Espera, and now she's here. Marrying *their* Crown Prince on the brink of what's sure to be a war, where she will ask the Hollowvanians to lay down their lives for her. We're toting this love story around like it's going to save the day but it's going to take more than that." She narrowed her gaze. *"You* should be throwing all the riches we can provide at their feet and begging them not to stone you."

"That's encouraging, Princess," Vixenya said through pursed lips. "Do *you* resort to such tactics when you are among the people?"

Shairi's blood heated at the implication of the question. "If you were ever allowed out of the harem, maybe you would know," she shot back.

"Shairi, really?" Zak's patience was wearing thin. He wasn't used to so much attention being on him. He was usually a silent observer type. To now be thrust into the spotlight to portray one of his closest friends? Honestly, she wasn't sure what Calix was thinking on this one. The ruse was paper thin, and rain clouds were gathering. She could feel it.

"Really, *Prince Calix,*" she hissed. "I am here because *you* wanted me to make sure *this,*" she gestured vaguely between the two imposters, "doesn't fall apart at the seams. That's what I'm doing, so give out the Metals, *your Majesties.*"

On the other side of the carriage, Eiren was smirking as she peered out the curtains. "We're arriving."

"Eiren, you stay back with me. Princess Issaria will exit first—"

"What if there's an attack?" Zak asked.

"Then *Princess Issaria* better duck," she said as she rolled her eyes. "The people are here to see her, first and foremost. Let them see her.

She's supposed to be some exotic beauty who's captured your heart, right?" When no one said anything, Shairi smiled and quirked her head to the side, a long braid falling over her shoulder. "My point precisely. Prince Calix, you will follow her and distribute the Metals as I have instructed. *We* will go meet your host and see to it that we have a room to rest before this evening's...*festivities,*" she said with distaste. "We can regroup in private there."

She did not envy Vixenya for having to take this role. Nor did she blame Issaria for having been mortified upon finding out this barbaric ritual was still honored and enforced. As if the girl hadn't endured enough, getting naked for a ritual bath in front of strangers was just as degrading as slavery. Had Shairi known of this little requirement of Calix's bride when it had been her betrothal, she might have been a bit less enthusiastic about the failed arrangement from the beginning.

The carriage rolled to a halt, jostling around as the horses stilled. They waited a moment, and then the footman opened the door.

Vixenya cast them one last wide-eyed glance before palming the pouch of metals and emerging from the carriage. Her indigo dress caught the sunlight like a peacock's feather as she lifted her free hand to wave to the gathered people. Cheers went up and then Zak—Prince Calix was climbing out beside her, falling into place with such ease that Shari's stomach churned a little.

He wasn't supposed to be comfortable with attention. He'd told her on several occasions—most recently at the *real* Calix's coronation party as they'd scavenged the buffet for sweets—that he never felt comfortable in front of a lot of people. It was why he preferred being a soldier and guard rather than some chancellor like his father. But there he was, his hand on Vixenya's lower back as if he'd been molded to fit. Zak's black hair, unlike the real Calix, shone highlights of blue in the sun.

"You coming?" Eiren said, startling her from her thoughts as she hunched over, dress gathered in her fists in the carriage doorway. "You took charge. Can't fall apart now, Princess Shairi."

"Yes, of course," she replied, following Eiren out of the coach.

Together they climbed a proverbial mountain of stairs to reach the temple's hall.

"Disrespectful, is what it is," Shairi murmured. "Making them climb all these stairs *before* we even see a representative?"

"You really read into it like that?"

Shairi shot the brunette a look. "I don't *read into it*," she hissed. "I know it. I was raised in this. Every look is a meaning, every word a carefully chosen weapon meant to enable an ally or disarm an opponent."

"You're rather like a spider, weaving all these webs, are you not?"

Shairi paled and it wasn't from the ridiculous amount of stairs she was climbing. "Why would you say that?"

Eiren blanched. "I mean no disrespect, I only…the way you view things is astute." She swallowed hard before saying, "I thought a spider to be a weaver of worlds. You make and unmake like them, seeing the whole when there is only a piece."

Oh. Shairi didn't get to reply as they crested the top of the stairs and found only two magicians, one dressed in the garb of a temple priest, the other in a tunic and pantaloon combination in a bold green pattern Shairi wouldn't be caught dead in, to receive them. She didn't look at Eiren as she mumbled, "Disrespectful. I told you."

As they neared, she sunk into a polite curtsey, and Eiren followed in turn. "Esteemed patrons of Nazarovo, we are so gracious for the generosity of your house for—"

"And who are you to extend such thanks?" The one draped in temple robes asked, voice laced with disdain.

Shairi's eye might have been twitching as she replied curtly, "I am Princess Shairi Chrysanthos of Ares. As you know, I have long lived in Hinhallow, and I am attending to Imperial Princess Issaria and Crown Prince Calix on this journey, so you would do well to address me, Lady Eiren, as well as the others in our retinue, with respect, lest we tell our charges how rude our hosts have been."

The magician with the bold tunic guffawed and pushed past the temple priest. "What Magistrate Elgideous means to say is that we were *expecting* the Prince and Princess to arrive at the head of their traveling party."

"As you can see, they're busy."

The Magistrate's beady eyes narrowed down the temple steps at them. "Yes, I can see that they're quite charitable."

"At least someone is," Eiren murmured.

At that moment, Cizabet, Asmy, and Cylise topped the stairs with boxes and luggage in tow. "I hope I can put these down soon. My arms are as tired as my legs after those stairs!" Cylise panted as they approached.

Shairi quirked an eyebrow at their hosts. "Will someone show these poor girls to our suites so they may relieve themselves of their parcels?"

The pair of Nazarovian leaders exchanged hesitant glances before the green-tunic-chancellor said, "We have prepared a banquet to receive the Prince and Princess. You and the other attendants may retire if you wish, but we had *expected* to exchange pleasantries with our guests."

Shairi resisted grinding her teeth as she said graciously, "I'm sure they'd love nothing more. I, of course, will accompany Princess Issaria anywhere she goes."

Magistrate Elgidious clapped his hands and a young acolyte, dressed plainly in grey robes, emerged from somewhere beyond the temple's massive quartz pillars. "Take them to the rooms we've prepared. Provide them with anything they need. Send our finest tea service at once for those who wish to rest."

As the acolyte led the members of their group bearing their belongings to their rooms, Prince Calix and Princess Issaria ascended the stairs arm in arm and flanked by two straight lines of soldiers in gold-colored alloy armor. Their heads were inclined together, foreheads nearly touching as they whispered conspiratorially. Shairi had to give it to them. Zak and Vixenya were playing this loving couple schtick *really* well. Very convincing the way he tucked her hair behind her ear, his thumb lingering across her cheek. Entirely believable, the way she blushed and held his gaze as if he had replaced the very planets themselves.

She ignored the lack of remorse she felt as she interrupted them. "Your Majesties, our hosts have prepared a banquet to receive you."

Zak grinned and said, "That's fantastic. I'm a bit peaky after the trip." He looked down to Vixenya and said, "And you, my love?"

She nodded her agreement. "Yes, I would love nothing more." As if just noticing their presence, Vixenya startled at the Magistrate and the…Shairi was fuming. These cads *still* hadn't introduced themselves! Had she fallen so far?

"You must be Chancellor Foristall," Vixenya said with a familiarity that surprised Shairi. "And Magistrate Volcimus, I'm so *pleased* you're officiating the ritual later today."

It was Chancellor Foristall, clearly flattered she'd taken the time to know who he was beforehand, who stepped forward and smoothed a hand over his slicked-back sandy hair before inclining his head toward the false princess. "Welcome to Nazarovo, Princess Issaria. Please, call me Takunda. We're to be friends while you're in my fair city." He then looked to Prince Calix and said, "And Prince Calix! My you've grown since last I was in Hinhallow! When your father wrote that you'd selected a bride, I confess I hadn't expected to see you so soon."

"What can I say, Takunda, I don't want to wait a moment more."

"How quaint." He folded his hands before him as if this pleased him. "You'll have to tell us more about how you two met. Such a magnificent union of houses, and after *so* long in the dark." He cast accusing eyes toward the princess and said with sunshine happiness, "Shall we head to the banquet hall? I think you'll find we've prepared all the best dishes the Hallowvanian empire has to offer.

They followed the pair of patrons into the temple and down a long hallway to an open doorway. The breeze was heavy with the scent of garlic and roasted meat, and as they entered the hall, strewn with large plush seating and dozens of servers ready to rotate amongst them as they…what did they want to talk about again? Shairi felt the hairs on the back of her neck prickle.

There was but one settee that was large enough for two, and Zak settled himself so that he could spring to his feet while Vixenya perched on the edge of the cushion, fixing the ruffles on her dress as their hosts found seats across from them. That left Shairi, Eiren, and about a dozen soldiers without seats. Again, *rude.* But she wasn't letting the offense keep her from her task. It only made her more indignant.

A server dipped in front of Issaria and Calix, offering honeyed figs wrapped with salted pork, of which Zak took two and Vixenya passed. As Zak hungrily wolfed down his figs, the assault began with a seemingly simple question.

"Princess Issaria, how *did* you two meet?"

Vixenya, the false Issaria who'd been selecting a cucumber sandwich from another server jolted, surprised by the inquiry, though they'd practiced for this very incident. The server left without her having taken anything from his offerings. "We didn't meet. Not until recently. But…I felt as though I'd known him for years already by the time I did."

Zak cleared his throat, bringing their attention back to him. "You see, my parents had written to the late Emperor Helios about an arrangement." He cocked an eyebrow in a way that was so very much Calix that Shairi wanted to snort. "We'd only exchanged…preliminary letters to each other when Hecate killed them. While my parents thought all was lost…" he looked over to where Issaria sat, chewing something from a tray Shairi had not seen. The tenderness in Zak's gaze made Shairi's throat feel as though she'd swallowed glass.

"We continued to send letters when we could. Sometimes I wouldn't hear from her for months, and I always feared the worst, but then another letter would come."

"And you kept this up for years?" It almost sounded incredulous, but the apples of their cheeks were rosy, their eyes glassy with that dumbstruck look of acceptance that officials got when royals were present.

Zak and Vixenya nodded as if it were the most obvious thing in the world.

"By now, I was well accustomed to how Issaria had to sneak to send me letters so I waited on the days I knew the hawks were coming from our...representatives in the Evernight. I would take her scroll before the Post Master retrieved the correspondence," Zakarian said, bringing Vixenya's hand to his mouth with his gloved hand. "She took great risks, and greater still when she crossed the Glass, *alone*, to reach me." Her pressed his lips against her knuckles as he gazed into his beloved's eyes. "My brave, darling girl."

Mythos above this was as disgusting to watch as if it were the *real* prince and princess. Shairi kept her pleasant smile as she stared longingly at the sweet couple. The fact that this false story was not so far from the truth stung like nettles. Shairi knew in her heart that had Calix known that his parents had tried to broker a marriage with Issaria and himself before everything changed, he *would* have written to her. Cosmos, he might have even hopped on a ship and sailed there himself when her parents had been assassinated.

Calix wasn't that creative. He came up with this tale because it's what he *would* have done. *For her.*

Tears tightened her throat and she cleared her throat. "Excuse me," she murmured when Eiren and Cizabet cast concerned glances her way. "Must be...dust from the road in my throat."

Vixenya caught some unintended implication and parted with Calix, her hand dragging across the back of his shoulders with warm familiarity as she passed behind their settee. "Princess Shairi, are you well?"

She cleared her throat again. "I am, Princess. Thank you, for inquiring. The trek was a bit trying, that's all. I'm not used to such lengthy journeys. Please, don't concern yourself with me."

"My dear, I am concerned with *all* my friends. If you're weary, we can adjourn and take to our..." she looked about the room expectantly, "suite? I would assume? Since there are so many of our staff to attend us on this purification pilgrimage your tradition demands."

Chancellor Takunda nodded enthusiastically. "Oh yes, Princess Issaria, Prince Calix, we have prepared a suite for your party. Allow us to escort you."

When they were finally alone, the girls collapsed into various seats around a spacious sitting room with a once-picturesque view of the now near-depleted mountain-fed lake. The men snooped about the space for secret entrances or spaces where listening ears could be waiting.

Shairi draped herself across the nearest chaise and sighed dramatically, one arm slung across her brow. "Tea, please. Someone. Anyone."

"What's got you so drained?" Zak asked as he returned to the sitting room from one of the adjoining bedrooms. "Distributing Metals went well. A mother even let Vixenya hold her infant. I would have thought you'd be pleased."

Shairi sat up as Asmy brought a steaming porcelain cup and saucer over. "I knew no one this side of the Timeline was going to like the idea of Issaria, but I didn't think their dislike of her would extend to the Ballentines as well." Shairi took a bracing sip as she considered the behavior of the Nazarovian officials.

"Come again?" Khodri, another of Calix's guards who'd joined their group to add to the facade that Zak and Vixenya were indeed Prince Calix and Princess Issaria. "I thought they bought it well enough."

"You would think that. Tell me Khodri, when was the last time only two people came to greet Calix?" The soldier's mouth pressed into a thin line. "Exactly. It's never happened. It only happened here and now because he's aligned himself with her, and while it seems the common folk are easily swayed with bribes and kissing babes, the city lords and ladies will not be so easily won. Not when they think she's cast some love spell over their prince."

"But she didn't! Prince Calix and Princess Issaria really love each other!" Asmy objected as she brought teacups around the room.

Shairi resisted the urge to roll her eyes at the young girl's naivety, but it was Zak who said, "It doesn't matter what Calix and Issaria truly feel if Vixenya and I cannot convince them that Issaria stands against the Eventide, or I suppose, against this new threat, whatever it may be."

"What new threat?" Cizabet asked from her seat near the windows.

Zak's mouth opened a fraction before he snapped his jaw closed. Across the room, Khodri groaned.

Shairi sat up straighter. "What new threat?" she echoed.

"Good going, Zak," Khodri shot. "It was the *one* thing Calix asked us not to say."

"Now you *have* to tell us," Eiren said, her knuckles white as she gripped her cup.

Zak groaned and examined his hands before shucking the gloves and tossing them on the table beside the tea service. "Right before Calix and I switched places when it was just us and Vixenya in the carriage…he told me his father withdrew the army's support."

Cizabet gasped. Asmy dropped her spoon, the alloy clattering across the marble floor.

"King Akintunde wouldn't pull out of an alliance like that if there wasn't a logical reason," Shairi stated. He was ruthless, but not unwise. To pull his alliance meant something larger was at play.

Zak nodded. "Espera was attacked. They're saying the city has fallen to some…abomination or something."

"The prince asked us not to share the information until he'd had a chance to speak to Issaria," Vixenya added hastily. "I think he was afraid of her response to the news."

"As he should be!" Shairi replied, surprised by her vexation with the news. She might not have liked the princess, and *maybe* she poisoned her that one time, but the thought that she'd lost the prince to a slip of a girl who didn't even get what *she'd* bargained for in the trade was just…well it wasn't right. "And did he tell her?"

Zak shrugged. "I'd assume so?"

"Hopefully she doesn't kill him!" Cizabet joked, but when no one joined her laughter she fell silent and turned mossy eyes back to her tea with a grimace.

It was then that Eiren looked around the room, her teacup halfway to her lips when her blue eyes went wide. "Has anyone seen Rhaminta?"

1 4

CALIX

At the helm, Jallah called out, "There she is! The Siren's Song." He shook an angry fist at the sky as lightning flashed in the clouds and a series of thunderclaps popped off like festival fireworks. "Siyari Crowsong! Cosmos damn you, storm bitch!"

As if in reply to the taunt, the winds buffeting the ship intensified, sending needle-like drops of rain against their frigid flesh like daggers. Calix grit his teeth as one sliced across his face below his eye. He wiped the back of his hand across his wet cheek to find blood congealing with the rain.

This was not ordinary rain. Magicians were behind these razor-sharp raindrops. They were weaponizing the storm.

At last, a ship appeared off the starboard bow, ghostly dark in the rain and fog of the storm that enveloped them. Black sails glittered, slick with water as a silent filament of lightning slashed out of the sky and ignited the mizzenmast of *The Henrietta* in a shower of sparks. Flames surged to life, more potent than a naturally burning fire, and began to consume the wood despite the raging storm.

Several men went scurrying up into the rigging, but Calix stayed alert as the ship approached.

Raif and Alander took up posts by Calix's side. Even in his peripheral, he could see that Raif's bow of fire was greatly subdued by the conditions. Steam and white smoke churned up from his drawn weapon, flaming arrow guttered feebly against the wind and water. They were both at a disadvantage in these conditions.

Alander Lunawot was more at home with the wetness. The alloy hilt of his sword bore no blade. Instead, a gleaming, sapphire-hued oval of an aquathyst was mounted below the guard. He raised the empty hilt to his shoulders and leveled it, poised to attack. Frost crackled out from the elementia stone, claiming each raindrop for itself until a shining broadsword of glistening ice emitted a soft blue glow.

"Stay with us, Calix. You are still the Crown Prince, and we're here to protect you."

Calix said nothing. On the prow of the pirate's ship, a crimson-haired woman bore a fierce scowl and held aloft an alloy blade. The *Siren's Song* circled wide alongside the *Henrietta*, both ships matched for size. As Calix glared into the faces of his foes, he was surprised to find the enraged faces of women crowding the deck. Not a single man among them.

Some bore alloy weapons, but others raised hands to wield their mana. A barrage of arrows hailed from a single shaft shot from their crow's nest, flowering twigs that battered into the deck and forced Calix and his friends back several steps.

Ocean waves sloshed over the sides of the ship as pirates began to board, swinging in on ropes and flowering vines that turned thorny when touched by foes. And then the clash of alloy and the glamour of battle was as rife on the wind as the thunder that rattled their bones.

Calix went up against a broad woman with a nasty scowl and black hair shorn close to her scalp. Two short blades of lightning crackled and sparked in her grasp. His swords met the filament with pops and snapping light that zinged along his skin as she thrust and lunged at him time and time again.

Beside him, Alander's ice broadsword sliced through a midnight-skinned warrior's arm, the severed limb flopping about the deck like a fish as the woman howled in pain. He'd lost sight of Raif but could hear his throaty cries from nearby. The fray was thick with bodies and the storm was friend to none.

Lightning strobed the sky in monochrome madness as the swells tossed the ship like a toy. Rain came in torrents, and buffeted against them like razors on the wind. Magic flared around them as they battled, visible in bursts and shimmers of blues, greens, and reds amidst the storm.

Parry exchanged for thrust and pivot; brute force met with evasive skill. He did not want to hurt his opponent, he hardly thought this was his battle, but he *would* protect Issaria, even if she loathed him for it. Instead of going on the offensive and attacking her, he evaded his opponent's attacks but the danger of being skewered by a dagger of electricity became very real as his parries and dodges began to slow, his footing unsure on the rain-slick deck.

Swift as cobra, the series of punch-strikes that the scowling woman advanced with had Calix backing up against the gunwale. An angry ocean swirled at his back as he struggled to keep his footing.

Thunder clapped overhead like bronze bells in Sol Caravali as a flurry of black hair dashing across the deck caught his eye.

Cosmos be damned, he'd know that mane of hair anywhere. She'd found a way out.

"Issaria!" he shouted into the storm, but the wind ripped his cry away.

"Keep your focus on me, *filth*," his opponent snarled.

He ducked and dodged, but the ferocious woman was relentless in her assault. A rapid thrust-and-jab of zinging electricity that set every hair on his body on end had Calix twisting and flinging himself to avoid her daggers. It was like fighting a wild animal—unpredictable.

"Calix! Issaria's on the deck!" Raif cried from somewhere, he couldn't break his attention from his electric foe or he was done for.

"Find her!" he managed to shout as he dropped his body to the deck and rolled to avoid what surely would have pierced his heart had he lingered. Her aim was impeccable. "Don't you ever get tired?" He asked as he sprang to his feet.

"Never get tired of sticking slaver pigs!"

"Slaver? I'm no slaver! I'm the Mythos-forsaken Crown Prince of Hinhallow!"

His admission gave her momentary pause, but it was enough. Calix extinguished his talent and launched himself inside her guard. To fight him off, she too had to dismiss her weapons with crackling pops as the air pressures dissolved her bolts. As soon as she put them out and tried to grapple with him, he grinned and tossed her over the railing into the sea. She was big, but he was bigger and no stranger to brawling.

From down on the main deck he heard Raif's warning amid the song of battle and bloodshed. "Issaria! Run!" He wrestled with a woman on the deck. One hand gripped her long braid, the other wrapped around her neck as he clung to her waist with his legs. "It sees you!"

Issaria scrambled to her feet but the unnatural angle of the deck sent her backwards. Her skull smashed off the deck and she rolled to her side, head in her hand. Calix didn't want to look away from her, but he had to know.

Across the fray, a bull of fire and ash stomped cloven hooves into the ship's deck as he readied to charge.

There must be a Beastmaester somewhere, he thought blindly as he scoured the faces for one locked in concentration. He caught sight of Sethik, his fire extinguished by the torrents of rain, blade-locked against a dreadlocked axe-wielding warrior-woman. A red-headed girl far too young for this mess wept beneath the stairs, seeming to plead to the skies. Alander wielded his wintry sword against an archer who used her flowering bow to block his attacks.

And then there was no time to seek the magician.

The fiery beast barreled ahead, churning cinders in its wake.

Hoofbeats sounded like each heartbeat between them as he lurched into motion.

Issaria floundered as she brought herself to her knees. Still stunned from her fall she stared down the bull with an odd expression as it bore down upon her.

He wasn't going to make it in time.

15

ISSARIA

Issaria turned from the door, fists sore from demanding her release, and examined the Captain's quarters at last. There had to be something in here to get the door unlocked. A key, perhaps. Jallah's space was lavish, as expected, she thought as she scowled. Scrolls littered the heavy table in the center of the room, and thick velvet curtains swayed against the windows. Outside the sea raged, smashed against the glass with titan force. Surprised it didn't break, she hastily rummaged across the table, tossing scrolls to the floor. Maps and charts unfurled at her feet as she took to a desk and started pulling drawers out of their places and emptying them onto the desktop. Rings, loose gems, and coins spilled out. A series of letters penned delicately in cursive, all tied with a blue satin bow. Bottles of ink, melting wax for sealing documents, a letter opener with a porcelain handle in the shape of a red and orange spotted fish, and a thick leather ledger with yellowed pages askew.

She gasped.

Issaria rushed back to the door, letter opener fisted at her side. She banged on the door thrice. "Sethik! Jallah!" No one replied. She banged once more and listened to the clamor of battle on the other side of the door. "Calix! Let me out!" When no one replied, Issaria knelt at the doorknob and jammed the thin blade into the open keyhole, and shifted it around, searching for what, she wasn't sure.

Seconds ticked by. Above her, the ceiling rumbled with the steps of people rushing about. They shouted, their cries washed out by the roar of the sea and the clash of thunder and lightning searing the sky.

The blade clicked into place and the door swung open with the motion of the ship.

Issaria bolted into the fray, letter opener brandished like a dagger.

The sea attacked the ship. Waves crashed over the railings, sucked unlucky souls overboard. Rain came down so thick and fast she could hardly see inches in front of her face. Icy drops sliced like knives, and soon her cold skin was peppered with little beads of blood. Thunder boomed, a wildcat screaming in her ears while lightning cast the ship in flashes of brilliance and pitch. Men battled the elements in more ways than one. A flaming arrow struck the foremast, lighting it ablaze. Cinders rained down on the sails below, smoldering in patches that ate holes into the sails like moths. Jallah's men in the rigging clung to the ropes, trying to tie the sails down, but the wind ripped the sheets from their hands and battered them with rain, making the task nearly impossible.

Issaria ran to the railing of the quarter deck and took in the battle raging below.

Beasts were afoot on the main deck. A bull of fire and ash stomped its hooves and charged a group of Jallah's men as they descended the rigging. Smoldering hoof prints branded the deck in its wake. Sethik, embers smoldering on his jacket, ripped his hood from his shoulders, tossing it away so as not to be burned.

Lightning illuminated the sky. Beyond the swirling vortex of angry thunderheads, Issaria glimpsed the silhouette of a giant bird in the sky, wings spread as wide as the storm itself. Lightning filaments cracked down from its wings like feathers lost in flight. A bolt struck the charred mizzenmast, igniting the cinders doused by the storm. Another clap of thunder and a cage of lighting circled the ship, trapping them in the maelstrom.

A trio of arrows struck the deck in front of her, forcing Issaria back. The shafts bore budding flowers. Curiously, the flowers trembled, then the blossoms exploded. Branches snaked out across the deck like living vines, disappearing through the cannon ports and down the side of the ship before coming up the other side like a flowering maw.

Letter opener still in hand, Issaria threw herself on the branches, hacking at them with the dull blade. They fought back, growing thorns that sliced her hands with each stroke. Still, she did not relent. Branch in hand, she grimaced as thorns pierced her palm and bit into her fingers. Slick with blood she raked the blade across the vines like a saw, determined to cut through them.

The vines were going to crush the ship in half.

"Take the loot! Kill the men!" A woman's voice shouted from behind her. "He's just been to port so he shouldn't have slaves! Jallah Coppernolle!" Her war cry echoed against the grey-black sky. "Maggot man! You've sold your last girl!"

The woman shouting commands stood on the bulwark, braced by the rigging of her ship. Crimson hair snapped in the wind as her wild grey eyes met Issaria's. The woman's feral smile turned ravenous. "Bring me the girl."

Issaria abandoned the vines, letter opener still wedged deep into a thick bough, and scrambled into a run as a fierce-looking blonde woman with a long blonde braid charged after her. Down the stairs and into the melee on the main deck. The ship buckled underfoot as vines shattered the hull.

Water rushed into the bilge. *The Henrietta* groaned and began to tilt as the ocean filled its belly. Issaria skidded across the deck, ducking errant blades and elements as slavers and pirates fought to regain their footing on the storm-slick wood.

"Issaria! Run!" Raif shouted from where he grappled with the woman who'd been chasing her. "It sees you!"

Across the main deck, the bull stamped its cloven hooves into the planks, stirring flames out of the embers of the deck underfoot. Issaria clambered to her feet but the rain-slick deck and the slant of the ship kept her unbalanced. Falling hard, her skull cracked against the deck, dazzling her vision with starbursts of light. Snorting ash and sulfur gases, the flaming bull lowered its head, long fiery horns seeking a target.

Dizzy, she swayed, coming to her knees as she tried to steady herself.

The cacophony of hoofbeats as it charged her across the deck swallowed her as she thought of the paper cow she'd folded with Kidalma what felt like a lifetime ago.

The old slave seer had said she'd know the red-cow moment when she reached it. If the path she is on was the one true path, the one the Cosmos had lain at her feet.

Well, she thought as the fire bull's searing heat warmed her cheeks, *it's not a cow, but he certainly is red.*

And then Prince Calix was there, grunting as he took the brunt of the charge. *Fervent*-black hands locked around flaming horns as he wrestled the beast. "Issa! Get out of here now!" He ordered through clenched teeth as he risked a glance over his shoulder.

The heat of the mana inside him kept a halo of silver steam billowing off into the storm. Sweat glossed his brow and blood had dried in tiny rivers on his face from a shallow cut beneath his eye. Flames from the bull's horns lapped eagerly at the prince's hands.

Golden eyes flickered.

Fissures in his hands spewed cinders as the bull wrenched its head back, trying to free itself.

"The Beastmaester is too strong. I can't hold him off—" Prince Calix slid backward on the storm-drenched planks.

The bull snapped its head to the left, and again to the right, before rearing back and wresting his horns from the prince's hands in a mighty tug that sent him reeling backward.

Issaria felt all the oxygen suck out of the sky as the bull's hooves met the deck and he barreled forward, strength renewed by vengeful vigor. She didn't hear her scream, swallowed by the riotous clap of thunder erupting from the sky as the fire bull's longhorn punctured his abdomen, clean through to the other side.

"CALIX!" Raif's tortured cry ripped across the deck through the storm. He'd released the braided warrior and scrambled across the deck on hands and knees toward them.

Issaria felt her heart crack in two as the bull jerked its head back and Calix dropped to the ship's deck like a rag doll, the stench of burning flesh rank on the wind. The prince did not stir and the bull smoldered over him, snorting cinders, as if momentarily satisfied by the damage it had done.

"Cosmos, Calix! You idiot!" Raif lamented. "You Mythos forsaken fool!"

Tears wet her cheeks as she whispered, "Aurelia." The void inside herself where the wrathful deity lay dormant since the assassination attempt shimmered feebly in reply. Sulking or weak, Issaria wasn't sure. But she had to try. "Please."

The shimmer faded into the chasm where her mana should be.

She would not come without a price.

"I'll do anything."

Issaria saw the surge of white light from her own dead eye before velvet softness snuffed her out.

16

AURELIA

Aurelia was happy to answer the plea of her *Sanguinem Descendia.*

After all, now that the Saros Curse was broken with her eighteenth orbit, each welcome union of her soul with her vessel solidified her in this realm once more. Soon they would be inseparable.

The prayer on sweet, naive, Issaria's lips brought Aurelia forth like a tsunami of unbridled might. Radiant light burned away the beast-maester's rain like a second sun branding the world in a new dawn. Disintegrated the flaming beast that had dealt the near-fatal damage to the fire prince. Thunderheads rolled back on the horizon as if the sky itself recanted the tempest. Furious winds calmed. The storm bird that had caused it all shrieked against an azure sky as it too dissolved from hard bands of silver wind into an unfurling ribbon of shimmering dust that returned to the pirate queen, jaw slackened in awe at the sight of her true manifestation.

As it should be, Aurelia thought. Primordials are magnificent, unlike these frail mortal magicians that have broken Ellorhys so completely. They *should* be in awe of her primordial power. Fear what

128

she may do if they do not come to heel. She would ensure there would be no question of her authority.

"Aurelia! Please save him," a man she knew through the eye of her vessel to be Raif Evanoff begged as he pulled the inert prince into his lap, hands trembling over the cauterized wound. "Don't let him die for you like this. You can't let him die like this!"

Hush, Son of Tarlix. You need not beg for what I would do for my descendia's *guardian a thousand times over. Be at peace while I remedy this wayward journey. Your Prince Calix is precious to us both, and I will not fail him.*

Aurelia said without speaking, and all who were present, trapped by a fallen crate in a flooding bilge or bowing in reverence as she levitated just above their heads, heard her as if she had whispered into their hearts.

Storm daughter. Your fight against the Baelfor-blessed one called Jallah Coppernolle is valiant and noble. Too true, he is a blight upon the women of Ellorhys. She brought her hand to touch the too-smooth ridge of scar tissue that ringed Issaria's throat where her slave collar had been. *My vessel knows firsthand what it means to be degraded to that of an object. To be devalued, dehumanized, and mocked.*

The crimson-haired pirate queen knelt before her, head bowed. "Forgive me, Radiance. I thought he was off to raid more villages. Had I known he was ferrying—"

The prince paid for passage for himself and my descendia. *You will take them, and those who survive this skirmish the rest of the way. Only one need pay the toll to even the scales.*

"Yes! Of course! We've a healer, we'll tend to the prince's wounds as well. Anything you ask of us, it is done."

There is a stowaway trapped in the bilge of Jallah's ship. She's quite close to drowning. See that she makes it aboard your vessel, Storm daughter.

Siyari Crowsong barked orders to retrieve the foolish slave girl, and a team of magicians disappeared into the bowels of the flooded ship. The storm magician herself helped a trio of men bring the mortally wounded prince aboard the pirate's ship.

Everything suffers for the wants of man.

She sounded tired, weary. But Aurelia's voice grew cold and cruel as she turned her holy fire gaze upon the one who had broken souls for profit, her fury and outrage plain as the disgusted scowl on her face.

Jallah Coppernolle.

He crouched on the sterncastle deck, using the helm as an anchor to keep himself from sliding across the near-vertical angle of the deck. "I didn't hurt her! I knew!" he wailed. "I got her to where she was going! I did her a favor! Had I but known—"

Had you known I dwelled within my silver-tongued vessel, you would have sold me to those you know to hunt me. You can not lie to me, Maggot Man. Jallah, a fearsome man to her vessel, shrank at her slur. *Merchant of Men is a name you coined yourself. A false moniker for one who wishes to erase what they cannot escape. Behind your back, they call you Maggot Man. Feeding off of the carcasses of more evolved beings.*

"Yes, yes they call me Maggot Man. Is this what you want? I'll tell you anything. Anything at all."

Aurelia narrowed her eyes. *Do you think your confessions will redeem you? I watched from within my vessel as you belittled souls to that of barter. I have seen into your harrowed, hollow soul, Jallah Coppernolle. I can taste the lies on your tongue before they touch the air. You are a foul, vile, little man, and you shall plague my realm no more.*

"What are you going to do to me?"

Funny you should ask that of me, Maggot Man. I recall another monster asking you the same thing.

A trio of tiny ceramic jars that hung just below Jallah's zoster began to emit a low hum. The hum began to grow. The jars shattered each with a satisfying pop and the inhabitants, an assortment of moon-pale and bruised-grey grubs scattered across the slaver's clothes. A pitiful sob keened from inside the mustachioed man who'd terrorized so many. He flailed, trying to free them from the folds of his jerkin and pants, but the maggots were no longer influenced by the mana that had sustained them within the jars.

They had new commands now, and within seconds, they had wriggled under Coppernolle's clothing and began their dirty work. He writhed on the deck, scratching and slapping madly at his skin. He tore his shirt from his back and spun wildly, trying to reach his bodily invaders. Dug his nails into his flesh until they peeled back bloody trenches.

Jallah backed into the railing and toppled backward over onto the quarter deck where he squirmed and thrashed. Agonized moans and screeches resounded across the sea until his flesh appeared moth-eaten and his carcass only moved where thousands of maggots were feasting upon him.

Satisfied with his gruesome but fitting end, Aurelia turned from the vessel and glided over to the larger of the remaining ships. As her aura of power abandoned the sinking vessel, the stern snapped off the bow, weighted down with too much water. The storm darkened Lanzauve sucked it into the black as the bow splashed down upon floating corpses fresh from the skirmish.

Those who could be saved had already been evacuated. As Aurelia touched down upon the deck of the pirate queen's ship, she turned to the nearest magician, a young freckled girl with doe eyes and a skittish way about her. Guilt clouded her soul like a poison fog.

Bring me to him. When he is well, you can seek forgiveness.

The girl nodded and tentatively reached out, taking three of Aurelia's fingers in her small hand. She looked back at Aurelia only once as she led her below deck.

They had brought him to a dimly lit infirmary at the stern of the ship. It was at the vessel's waterline, so no windows brought sunlight to the space. Instead, melted candles obscured most of the shelf space around the cabin. New pillars were mashed into the old while still hot and pliable, making a jagged mountain range of multicolored wax dribbling and flickering along the perimeter of the room. Any space that wasn't occupied by candles was cluttered with jars and canisters of varied sizes and mediums. Glass, clay, silver, brass, copper, and porcelain: all filled with fresh and dried herbs. The air in the space was thick with the metallic tang of blood and the musty, earthen aroma of healing magic.

Behind a patchwork curtain of intersecting patterns, a small gathering pressed into the tight quarters around a narrow cot in the corner. Bloody bandages were left abandoned on the floor, and a half-empty basin of crimson water sat on a small table built into the wall of the ship. A blood-stained cloth hung off of the rim, dripping into a pale pink puddle. Aurelia peeled back the curtain. Raif, Alander, Siyari Crowsong, and the injured stowaway parted to make space for her beside the healer. Thankfully, the prince did not stir as the healer's deft hands peeled back pieces of charred skin. Black blood and viscous liquids seeped from the circular, fist-sized wound.

The midnight-skinned healer met her gaze and shook her head. "This is very bad, Radiance. The injury is deep, many organs were obliterated when the horn," she broke off, burying her mouth in the crook of her elbow, bloody hands extended away from her face as she gagged on the stench of burning tissue.

You've done well, healer. See to the other injured. I'll take over here. This was always meant for me.

Muscles in his abdomen contracted as Aurelia lay her hands upon his ravaged flesh. Slow at first, like the first sparks of a new flame, her fingertips began to glow a soft lilac-white. Effervescence bled up her fingers to her palms, her wrists, and up her arms in shimmering prisms of light.

The small cabin grew stifling hot. Sweat beaded down spines and ran rivulets down temples as they watched as the Primordial Mythos' hands emanated steady light bright as a newly forged star.

Calix groaned, his jaw clenched.

"Make sure he doesn't bite his tongue out!" The healer called from across the cabin with the stowaway.

Raif leaped across and pinned his shoulders to the bed. "Alander, the spoon!"

The water magician snatched a wooden ladle from a bowl bearing a thick green paste and wedged it between the prince's teeth as he wailed against the pain. Prince Calix bucked as the necromancy reached inside him and repaired ruined tissue. Stitched together organs and reconnected nerves; grafted bone and knit muscle like a weaver at the loom.

At last, he fell silent and Aurelia leaned back. She removed her hands, still radiating with afterglow, from his stomach, leaving behind a gristly white circle of scar tissue.

He will never be as he was, and some days the pain will wear on him, but he will live. She looked to the two men who had restrained him as she worked and added, *For his loyalty, I have granted him a boon to maintain the balance of give and take. I cannot undo what has been done, but I can stem the damage to his hands. After wresting the bull that surely would have ended my vessel's existence, the bloodfire fever would have claimed his left arm by the next new moon. The right shortly after.*

"Cosmos, you stopped the *Sanguignis Fervent* just like that?" Raif gaped.

It was not just like that, *as you say. But yes, his fire remains intact, and it will no longer consume his mortal flesh as he calls upon his gifts. As it always should have been.*

"My Lady? Your glow is, forgive me," Alander said as he cautiously reached to steady her. "You're fading rather fast, Eminence. Are you well?"

Aurelia wobbled in place on her knees beside the prince's cot. *I believe I've overtaxed this body,* she said as the light in her eyes flickered out, leaving Issaria's violet and ivory gaze stunned and deadpan in the wake of cosmic radiance.

Her eyes rolled to the back of her head as she collapsed into Alander's arms. Black hair seeped into white from the root like ink staining parchment until all that remained of Aurelia's presence in the cabin was the full moon scar on Prince Calix's stomach and the starlit radiance that encased her vessel's hands like gloves.

17

ELON

The rebel encampment in the Baelforia was abandoned when Elon and the nineteen people he'd convinced to follow him out of Espera after King Shura's proclamations arrived. Nineteen. It was a shameful number, but he didn't blame the people for their fear. The machines the usurper brought to Espera were unlike any weapon Ellorhys had ever seen, and they'd doled out devastation beyond belief. Taking out a few of them had cost their rebellion precious friends and thoroughly broke the spirit of the ragtag rebellion he'd been building in the wood.

Elon could still hear that monster's voice in his head. The Khaosson, he called himself. Obsidia's *son*. He intended to find Issaria and end her life. She was no safer now than she had been when her aunt had held her close and whispered falsities in her ear.

The paddock he'd built had been dismantled on the northern side, and glossy green new growth carefully camouflaged a trail of trampled brush that led west. The trodden path, poorly disguised, was easily spotted. A false trail, should pursuers find the remnants of their camp. Motes of light still clung to the curling fiddleheads like dew and dusted the pale blue star creeper flowers that coated the forest floor like a carpet.

"I thought you said there were more of you?" a thick-necked black-smith called Quinlann asked from the back of the group. "Aint nothing here. No one."

"They evacuated," was all Elon said as he trudged east, picking up subtle signs of a mass exodus. Gravel in a gully that was upturned. Flowers that had bruised petals, or the contrary branches that bloomed out-of-season—clear evidence of terran magic used to disguise their passing.

Nineteen. They followed him with wary trepidation.

Elon hoped that they were able to evacuate more than nineteen people in the initial excursion into Espera, but the corpses that dotted the countryside between the fallen city and the forest told him a different story. Unfortunate souls had encountered those monstrosities in open battle, likely unprepared for the level of destruction they were capable of.

He lamented being glad he didn't recognize any, but it was a small consolation. Most of the dead had been charred beyond recognition or were buried in effective trench-like graves, mangled limbs protruding at odd angles from rocky tombs.

Elon resisted the overwhelming urge to hang his head in defeat. It had seemed so simple when they conceived the idea of a rebellion. Resisting Hecate had been an attainable goal. The conniving scheme to sneak past Espera's watches in a storm cloud and steal into the bay with those abominations was the blindside assault that Elon hadn't calculated in his strategies. The unknown factor that devastated everything he'd strived to protect.

After witnessing this Khaosson's power for himself, Elon feared the worst.

Perhaps Issaria was outmatched after all.

THE TIMELINE STAINED WHAT LITTLE SKY WAS VISIBLE THROUGH THE canopy of the Baelforia in wispy swaths of tangerine and honey when Elon first smelled the woodsmoke. He led his pitiful gathering of refugees to the top of a ridge and spotted a smattering of campfires across a shallow stream at the bottom of the gully.

Sad silhouettes slumped around the flames. Muffled sobs broke the quiet sanctum of the forest.

They'd caught up with the others at last, and there were far fewer bodies than he'd even dared to hope. The sight shattered the remnants of his broken heart.

This was not how he'd intended to protect Espera.

"Elon!"

Safaiya's voice reached him in the twilight, breaking him from his melancholia. She'd nearly crossed the glen and trundled over to him through the undergrowth with a thin green blanket wrapped around her shoulders when Elon snapped to. The refugees had passed by him and joined the others at the fires, filling vacant places without a word.

"Thank the Cosmos, you made it." She offered him a tight-lipped smile. "We were beginning to fear you wouldn't, but I told them to have more faith in you."

Her confidence, Elon thought, was sorely misplaced.

"How is Maiyra?"

Safaiya cast a weighted glance over her shoulder before shaking her head. "She hasn't woken up. The boy, Jahvari, told me she pushed him out of the way of some…Elon he didn't make sense. None of the refugees do. I thought it was shock. Trauma, maybe. But…"

Maybe it was the haunted look in his eyes or the way he reeked of death, but she didn't push him to tell her what had happened to cause so much devastation, so much pointless sacrifice.

They should have just turned back. He was supposed to be their leader.

This was his fault.

Born to shovel shit and be grateful for it. Traitorous Flynt's ruthless taunts had haunted him. Now Elon heard a truth in the words.

"Elon, come sit down." She took him by the hand, leading him toward the fires. "I'll heal you best I can. I'm pretty tapped out after…" Safaiya gestured around them and didn't say more. Didn't need to. She wasn't a healer by trade but had picked up a few skills from the healers in the Crystal Palace. She'd probably exhausted her Terran magic trying to heal everyone who'd sought shelter by her fire.

They settled beside a feebly constructed fire that sputtered cinders with each shifting twig. Maiyra was laid out beside it, with a blood-stained cloak rolled beneath her head. Her armor had been removed, presumably by her sister as she'd tried to heal her non-existent wounds. Maiyra looked peaceful, wiped clean of blood, even if dust still clung to her scarlet hair. Safaiya knelt beside her sister and draped her blanket over her still form.

"I'm worried about her, Elon," she confessed in a whisper as she tried to swipe the debris from Maiyra's hair. "I *told* her not to do anything reckless. I should have told her not to go at all."

"I've only known Maiyra a short time, Saf," Elon started, "Honestly didn't know you had a sister before you told me she'd be meeting me at the Amber Rose." He chuckled at the memory, reaching out to tuck the blanket around Maiyra's feet. "But I know she wouldn't have listened to you even if you did tell her. Maiyra isn't the sort of woman to sit by and watch bad things happen to undeserving people. If she got hurt saving Jahvari, she accepted the risk and consequences willingly. You can't blame yourself."

"You're right," she agreed, a sideways smile pulled taught across her face. Safaia took a deep breath as if she could inhale Elon's absolution in the smoky air before releasing a great sigh. "There was blood in her ears. I'm not a healer. You know I'm better with food. There's no one here who can look at her properly. I hope someone in Ares can do something for her…that it won't be too late to repair any damage."

Safaiya's concern was well-placed. Magic could only heal fresh injuries. The newer the better. The longer damage was left to fester, the more difficult it became to repair. If Maiyra's injuries were internal, they were on a countdown to get her to a healer who could assess her condition.

"We covered a lot of ground. Ares lies on the Timeline…I would gather that if we continue east we'll intersect the city at some point. We'll find a healer for her straight away," he offered, reaching out to rest a comforting hand on her knee. "It'll be okay," he said with a confidence he didn't quite feel.

Safaia laid her hand atop his, nodding her agreement, though the crease in her brow spoke volumes of her own hopelessness. "And then you'll speak with the King?"

Elon had entirely forgotten that was why they'd headed in this direction in the first place. "Where's Rhori, Saf?" he asked, realizing at last who was missing from the conglomeration of rebels and refugees gathered in the twilight wood.

Safaiya sprung to her feet and spun around, counting the faces around them, perhaps noticing their friend hadn't accompanied Elon in his return. "He…he went back for you with some of the others. They hated the thought of leaving the city to fend for itself. You…" She faced him, grief-stricken eyes wide and glassy with tears in the scarlet glow of fire and perpetual sunset. "You didn't see him in Espera?"

Elon didn't have to tell her he hadn't. Silent tears burned his vision as he dropped his head into his hands. Another name etched into his heart. He wondered if Rhori had been among the corpses that littered the countryside, or if he was now trapped within the fallen city, left behind and unaware that Elon had evacuated as many as he dared without arousing suspicion from metal monstrosities and the magicians that controlled them. Safaia shuffled to his side and wrapped her arms around his shoulders to comfort him as best as she was able.

<h1 style="text-align:center">18</h1>

<h1 style="text-align:center">SHAIRI</h1>

Ultimately, their time in Nazarovo went by without major incident. Vixenya played a perfect Princess Issaria and endured the barbaric purification ritual with a grace that Shairi was certain not many could muster.

Even for a concubine, she had to admit.

Zak maintained an aloofness that was an acceptable replication of Prince Calix, though Shairi may have been a bit biased on that point. The interrogation continued at each encounter with officials, but the Chancellors were either incredibly good liars themselves—doubtful— or they genuinely believed the imposters to be the Ballentine prince and his intended.

The missing Rhaminta, though Shairi admitted she was elated to know the abrasive Aresian girl wasn't among their retinue, had caused some alarm between Issaria's girls, even the decoy. Then Eiren uncovered a note tucked into her satchel that Rhaminta had penned before she slipped away after the real Princess Issaria, well before they'd even left Hinhallow. Each carriage of girls had assumed Rhaminta was in the other carriage, and the men hadn't noticed their party was down one of several unnecessary handmaidens. There'd been such relief that the missing "Mint" was safe—or as safe as they could assume—

139

and they'd all shared secret relief that Princess Issaria and Prince Calix would have another set of hands on their impossible quest.

Shairi could hardly understand all their willingness to throw themselves in harm's way for some pampered princess from the Eventide. Every private conversation was about them: what they might be doing, where they might be that very instant if they'd had the epic blowout that was bound to happen—the princess was known to have an explosive temper when pushed to her limits, much to the amusement of Shairi's traveling companions.

By the time they arrived in Sol Caravali, once a beautiful commune of healers nestled against a picturesque backdrop of cascading waterfalls and misty rainbows, now a husk of shriveled palm oasis that reminded her of sun-dried grape, Shairi found it near impossible to ignore the sour mood that accompanied intrusive thoughts.

She would always be second best.

First degraded to the handmaiden of a younger princess after being trapped in Hinhallow following the Eventide; then cast aside as Prince Calix's affianced the instant a more valuable option appeared. It hardly mattered now that Calix never returned her feelings, the sting of rejection was felt all the same. Now even a servant girl would stow away on her former slaveship to help that raggedy urchin of a princess after she'd already walked away with everything Shairi craved for herself.

Even this charade of being an attendant to her was insulting, heartbreaking, and infuriating.

Hadn't she earned more than this sham of a reward? Hadn't her patience, her dedication, and loyalty merited more than this?

Princess poisoning aside, she'd been the epitome of a perfect princess, even half a continent away from her family's seat of power. As far as anyone knew, she was the ideal candidate for a strategic marriage. Poised, a skilled conversationalist, and while she wasn't barbaric enough to dance like the little nighttime princess, Shairi *was* an accomplished ballroom dancer.

So how was it that she was constantly being cast aside?

Her foul mood had tainted the carriage like a toxic fog. Even conspiratory whispers among the girls had stalled so as not to irk her ire.

There was palatable relief from Cizabet, Asmy, and Cylise when the carriage finally rolled to a halt and they practically fell out in their hurry to be away from her dark cloud and venomous glares.

The message was received. They were friendly, *not* friends. And clearly, her moroseness was too much for them, but they'd be happy to deceive countless officials if it meant helping *Princess Issaria.*

"You're in a fit," Zak commented as soon as she'd stepped down from the coach.

"How observant of you." She barely glanced at him as she started for the back of the carriage to start instructing the assembling staff where their luggage was to go—at least Sol Caravali hadn't skimped on the hospitalities like Nazarovo's officials had. A full retinue of attendants had gathered to welcome their party to the once-blessed acropolis, and she could already hear Eiren's commanding tone emanating from the other coach. Thankfully they wouldn't need to ply the public with Metals this time, but it might not hurt to reinforce the crown's generosity.

"Hey, Shairi," Zak exclaimed as he followed her. "What happened? Were the other girls rude to you? I'll talk—"

She whirled on him, scowling. "You think I'd care if some *servants* were mean to me?" She snorted and shook her head, smirking at him with all the bravado she could muster. "They weren't rude to me. They're *afraid* of me. They should be. I'm poisonous."

"Poisonous?"

What would he do, she wondered. What would Zak do if he knew she'd been the one to poison their precious princess, not her wretched Aunt stuck far beyond the Timeline. He probably wouldn't be looking at her like—like *that* if he knew what she'd done, what she was capable of. What lethal promises she'd vowed to Aunt Emmaleigh for Hinhallow, for *Ares* if only she could secure a place at Calix's side.

She could have rivaled that half-blind brat. Together, they could have easily stood against the Eventide, and Shairi could have been an

Empress Above the Timeline. A distant daydream that slipped through her grasp like grains of sand.

Ruefully she shook her head, banishing the confession before it cemented itself on her lips. "I'm *toxic,* Zak. Don't you see that? The others must. Something about me keeps them away."

"Shairi, you're not a bad person," he said with a confidence that annoyed her.

"How would you know?"

"I know you, Princess," he said with a sincerity that alarmed her. "Probably better than you think I do."

"Oh?" She could feel the heat rising in her cheeks. Nervous they'd be seen in a compromising position, she glanced about the courtyard, but everyone seemed to be busy. Vixenya was chatting amicably with their hosts—she'd leaned into the role of Princess Issaria in her performances, even carrying on in their quarters in case they were being watched. Shairi shuddered to think the former concubine's acting may have kept her in Akintunde's favor these past years. The other girls were catering to her skirts, hovering at her back, their attention thoroughly fixed. She wasn't sure why she bothered to be irritated at finding herself invisible once again. It was pitiable.

"What is it that you think you know about me?" Shairi snapped, turning her attention back to Zak.

"You just…*want* things," he said carefully. "Sometimes you can't have those things. And sometimes you go to extremes to try and get it." Zak chuckled as he smirked, cobalt eyes alight a secret only he knew. "Calix," he whispered, leaning in a bit, "once called you calculating."

Shairi's glare frosted at the Prince's more than accurate assessment. Maybe Calix wasn't as obtuse as she believed him to be.

"I don't think that's a poisonous trait," he added hastily. Shairi scoffed, but Zak cast a wary glance around them before he brushed the back of her hand with tentative fingers. She gasped at the contact, eyes snapping back up to meet his. "I understand that desire, and I've always liked that about you."

And then he was gone, walking across the courtyard toward their retinue, his gait transforming into the confident stride of Prince Calix the further he got from her. Shairi watched as Zak, in perfect imitation of Prince Calix's casual affection for the princess, slid his gloved hand around Vixenya's waist and leaned down to press a kiss to her cheek. For an instant, across the crowded courtyard, Zak glanced back toward her before turning away and carrying on with his charade.

Eiren found her a few moments later and eyed her curiously as she unbuckled their trunks from the back of the coach. "What's got you so red? You don't look upset. The girls said—"

Shairi spun away from the courtyard, shaking her head as she tried to clear Zak's words from her mind. "It's nothing, never mind. I was being foolish."

But Shairi wondered idly if the only thing she had been foolish about was Zakarian.

19

SHURA

Shura stared down at the scale map of Ellorhys that some poor fool had carved into a massive crystal table. It was such an impractical piece, even if it was impressive. How this had functioned as a council chamber was beyond him. Certainly, there was enough space for everyone, but this table was problematic.

How ever did one *use* it? It was more an art installation than functional furniture.

He was considering having it destroyed. Removed and replaced, at the very least.

Shura had taken to exploring his new palace, but the more he uncovered about the behemoth Crystal Palace the more he understood that its original inhabitants had garish taste.

Everything was so…*reflective.* The floors, the walls, the stairs—he was shocked the toilets weren't crystal as well.

"Ah, here you are." Risa's sultry voice broke him from his contemplations. She sauntered along the table until she was beside him. "I know this is your ancestral seat and all, " she gestured vaguely at the tabletop map, aquathyst bangles clattering together musically, "but we've got a whole continent to bring to heel." She cut him an assessing, predatory glare and asked, "Is there a reason we're sitting on our heels in the Eventide when we have a fleet of warships ready to move on Ares at your command?"

"Mind your tone, Risa," Shura cautioned with a pointed stare that had Risa averting her golden eyes and fingering the fringe of one of her long white coils.

"And there *is* a reason why we're waiting here, but Espera is *not* my ancestral seat, as you're so quick to err." He unfolded his arms and paced the length of the table north, dragging his fingers along the rim of the crystal basin that surrounded the carved map. "My *ancestors* never held power in the south. In Espera, Aurelia and her Endymion held the people's love. My mother and her lover fled to the northern continent and thought they would build their kingdom as far from Aurelia and her light as they could."

Shura stopped at the head of the table, his gaze fixed on the northernmost shore, nestled against the Salt Ice. He'd been that far north. Once as a boy, tied to an ancient tree by a man foolish enough to raise a monster as his son, and again as a man to see the place he'd been born with a vengeful heart. He knew there was no palace of ice and shadow anchored into the bay, but he knew a great many things that should have been. Things that he was fated to bring to pass, reweaving the Cosmos in his own pattern.

"Well?" She prompted, bored with waiting for his explanation. "Are you going to enlighten me, Shura? I thought we didn't keep secrets from one another," she pouted.

"I wasn't keeping secrets, pet. I was hoping to make a surprise of it."

Risa's eyes lit up and a wolfish grin pulled at her lips. "A surprise? For me?"

"Well, not *for* you," he conceded with a shrug.

Risa's pout turned into a glower. "Shura—"

"*King* Shura."

"*King* Shura," Risa corrected with only a moment's hesitation. "That doesn't count as a surprise, that sounds like a secret. When I came to you, I *told* you there were to be no secrets if I was to be your weapon." Her golden gaze was hard. "It was my only ask besides protecting me from *her.*"

"And I've upheld both, Risa, I assure you. I've not kept this from you maliciously, I simply wasn't sure when, or if ever, it will come to fruition, and it's best not to speak of things before their time lest we tempt the Cosmos to interfere," he cautioned. Seers were always peering into scrying pools trying to untangle the fates written in the stars, and simply speaking, to speak of a thing before its due could be the whisper that is heard across time.

Such things could not be allowed. It allowed too much room for error. It allowed too much room for resistance.

Risa stayed silent but her frown made her annoyance clear. He hoped he'd make it up to her. He didn't want the dark sorceress unhappy with her role in his court. She had been loyal and cunning and he would reward her patience.

"Shura!" Phelix's eager shout proceeded him barreling into the room, fur-lined cloak swirling around him. He spotted Shura and thrust a scroll out. "We've had a falcon from one of our hunting parties."

Shura had to resist the urge to gloat, but he did love it when things aligned. "Have they found the princess so soon?"

"Better."

There was only one thing that would be better than finding his wayward niece somewhere beyond protective walls. "Tell me, Phelix. Tell me it's time."

"Time? Is this the surprise?" Risa asked, anticipation sweetening her mood.

"With pleasure, Sire," Phelix grinned as he read the missive, eyes scanning the parchment twice before meeting his liege's expectant gaze with excitement. "We've found one of them."

"Them?" Risa asked.

"This, Risa dear, is what I've been waiting for. What I *need* more than I need to take Ares, or move against that bloody buffoon Akintunde," Shura explained as he turned to Phelix with eager eyes. "Where?"

"If we cut through the Baelforia there's a chance we could intersect it before it reaches the Ascalith," Phelix offered.

Shura glanced at the tabletop map of Ellorhys and suddenly understood the appeal of such a massive, impractical piece of furniture. It was absolutely *perfect* for planning a conquest. The world at his fingertips.

At his feet.

The sigil branded into his chest grew warm, a pleasant buzz of magic rushing through him. Shura loathed to disappoint and relished the thrum of approval that radiated through him.

Gather the pieces.

Shura had waited a long time for this opportunity to prove himself worthy of the favor bestowed upon him. Of all his mother's children, only he was gifted with the Saros Curse, a misnomer meant to discourage small-minded magicians from accomplishing great workings over multiple lifetimes. Hardly necessary, one would think, when magic enhanced the average lifespan to centuries, but the ambition of great minds had never been limited by only what they can achieve in one life, but challenged by the concept of how far into the future they can make their impact last.

Make their name live among the Mythos themselves.

Immortality. A reign that lasted forever. Worthy of his name.

"Risa, in my absence, you are the Queen Regent of Espera."

Risa squealed in delight and sprang from her chair and down the length of the table before crushing Shura into a hug. "You said the surprise wasn't for me!"

"Try not to burn it down, or kill too many people," he advised when she released him. But really, who was he to judge?

"I'll take excellent care of the city, King Shura."

"When we return, Risa," he added as he headed toward Phelix, still lingering on the threshold of the room, "We take the Titan Project to Ares."

The echo of her celebration followed Shura into the hallway. Phelix kept pace with him as he took the spiral stairs down to the more public spaces of the palace. "Ready a contingent of of our most daring magicians. We're going to be hunting something a bit more challenging than princess."

"With pleasure, sire," Phelix said with a wicked grin before departing down another garish and glaring crystal corridor to fulfill his orders.

As Phelix reached the end of the hall, Shura called out unable to resist knowing his prey, "Which one is it, Phelix?"

"Baelfor."

20

ISSARIA

She woke in a dim cabin, tucked in up to her chin underneath a faded green blanket. Painted on the ceiling above her bed was a crude swath of indigo blue, studded with yellow orbs and white specks meant to be the night sky. Issaria picked out familiar constellations among a scatter-shot of stars as bleary vision gave way to an assault of violent imagery:

Storm birds and sinking ships. Blood in the water, and flames on the deck. Red bulls and—she gasped aloud as she jolted upright.

"Calix!"

Calix had saved her. He was wounded, very badly. He might even be dead. For her. She could still taste the stench of burning flesh on her tongue. And she…what had she done? Clutching the thin blanket to her chest, her hands tingled strangely beneath layers of linen bandages.

"Issa!" Rhaminta's voice brought her attention to the corner of the room where she reclined against the wall on a three-legged stool. Her left leg stuck out straight out in front of her, framed and bound in a wooden brace. "Thank the Cosmos you're okay."

"Mint?"

"I'm so glad you're awake." Rhaminta's smile was weary, strained. Her dark eyes flickered between Issaria's face and her bound hands. "How are you feeling?"

"What are you doing here? Where is—what happened? Calix? Is he—"

"He's okay," she replied quickly. "We all are. Thanks to you."

The relief that doused the flame of concern building in her chest was momentary. This cabin was unfamiliar, the events that brought them to this moment were hazy in her mind. "What...what did she do?" Because Issaria knew it wasn't by her own grace that, wherever they were, they were whole.

"She stopped everything. It was incredible, Issa. She knew things. Things she shouldn't have, *couldn't* have known. Knew about Coppernolle and the pirate queen. Knew I was hiding in *Henrietta's* bilge—"

"Rhaminta!" Issaria scolded. "I told you to go with Vixenya! What about Eiren?"

"I know what you said." She offered a dismissive shrug. "But I thought you didn't mean it. Eiren will take care of the other girls and Vixenya, and *that* whole mess. They don't need me to sell the ruse. Besides, I thought you could use another set of hands in your whole save-the-world quest." She gestured to her injured leg. "Or I did before a crate fell on me."

"There's no healer for you?"

"There is. Mikko. She needs to rest after seeing to Calix and you." Rhaminta laughed ruefully. "Being far less important than the two of you, and a few of her own crew, I am last in queue for treatment. I'm going to require a few sessions as she builds her mana back up." Smiling thinly she added, "I'm okay. It's nothing, really. Just a break. Nice and clean, I'm told. Should be an easy enough fix. Just time-consuming."

Assured as much as she could be, Issaria looked around the room. The painting on the ceiling was not the only artwork. A sunset cove in crimson and saffron, a sea aflame with color, and a silhouetted pair of lovers walking the beach were rendered above a modest worktable secured to the floor. "Where...where are we?"

"Captain Crowsong took us aboard her ship at...at your command, sort of. Siyari's been waiting for you to wake up. She's very interested in you."

"Is that a good thing?"

Rhaminta considered for a moment before saying, "Well, I don't think it's a bad thing." With some effort, she pushed herself up off of the stool and limped over, leaning heavily on a crooked cane Issaria hadn't noticed before. "C'mon. I'll bring you to meet her. There's a few among the crew anxious to see you after..."

"After Aurelia came out of me." Issaria finished for her as she ducked under her friend's arm to help her walk.

"More than that, Issa." Rhaminta's voice was taught as a bowstring as she continued. "I heard the light coming off of you was more brilliant than the sun itself. I heard you rolled back the storm and forced *all* the mana back to magician. I heard you *were* a Mythos." She took a harrowing breath as they exited the room and into a long hallway studded with doors. "And then I saw you and I knew you were."

Issaria was silent, as they hobbled down a narrow corridor in the belly of the ship. Every door they passed bore a different pair of woman's names: *Cionè. Farrah. Mikko. Mia. Aleta. Gliss. Daya.* Each was uniquely decorated with shells, colorful sprays of flowers preserved with magic, lace ribbons torn from elegant gowns, and chains of gold and silver dripping with gems.

"These bandages," Issaria started as they came to the foot of a steep staircase meant for one person at a time. "Do I want to know what's underneath?"

Rhaminta took the cane from her and leaned in the doorframe before meeting her eye. The pity reflected in Mint's dark eyes swallowed Issaria as her friend said, "What you accomplished was nothing short of a miracle, Issaria. He would have died. I'm sorry for what it cost you." With her free hand, Mint caressed her cheek beneath her blind eye. "Then, and now." Her hand fell away and she limped up the stairs, gait slow and awkward as she maneuvered her leg.

Issaria followed, steadying Rhaminta when needed, and when they emerged on the quarter-deck Mint leaned against the main mast to catch her breath while Issaria took in her surroundings. The ship was on open cobalt seas—the Lanzauve or Norvenello she wasn't certain. Blue sky swallowed the horizon all around them, not a speck of land in sight. On the deck, and in the rigging, sailors from Jallah's crew were among unfamiliar faces of women. They chatted in low tones as they went about their tasks; tarring ropes, mending holes in the sail with bone needle and sinew, scrubbing blood from the main deck. Among them, she saw Raif and Alander, each sporting superficial wounds and bandages but otherwise alive and well, working with a group of women on the forecastle. Alander adjusted stances and elbows while Raif demonstrated different attacks.

"Everyone seems so…normal. How long have I been out?"

"It's been a few days, Issa," Mint wheezed as she pointed toward the stairs that lead to the rear decks of the ship. "The captain will be aloft."

Days. The realization felt like an anvil sitting on her chest. She'd been out for days and Calix—she'd yet to see him. If anything was to be gleaned from Rhaminta's avoidance of the topic it was that the prince had very nearly died. Could have, maybe should have died, had it not been for *her* interference.

It had very little to do with Issaria herself.

Issaria turned to take the stairs when a small, freckled girl with a knot of brown hair atop her head and too-big corduroy trousers rushed up and seized her bandaged hand.

"I didn't mean to! I told Vasha not to hurt him but he's so ornery!" Wide brown eyes rimmed with tears overtook her heart-shaped face as she pleaded. "I'm so sorry. He wouldn't listen to me!"

Issaria shook her head, confused but endeared. She crouched down to level herself with the girl, maybe no more than ten or twelve, and offered her a kind smile. "I'm sorry, I've only just woken up. What are you talking about? Who's Vasha?"

"Mia." A stern voice from above silenced their conversation. The redhead with storm-grey eyes who could only be Captain Siyari Crowsong overlooked them from the deck above. The tails of her cloak snapped in the wind, revealing two brutal-looking alloy daggers and a wineskin affixed to her hip on a leather zoster. She wore a man's trousers and had another dagger wedged into the calf of her knee-high boots. "I told you that when she wakes, I will be the first to speak with her."

Mia released Issaria's hand. "I'm sorry, Captain, I just…"

"Guilt is a humbling thing, Mia. Do not forget what this feels like, to be responsible for your actions, and your inactions. You lost control of your beast and many have suffered for it. If not for this woman's power, a *prince* would have died at your hands. The fallout from that would destroy us all. Even I would not be able to spare us from Akintunde's wrath."

A gasp caught in Issaria's throat as she wrenched her attention back to the sheepish young girl before her. Vasha…the red bull belonged to this…this *child*.

Mia swallowed hard as recognition of her crimes dawned across Issaria's face. She looked back to her captain. "I understand, Siya—Captain. I…I won't let it happen again. I'll work with Vasha until he's tamed." To Issaria she added, "I'll bring you news if your prince wakes. Mikko is with him now. I promise he's in good hands." Her eyes dropped to Issaria's own. "I mean…well, you know what I mean. I'm sorry!" She said again before thundering down the narrow stairs.

Issaria looked up toward the pirate captain to find herself pinned by those steely eyes. "Captain Crowsong, I take it?"

"I am," she replied, voice laced with pride. "But what manner of creature are *you?*"

"Creature?" Issaria laughed outright. "Do I look like some sort of beast to you?"

"Not now you don't. But when you blazed radiant with holy fire and set a man's own mana against him, making a corpse of him in minutes, one begins to wonder about the nature of beasts."

"Well, I assure you I am no creature."

"And a beast?"

Issaria smirked and held up her bandaged hands. "That remains to be seen, doesn't it?"

"Aye. It does." She held her gaze for a moment longer then smiled wide, a gold tooth showing in her grin. "Join me aloft. I've some news that will interest you if you are who they claim you to be, Princess."

At the moniker, Issaria looked to Rhaminta, eyebrows raised in silent question.

"What? Don't look at me like that. I had to tell her. She already knew who Calix was thanks to Raif and his big mouth." Mint rolled her eyes. "She's not as bad as she seems." Issaria arched an eyebrow at her. "I think."

Issaria huffed and ascended the short stairs to one of the ship's upper decks. Captain Crowsong kept one hand on the helm, and one before her, a compass palmed against the horizon. Her attention remained focused, so Issaria's wandered. Behind the crimson-haired captain, a dark-skinned woman with thick coils studded with glass beads and shells leaned against the mast. Her posture was relaxed, but the way she white-knuckled a bow crafted from a flowering dogwood branch and strung with something that appeared to be a thread of gold, Issaria knew she was anything but.

"Captain Crowsong, I am—"

"Call me Siyari, Princess," she said without looking. "I've never had royalty aboard my vessel before, but I imagine it negates the need for titles. This is Farrah, my first mate. You've met Amelia—Mia—who is responsible for your prince's wounds—and yes, your stow-away Rhaminta has informed me exactly how precious the cargo I carry is." She snapped the compass closed and tucked it into a pocket on her leather vest. "The question becomes, do you know how valuable you are at this moment?"

"Valuable?" Issaria questioned. "To whom? My aunt?"

Siyari shook her head. "Nay. Your aunt was executed shortly after Espera fell. Quite violently, I'm told. You're hunted by the one who calls himself True King."

Issaria blinked at the news. Aunt Cate—Hecate Messorem, Empress Regent and *murderer* of her parents was dead. Just like that. It seemed she owed someone a debt of gratitude for saving her the effort. Her heart ought to be made of stone for all the pain she felt at that woman's death. Not after what she must've done to Elon. What she had done to so many innocents. She swallowed her rage and scoffed. "True King? Who is this man? If he liberated Espera, why is he an enemy of mine?"

Siyari looked to Farrah who only shrugged in return, leaving the bulk of the conversation to her captain. "He's got an army of beasts. He made them, controls them. And they leveled your city to ash. He plans to turn them on the world to find you. Half the fleets out there are looking to bring you in for a reward and put a stop to this war before it starts."

"Who is he? Where did he come from to have such an army?"

"He's the bastard prince of Rhunmesc. Denounced the Wintersea name. He's claiming to be your family. Cousin or uncle or some such nonsense. Says he's the last son of Obsidia."

"Well that's impossible," Issaria refuted. "My family is infamous. Had there been another Imperial child, we would know about it, we would—"

"Impossible or not. He claims to have the blood of the Mythos, just as you do. And more, he claims your blood is the seal on the Eventide Curse. He intends to unravel it by sacrificing you."

Issaria was stunned into silence. It was improbable, but she knew that it wasn't impossible. There had been a rift between Aurelia and Obsidia for over a century. Even Aurelia had told her she'd hoped not to lose her sister, but Obsidia and Erebus had vanished. Helios, Issaria's father, had hunted them at Aurelia's request but they'd never been found. Before their assault on Espera the night Issaria's parents ascended to power, they hadn't been seen on the southern continent for a decade or more.

They very well could have hidden an Imperial baby in the wild north.

Issaria knew very little of Rhunmesc, the Winterseas who governed the capital city, or the frozen wastes beyond its walls. To think that some distant relative had done away with Aunt Cate so abruptly, had attacked her city and sought to hunt her down like an animal for slaughter…

Issaria turned to the captain, wary words on her tongue. "And you would tell me this because you intend to help me evade this True King?"

The wicked curve of Siyari's mouth set a cold shiver down her spine. "That remains to be seen, doesn't it?"

2 1

SHURA

Day broke across the Timeline as Shura and the hunting party rode hard into the shadow of the Mythos. Chunks of soil, felled branches, and occasional boulders rained down from Baelfor's lumbering form as he strode across Ellorhys, hindering their pursuit with a maelstrom of shed earth.

They had traveled far, and ridden hard across the darkness, led only by the glow of the half-moon and pinpricks of stars. Two horses had stumbled in the Baelforia, breaking their legs. The riders took their squire's steeds and left the boys to end the wounded animal's misery and make their way back to Espera on foot. Shura did not stop, his eyes locked onto his target.

Terran Mythos Baelfor was a titan of rock and vines. Dirt and clay fell from his lumbering form like rain and smashed into the ground with avalanche-like force. Green light wrapped around boulders and bones that made up his massive form, binding him together. Wiry white roots stuck out like hairs on his massive legs, while moss and leaves spiraled up his calves and thighs. On his back, a great forest grew, gilt with the golden leaves of the harvest season. Thick branches and vines wound around his broad chest like armor, and his eyes were brilliant orbs of green light.

The men gave chase after the Titan on horseback, wrapped alloy chains around its legs in an effort to bring it to the ground. Shura watched as the links cracked tight, twanging with pressure before shattering like shards of glass as the Mythos continued to stride onward, unfazed and unperturbed by their assault.

"Keep after him! Bring him to the ground!" Shura shouted as he dug his heels into his steed's side once more. "Faster! Faster, you stupid beast!"

Without hesitation, his soldiers tried again and again to bring the Mythos down. Arrows that held true to their target brought no reaction, though with a creature as colossal as this, Shura wasn't surprised.

Baelfor continued without pause, one gargantuan foot swinging in front of the other.

One brazen soldier foolishly rode out in front of the Mythos, blade catching the blazing sun like stars burning out across the universe. Crazed with loyalty, he cried "Long live the Khaosson!" and charged Baelfor's mountainous leg.

There was hardly a sound as the god crushed him underfoot.

Ellorhys trembled with his steps. Horses reared and whinnied each time a foot landed. Eyes bulged in panic as every instinct told them to flee. If mortal means and meager magic could not bring down the Mythos, then perhaps Shura could.

While Shura had no magic of his own, over the years he'd bargained and bartered, siphoned and bled it from his victims until he'd amassed enough mana to use independently of his dark ancestors. He wasn't nearly as powerful as that sweet, sinful magic that flowed through him when he communed with the dark void of magic his lineage gave him access to, but Shura knew the risks of relying too heavily on that unforgiving, primordial magic.

He had no intention of losing himself to the past.

Not when his vision for the future of Ellorhys was so clear.

Despite the radiance of day bearing down on them, tapping into his late sister's magic came easier than other elemental talents, almost like it wanted him to use it. Like it was always destined for his dark workings.

Shura thrust a fist toward the sky like a claw, twisted malevolently to the left as he summoned the stark shadows of the sparse country-side to rise to his bidding. They came, lurching and streaking to his call like the hills themselves had grown a thousand grasping claws to trap the Mythos' leg.

Still, the titan carried on his pilgrimage, seemingly unaware that it was under attack.

"Enough!" The dark King spat, recanting his mana. Shadows pulled apart like black mist burning off in the morning light. "I will handle this my way. Follow the immortal as far as he goes. Do not relent. Keep him in your sights," he commanded.

Shura urged his steed forward as he raised himself out of the saddle. His eyes narrowed in focus. His horse moved tentatively at first, resisting the reins as he edged closer to Baelfor's leg. With care-ful, steady movements, Shura lifted himself out of the saddle and stood on his horse's back. With arms wide, he held his balance before he leaped onto the leg just as it lifted in stride.

Wind roared around him as his horse's panicked whinny ripped away from him. Shura dug his fingers into the crevasses between rock and withered vines. His feet struggled to find footholds before his left found the shaft of an arrow to steady himself. He buried his face against stone and held tight as velocity pushed against him until his very bones hurt with the force of it. When the crushing weight of motion stopped, he climbed up as far as he could until Baelfor again stepped forward with his left leg, and Shura pressed himself against the boulders, wriggled under vines and roots, and waited until he could begin his ascent all over again.

Far beneath him, the whooping and cheers of his men faded away to wind whispers as the Mythos out-strode them. Shura looked out for the first time since he leaped onto the Baelfor's leg. Blood drained from his face. Small figures that chased the true titan were no larger than the nail on his little finger.

Each time the leg stopped, upward he climbed until, breathless and bone-weary, Shura reached the edge of the forest. Dirt and bramble clung to him like a second skin. His lungs burned with the effort of his monumental vertical climb.

And if he had to judge, he was only halfway there.

So he tethered himself to a tree to rest.

PART III
GODSBLOOD

22

SHURA

It was long believed that all the creatures of Ellorhys once lived in the sacred forest that grew upon Baelfor's back. As he bent to carve the rivers and valleys of Ellorhys, they leaped from him and soared from treetops, sewing seeds from the original forest that grew along the Mythos' spine. It was said that not all the creatures that ventured forth on Baelfor's behalf returned to his side. By chance or choice, many of the beasts wandered into the woods they grew and became of Ellorhys instead.

Shura awoke to see a strange sort of beast peering at him from a nearby tree. A fox-faced owl with glowing purple fungi gilding tawny wings. It blinked onyx eyes and cocked its head at an unnatural angle before screaming into the forest with agonizingly painful human resemblance. Then, it spread its shimmering feathers and winged into the trees with surprising agility.

Shura swallowed hard and brought himself to his feet. He coiled the length of rope and ducked into it, settling the weight evenly across his shoulder before taking daggers from his boots and gripping them tight. He sucked in a breath and propelled himself up through the forest, digging his blades into trees to keep himself steady.

Greenish-gold Terran magic seeped from the wounds he inflicted on the trees like blood beading at the surface of a fresh cut, only to burst into shimmers of light instead of weeping like an open sore.

He pushed forward, upward against gravity.

Shura had always loved the scent of the woods. But this forest was different than the crisp scent of frost and pine he was accustomed to in the Ferrofrost. Rich and green, this forest smelled like dirt and loam, and the gentle aroma of wildflowers. Around him, the woods brimmed with life. Birds flit among the branches overhead, chirruping and chattering. Moss and leaves, fallen branches and shrubs entangled themselves into the Mythos' woods. He saw the fox-faced owl among the trees but was uncertain if it was the same one as when he awoke or if there were more of the strange creatures watching him from the trees.

He glimpsed a herd of crystal-horned elk with sweeping peacock tails in every color of winter and frost he'd ever seen. Fur-covered creatures with human faces, elongated necks, and long winding tails crouched among the leaves of the fruit-bearing trees, cackling and howling as he passed.

Streams bubbled and gurgled, trailing silver threads through the expanse of the forest. The little light that penetrated the canopy came through in piercing yellow rays, streaming through the darkness. Overhead, the leaves glowed every hue of green, glittering gems illuminated by distant sunshine.

If Shura didn't know, hadn't been struggling for each step against the constant pull of gravity, he would have thought this any ordinary forest, despite the bizarre fauna that lurked in his peripheral vision, watching him closely, only to vanish when he turned his head. Curious little things. Perhaps they would warn their warden the wolf had come to play, or perhaps he was the prey, and they only bided their time.

The very thought brought an unbidden chuckle to his lips.

As he carried on through Baelfor's woods, the animals began to pull back. As if sensing that the magician among them was more predator than prey, his presence silenced the forest. Birds ceased to sing. Strange creatures vanished from the brush, leaving shimmering motes of Terran magic in their wake. The forest's fragrance struck him. Before it had smelled loamy, and fresh, trees and earth all working together to create a thriving ecosystem. Here the only scents were the breeze that rushed across the leaves, carrying with it the dry grit of sand and the salt sea.

The forest was breaking. Soon he would crest the crown of Baelfor's head.

Shura broke through the brush and realized that, for the first time since he began his treacherous ascent, gravity wasn't pulling him back down the giant's back. He stood upright and stretched aching arms above his head. As Baelfor lurched forward, Shura swayed with his motions, easily keeping balance in the dim dappled light of Baelfor's forest.

A shifting, shimmering aura in hues of gold and umber, sage, jade, evergreen, and wheat-stalk yellow danced beyond the tree line, illuminating the dense canopy from underneath. The sight of it, radiant and ever-bright, made the dark star burned into his chest flare to life even as Shura was reminded of the night rainbow, the ribbons of light that had danced above the Averhame's peaks on clear winter nights.

Hungry and wanting, it urged him forward. They were so close. Memories could wait. He would bring back the night and they would all see the night rainbow again.

Tentative, Shura crouched low and shifted the bramble and shrubs aside as he made his way toward the source.

A circle of wiry young trees with golden leaves framed a small glade. White bell-shaped flowers sprouted around the base of each sapling, and glowing moss gilt stone and bark alike. Before him, in the center of the grove was the source of the light. A sunburst-shaped pool filled to the brim with luminescence. Too many colors to focus on at once, Shura tore his eyes from the hypnotizing depths of the pond and realized that from here, the forest thinned over what must be Baelfor's brow. Beyond the tree line, he could see bright sun, and red sand for kilometers.

They had reached the Ascalith, the red sand desert nestled between the Rilaan and Wildrine mountain ranges. There was nothing out here but hot sun, hotter sand, scorpions, and if legends were to be believed, *sandsharks.* His men, though loyal and skilled, would not have been able to follow the Mythos this far. Baelfor had covered nearly the length of the continent in just one day.

He needed to end this quest. But how?

Shura knelt next to the pond and reached out to touch it. Green light leaped out of the pond like an eager fish and splashed back down, only a hair's breadth from his fingertips. The magic responded to his presence. He wondered if that meant the Mythos knew he was there, crouched on his skull. It would only take Baelfor a moment to strike him down and leave only a bloody smear amidst the trees.

You must draw ichor to harness the original Terran Magic as your own.

Behind him, a frightening screech rattled the trees. He turned, unsurprised to the fox-faced owl watching him from just inside the forest.

"If you're here to stop me, you'll have to do more than that, bird."

Drawing his sword from his hip, Shura waded into the pool. Light seeped into his clothes like bathwater, and caressed him with champagne fizziness as motes of emerald and ochre light shimmered up in his wake. Beneath him, Shura felt Baelfor slow, and he imagined the great beast having the grand realization that he did not walk alone.

The Mythos stopped.

Shura grinned. *Too late.*

He raised his sword above his head and plunged it down into the center of the pool. The light that had filled the pool went out as if someone had doused a candle, leaving Shura crouched in the basin, shrouded in the twilight of the dense canopy

The sky cried out a thunderous groan that sounded like some abyssal beast had been summoned up from the depths of the Cosmos —and then Shura realized that sound wasn't the sky. The cry that could shatter the earth itself came from Baelfor. Curtains of light poured into the sky from below his vantage point in shades of green and gold he'd never imagined before. They stretched out and sped toward the horizon as if trying to escape the pull of whatever cataclysm he'd unleashed. Gold oozed from the gash in the bottom of the pool, congealing like bubbles of oil against his blade. He yanked the sword to the side and twisted it in place as he thrust down, putting all his weight into driving it as deep as he could. Shimmering ichor spurted from the wound, and splattered the leaves on the trees, the rocks and moss that surrounded the pool.

The wound gushed gold.

With a mighty heave, Shura wrenched his sword from the fissure and sheathed it at his side without cleaning it. He wanted proof that it was he who'd conquered the Mythos.

Ichor bubbled up like a spring at his feet, lapping at his boots like a sea of sparkling honey. It rose to his knees, his thighs. Soon there was more gold in the pool than not, and like crude waste, it spilled over the edge of the pool and onto the crown of the Mythos head, leaking out from the pool like blood from a wound.

Shura cupped his hands and dipped into the Godsblood. He paused, only for a moment, before bringing his hands to his mouth and parting his lips for the shimmering nectar. It tasted nothing like honey, instead, it was rich, loamy, and fresh, and reminded him of the first time he'd seen a spring thaw in Rhunmesc as a boy. Ichor dribbled down his chin as he guzzled handful after handful.

Overhead, the ribbons of light that had spread from horizon to horizon rushed backward toward his epicenter like the tide pulling back into the sea. Another pulse of light erupted across the sky as the colorful ribbons of mana collided. Flickering motes of effervescent fluttered down like errant feathers from the Cosmos.

Beneath it all, Shura felt the Mythos sway.

This was it.

Shura retreated to the forest. Toward the back of the titan's skull, drove his daggers to their hilts into the trunk of a gnarled ancient oak and wedged himself into a crevasse between its roots, and held tight. Just waiting for the collapse. He considered tying himself with the rope but images of being crushed by debris he could have avoided flashed through his mind, and he left the rope coiled across his chest instead.

It happened much faster than he anticipated. One moment he was above the clouds, riding on the top of the Terran Mythos' head, and the next he was careening toward Ellorhys, inertia ripping all thoughts from his mind but one: Shura wasn't positive the massive body of earth and forest between him and the ground would save him.

Birds and flying beasts took wing in a riotous flock of fur and feathers. Animals trapped in the forest cried out in howls and wails as the world around them detonated. Trees ripped up by their roots, were upended and split with lightning-sharp cracks as the Mythos' body crumpled.

A mountain of a creature came apart at the seams.

Dust and dirt clouded the air, and choked his senses as he careened through the sky. Velocity crushed his stomach against his spine, made his head light as clouds, and tried to pry him from his crevice with the cloying desperation of a jilted lover.

Sand exploded upwards with the massive impact of the Mythos' body. It rained down on Shura and coated him in red. He drowned in grit and debris. Breathed dust and sand, and felt the shockwave of impact in his spine like he'd been struck by lightning and buried in an avalanche at the same moment.

Take what has not been given. The voice within the chasm of his mana spoke with the same fervent hunger that had driven him these past years. *Fill your mana before they are able to yield to the Maiden of Light.*

23

ISSARIA

Issaria grimaced at the malice lacing Siyari Crowsong's voice. "I take it the bounty is quite generous, then."

"You could make that assumption," Farrah simpered from where she reclined against the mast.

"Could I also make the assumption that because of…my actions you think I would be better off traded to someone who could end me?"

"I did say I had been wondering about the nature of beasts, did I not?" Siyari's grey eyes held no remorse, no fear, as she looked upon her. "Lucky stars shine on you, then. It's been a few days since you've been awake, but I've put a great many leagues between you and the likes of what hunts you. There are some beasts, Princess, you do not choose to fight, but rather, you must."

"Be afraid, but then you must do it anyway," Issaria said as she nodded in understanding at the pirate queen.

"Aye. Something like that." Siyari swiped a hand through her thick swath of scarlet hair and turned her face toward the wind. "This True King, he calls himself. The Khaosson." The way she said his name was the same way Issaria spat Aunt Cate's. Pure disgust. Siyari shook her head as she looked out at the vast blue sea. "I met him once, delivered

169

a hefty shipment of lava rock from the volcanic islands east of Sorair. Had to contract myself a second ship to make the deadline. I didn't know he was anyone other than a merchant when his business associate called him 'sire.'" The look in her eyes was all the confirmation that Issaria needed. The infamous Captain Crowsong regretted the encounter with this Khaosson. "When he said he could revolutionize the world I thought he was eccentric, but harmless."

"Yeah, well, he gave me the creeps," Farrah said.

"He is no friend of ours," Siyari continued, "We glimpsed his fleet as they prepared to sail south under the cover of storm clouds. We knew they were no one to trifle with, but had we known what monstrosities they bore..." Her voice was tight as she hung her head. "We should have warned them they were coming. Sent a falcon to our contacts, tried to reach the harbor first. Something besides turning tail and keeping to our side of the horizon."

Issaria knew what that gnawing guilt felt like. She reached out, Farrah straightened, eyes narrowed at the movement, but allowed Issaria's hand to fall on Siyari's shoulder. "My people are not weak. Though it seems many above the Timeline believe a knee bent means a broken spine. Perhaps a wounded spirit, but *I* heard there was a rebellion."

"Aye. I heard that too." Captain Crowsong shrugged Issaria's hand away. "And I heard they were thoroughly wiped out. Massacred. The *things* he brought with him followed the stragglers out past the city limits and left corpses scattered across the hillside for the crows."

Issaria gasped. She hadn't known *that.* Her horror must have shown on her face because the Captain's face softened, but only just.

"Your girl also led me to believe that you and your prince are on your way to save the world. Because that thing inside you told you to."

Issaria resisted the urge to turn and glare at Mint. She was going to have to have a word with her about her inability to keep secrets. "I wouldn't go that far, truth be told, I'm not really sure what I'm doing by going all the way out here...maybe I'm damning us all to Tarlix's fires, or maybe I'll get caught by this True King and be sacrificed and the curse will be lifted and all will be well." The futility of her situation struck her then and she laughed. At first, it was just a giggle, but then it grew like a thousand butterflies escaping with her sanity. "Maybe I'm a sacrifice either way because Aurelia is taking my body bit by bit. Her *sanguinum descendia*."

She held up her bandaged hands. "You think I don't know what I'll find under these wrappings? You think I don't know why you call me beast? She *took my fucking eye*." Issaria gave a hollow laugh and looked piteously at Siyari. "I am not the beast. I am the lamb offered to *satiate* the beast. Culled for the good of us all. The more I need her, the more the world needs her, the more she will take from me. Until I am no more."

And there it was.

The truth clanged inside her head like a death knell.

She was not long for this world. But in her death, she would unleash light and peace if it was the last thing she did. This wicked, spiteful creature inside her would not harm a single magician, save those whose hearts were corrupted, their mana dark. "So maybe I will save the world. But it won't really be *me* who does it."

The sound of the sea thumping against the hull of the *Siren's Song* filled the silence between them. Across the deck, she met Mint's horrified gaze and knew she'd been loud enough to hear even over the wind. Issaria turned to the railing, her back to the pirate queen, and her face to the sun.

She closed her eyes and let herself feel the warmth. The way sunshine felt as though a hot glob of honeyed light had been spilled atop her head. The crisp sea breeze, salty but also smelling of wood, and the ship's pitch on the worn ropes. Canvas sails snapping in the wind, and the spray of the sea against her skin.

She was alive. And she was free. And every day on this planet she would drag her body toward the Vera Calum if only to take the satisfaction from Aurelia in taking *her* first.

"Where do you need to go?" Captain Crowsong asked after a long while. "I don't much care for that beast, but she's certainly made a warrior out of you. I'll keep my word and drop you where you're headed when your prince awakens."

Issaria didn't open her eyes. Didn't turn around. She bowed her head in thanks and said, "The Ascalith. We're headed into the Ascalith."

"We've been circling the same few leagues for the past day or so. I didn't want to rush bringing you anywhere you'd get sighted, and with the Lady inside you," she looked about the ship before finishing, "I didn't want to take any chances. We're about two days from Belxac, a little twilight town on the edge of the desert. You'll like it there, Princess."

Issaria didn't quite care where they were dropped off, but Belxac sounded as good as Pallis did. Maybe better, since there wasn't a chance of them intersecting their imposter-selves and the royal caravan.

"The girl, Mia."

The statement startled her and she turned to face the Captain and her first mate again. "The one who nearly killed Calix?" Issaria asked incredulously, resisting the urge to look around for the child.

"She's a good girl. Daughter of a city lord or some sort up in Kraznodar. Didn't like that her father had slaves so she set out to find me. Aye, and she did but that's another story for another time. The point is, we set them all free. All the girls, some younger than his daughter, that he kept like whores. All the ladies in the household who'd grown up under his reign of terror. Many of them had been pregnant, some more than once, and forced to terminate their pregnancies, lest his equally vile wife found out and had them punished. If they managed to hide it, well…I won't turn your stomach with what that sort of man is capable of, but sufficed to say he deserved everything that came upon him that day."

"That's…incredibly brave of her, and horrific. I never knew such things, such monstrous people existed in the world. My parents never would have stood for it. And I will not either."

"She is brave. And kind. Couldn't kill the sick son of a bitch herself, but that fire of hers." Siyari shook her head and let out a low whistle. "When that fire set loose for the first time, she *really* put her anger into it. The bull, the one she calls Vasha, I think that was the first time he took his true form. Before that, he was just...fire that she attempted to command. Vasha stampeded that wretched house into ash and I did not see her shed one tear."

"Why are you telling me this?"

"Because Vasha has done a lot of damage in the name of righteousness and vengeance and not once have I seen that girl feel the guilt of her actions. Until now. Until that man saved you for nothing more than love."

"That's a daring statement considering we were having quite the spat when you showed up."

"And despite your little lover's quarrel," she slid grey eyes to Farrah, whose mouth ticked up at the corner, the slightest, knowing smirk, before continuing, "you saved him right back. Cost you your hands to do it too. From what it sounds like you knew there was an asking price for her intervention and still, you let her out? And you did, didn't you? Let her out? She didn't just...do it of her own accord, now, did she?"

Issaria shook her head. "No, you're right. I...I bargained with her. Poorly it seems, as I may have said I'd give her anything to save him."

Farrah snorted. "If that's not love, Siya, I'm not sure what is."

Siyari shared a chuckle with her first mate at Issaria's expense before confirming, "Indeed, a poor bargain. Perhaps next time offer her a lock of your hair instead of a limb."

Farrah cleared her throat. "Speaking of limbs, Princess, you ought to know that your prince—"

"He lost a limb?" Issaria exclaimed, pushing herself off the railing to dash off to...wherever he was on the ship, she wasn't quite sure.

"No, actually...your other...self," she tried, unsure of what to call her.

"She has a name," Issaria said. "And as much as I'd like to withhold it to spite her, she might actually like hearing it. Her name is Aurelia, we should call her as such. You've likely heard of her."

"*The* Aurelia?" Issaria nodded and Farrah's eyebrows shot up. "Okay then," she replied, then tried it out. "*Aurelia* did do something pretty amazing for your prince. The damage his *fervent* had done to him was already nearing fatal, he must have known he didn't have long. Never knew the Crown Prince battled against such a condition with all his accolades." She shook her head in disbelief before meeting Issaria's gaze. "She stopped it. Said she couldn't undo what had already been done, after all, it must've been a lifetime of damage," Farrah elaborated. "But she stopped it. Must've shielded him somehow. As a gift for saving you in the first place."

"So, what, both Aurelia and Mia have a soft spot for tender feelings?"

"So you admit it, then?" Rhaminta said from all-too-near, though out of sight. "You have tender feelings for him?"

"Mint!" Issaria hissed and Mint hobbled out of the shadow of the sterncastle deck and out to the railing where she could watch Raif and Alander training with the ship's ladies on the deck below. "Very sorry about her. She's just *very nosy!*" she called out loud enough to ensure she heard.

"The point of all this was to tell you, Princess, that Mia acted rashly, and for her actions, your prince suffered greatly, and so too did you. But she is young, and you have taught her a valuable lesson about engaging others in life-taking combat."

"And what lesson is that?"

"That every side has a story. In theirs, *you* may be the villain. And sometimes that truth is hard to bear. But it is not *un*bearable."

Issaria considered it for a moment then nodded in agreement. "Perhaps I will be a villain in someone's story someday, but Mia, nor you or any of your crew, has anything to fear from me, as long as me and mine have nothing to fear from you."

"The same could be said of us. I believe a common enemy makes allies of even the most unlikely adversaries."

"Aye, there's truth in that," Issaria agreed with a smirk, parroting the pirate's own colloquialisms back at her. The three of them laughed and when they'd broken the tension she asked, "Where *are* we, anyway? Everything's just so…blue."

"Just north of Sorian Isles in the Norvenello. We'll head a little further south before cutting west across the isles and toward the continent. Hopefully, your prince will wake by then."

"Hopefully." She thought for a moment then dared to venture, "Were there any casualties at the confrontation besides Jallah?" How she knew it was he who'd perished, she couldn't say for sure, but it remained a fact all the same. Perhaps Aurelia had left the knowledge for her, or maybe they were closer to joining than she wanted to know.

"Aye. I lost two girls, two more wounded by alloy below deck. I heard that Jallah's side lost a man as well, though I know not his name. We try not to mourn slavers on this vessel, but it is strange times and strange company we keep these days."

Issaria had hoped to think Sethik was still alive, but the fact that she had not seen him among the rigging or the sails told her otherwise. Odd that her heart mourned him when he had once held her captive against her will. She didn't realize she'd lifted her hand until the scar on her collarbone was underneath her fingertips. "Strange indeed," Issaria murmured absently as an odd light on the horizon caught her attention. "What is—?"

Surging toward them like a rouge wave in the sky, tendrils of mana in every shade of greens and shimmering yellow-brown flashed and rippled like ribbons of wind and light.

"Mythos above."

"What in the Cosmos is *that?*" Alander asked from somewhere on the deck below.

Everyone looked up. Light spiraled overhead, brilliant in contrast against the azure sky. Extending out far beyond their ship, clear across the horizon, the jades and ochres shifted and coalesced with shimmering emerald and verdant mossy green. It was beautiful. The colors danced to music no one could hear, but if music were made into something that could be seen, this...*this* was it.

The menagerie of color was an artist's brush against the canvas of the sky.

Farrah was crying at the sight of such wondrous magic.

Gasps and questions went up around them as a burst of golden light like a second sunrise flashed against the distant horizon. A moment later there was a cataclysmic crack of thunder that had everyone ducking for cover. The mana rushed backward like the tide before a typhoon. The ocean rumbled long after the lights vanished. The deck of the *Siren's Song* quivered with the quake and bounced about on the sea as if someone had shaken the blanket of water that was the ocean.

Issaria and Siyari exchanged wary glances. All was quiet. The sea was calm enough, winds strong and sails taught, the day bright.

Farrah's scream sliced the tentative serenity like a forge-hot sword as she collapsed to her knees.

Bejeweled coils fell around her face, but Issaria could see the tears dampening her ashen cheeks as Captain Crowsong dropped to her side.

"Farrah!" Siyari cried, patting frantic hands along her bowed-over figure. Farrah moaned, her pain as palatable as if her bones were being ground to dust before them. She clenched at her stomach, her chest, and curled in on herself like a wilting blossom.

"What's wrong?" Siyari asked as she rocked Farrah into her lap and cradled the woman like an infant. "Show me where!"

"It hurts!" she cried out, curling her knees up to her chest as if being smaller would diminish the agony. "Mythos have mercy on me," Farrah wailed.

"Are you wounded? Mikko!" Her eyes darted frantically across the faces on the deck, "Where's Mikko? Get Mikko! Get me the damn healer!" A few of the women hurried away. Siyari looked back down at Farrah. "It's going to be okay, I promise."

The noises coming out of Farrah rivaled the most pitiful, wounded animal. Issaria backed up against the ship's railing. What in the Cosmos was going on? Farrah had been fine moments ago. Had she been poisoned as Issaria once had?

Farrah's hand clutched at the front of Siyari's vest. Her voice was strained, as though she'd swallowed hot coal, smoke plumed from her lips as she pleaded, "Cosmos, kill me, *please Siya.* Just kill me."

As her eyes fluttered closed, another pirate burst out from the stairs that led to the sleeping quarters.

"Captain! Farrah's not the only one!" A girl yelled from the lower deck. "Aleta and Gliss both blacked out from the pain below deck!"

Siyari locked furious eyes with Issaria over her first mate's pain-stricken form. "Do *something*," she hissed. "Anything!"

"I'm trying!" Issaria cried out. And she was. That place deep down inside her mana where Aurelia dwelled had frozen over. The light that had illuminated from within had gone dark. She could hammer her fists against it as hard as she wanted, but Issaria knew Aurelia would not, perhaps could not, answer her summons this time.

Not even to name her price.

Mikko, the healer, came though, from wherever she had been below deck.

The woman was dark-skinned, like most of the people above the Timeline. Though the healer was not just tan, her skin was the color of moonless, midnight skies. Likewise, her dark hair was pinned back in a tight bun beneath an orange headscarf. Her apron was stained with old blood and new, and her hands, though clean, were only freshly so. Still wet from whatever basin she's rinsed them in, blood still caked under her nails.

Kneeling beside Siyari and Farrah, Mikko pressed her ear to Farrah's chest and lingered, eyes closed as a faint blue glow surrounded Farrah's body. She drew back sharply. Brows pinched and mouth dipped into a scowl, Mikko glanced between them before throwing her hands up in frustration. "What are you waiting for? Bring her below deck! I've got to examine Farrah, along with the others."

And when they descended below deck, Mikko muttering, "Curious, curious," as she went, Issaria was still frozen against the gunwale, silently begging Aurelia to show herself.

24

WITHOUT

The tree line ended and suddenly the Esperian refugees were only separated from Ares by a fog-cloistered vineyard, lush with waxy clusters of maroon grapes and one *monumental* wall that loomed in the distance.

"Maiyra would love this," Safaiya said from the back of the donkey cart he pulled. She sat among the critically injured, Maiyra among the few they'd been able to fit in. "It looks lovely."

From a distance, the wall looked rosy in the glow of the sunset. Further down the wall, a pair of sharp turrets studded a well-guarded gate that was already rife with foot traffic entering the city. The lanes between grape trellises were just wide enough for the cart, so Elon took the lead, and the refugees fell in line behind the rambling cart.

As they neared, it became apparent the wall wasn't pink, but pale sandstone, and decorated with colorful shells. It wasn't until the refugees had nearly walked up to it that they recognized skulls cast into the gritty stone like mortar. Some were animal and Elon picked out the bizarrely long profile of a horse's skull among some smaller woodland creatures, but the next he spotted appeared eerily human.

It was easy to forget that each of the kingdoms were built in a time

178

before magic, when humans toiled beneath the command of the Mythos.

Elon didn't wait in the line of citizens waiting to gain entry to the city but led his ragtag group straight up to the gate. His arms ached from hauling the cart along, but he relished the pain. He deserved the torment and more for the lives he'd taken with carelessness.

At the gate, the city guard taking an inquiry of the people admitted into the city eyed Elon warily as he set the wagon down beside a cart laden with squawking chickens in wooden crates. Draped in chainmail studded with shiny green terramond stones in a pattern like snake scales, the guard was built like a mountain and resolute in his command as he eyed Elon from head to toe, "Back of the line, buddy."

"We need a healer, immediately," Elon said, gesturing toward the bed of the wagon behind him. "I'll also need to speak with your king—"

The second guard laughed, silver chainmail sparkling in the twilight. "What makes you think you're special enough to secure an audience with King Fraxinus?"

"I said back of the line," the first insisted from beneath his shiny alloy helmet as he peered around Elon and into the bed to see Maiyra, Safaiya, and the other wounded. "Some sort of accident?"

"I am Commander Elon Sainthart, *Sanguinem Defendier* of Princess Issaria. I come bearing news from the Imperial City. Espera's been attacked from the sea. We're probably the last to make it out before the perimeter went up. We need a healer," he said again as he hefted the wagon back up in his grasp, muscles aching with the prolonged weight of so many. "Please," he asked through clenched teeth. "My friend is hurt and we've been traveling for too long for her to wait."

"Let them in," said a farmer from the front of the line. Elon had barely seen him beside his crates of chickens. "You can't be so cruel as to make them wait."

"Yeah, let them in!" said another from further back in the line.

"They need help!"

"Closest House of Healing is up by the Temple of Baelfor," a freckled father with a small boy on his shoulders offered.

"It's got a big glass dome!" the child cried from his father's shoulders. "That way!" He pointed toward the city center, and in the distance over the tops of shops and homes was a glass dome covered in curling framework that glittered in the sunset.

The commanding guard shook his head as he stepped aside, clearly not wanting to incite a riot. "You're on your own with the King. Try the Gates. Maybe they'll run a messenger for you."

"Thanks," Elon said, not feeling at all grateful as he hauled the donkey cart through the arching gate.

"Wow! Papa look at that!" The child who'd pointed out the dome exclaimed. "The sky is dancing!" He clapped tiny hands together. "It's happy!"

Shimmering stripes of iridescent light spiraled across the sky. Elon tipped his head back to revel in the radiance above.

"Jahvari!" A woman's panicked scream pierced the blushing sky. Elon didn't want to stop, not when he was this close, but he knew that was the name of the kid Maiyra had saved, and Mythos be damned if that asshole guard had done anything—Elon felt his breath rush out of him like he'd been sucker punched.

Something was wrong. It felt as though he was suddenly wearing the wrong skin atop his skeleton. He hadn't even blinked but something had shifted in him, like dousing a light.

"Jahvari, wake up! Why won't he wake up?"

A pained keening came from the bed of the wagon, but Elon couldn't move. His body felt more foreign to him than when that water magician had taken control of him and the gathering of citizens in Espera. That felt as though his body had been invaded, possessed by an invisible assailant and forced to bend against its will, while this...

This felt like hearing his baby sister screaming, trapped inside his family's flaming house in Larkham. This felt like sifting through the ashes to find teeth and bones.

Like long ago death-bringer Zephyrus had passed through Elon on his way to take everything he ever would, or would ever come to love, leaving nothing but misery and a longing for the end.

"Safaiya!" A refugee from the trek caught her before she fell backward out of the wagon.

On the city street behind him, someone screamed as though they were being torn apart by wolves. Elon thought he might know something of that pain as he felt himself shatter like a mirror.

The agony engulfed his senses and cast his veins in frost and flame.

His knees hit the cobbled road like a meteor strike and the last thing Elon saw was the guard who'd wanted to deny him entry to the city collapsing to the ground, mouth agape around a horrific wail that echoed the rift of emptiness that was tearing open inside him.

THE GARDEN PARTY DELIGHTED IN THE RIBBONS OF LIGHT THAT DANCED across the sky. Even the musicians had stopped playing to watch what was surely another sign from the Cosmos. When the light show receded, words died on her tongue as Queen Emmaleigh Ballentine felt her magic, that quarry of mana within her that she associated with rich upturned earth and pale bones harvested in the moonlight, passed through her like a specter stealing off with a piece of her soul.

"Are you quite all right, your Majesty?" Commander Valente asked just as the porcelain teacup slipped from her grasp and shattered against the flagstone terrace.

It was gone.

The place where her magic had been was a burnt-out husk of a forest grove, so still with death that not even smoke stained the air.

An animalistic screech tore from within her as pain bent her in half, clutching her stomach as if she'd been gutted. Emmaleigh crumpled to the marble floor, vaguely aware she'd cut herself on shards of teacup, that her bejeweled crown had toppled from her head and rolled to a stop some distance away.

Agony assaulted her with the overwhelming sensation of emptiness, having been hollowed out like a rotten tree in a forest, festering all at once. There was an innate *wrongness* to her body. It was the absence that her body rejected, so wholly and completely that every fiber of her being felt as though she were being crushed beneath the heel of Baelfor himself.

"Mother!" Bexalynn cried as she sprang from her seat at a distant tea table and rushed to her side. "Mother, what's—"

"It's gone!" someone lamented.

Screams peppered the garden party, allowing some small part of her consciousness to glean that something was terribly wrong, not just with her, but broken with the world. Bexalynn's poor fingers were cranberry red and crushed in her grasp, but Emmaleigh couldn't make herself release her. So focused on how tightly she was clasping her daughter's hands, Emmaleigh's last thought was grateful for the darkness that swam up to take her from the torment of enduring existence without.

THE CARAVAN HAD STOPPED IN THE ZATLAN WOODS BETWEEN SOL Caravali and Tanzer to repair a wheel on a wagon hauling provisions. Zak, Khodri, and a handful of other soldiers were helping to change the wheel out, and the ladies were taking the opportunity to stretch their legs. Tall, shaggy-barked cedar trees were scraggly and browning but still clung desperately to their evergreen heritage where lucky branches and smaller trees hid from the unforgiving sun beneath the withering canopy. Princess Shairi, Vixenya, Cizabet, her sister Asmy, and Eiren, were circling the procession for the third time, wandering in and out of the sunbeams when rivers of green light spun dancing eddies over the treetops.

Shairi froze, mesmerized and stricken. She felt...queasy. It was more than just uneasiness at the sight in the sky. She felt it in her blood, in her bones and her muscles, a searing acidic burn, like everything was shrinking in on itself.

"Ciz—" Asmy barely began to speak, fear pitching her shy voice in alarm that twisted into a strangled cry as she dropped to the forest floor and began to seize, pitching back and forth like a shaken rag doll. Issaria had done the very same when Shairi had fed her oleander poison. And then Asmy stopped, falling so still it was as if she were dead.

It was all happening too fast. Not all of the soldiers had even turned to assess the commotion yet. Khodri was the closest, but his face was paling, his lips twisting in confusion as he neared.

Cizabet was shrieking, on her knees beside her sister when her cries of anguish turned into screams of pain. Bowed over Asmy's body, Cizabet's fiery hair obscured her face as she wrapped her arms around herself. Her nails dug gouges down her arms before she pitched forward, folding over her sister's body like a felled tree.

Khodri skidded to a stop, kicking up a spray of discarded pine needles from the forest floor. Hand on his sword he was already drawing his weapon and searching for the danger. Green light flared from the hilt of his sword as he tried to summon his armament magic, but like a shooting star swallowed by the horizon, it fizzled and faded.

"What in the Cosmos is going on?" Zak asked as he ran up beside his friend. "Khodri?"

Shairi wanted to know the answer to that, too.

Inside her body she felt as though some part of her was being starved, shriveling up without sustenance and splintering to dust like a dry tree branch. She took an unsteady step forward as Khodri dropped to his knees. A blade-less alloy sword hilt gripped so tightly his knuckles had gone bone white. The terramond mounted in the hilt was dull, cracked, and tarnished as if the magic inside had been sucked out. Blood dripped from his nose and his vacant eyes seemed to stare straight through her as he wobbled in place.

Shairi reached out a hand toward him, to catch him as he fell forward into the leaf litter but her fingertips caught her eye and she gasped. "What is happening?"

"Princess Shairi!" Cylise shrieked.

Was this…vengeance from the Cosmos for what she'd done?

Her flesh was turning green. The tips of her fingers were already a rich emerald, and it was spreading like a fungus across her palms and the tender flesh of her wrist like delicate lace gloves.

"Shairi!" Zak's alarm and proximity pulled her attention from her hands, but her vision was blurring—spotting like milky mist was pouring across her eyes.

Shairi whimpered, never having felt such caustic pain cleaving through her before.

"Princess?" Eiren's voice was close, right beside her, but gentle as she took her tainted hands.

"It's my magic," she gasped out. "It's—"

It was gone. And without her immunity, she was going to die a torturously slow death, poisoned by the toxins she'd ingested over the years. Sometimes for practice, sometimes for Hinhallow. *Always* for herself.

It was retribution. Shairi was sure of it now. She'd poisoned the last hope for the realm and now she was going to rot of poison herself.

She sniffled and sank to her knees as her consciousness swam in a storm of agony, bringing Eiren down with her to the forest floor.

Zak was there, beside her. She could smell the leather and salt of him. He always smelled a bit like the sea. "Shairi?" His voice was gentle as he clasped her free hand in his. "Shairi we're right here. I'm right here," his concern and comfort meant little. It wouldn't save her. But she was glad for it all the same.

"Zak?" She whispered, voice cracking as her throat blistered and a metallic tang coated her tongue. Metallic wetness bubbled at her lips. She felt him lean close and remembered his phantom touch and lingering glances in Sol Caravali. "Zak, I'm scared."

Shairi's eyes rolled back and she crumpled into Zak's arms like a flower blackening in a wildfire.

KIDALMA WAS ALONE IN HER CABIN ON JALLAH COPPERNOLLE'S flagship, *The Iron Tether,* and did not see the lights spin ribbons of shimmering magic across the cerulean sky. She'd used her Oracle magic earlier that day to read the path of a young slave girl Roark had picked up near Narwar.

The girl, Samirha, had used her Terran magic to wield thorny vines that snaked out of the sun-softened Snowflats and snared the slaver in a fool's trap, slung up by one ankle in a gnarled and knotted tree she'd grown in the same instant. She'd put up enough of a fight that Kidlama thought Roark and his tribe of huntsmen would abandon their quarry.

Samirha's resistance only stoked the fire of their determination to subdue her.

Curwin's aim was impeccable with a slingshot and a pellet imbued with his own Terran magic. He'd dropped her with a single shot, landed neatly between her eyes. A soft projectile of sand wasn't enough to kill her, but stunned, her vines fell slack and Roark was able to burn them away with his fire magic before restraining the girl and hauling her into a wagon in chains.

Samirha's reading had…worried Kidalma.

Her weathered face creased in concern as she peered at the folded miniature cradled against the hills and valleys of her palm. She hadn't let the girl keep the little gollum. A first. Kidalma always let her patrons keep their folded fortunes.

It wasn't entirely Samirha's gollum, folded carefully out of shimmering golden linen starched so flat it held the smallest indentations in its replica. There was no doubt in Kidalma's mind who the paper creature represented. Baelfor had been seen striding across the horizon when Master Jallah's fleets had been in Hinhallow.

In all her centuries, Kidalma had never laid eyes on a Mythos.

At the time it had felt more like a warning than the blessing everyone seemed to think it.

Kidalma opened her other hand, trembling with the weight of the petite, purple girl she'd folded in turn. A small dancing girl with a brave smile and a fierce heart.

Issaria Elysitao.

Kidalma wasn't sure if she'd folded the replica of the former slave-girl because Samirha's fight with Roark on the Snowflats reminded her of when the moonlight princess, poorly disguised as a dancer, fought with a dangerous beast of a man on the Glass; or if there was another reason she was folding bullheaded princesses and Mythos on the same day.

She always saw flashes of possibilities when she called upon the stars. It was usually a meteor shower of paths, so many options diverging through the Cosmos like new constellations begging to have their stories told among the legends. But this reading was different.

There was only one possibility. *One* future.

And in that future, Baelfor the gentle forest sower, mighty carver of the world, and guardian of all Terran magic, falls.

In one hand she held the future, and in the other…

Kidalma lifted the purple dancing girl into the light that shifted through her cabin's small window. She wondered how little Kai was doing…if she'd had her red-cow moment yet. Kidalma had seen the bull charging across the deck of a ship not so unlike *The Iron Tether…* and she'd seen the young man with the strength of the first flame intercept the beast. Kidalma knew the choice that would be presented in that moment. What the princess chose would bind the fates of both herself and her fiery protector together, and the path before them would not be kind.

The little dancer girl would need that fierce heart, but having the unyielding support of another…she would need that too, to face the dark days before her.

Kidalma did not see the lights spangle the sky with verdant magic that receded like the sea called away by the moon. But she heard the first screams of those whose magic went out with the tide, leaving them an empty shell that not even a mollusk could make into a home.

When the golden thread binding her Terran mana to the stars snapped like a frayed piece of twine, Kidalma was not as surprised as she thought she'd be, but the stab of loss that pierced her heart was more than her fragile body could bear without mana to give her strength.

She did not feel the pain that seized her as her flesh withered with the weight of her years.

She did not feel her last ragged breath sag out of her chest like a ghost's whisper.

Kidalma did not feel the moment her shriveled corpse impacted the floor of her cabin and exploded into a cloud of ash that left her colorful silk robe deserted of its wearer and splayed across the floor as though it had only been dropped.

Two destinies, folded of violet and gold, lay abandoned in a grey snowfall of death.

2 5

CALIX

He thought he heard someone speaking. It was difficult, like wading through tar but he slogged his way through the dark, blindly seeking out the echo of a whisper. Sometimes all was silent, and he was lost again. How did he get here? All he remembered was fire. He was of it. From it. One with it.

He'd heard once, as a child probably, that if he was ever lost he should stay in one place, and someone would find him.

He did not think anyone was coming to find him.

So even when the speaking stopped, he went on, hoping he'd located the source and wasn't stumbling in circles. He was getting closer though, he knew, because now he knew it was *her*. He wasn't sure who she was, of course, but there was a gentle voice that called a name that felt like it belonged to him when it fell upon his ears.

Maybe he didn't care if it wasn't his name, as long as it was her voice.

And he wanted to see her again. He'd always want to see her again. Even if it was forbidden. That was why he gave up his life, his immortality, and cast it into the forge to sustain the covenant until their return. He'd known she was coming back. He'd wanted to greet her as an equal at last.

188

Maybe then they could…

But first, he had to claw his way out of the dark.

THE FIRST THING CALIX SAW WHEN HE OPENED HIS EYES WAS THE MOST garish orange and green stripes he'd ever seen intersecting navy blue velvet in a hasty stitch of twine. A curtain, he realized, as he blinked and attempted to focus his attention on anything except the pit of fiery pain that was radiating from his stomach, just begging him to peek at whatever had laid him out long enough that no one thought his eyes would burn upon waking and seeing this offensive color scheme. He wouldn't do it.

Maybe he couldn't.

This was by far the worst pain he'd ever been in, and he'd shattered his leg in a botched hunting excursion with Raif and Zak. Took the healers three weeks to heal him completely, but not one of them ever said it *couldn't* be done. Maybe it was the fear of what Akintunde Ballentine would do if they didn't heal his firstborn son to perfection after a foolish youthful stunt. The pain had been excruciating, night after night after night. Until now, he had measured all other pain against those long weeks of healing sessions. It had diminished it and made it bearable, for he had endured worse.

Now he knew greater pain existed. It existed, and he had somehow encountered it and had very clearly lost. If he didn't hurt so much, he might think he was lucky to be alive.

"Is she going to be okay?" A concerned voice whispered from the other side of the curtain. There was no hiding the tremor of fear in her question. Whatever was going on, she didn't believe it would end well.

"I don't know," another voice replied. Women. They're both women. *Where is Issaria?* "I'm trying, but this is…strange. I don't know what's wrong with her, Siyari."

At the mention of the infamous pirate queen who'd attacked their ship, Calix bolted upright, the thin blanket that had been covering him falling around his hips. Lightning sliced across his stomach, up his spine, and shot down to his toes. He groaned in agony as he gripped his side and fell back against his pillow. "Mythos be damned, what *is this?*" he moaned.

"Thank the Cosmos. You're alive," the second voice said as the curtain dividing the cabin pulled back on its line. It belonged to a woman wearing a blood-stained apron. Her hair was pulled back in a vibrant kerchief. Immediately he knew the offensive curtain was her doing.

Relief was apparent in her clear eyes as she raised a hand beside him, allowing a faint aqua glow to encompass her hand as she reached for his bandages."My name is Mikko, and I'm the healer on this ship. I'll kindly ask you not to wrestle any more familiars." Her touch was cool and instantly he started to feel the pain begin to subside.

Meeting a healer upon waking was never a good sign, but in his case, he was lucky a healer was nearby. "Is that what I did? Cosmos, I might deserve this. Are we certain I'm alive?" he asked through clenched teeth. "I feel I would have liked the alternative."

"Don't temp fate, Prince. You very nearly ended up with the alternative," said the pirate queen Siyari Crowsong. She crossed her arms over her chest and though her voice had lost its tremor, Calix was sure she was trying to hold herself together. "You would a make certain princess very upset if you were you leave this realm."

At the mention of Issaria, it was as though a forge was stoked inside him. Instantly he was back up, pushing through the stab of torment that twisted up his spine. Shaking her head, Mikko helped him sit up and adjust the pillow. "Where is she?" He asked when he was settled.

"She's alive. Mia scampered off when you were cursing the Cosmos so I'm sure she'll be along shortly."

Calix cast his eyes to the cot behind them. A dark-skinned woman lay prone, with a flowered quilt pulled up to her neck. Her face was ashen, far too pale. "And her?"

Siyari ran a hand through her hair. Her distress was evident as she rubbed the nape of her neck, her gaze fixed on the comatose woman Calix recognized now as the dogwood archer from the battle.

"I don't know how to explain it. It was beautiful," her voice echoed with awe at the memory. The fierce captain sounded mesmerized as she stared into middle space and finished, "And then something happened. There are two more with the same symptoms down the hall." The captain shook her head and looked back to the healer, her loss and confusion clear. "What do you see within her, Mikko?"

"That's what is strange, Captain. I see everything is well. She does not bleed, nor is she pregnant, or wounded, or ill. Her blood flows, and her organs breathe it in. Bones are sturdy, her strength is there within her muscles. There is *nothing* wrong with her." She could have stopped there, but her voice didn't sound as though she were done speaking.

"Nothing except?" Siyari asked, urging her to continue her diagnosis.

Mikko's gaze slid to her patient. Worry furrowed her brow, a puzzle she couldn't solve, and Calix imagined that might be a first for the healer. "Except I do not see her mana. Nor Gliss, or Aleta. They are all without."

"You can see magic within a person?" Calix asked, astonished that something could be possible. As a fire magician, he had no possibility of wielding the healing arts, and thus, the magic remained a necessary mystery to him.

"Calix!"

His attention snapped from the healer to the doorway, where Issaria stood just beyond the threshold, lantern light from the corridor casting her in drastic shadows. Tears wobbled in her eyes, and her hands—her very bandaged hands, he could not help but notice—covered her mouth as if she couldn't quite believe he was awake. Cosmos, how close had he come? She'd been furious with him before.

He would face death every day if only she would look at him like that for the rest of their lives.

"You idiot!" she cried as she dashed across the cabin and crumpled against him. His eyes rolled back in his head at the shooting pain that sliced through his center even as he folded his arms around her. "You stupid, overconfident, foolish man!" Each word was accentuated by tears on his neck as she berated him. Issaria pulled back their faces barely a breath apart as she searched his eyes, for what, he wasn't sure. Whatever it was, she didn't find it. She threw her arms around his neck again, and he draped his hands around her waist. "Why would you do that? You almost *died!*"

"I didn't, though," he murmured. She had to know why he would do something so reckless.

"Princess," Mikko said, "please go easy on him. He's going to be in a lot of pain after such an ordeal. I'll need to change the bandages on his wounds."

"Oh!" She pulled back, wiping her cheeks on the back of her hand. "I'm sorry! Are you okay?" Her gaze dropped to his stomach and finally, he allowed himself to look at what felt like hot razors in his gut.

His abdomen was wrapped tightly with white gauze. For some reason, it made the many tiny scars he'd managed to collect over the years stark against the dark of his sun-drenched skin. Calix felt as though he had been torn in half and hastily reassembled like the curtains he'd awoken to. He hoped that underneath all that padding he didn't look like it.

"I must have you to thank for my miraculous survival?" Issaria wouldn't meet his gaze but she nodded, her eye fixed on her bandaged fingertips. He didn't want to ask. He really didn't. "What happened?"

"I asked her to save you. And she did."

She said it so matter-of-factly. He took her hands and held them between his own. "She did this to you in return?"

Issaria nodded. "I still haven't looked."

He nodded in understanding. "Me neither," he confessed, even though she probably knew he hadn't had the chance to see beneath the bandage. Mikko lingered behind Issaria with fresh bandages. "Guess I'm going to go first," he said as she withdrew to make room for the healer.

Issaria offered up a half smile. "Such a brave volunteer. I suppose we should see what I accomplished with my sacrifice."

But the word dropped into his stomach like a hot coal. *Sacrifice.* Is that really what she was? The thought soured in his mind. That… could *not* happen.

Mikko had him sit forward as she cut the first layer before unwrapping his abdomen. As soon as the pressure released on it, the wound throbbed, muscles settling into place. Calix hissed and threw his head back. "Just do it." And she did. Both bandages, one on his front and one on his back, ripped off with ease.

White scar tissue rippled across his side in a near-perfect circle, one on either side.

"That is disgusting, Calix," Raif taunted from the doorway. "You've finally won the gruesome scar contest that we weren't having."

"I am happy to see you awake, Highness," Alander said from beside him.

He chuckled, but the motion hurt, so he winced, which made Raif laugh. "Good to see you too."

Raif strode into the small cabin, getting even smaller as more people squeezed in to see him. "You idiot," he said.

"That's what I said!" exclaimed Issaria.

Raif cut her an appreciative glance. "Finally, we agree on something."

Mikko stood abruptly and clapped her hands. "Everyone except patients and royalty out! I need space to work. If I thought it was good to have this many bodies in my infirmary, I would bring in my other two patients!"

Huffing their feeble protests, Raif and Alander filed back out, Rhaminta—when had she gotten here? How long had he been asleep? —followed behind them, leaning heavily on a crutch.

"Wait," Raif said poking his head back in. "Why does she get to stay?" He asked, nodding at Siyari.

"Really?" The captain asked, astounded. "It's my ship, you idiot."

Raif flushed. "Oh. Right. Of course. As you were." He ducked out again.

When they were as alone as they were ever going to be in an infirmary, it was Issaria who broke the thick silence, her attention fixed on the archer in the other bed. "I don't know how to help her. Aurelia won't come. I think she's...tired or weak or something. Maybe. It happened after I was poisoned."

An even-tempered deity she was not. Aurelia was more like a toddler throwing a tantrum. Impossible to appease for long and bound for trouble.

"Mikko," he tried, addressing the healer. "You said her mana was gone? And you can see that? Sense it?" He asked again, still perplexed by the concept. He knew the healing arts were mystical and complex, but he never imagined healers were able to envision a magician's mana in their very bodies.

Mikko nodded. "As a healer, I can. Magic is a part of a person as much as bone or blood. I can see it flowing through the body, its own network of channels and burrows, reaching out to the furthest portions of our bodies, all stemming from the strength of one's heart." She smiles. "That's where the legend of the Mythos' touching a Magi's heart to give them their power came from."

"And hers is...gone? Just like that?" Issaria asked. It's not just... blocked or..." she looked helplessly between Siyari and himself, waiting for them to offer suggestions.

"Gone," Mikko repeated firmly, closing her eyes as if it could shield against what this would mean for these poor women.

"What could do such a thing?" Issaria asked.

"A Mythos," he suggested, thinking of Baelfor walking the Hollovanian countryside not long ago. He'd seen the colossal being with his own two eyes, and it hadn't been the first time.

"They're all Terran magicians," Siyari announced. "Farrah is an armament magician. Gliss has a talent for fabrics. She works on my sails. And Aleta is a healer."

"She's my apprentice," Mikko confessed. "She was quite good, too, even if our talents differ."

Silence enveloped them. Three vastly different affinities. All Terran by element.

What could the loss of their mana mean? Was it a solitary event? Was it widespread? He thought of his mother. The loss of her mana would devastate her. What would his father do? And what of his younger brother? Darres was but a child. He had yet to show an affinity for either element. What if he had been stripped of his mana even before he'd had a chance to learn it? And what could he even do about it?

"You need to get me to the Ascalith as soon as possible. We can't delay anymore. I have a horrible feeling this is connected to Aurelia," Issaria announced. "We saw something, and it *felt* like magic. Like Terran magic." Her mouth pressed into a firm line. "I can't let this happen again. And I'm terrified it will."

"We'll head for Belxac immediately," Siyari agreed. "I knew an old scholar once who said there was an old priest's path along the foothills of the Rilaan mountains. He said the path led right into the sky. I never believed the story...but I think you might find better use of the tale than I will."

"When will we arrive?" Issaria asked eagerly.

"Three days."

"Three days," she repeated like a solemn vow, her fist clenched over her heart.

2 6

SHURA

Shura crawled from the debris like an animal. Clawing and scraping, he dug his way free of the rubble and rose on shaky legs. Dried blood stained the side of his face from a gash in his hairline. Red sand matted his hair and skin in a cake-batter coating. Dust clouds billowed out of the wreckage around him, and he stumbled on uneven footing. He coughed into his hand and winced at the sharp pain in his ribs. Probably broken, he thought. He'd have to find a healer to correct that sort of damage or heal the natural way, which seemed curiously unnatural in itself.

Picking his way out of the carcass of the fallen god was no easy feat. Felled trees made a labyrinth of the carnage, bringing Shura to impassable crags of ruined stone and bloated corpses of the furred beasts he'd spied upon his ascent before he picked his way to the peak of a jagged slab of stone and cast his gaze across the Ascalith.

Rolling dunes of red sand stretched beyond the western horizon. In the south, the peaks of the Rilaan Mountains bit into a vermillion sky like bloody fangs. He could just make out the golden smudge of grain fields wavering beyond the desert heat. And where there was a farm, there were farmers. Perhaps a healer, but more importantly, he could navigate back to Espera.

Clambering down from his vantage point, Shura became acutely aware that the sigil on his chest was eerily calm in the aftermath.

Silent. Satiated. As if a yearning emptiness had been momentarily filled.

But for all the serenity of his brand, his hands practically vibrated with power. He could feel it beneath his skin like a prowling beast, straining against the confines of his skin. It didn't feel like the borrowed might of the Cosmos flowing through his veins.

No. This was raw magic. It dwelled within *him.*

It wasn't borrowed.

Not anymore.

This magic wouldn't eat him, steal pieces of him like a thief in the night. It was his, at last. The thought settled in him like a stone.

He didn't think he was free of the burden, by any means, nor did he wish to be. For a boy who'd never felt as though he had a family, there was a strange pleasure to be had in knowing that his true family, the dark power they'd cultivated, had been with him all along, just waiting for the time when it would be awakened. The gift of his mother's curse had been the answer to all his secret prayers, even if it came with a heavy price.

It was learning to achieve without it that was the real struggle, to not fall headfirst into it. It was so easy to gorge oneself on power, to get drunk off it.

Shura wondered, only for a second, if his sweet niece was navigating her newfound powers with as much trepidation as he had, or if she was already losing herself. He wondered if it would matter when he eventually caught up with her. Would it be the raven-haired princess he met, or would it be her *other?* He imagined each posed their own unique obstacles, but he had to admit some part of him wanted to see his niece across a battlefield instead of some cosmic creature wearing her skin.

Setting himself eastward, Shura began a long trudge toward a line of smoke billowing from that smudge of gold farmland.

✦ ✱ ✦

THE WOODEN CABIN WAS IN DANGER OF BEING SWALLOWED BY THE Ascalith. Red sand encroached on the meager grasses that tufted through growing dunes. A piebald goat brayed from a fenced paddock beside the stout little house. A pair of brown horses grazed in a pasture beyond a sagging barn. A barrel full of water stood near an open window. Surrounded by golden tufts of grasses, the little farm looked idyllic from a distance, but there was a preternatural stillness about the scene as Shura approached.

If it weren't for the calm, healthy animals and the woodsmoke billowing from the chimney, Shura would have been sure the place was abandoned, or the site of some tragedy that silenced even the wind.

Despite the stillness, Shura approached the wooden door and rapped his knuckles against it, leaning in to listen for any shuffling within. Floorboards creaked, and before long an old man with brown sunspots speckling his bald head like a hen's egg opened the door. His wrinkled face was ruddy with sorrow as he peered at Shura on his doorstep.

Caked in dust and sand like the desert itself had spit him out, he imagined he cast a formidable figure, but the old man only threw the door wider and pulled him inside. "Cosmos, fella, you must've been in the desert when that quake hit! Come in, come in. Name's Eitan." He was a frail man, thin as a reed, but he moved about without too much trouble. He settled Shura onto a bench beside a square table and doddered into his kitchen.

"Phelix," he introduced himself with his captain's name. "You mentioned a quake?"

Shura knew the man must've meant Baelfor's impact with the earth, but he wanted to know how his feat had resonated among the people. If they even knew what he'd done yet, how far his name would echo in history.

"You didn't feel it?" The old man asked incredulously.

"The sand must have muffled it," Shura supplied by way of explanation.

Eitan shrugged and retrieved a clay mug from a wooden cabinet and with a wobbly flick of his wrist, he sent a spiral of rainwater from the barrel Shura had seen outside through the kitchen window and into the waiting vessel. "Have a drink, you look worse than you think, friend. I'll get you some fresh clothes, and then you can rinse off behind the barn." He offered Shura the cup and thumped his bent back as he added, "I was about your size when I was younger. Indra, my wife, she was always sentimental about the old days."

Shura accepted the drink from his gracious host and drained it, finding his mouth as parched as the desert he'd left behind. "I'm not sure where I am. Got lost in the Ascalith," he called after his host.

Eitan shuffled across the cabin and disappeared into what had to be the bedroom. "Oh, you're a ways from everywhere out here. Last Aresian farm this side of the Rilaans," Eitan replied from the other room. "Closest town is Belxac, out on the coast. Unless you want to cross the peaks to Ayvis, but that'll take twice as long."

Shura listened intently as the old man rummaged. He seemed friendly enough, lonely and talkative, but friendly. But Shura knew better than most that enemies often hid behind the friendliest of faces. He returned after a spell with a folded set of black trousers, and a green tunic. It was Aresian in style, an outdated fashion that had long shirttails and required the wearer to secure the garment around their waist or hips with a belt of some sort.

Eitan set the clothes on the table and refilled Shura's cup before he asked, "What brings you all the way out here?"

"Hunting."

The old man nodded knowingly. "There used to be some good game up in the hills, rabbits and some fox and the occasional deer. Pheasants too, if you knew where to look." He gave a heaving sigh as he settled onto the bench beside Shura. "Things just ain't the same anymore. Didja happen to catch anything?" He examined Shura with fresh eyes as if he may have been smuggling a hare in his coat.

"I did, before the quake," Shura said with a nod.

"Must've lost it in the sandstorm?"

"Sandstorm?"

"I only assumed..." Eitan said as he gestured to Shura's crumbing crust of red sand, sweat, and blood. "Well, if you didn't feel the quake, you must've seen the sky?"

"You mean the bands of green light?"

Eitan nodded. "It was right before my Indra," he took a heaving breath before his voice warbled, "Before my Indra died."

The man's grief ran rivers down his cheeks as he cradled his freckled head in gnarled hands—hands that had likely built this home and worked these lands beside his late wife. "She was all I had left in the world and she didn't deserve what happened to her, ya hear me? She wasn't nothin' but a sweet old woman who asked for nothing from the Cosmos but a good harvest and a child. Those forlorn stars only saw fit to grant one of those, and now I'm alone."

"I'm sorry to hear of your Indra's passing, but grateful for your hospitality when your heart must be so heavy," he offered. He avoided the obvious question of *what* and settled on, "When did this happen?"

"Yesterday. After the quake. The Mythos called her into the Cosmos with those beautiful lights...It was the last thing she saw before she just..." He broke down into sobs.

Unaccustomed to such unbridled emotion, especially from a stranger, Shura was unprepared for Eitan to collapse on him and caught the old man in a stiff embrace. Awkwardly, he extracted himself from the soggy man and patted him on the shoulder.

"She...Indra's in the barn. It's why the horses are out in the pasture, they're too frightened of her to stay in their stalls."

That piqued Shura's curiosity. Bizarre. "They're afraid of her body?"

Eitan couldn't meet Shura's gaze. He hung his head into his hands and shook his head. "It's not just a body."

Shura claimed the borrowed clothes from the table and rose from the bench. "I wouldn't claim to be any sort of expert but I'd like to take a look after I've cleaned off, if that's okay with you, Eitan." He wanted to tread carefully, but he would have a look at this corpse even if he was denied.

"She was a good woman, Phelix. I don't pretend to know the will of the Cosmos, but she was a good woman and they *stole* her from me."

Out in the yard, Shura could see a dark death shroud draped over a shape in the dim barn, but circled around the back and found a deep trough and hand pump. This far from any cities or rivers, he was shocked to see water beyond the rain barrel at all, but when he cranked the lever and water began to spew from the spigot, it was thick with sediments and yellowed from the earth.

Magic was never Shura's calling, but big workings, the void blade among them, came easily to Shura. The more destruction and mayhem he wanted to cause, the more freely his mana flowed. Small magic, however, like trying to harness his new powers to separate earth from water was like threading a needle in the dark. Ultimately, he was able to use a bucket to capture enough water to dump over his head three times.

He wasn't clean. His skin and hair felt more filthy if that was even possible, but as he dressed in the clothes Eitan had provided, Shura had to admit fresh clothes felt better than the grit that continued to pour out of his own. Strapping his sword around his waist, Shura shook the grime out of his clothes as best he was able, before he folded them and made his way back around the barn. At the front, he lay his clothes on the fencepost, cast a wary glance back toward the cabin, and stepped into the barn.

Even knowing the shape on the table against the far wall was a woman, Eitan's wife Indra, Shura had a difficult time identifying the misshapen lump as a person. He peeled back the black linen shroud and jerked away as if he'd been burned. The death shroud fluttered down like a bride's veil, but it didn't obscure the desiccated corpse curled in on itself like the pain had been too much to bear with such frail bones.

"Cosmos above," Shura whispered as he examined her. Waxen skin was stretched thin as tissue paper across her skeleton and a look of agony was etched into her sunken eyes.

It was nearly identical to what his sister had looked like after he'd leached her mana with the void blade. After, he'd shoved the husk of her body off the balcony and she'd practically disintegrated on impact. Shura had assumed it was because he'd taken everything from her, every last drop, but maybe…

He barely touched the corpse and Indra's body began to fall to ash as if she'd been molded of sand and was crumbling with the rising tide.

"I thank you for your sacrifice," he whispered over the remains. "I'll make use of what I took from you."

"You *thank* her?" Eitan exclaimed from behind him. He'd come to see what Shura made of the state of his wife's body. "What did you take? What's that mean, Phelix—did you have something to do with —" his gaze caught on the dust that was now on the table behind Shura. "What—Indra!" He threw himself across the barn, stumbling into the table.

"What have you done? What did you do?" Eitan's wail was harrowing as he sank to his knees. "Indra!"

Shura backed out of the barn while his host was sifting through his wife's ashes. Eitan, feeble, freckle-headed Eitan, spun on Shura with rage carved deep into his wrinkled face. "I'll kill you, Phelix!"

Opening himself to the Terran magic that stalked beneath his flesh was easier than Shura thought. It wanted to get out, and now he had the opportunity to wield it.

It sprang free with bowed haunches of timber and mossy paws bearing granite claws. A ridge of dark, jagged stone protruded from its spine like a mane of tufted hair. Skeletal canine faces laureled with inky black mushrooms tipped to the side as they focused hungry eye sockets on Eitan, frozen in place in the face of not one, but several beasts crafted from Shura's stolen Terran magic. A gravelly cackle that sounded like hysteria began with the first, a wolfish-looking creature of lichen and fallen trees, was taken up by its compatriots like a chilling song.

From out in the yard, Shura met Eitan's hopeless gaze.

"Go on, then!" Eitan cried, pounding a gnarled fist against his skinny chest. "Go on, Phelix! You'll have to kill me too!"

"If you insist, friend."

The beasts were on him before Shura had turned away. Eitan's screams had the horses stomping and running circles in their pasture. The goat had fainted, or perhaps it had died of fright. The screams stopped, but a thick wet slop accompanied by the crunch of bones and cartilage was audible over the yips and growls of the pack of canids.

"And thank you for the heading," Shura said as he opened the pasture and helped himself to the broader of the two horses.

Saddled and feeling refreshed, Shura mounted the beast and set out for Belxac, calling his feral magic back to him as he rode past the barn.

27

ISSARIA

Much to Prince Calix's dismay, Mikko insisted that he be sequestered in the infirmary for the remainder of their voyage for recovery. He was still far too weak to even think about traipsing across the Ascalith. Issaria tried to let him rest, but often found herself lingering on the threshold of the infirmary while he slept.

"He did the same for you, you know," Rhaminta commented on the second day after he'd woken. "Stayed by your side when you were poisoned."

"We really must stop being incapacitated." Issaria's tone was joking, but her expression remained solemn. They'd barely begun their journey and already it had proven near deadly. She loathed to think how she would bear the guilt of Calix's death on top of Elon's. It would be crippling, and for all her steely resolve, she knew Aurelia would have no problem overtaking her consciousness if she were to lose both of the men she loved to this war.

"It would do something for my nerves if you did," Mint replied.

Issaria turned to Mint and saw that wrinkle of concern form between her friend's eyebrows. "Oh come now, admitting you care, Mint?" She tried to deflect, but Mint was having none of it.

"I heard what you said, about being culled by Aurelia."

Issaria held her friend's concerned gaze for as long as she could bear before she elbowed past her into the narrow corridor. "What of it? It's the truth. She's taken my eye, now my hands."

She'd peeked beneath the bandages in the guise of changing them and knew she'd never pass for normal again. If she ever was. "What next? Which limb will she demand?" She heard Mint hobbling after her and slowed only a little to allow her to keep up despite her unwillingness to dwell on this topic. "She's consuming a little bit of me until she *is* me. She practically told me so herself, I was just a little distracted by the whole 'razing of the planet' bit at the time to hear her."

It was hard to keep the sour notes from her tongue as she thought about this unwanted destiny dragging her toward inevitability.

"Aurelia will *never* be you, Issa," Rhaminta said from behind her and Issaria froze at the top of the narrow staircase that led up to the sleeping cabins and the main deck above. "I didn't think you'd surrender to her like this, though."

"Surrender?" Issaria whipped around. "Is that what you think I'm doing by dragging myself across the continent?"

Mint leveled her with a knowing stare. "You've been quiet since you woke up, Issa. I feel like I'm getting some play actor's version of who you think I want you to be. I can't help but think this is how Hecate made you behave, some royal farce to project stability and poise, but I see that you're scared," she said with eviscerating accuracy. "It's okay to be frightened, Issa."

And she was frightened. Hurtling toward what she could only see as her demise was debilitating if she thought about it too much. How could she possibly bring herself to death's doorstep knowing there would be no one left to fight for the goodness in Ellorhys in her absence?

"I can never pretend to understand the weight you're shouldering. But you do have friends who want to help you." She chuckled a little. "You were so stubborn about even telling us who you were, Issa. Look how that turned out. Eiren, Cizabet, and the others are out playing decoy for you. I stowed away in the bilge of a slave ship to try and help you, even when you told us to go the other way. You don't have to push us away to save us. We're trying to save *you*."

Issaria was back at the bottom of the stairs, throwing her arms around Rhaminta as they collided. Mint's crutch hit the wood as she wrapped her arms around Issaria.

"I'm so sorry, Mint." Issaria clung to her friend, trying not to let her terror consume her. "I don't mean to push you away I just…I feel like I'm losing myself. Like I've already lost."

"Then let's reclaim your identity a little, shall we?" Rhaminta asked with a fiendish grin as she pulled back from their embrace. Issaria knelt to retrieve Mint's crutch and allowed her to take the lead as she headed up the staircase.

"What do you mean?"

"C'mon. I was discussing the next league of your journey with Raif and I got a brilliant idea."

"Raif, huh?" Issaria asked coyly as she followed Rhaminta up the stairs and into the corridor of cabins. "You two sure are friendly. What happened with you two when I was out?"

"Friendly? With him? Hardly. He's infuriating," Mint replied with finality as she made her way down the hall, her injured leg only hindering her progress a little now that Mikko had been able to begin her healing sessions.

They stopped at a door labeled with the names Mia and Aleta and decorated with pink lace and the husks of withering flowers, the Terran magic that had kept them preserved gone with the rest of the magic. Rhaminta knocked gently a few times before the door cracked open and Issaria spied a familiar freckled face peeking out at her.

"Oh!" The door flung open and Mia practically dragged them inside. "I wasn't expecting you so soon, Mint."

"You two know each other, now?" Issaria questioned.

Mint gave her a lopsided grin. "You missed a few things while you were out."

"Apparently," she mused as she took in the girl's cabin.

It was much smaller than the Captain's quarters she'd woken up in, but no less comfortable. A makeshift curtain had been pulled aside to allow daylight in through a small round window. Amid a plethora of maps and Aresian playbills tacked to the walls, two narrow cots were bolted to the floor, but above one of them hung a multicolored hammock overflowing with soft, knitted blankets and frayed pillows. In the second cot, a pale, dark-haired woman was tucked in to her chest and completely comatose. Her skin looked like wax, her breathing so shallow Issaria had to focus intently upon her chest to see it rising and falling.

"None of them have woken up yet?" Mint asked though the answer was obvious.

Mia shook her head. "It's too quiet without Aleta awake." She offered them a sad smile. "Thanks for coming by."

"Of course," said Mint. "You know Issa, right Mia?" She gestured to Issaria, who smiled on cue and tried not to think that this little girl almost killed Calix a few days past.

Mia offered a tight-lipped smile and said, "Mint said you walked across the entire Glass to try and stop all this. Is that true?"

"Not the *entire* thing," Issaria conceded, looking to Rhaminta for confirmation. "I got pretty far, though, I think."

"Well, if it'll help you do whatever it is you need to do…you can help yourself to Aleta's closet. She loved fashion. Collected them from every port we've made like it was a game. She was so excited you were aboard, and couldn't wait to meet you." Mia cast a forlorn glance at her cabin mate. "I'm not sure if she's going to wake up, but if she does, she'd be thrilled to know you're out there wearing her clothes. That she could help you at all would be a comfort to her."

"Wait, what?" Issaria wasn't sure she understood the purpose of their visit.

"I was thinking that with this…Khaosson or whatever searching for you, we could make it a little more of a challenge if you didn't look like you." Mint's grin grew wicked. "And I *also* think that Aurelia looks a bit too comfortable wearing your skin, no matter what great deeds she's done for Ellorhys." She tugged Issaria into the room and sat her on the edge of Mia's cot, where her hammock barely grazed the top of her head.

From under Aleta's bed, Mint and Mia pulled a heavy black velvet trunk that left scuffs in its wake. They opened the alloy clasps that held the lid closed and Issaria gasped at the volumes of lace, leather, and silk that spilled from inside. The makings of a pirate queen's wardrobe had been stuffed inside, a dragon's hoard of dresses, corsets, and breeches.

"Mia, I couldn't possibly," Issaria began, but Mia's eyes were expectant, Mint beside her practically vibrated with excitement for whatever they had envisioned. "You think that this will make a difference?"

"Oh, Issaria. We're not stopping with the clothes," Mint said as she pushed a hand into Issaria's sea-swept curls. "He won't even recognize you if you're standing in the same room."

ISSARIA *DEFINITELY* DIDN'T LOOK LIKE HERSELF, AND IT WASN'T JUST THE kohl that Mint had smudged along her eyelids.

She tugged at the black gloves Mia had pressed upon her after they wrapped her hands in bandages up past her elbows. It was a challenge to wrap her fingers, so they settled for wrapping her palms and continuing the bandages up to nearly her elbow, but the gloves took care of that little problem. Her side-swept bangs almost hid the lacy black eyepatch they'd crafted from some dress scraps, but it was quite fetching, if she forgot that princesses did not wear eyepatches or carry swords they did not know how to wield on their hips, but Issaria was doing all of the above and more.

She looked positively roguish with her new haircut. Gloved fingers skimmed the short fuzz on the right side of her head. Princesses most certainly did *not* shave a quarter of their head.

A feral sort of smile twisted Issaria's lips as she made her way down the corridor toward the infirmary with a bowl of jasmine rice and spicy curry for the invalid prince. She wasn't sure what he would say about her new look, but Issaria had to admit that Mint was right.

She felt a little better. Solid in her skin for the first time in what felt like a long time.

Mint and young Mia had selected soft grey breeches, and a linen long-sleeved blouse that hung off her shoulders, bearing the crescent-shaped scar on her collarbone where she'd once worn a slave collar for all to see as if it were a battle scar she'd earned. She probably could have done without the black leather corset that pinched her waist and did incredible things for her already ample bosom, but without it, the linen blouse practically fell off of her. While Aleta and she shared similar statures, their figures differed greatly in one area. The white blouse was the only shirt in the entire trunk that fit Issaria comfortably enough.

Calix was sitting up in his cot when she arrived, plotting with Raif over a map spread across his lap.

"Belxac might be a better landing than Pallis. Siyari is doing us a favor by bringing us further into the Straights. It's closer to Ares, and —" Calix's thoughts died on his lips as he caught sight of her in the doorway.

A sideways smile pulled at his gaping mouth and a thrill ran down her spine as she smirked at his speechlessness. "If I'd known Raif was here I would have brought two bowls," she said as she pushed into the infirmary.

Raif loosed a wolf whistle that earned him a cuff upside the head from Calix. "A few days unsupervised at sea and you're already a pirate. I knew you were trouble as soon as I saw you, Princess."

Issaria scrunched her nose and stuck her tongue out at Raif as she crossed the space and handed off the steaming bowl of curry, but even his teasing couldn't steal the smirk from her face, the confidence from her stride.

"That smells delicious, though," Raif said as he rose from his stool, and gathered the map off of the bed. "And judging by Calix's stunned silence, I think I'll leave you two lovebirds to...whatever it is you want to do, really. I won't tell," he added with a wink as he made for the door before either of them could protest.

But neither of them did, she noticed. She bit her bottom lip and shifted her weight back and forth as Calix gripped his bowl with blackened hands and continued to contemplate her with a bemused expression.

"Well? Are you going to say anything or just stare at me?" Issaria asked as she ran nervous fingers over the newly shaved portion of her scalp long after Raif had cleared the room.

As if she'd permitted him, he let his golden eyes fall over her in grateful assessment. His gaze glazed with a hunger that wouldn't be satiated by curry as he met her eyes again.

"You look dangerous," Calix said at last.

"Thank you," Issaria grinned. "That may be the finest compliment I've ever been paid."

"A shame you had to wait so long for it," he mused as he put the bowl aside and beckoned her to sit beside him.

Blackened fingertips skimmed the soft shorn hair on her scalp before trailing along her jaw. "It was Mint's idea," she confessed softly as he coaxed her to meet his near-feral gaze. "But I rather like it."

Calix nodded his agreement. "I like this fierce you, Issa. It suits you."

"The hair?"

"The bravery."

28

SHAIRI

Shairi was sure she was dead. If she wasn't, she desperately wanted to be. Even in the strange place between waking and sleeping, the absence of her mana rang through her like a frosted echo in an empty cavern. This was no way for a magician to feel.

Empty.

Everything else was there. Her heartbeat, her muscles, her bones… but to live without her magic would be…

How was she even alive? She tried to open her eyes but found herself in a marbled white murk. She felt like she'd been cocooned in a fog of spider silk. Her hands…felt so far away. Detached from her while somehow still being hers. The hands of a ghost. She knew without trying that she lacked the strength to lift even her littlest finger. Her feet? Did she even have them? She couldn't remember.

Maybe she wasn't alive. The pain told her otherwise, but she'd done wretched things in the name of the future she'd desired. After everything Auntie Emmaleigh had done for her and Calix to be wed, that one small act had seemed…frivolous in comparison. It was never meant to come to *poison*, but Issaria had arrived so suddenly and Shairi had seen it at the coronation when Calix crossed the room to help her up. The jealousy that simple kindness had flared in her…she needed to get rid of her. It was obvious even then that her fragile position had shattered like glass.

Perhaps this was some form of perdition wrought upon her by the Mythos. She'd tried to kill their last descendant, after all. Enduring her cosmic punishment with the loss of her magic seemed fair.

But what of the others?

She'd seen little Asmy, barely able to grow a flower but Terran all the same—she'd dropped like she'd been struck down where she stood. Her sister Cizabet too. Soldiers in their retinue had fallen like trees in a rotting forest.

What of Aunt Emmaleigh in Hinhallow—what of her own parents in Ares? What of all the other Terran magicians?

It wasn't fair for them to lose their mana for her transgressions. She could not have sullied the magic so far as to recant it *all*. Bitter tears stung her eyes and rolled down her temple into her hairline.

"Princess Shairi?" Eiren's familiar voice broke through the white expanse.

"Eiren?" Shairi's voice cracked, parched, and fearful as she choked out, "Where are you?"

Some invisible phantom in the fog took her hand. "She's awake," Eiren said in a calm whisper.

That made Shairi's panic quicken. "What is it, Eiren?"

"Shairi!" Zak's alarm cut through her as he drew closer. "Thank the Cosmos you're awake." He was beside her, but still, she could not see him. "Here, have some water." And then there was sweet, clean water at her lips like a trickling river—it fizzed and shimmered with Zak's water mana as he spun it directly to her mouth until she'd had her fill.

Swallowing hard, she tried again, "I…What's happening, Zak?" Terror wobbled on her lips.

"Shairi…Terran magic is gone," Zak whispered with absolution.

She already knew this, so she said nothing. That wasn't what he was afraid to tell her.

"A lot of elderly magicians have died. Withered away into dust on the wind." The loss of ancient peoples was devastating, and loss stabbed through her. Her grandmother would have been struck then. And maybe her father too. King Fraxinus was the oldest king in Ellorhys. Her mother was young enough, she hoped, but what was young when one could live for centuries?

Longevity of life was meant to make magicians peaceful creatures of Ellorhys. With ample time at their disposal…why would they wage evils upon each other as they had done in dynasties of old?

"Shairi…I have to ask you because your symptoms are very different than the others," he explained as if he were speaking with a child. "Though it's not uncommon for royals to be secretive about their talents, no one here knows exactly what it is you can do," Zak hesitated before he added, "Even me."

Shairi couldn't see him, Eiren, or any others in this strange white purgatory but she felt the heavy stare of many as he asked, "What exactly was your Terran magic?"

She would have shaken her head if she could but the gesture was beyond her. Her silence must have conveyed enough as he asked again with desperation cloying his tenor, "Shairi, please. I need to know to help you…with whatever this is. What was your magic?"

Her tongue felt like a lead weight in her mouth. She would almost rather choke on it than admit her gift aloud. It was as good as claiming her crimes for all to see. And where there's one, there's many. How many illnesses and ailments would be traced back to her?

Walk with graceful death.

But Shairi knew there was nothing graceful about poisons that ate away at your mind, your senses, and your life. What she did to others with her magic was often humiliating, always horrific.

They would forsake her.

They all would in the end.

"I can't tell you."

"Shairi," Zak sounded resigned. She pictured him at her bedside—she must be in a bed, as she was laying on something soft, and her tears had wet her ears as they fell—head hung and clasping her hand—

At once, Shairi remembered her hands, the fine lace of green rot spreading up her hands like she was slipping on delicate gloves of decay. "And you *can't* help me," she bit out.

No one could.

"Shairi, do you know how I knew you were awake?" Eiren's soft voice came from somewhere near her feet. She sounded as defeated as Zak, if not more so. Eiren didn't wait for an answer as she supplied it for a silent Shairi. "Your eyes are open. I know you can't see anything. But your eyes are open Shairi. You're blind."

The realization stunned her as she grasped at her hazy final memories of a life with powerful, terrifying Terran magic flowing through her. She was blind. The mist obscuring her vision hadn't been unconsciousness, though that had come too. It had been her gift stealing the first of its prizes from her body.

"And because you're blind you don't know that there is some...*fungus* crawling its way up your body." Eiren took a deep breath before she finished, "Princess it's headed toward your brain and when it gets there we think you're going to die."

Silence was heavier when all she could do was listen to the rhythmic breathing of all the people around her.

"Shairi, please let us help you," Zak begged.

"It's poison," said the concubine Vixenya, her voice unmistakable among the others. She sounded like herself instead of Issaria's breathy cadence. "Isn't it? Your talent has been cultivating toxins. Which means you must possess an immunity, and without it, your gift has become a curse."

When Shairi didn't respond, guilt eating away at her insides like acid, someone gasped and hissed, "How could you?" As they fled, she identified the now-familiar rustle of tent canvas and scented the distinct fragrance of the Day-burnt pines of the Zatlan Woods on the breeze that spiraled in behind them.

"How did you know?"

"You all forget I've been in the palace a long time. I have watched too many of my friends in King Akintunde's Seraglio die miserable deaths because they became too favored by the king," she said. The accusation hung in the air.

"The queen may have gotten her potions from me," Shairi confessed in a whisper. As close to admitting it as she could come. "When she didn't have the means or the access herself."

"I wished it weren't true, Princess." Eiren's disappointment hung in the space between them. She felt the weight of regret in her heart as she heard the canvas rustle again.

The pressure of bodies in the space around her was ebbing. Disgusted by her, no doubt.

"I had suspicions, I'm afraid," Zak said after a while. She'd almost forgotten he was there, clasping her wretched hand. "I sent a few soldiers ahead to Tanzer to fetch a healer, but we're stuck here until more of our people recover. A few have started to come around, but… Shairi you're by far the worst case we have. I'm afraid to move you from this tent."

"A healer can't help me, either."

"Are you not even going to try then?"

"What for?"

The question shocked them both.

"What…for? You can't mean that."

"Can't I? It's all gone, Zak. My magic…*Terran* magic," she corrected. "My family is ruined without it. I'm…ruined either way."

"It was you, wasn't it." It wasn't a question, but she knew what he was asking all the same. Still, he carried on. "You'd said as much at the time, but everyone thought it was just the pressure of the situation getting to you…fear of implication or something of the sort. I had thought it was odd at the time, but then the assassin came back to finish her, or so it seemed," Zak sounded as astonished at her luck as she had been, but then he said, "Shairi…poisoning her? Did you have to do that?" And she heard the condemnation in his tone, and that shamed her beyond anything she thought she could imagine.

Zakarian thought her reproachful.

Her throat felt as though it had been cinched in a corset. "I didn't think I had a choice," she murmured.

"You've always had a choice, Princess," Vixenya said, startling Shairi with her lingering presence. "I think you were led to believe you were making the right one. Cruel hearts are rarely forged on their own." Her wisdom was punctuated by the snap and rustle of the tent flap.

"I was jealous of Calix," Zak said in a voice so soft that she would have flinched when his breath tickled her ear with the confession if she could have. "I always knew you were out of my reach, a princess, destined for a crown I could never wear. And I was jealous, Shairi. I was envious of my charge, my *friend* because he had *your* affections. And he didn't even want them," he said so matter-of-factly that it stung. There was a long, weighted pause before he said, "I understand the jealousy that drove you to do it, Shairi. I do." He sighed. "I just wish you'd been strong enough to resist its dark temptation. I know you're better than that."

"I'm not, though. Am I?" she reasoned. "I didn't resist. Not once. Not if it would give me what I wanted."

"And is this what you wanted, Shairi?" He asked. "Is laying here waiting to die of your *own poisons* what you want now?" Zak dared with contempt in his voice.

"It's not what I want, but it might be what I deserve," she resigned.

"You may have given up, Shairi, but I haven't," he challenged. "Asmy woke up and she's fine. She doesn't have magic, but otherwise she's *fine*. Ciz is fine too. Upset, distraught, but they've recovered."

Shairi knew what he wasn't saying.

They recovered, but she might not. Because of the nature of her magic. For all her confidence in her immunity, it had tainted her after all. All the time she had before her was coming to a crushing halt and all she had room left for was regrets. "I'm sorry," she whispered.

"Good, because you'll apologize to the real Issaria when we see her back in Hinhallow when this is all over," he concluded with a confidence she didn't feel.

Zak released her hand, gently laying it back down beside her. "I'm not giving up on you, Shairi. Not yet."

When he was gone, taking with him the scent of leather and salt water, Shairi knew she was alone because the silence compressed around her like a fist. It seemed sharper, more foreign, and acute now that she had to rely fully on her hearing. It seemed to pierce the very emptiness inside her and remind her how forsaken she truly was.

"Baelfor," she petitioned with trembling lips. "Please release me from this. I will make better choices if only you save me from this misery."

But only silence answered her prayer, and Shairi knew in her heart that she was well and truly alone.

29

CALIX

Belxac was aglow with the fire of perpetual sunset. Gold glinted off of copper roofs and diamond-paned windows. Pops of color waved whimsy in the breeze. Scarlet, carmine, and canary-colored blossoms spilled from window boxes, across trellises and balustrades. Paper lanterns were strung haphazardly between buildings, crisscrossing over the roads and bathing the stalls and storefronts in a warm, amber haze. A peaceful little twilight town.

Siyari and crew docked the *Siren's Song* in the indigo bay, and they made their way to a tavern near the docks in pairs of two and three. The sign hanging from an exposed beam dubbed the place The Hanged Hare alongside a crude depiction of a jackalope strung up by one hind leg. Raif had escorted a limping Rhaminta, and Calix noted the familiar banter between the two as they vanished into the crowded thoroughfare. He and Issaria followed not too far behind with her tucked in against his side, his arm around her shoulders.

The Hanged Hare was a racket of boisterous conversations, wagers over cards, and a ramshackle trio of musicians alternating between singing drunken ditties and drinking themselves. Candles flickered on the table tops and fire from the long hearth warmed the space. Shadows loomed and without discussing it, Issaria ended up in the corner of their booth with Calix beside her, and Siyari Crowsong sitting across the table.

Immediately voices behind them caught his ear.

"The healer doesn't know what to do. She says Bhani's mana...it's just gone."

There was a pregnant silence, both at the stranger's table and theirs. One glance at Crowsong and he knew she was thinking of Farrah, and Issaria of their friends, probably in a *very* precarious place as her decoys in a caravan Cosmos-knows where in Hinhallow.

An empty mug clanked on the table as his companion replied, "How is Bahni taking it?"

A pitiful moan escaped the man as his head hung between his shoulders.

The barmaid saved them all the torment of listening to him lament what they were all keenly trying to avoid themselves as she approached with well-balanced trays laden with mugs of ale, one for each of them. She passed them out and greeted their crew, "You're in luck this evening! We've got hand pies and the cook made a fresh batch of rabbit stew just today!" Her warm brown eyes widened as she met Siyari's gaze, and she nodded in recognition, a gesture of deference Calix was accustomed to seeing someone give to him.

Oh, how far from home they were now.

"Good to see you again, Captain. Should I reserve the usual rooms upstairs for you and your..." finally she looked at the company kept and realized men accompanied her for perhaps the first time. He wondered what the barmaid thought about that. "Crew?" She finished with an arched eyebrow.

"Aye, they were a fine crew coming into the bay. We won't be staying though, Khora. I picked them up as a favor to an old friend. Her niece," she gestured vaguely to Issaria, and then to Calix before finishing, "and her new husband are moving to Mera Vino and I promised I would deliver them. Been on the sea since Snovic, so we're just stopping for a hot meal." She didn't even glance at Calix as she dropped a very familiar, very *heavy* pouch of Metals on the table with a dense thud.

He forced his mouth not to twitch as she slid cool grey eyes to him and said to Khora, "Hand pies, stew, and ale for *all*." She held the silence long enough, her hand still firm atop the pouch as she implied all was not just their table, but the patrons of the Hanged Hare. Siyari smiled warmly, gold tooth glinting in the light as her hand slid off of *his* Metal pouch.

Flushed and beaming, Khora tucked the leather pouch away in her skirts. "Right away, Captain!"

When the barmaid had gone, she said to Calix, grin feral, but friendly. A wild animal sharing the same fire for survival. "We're here to celebrate, despite the dark times upon us. A wedding present for you both. I wish you many happy returns."

THE HAND PIES WERE DELICIOUS. FILLED WITH WHIPPED POTATOES AND AN assortment of crunchy vegetables, Khora had to bring their table three dozen before they didn't instantly vanish into hungry hands. Warm stew in their stomachs, Calix realized how famished he was when he helped himself to his second bowl after devouring several hand pies himself.

By the time they'd had their fill, the mood in the Hanged Hare had changed dramatically. Food and drink had been generously distributed. The lights seemed brighter, the people warmer. Even the poor sod behind them who'd grieved Bahni's loss of mana was tapping his foot on the floor as the musicians in the corner struck up a jaunty tune that reminded him of the wild pine forests of the Zatlan Woods, and scaling waterfalls with the wind in his face.

Siyari was halfway through a story about how she and Farrah smuggled a shipment of goats from one of the chancellors in Drusi for the sheer purpose of bringing them to Sorair, only to be sold back to the same chancellors at twice the price when Calix realized Issaria wasn't laughing with the rest of them.

Though she'd enjoyed her fair share of ale and food, her cheeks were flush, her gaze was fixed. Focused beyond the settlement of tables that crowded the bar, to the musicians in the corner that had gathered a few couples, bouncing and laughing as they spun and twirled with the melody. Eye alight with a desire he'd not seen before, Calix was reminded of how graceful she was when she danced. How well her lithe form writhed against the beat. Her long, pale legs had leapt like a lean desert gazelle leading the spotted cat on a wild, spinning chase for its life. On the tabletop, her fingers absently drummed to the beat, as if she'd play alongside them.

"Do you," Calix started, but she didn't hear. He cleared his throat to get her attention and found not only Issaria pivoting her gaze to him, but all of their companion's attention focused as well. He swallowed once then said with forced calm, "Would you want to dance? With me?"

Issaria's eye widened, her smile resplendent as the sun, she nodded and said in a low tone, as her gaze swept across the room, "Is it…Is it safe if we do?"

He chuckled, took her hand, and whispered back, "No one knows who we are. One dance isn't going to reveal us. Not with that fetching eyepatch of yours."

Beside him, Raif snorted. "Eyepatch or no, no one will know who you are. Not the way you dance, Issa."

Rhaminta socked him in the arm with a solid punch that immediately dissolved into familiar bickering. Issaria glared daggers at Raif, wrinkling her nose at his taunt, but said nothing about how she danced. The memory made Calix's blood run hot, but he only stood, taking her with him, and announced rather loudly, "I'm going to dance with my wife."

Rhaminta's eyebrows shot up and a smile tugged the corner of her mouth.

Calix led Issaria by the hand as they wended through the tables and gathered patrons of the tavern.

"Can you even dance, Blaze?" Issaria teased, her smile hesitant as he brought her to the edge of the cleared floor, just a few square meters surrounding a wooden support in the center of the tavern. The minstrel's song came to a fluttering, high-note end when the drums began a steady, thundering pace for the next.

Calix only gave her a wicked smile and an arched eyebrow before he seized her waist and brought her out onto the floor between another set of dancers. They fell in line as they circled a wooden pillar supporting the roof beams. The surprise on her face at the first lift was more than worth withholding that his mother had him ballroom dancing from the time he was a lad until he was more suited for feats of strength and violence than politics and courtiers. But the steps never left him.

This was different than the ballroom. The beat was more wild, the sitar drone so strange compared to lyres and flutes. But the frenzied pace of the drum made it easy to keep time, circling, spinning, lifting her, and laughing. Pink tinted her cheeks, and black curls whipped wildly as she spun into him. A dizzy, delirious bliss had glassed her eye, and he swore at how Mythos-damned gorgeous she was that he cursed aloud.

Small concern furrowed her brow, but her smile did not fade as she gazed up at him. "What?"

"When you look at me like that…"

Issaria wet her lips, glancing between his mouth and his heated stare as she murmured, "When I look at you like what?"

Perhaps she didn't know.

Didn't know how she made him feel, how she infuriated him with her stubbornness, astounded him with her capacity for kindness. How the thought of allowing her to take on this monumental responsibility that had been thrust upon her, *alone,* had turned him into the sort of man who would scheme against his own flesh and blood with nary a second thought. How could she *not?* His thumb passed over her lower lip, and he knew he must look pitifully sad as he said, "When you look at me like you might feel even a fraction of what I do for you."

He swallowed hard as he sent her out in another spin that brought her snapping back against his chest. He leaned down to whisper against her hair, "Hope makes me greedy for more."

They dipped and bobbed with the other dancers, keeping the spinning circle going as they stomped their melody against the musicians' frenzied phrase, but they may as well have been the only ones in the room, in this little village, maybe even the world.

"And what if…what if I do?" She said brazenly as they came face to face in the final notes of the song.

He could barely breathe. Barely move. Everything in his being told him this was it. The moment it changed for them. He felt as though he'd been charged with electricity as Issaria murmured, "What if I think that it's hard not to want to be loved by you? What if I feel my traitorous heart throb every time you say something charming, or you cleverly help me deceive your parents out of humiliating me at their horrific purity ritual, or you do something stupidly, *foolishly* heroic, or—"

Calix kissed her.

He felt her shock, knew her blind spot had yielded a little weakness for him, and allowed him to close the distance before she could object, but as Issaria melted into him, he knew she'd wanted him as much as he had wanted her. Guilt would have held her in check, afraid of betraying one who'd already gone. She wanted to want him and her shame was *nothing* to be ashamed of. The moment her lips curved into a smile as she pressed her mouth against his, a heady rush of heat curled through him like molten gold.

She tasted like champagne and lavender, like moonlight and dark autumn honey. He had his fingers tangled in her hair when he slowed, pulled back, pressed another firm kiss to her swollen lips, and said, "You think I'm heroic?"

"Calix!" She cried, her grin wide as she pushed him—all for show, she barely pushed at all. "You're incorrigible."

He pressed her gloved fingertips to his mouth, silently reminding her to be quiet about his name, just as Raif slid up beside them and whispered, "The Captain just confirmed that the new patron is exactly the person we don't want to meet right now."

Issaria jerked, nearly spinning to take in the tavern's entrance before Calix snatched her back and crushed her against his chest.

"Does he know we're here?"

Raif shook his head. "We don't think so. But we would like to keep it that way." He pressed Calix's pouch of Metals into his hand. "Captain says you should leave. Now. Right now, with her. She'll handle him."

"Calix, I won't leave Rhaminta," Issaria protested loudly, alcohol plying her lips with carelessness.

Raif scowled as he leaned in. "You think I would let her get hurt?" By his low tone alone, Calix knew he wouldn't. At least not more than the damage she'd already sustained. "You have my word," he promised solemnly. "I'll take her and intersect Zak and the others in Pallas once we're sure you're both far from here and this True King stays put."

"Oh! Shairi is in Pallas!" She giggled looking dreamily up at Calix. "We're supposed to be in Pallas," she whispered conspiratorially before biting her bottom lip.

"This isn't up for discussion," Calix said and immediately began to steer Issaria toward the door, keeping himself between her and the bulk of the patrons. "That man wants you dead and I'll be damned if I let him anywhere near you," he hissed.

Across the tavern, he met the pointed gaze of Siyari Crowsong who nodded him toward the door before turning her attention to their foe—Calix noted a swath of blond hair crusted with red sand, and the distinct aura of dominance before he herded Issaria out into the twilight like a mewling cat.

Hitched to the post outside, Calix spotted a brown horse drinking greedily at the trough. In the crimson glow of the sunset, red sand shimmered like rubies on its sweaty flanks. He'd bet Metals this was the horse their nemesis rode in on. He untethered the horse from the hitching post and gave him a hearty pat on the neck.

"We can't steal a horse!" Issaria said in a loud hiss that he presumed to indicate she was whispering but had missed the mark horrifically.

"We're not stealing him. We're borrowing him," he said as he checked the saddle bags coming up with a map drawn on a leather roll, the charcoal nib that likely created the map, and a leather pouch of some sort of—he sniffed the contents—peppered meat jerky. It would have to do.

"Borrowing means we have an intent to return him!" Issaria chastised in her not-whisper.

"You've got a point there. I guess we *are* stealing him."

"Calix!"

Calix snatched a shrieking Issaria around the waist. "Up you go!" He hoisted her up into the supple leather saddle and climbed up behind her. "Now hush or you'll get us in trouble."

Taking the reins, Calix caged Issaria in against his chest. She leaned back against his chest and he pressed a gentle kiss to the side of her head. The horse plodded willingly west through the cobbled streets of Belxac.

"Didn't I tell you?" she asked when they were halfway through the town, taking an easy, casual gait to not draw suspicion to themselves or their theft.

"Tell me what?"

"You're the only person I want to get into trouble with these days, Calix."

A grin split his face. "That's probably a good thing because all I seem to do these days is get into trouble with you. Look at me! A prince! Stealing a horse!"

"Corrupt as they come, I'm sure," she chided in jest.

"You've no idea what I'd do to keep you safe," he said too quickly.

Issaria didn't have to reply. He already knew what she'd give to keep him safe.

Calix waited until they were well beyond the town's edge, vanishing into a hillside of golden grasses to give the beast a nudge with his boot and a snap of the reins. "Let's get out of here," he said as the horse broke into a gallop that had Belxac vanishing into the sunset behind them.

SHURA

Shura was grateful his stolen horse knew the way to Belxac because he dozed off in the saddle, waking to the laughter of children playing in a yellow field pocked with vibrant wildflowers with delicate carmine petals and pitch-black centers. He patted his steed's neck and straightened as he rode into the small town.

Copper rooftops gilded gold in the glow of the blood-red sky. In the distance, Shura could make out the edge of the Timeline, draped across the land like a curtain of twilight. Beyond the veil of the Timeline, cotton tufts of clouds lazed across the brilliant blue expanse of sky. So unnatural, this little sunset settlement wreathed in vibrant paper lanterns and laced with the glow of contented citizens.

So unlike the turmoil and unrest he'd left in Rhunmesc.

It was easy enough to find the town tavern. The lively music carried through the streets and soon the aroma of baked goods filled his nose with a savory scent that had his stomach gurgling in anticipation. He couldn't remember the last time he'd eaten.

Felling Baelfor felt like eons ago. He'd not quite cleaned up at Eitan's farm and was sure he looked worse for wear, crusted with blood and sand, but Shura's appearance was the last thing on his mind when he slipped from his saddle in front of The Hanged Hare and tied his horse to the hitching post out front.

Inside, a trio of magicians had ensorcelled a smattering of patrons in a dynamic, bouncing dance. The rhythmic stomp of feet had the warped and stained floor vibrating in time with the jaunty tune. A barkeep with dark hair piled atop her head wove deftly through the spirited crowd with flagons of ale and a plate of crisp, steaming hand pies with golden crust. Glasses clinked together and laughter rumbled through the tavern like a jovial storm.

Claiming an open seat at the bartop, Shura settled himself with his back to the bar so he could observe the room. He'd never leave himself exposed, let alone in a place full of potential enemies. Beside him sat a morose-looking fellow with a drooping mustache that he wore like a second frown. He cupped his hands around a flagon of ale, nearly gone, his stare vacant.

He'd be a perfect companion.

"We've got hand pies and rabbit stew if you're hungry, barrels of ale and mead if you're more the thirsty sort," The barkeep said as she stepped behind the countertop and procured a glass flagon in anticipation of his answer. "Can rent you a room upstairs too, traveler," she added when took in his haggard appearance.

His stomach growled loudly as he ordered the stew, a trio of hand pies, and took the foaming mug of ale she slid across the sticky counter in exchange for the metal coins Shura procured from a pouch tucked inside his jacket.

Flagon in hand, Shura sipped at his drink as he scanned the room. Several couples stomped and swayed along with the musicians. Among them, a dark-haired couple lost themselves in a passionate embrace. Dancers continued to flow around them like water. Tables were crowded, and games of cards spread between friends. Wagers and the clamor of voices created a chaotic melody that filled the tavern with a warmth that didn't quite touch Shura's soul.

The barkeep returned with Shura's order and he turned his back on the room, no threats were housed in these walls save drunkards carousing. The stew was warm, chunks of rabbit were charred but savory and crusted with garlic and pepper. The crust of the hand pie was flaky and buttery, and Shura was using them to sop up the dregs of stew gravy when the barkeep leaned over the bar to speak to the somber fellow beside him.

"I'm sorry, Xhulio, I've got to cut you off," the barkeep said in a low tone.

The mustachioed man didn't look up from the shallow remains of his ale. "Khora…just one more. Please." He hung his head and pushed his flagon across the bar toward her. She snatched it off the counter as Xhulio continued, "I can't…I can't go back. I can't help her and I can't face her until…" Emotion caught in his throat.

The barkeep shook her head but poured another all the same. "Elaria would want you by her side, even if you can't help her. She needs you, Xhulio. She's pregnant. What if this sickness affects the baby?"

Xhulio nodded solemnly. "Her mother says the baby is strong, despite Elaria being…" he couldn't bring himself to finish. "You're right, though. You're always right, Khora." Xhulio pushed himself up from the bar, watery gaze skipping right over Shura as though he weren't even there.

The man wore his misery like a death shroud.

When he was gone Shura asked curiously, "Khora, is it? What was that man, Xhulio, what was he so morose about?"

Khora shook her head sadly as she emptied and began to clean the mug with water magic at a sink behind the bar. Her rhythms were tried and true, meticulous hand motions summoned water to swirl about the mug before being washed down the drain like soapy slurry. "His wife's part of the Godsplague."

"Godsplague?" Shura wasn't sure he'd heard her right. The Godsplague was centuries old and responsible for the gift of elemental magic in magicians.

She looked at him incredulously. "How long have you been traveling that you haven't heard?"

"A fair while." Shura shrugged. "I was in the Ascalith until recently. I stopped at the first farm I passed on my way into town, way out on the outskirts. Was hoping to rest in their barn, but no one seemed to be home so I let my horse drink beside theirs and then carried on. Haven't spoken to a soul since the sandstorm separated me from my hunting party."

Khora's mouth pulled into a taught line at Shura's offhanded comment about Eitan's farm. "The Terran magic is gone. Everyone's either dead or…real sick."

"Or they wish they were," another man at the bar added as he nursed his mug.

"Cosmos above," he gaped. "Really?" Shaking his head he took a healthy swig from his drink before asking, "But it's just Terran magic so far? No other elements have been afflicted?"

"Not yet," Khora replied. "Pray to the Cosmos that no one else has their magic taken." She looked back to her work. "You won't have seen it, being out on the sands. It's horrific."

"No doubt," Shura agreed. "For anyone to lose something so vital…" He knew what losing magic could do to someone. But he also knew what *gaining* magic could do for him, and in turn what he could do for Ellorhys.

"Yeah, well I'm going to go see Prince Calix and Princess Issaria in Pallis in two days and see what they have to say about it," the bar patron on the stool to the right of where Zhulio had been sitting announced.

"Prince Calix and Princess Issaria in Pallis?" Shura asked, turning his attention to the fellow. It couldn't possibly be so easy…and yet Shura knew that he was following his path, written in the Cosmos. Perhaps it could be this easy.

Hunched over his lager, he didn't even glance at Shura as he drained the mug and pushed it out for another pour. "My kid sister slit her wrists when she woke up and realized she couldn't summon her beast anymore. We didn't even know she'd woken up. Someone's gotta answer for that," he said with a stomach full of rage.

"Shura Wintersea?" His name cracked through the bar like lightning. "Prince Shura, is that you?"

Shura's spine prickled as he turned on his stool. The bar quieted as a stunning redhead approached.

"It is! I knew I recognized you!"

Instinctively, Shura scanned her for weapons. The woman was tall, a leather corset cinched tight over a tattered grey blouse, with stormy eyes and a wicked smile. Siyari Crowsong, the pirate queen who'd provided him with the lava rock that had become the lodestones for his magnificent Titan Project. She wore a rapier on her hip, a fat yellow zephyrite crystal embedded into the base of the handle sparkled in the candlelight.

"You know I *had* heard rumors that there was a foreign prince on southern soil, but I wasn't sure it was you until now!" She looked him up and down in turn, taking in his less-than-upstanding appearance. His lack of entourage, and attendants. Guards.

The hair on Shura's neck stood on end as the pirate queen asked, "Are you here alone, sire? Is your ship in the harbor?"

At his hesitation, the pirate queen's smile glinted into a razor-sharp snarl. "No need to fret, princeling. I intend you no harm," she said with her hands spread wide despite her feral grin. "I only thought I saw a friend across a crowded bar, but I sense your trepidation…" She stopped a good distance away. Oblivious bar patrons passed between them, none the wiser of the lightning sparking in her eyes. "If you'd rather dine alone, I'll return to my crew," she gestured with one hand to a riotous table in the back corner crowded with sea-salted and sun-drenched pirates.

Shura noted that the infamous Captain Crowsong's second, the dreadlocked archer Farrah was missing from her retinue, but she came from a group of familiar faces, though she seemed to have acquired several male hands among her crew. "I wasn't aware you hired men, Captain."

She burst out laughing. "You think those pretty boys are mine?" Siyari continued to laugh uproariously. "No. No, those boys are paid for. Not all my girls like girls, but most of 'em do. Some like a little meat now and then." She cast a secondary glance over him and added with a little wink, "*I* might still like a little meat now and then."

"I thought your second—"

"Aye, Farrah has my heart as much as I have hers." She took a step closer, then another. Enough that bar patrons could no longer pass between them. "But I don't see her here right now, and I don't think hearts need to be involved all the time." And then she stepped back, an easy smile on her face. "Kidding, princeling. You look so serious, I couldn't help it." She jerked her chin back toward her crew and their guests. "I was going to invite you to join us is all. We're northbound when we leave port tomorrow if you're seeking to return to Rhunmesc?"

He shook his head at the offer. "I'm not going to Rhunmesc." The pirate queen's ship might have delivered him to Pallis faster than his horse, but Shura wasn't dazed. He hadn't liked the pirate knowing his name in their dealings over the lava rock, and he disliked it even more now. He'd be a fool to get aboard a ship at her command.

"Oh? What's your heading if not north?"

"I'm headed north, Captain. Just not that far." It was his turn to offer her a reproachful smile full of fangs. "I'll make my own way."

"It won't be any trouble to make a stop," she offered again. Too hastily.

Shura cast a wary eye around the room. Nothing seemed amiss. Dancers stomped along to a sunny tune. Patrons were flush with drink, happy with the food and company. Only a few grim faces remained among the tavern crowd. But still, he knew she was up to something.

"I'm not sure what you're playing at, Captain Crowsong, but I assure you this isn't a battle you want to wage," he leveled with her.

"Hey!" Khora slapped her hand down on the bar. "I don't care if you're the Lady of Light herself, there is *no* fighting in this establishment!"

Shura cast a glance at the barkeep, her stern face creased in anger, before looking back to the pirate queen. "You heard her, Captain. There will be no fighting. So return to your crew, and I'll return to my drink, and then we'll both go our merry ways." He narrowed his gaze. "And no one will get hurt."

Threat or promise, Shura waited until the pirate queen rolled her eyes and whirled about, retreating to her table before turning his back on the room again. Now that they knew who he was, he'd better not dawdle.

He finished his lager and placed a few more copper metals on the table. "For your trouble, Khora," he said before he turned to the man who'd spoken so roguishly about the Hallovanian prince and Shura's niece and placed a similar stack beside him. He left his hands atop the coin and said, "Yours, if you'll tell me about the princess. Why is she so far from the palace?"

"She's marrying the prince. She's on a pilgrimage with him around the kingdom to purify herself before they wed. They're to be in Pallis in two days. I was going to ride up the coast and see if I could ask 'em what's happened." He looked down at the metals on the counter and licked his lips before looking back to Shura. "You don't know what happened, do you, Your Highness?"

Shura didn't hesitate as he shook his head. "No, I'm sorry, but I don't. I heard rumors of some strange creatures and came north with a small hunting party. But we were separated in a sandstorm and I've only just learned of this atrocity," he lied as he pushed the stack of coins across the counter with two fingers. "I'm sorry to hear of your sister. Beastmaesters are rare and powerful. To lose such a magician before they'd even begun to harness their magic..." he shook his head. "Tragic."

"North?" Khora asked from behind the bar, rapt with attention as she eavesdropped on Shura's inquiry, a mug full of ale forgotten in her grasp. "If you're a Wintersea...what are you doing so far south?" Shura could tell by the glassy concern in her eyes that she didn't really want to know the answer to that question.

Shura pushed himself off the bar and tried to straighten himself up as much as he was able, despite being dressed in the borrowed clothes of a man he'd murdered to keep his new secret. "I'm liberating Espera from my sister. The Evernight Witch is dead," he announced.

The mug slipped from Khora's hand and shattered against the

floor as her hands flew to cover her mouth. "Cosmos above," she breathed.

"I seek the Princess Issaria to end this Eventide curse and set Ellorhys free," he said turning to the rest of the bar, silent with the news of his proclamation. "And Captain, I should have corrected you, but it's not Prince Shura anymore. It's King Shura. Of Ellorhys."

Across the room, he watched the Captain pale and he smiled. "But it's as I said. No one needs to get hurt," he said as he raised his hands and moved steadily toward the door.

He'd kill them all if anyone so much as moved in his direction, but the tavern was full of statues with owl-like stares as he backed out of The Hanged Hare.

Out in the scarlet tide of twilight that enveloped Belxac, Shura turned to find his horse missing. Frustration kindled in him like a lit wick. This had to be the pirate's doing. She'd been distracting him for a purpose, and he'd uncovered her plot too late.

Seething, but not defeated, Shura marshaled his emotions. A horse was only a means of transport. If his was gone, he would come up with another manner of travel.

The pirate's ship was out of the question. She'd gut him as soon as he left his guard down. But magic could solve many a problem.

Shura meandered the lamp-lit streets until he reached the beach. A couple walked hand in hand, mere silhouettes on the sand. Gulls flapped in the cloud-streaked sky. Ocean waves lapped against the shore, and red sand stretched north as far as the eye could see.

"Volubilefluctus," he commanded the earth, releasing Terran energy from his grasp. Origin magic was simple enough if you knew the old tongue, but finding the right combination of words was a bit more difficult. Too complex of an incantation, and he'd need a coven—other magicians—to fulfill his request. Being Imperial, he imagined his confidence that the command would work sufficed because the sand bucked beneath his boots like it wished to be rid of him.

A fisherman wading into the surf with a net turned at the strange sensation of the earth writhing as Shura pushed more Terran mana into the *mandatum.* "*Volebilefluctus!*" An amber-green glow emanated from the sand as his mana took control.

The fisherman's hat tipped back into the shallows as the sand surged up like a dune, Shura firmly atop the crest like a golden crown. "Mythos above," the fisherman exclaimed.

"Not a Mythos," Shura called down to him. "A Mythos Slayer. Tell your traitorous little town that when I return, I'll bring unimaginable death."

Riding a rolling wave of sand like a dolphin surfs an ocean curl, Shura made his way north in search of Aurelia's *descendia* and the end of the Eventide Curse that divided his kingdom like a bloody scar.

31

ISSARIA

Calix had pushed their stolen horse until they'd covered enough distance that he let the beast slow to an amble. It was then that Issaria had fallen asleep, lulled into drowsiness by the easy gait of the horse and being tucked into the safety between Calix's arms.

Perhaps she had been plied with too much ale from the Hanged Hare too, as her head felt like it was going to shatter with stabbing pain when she awoke.

She groaned and pried her eyes open.

The arid landscape was gridded into strips of farmland that framed the dusty road on either side. A sad sliver of river sliced through the countryside beyond the sparse crops. In the distance, white smoke churned up from beyond a hillside, indicating the presence of some sort of farmhouse. Still stained in blushing sunset, she knew instantly they'd traveled far, but were still parallel with the Timeline.

"Cosmos above, why does my head hurt so much?" she asked as a wave of nausea rolled through her stomach.

"Good morning, love." Calix chuckled, offering her a strip of smoked meat. "Want some?" Her stomach churned at the scent and

235

she grimaced, shaking her head vigorously. "Bit of a hangover?" he asked as he tore off a chunk with his molars.

"Is that what this is? Oh, sweet Mythos. I'm *never* drinking again."

"We all say that. It's hardly ever true," he mused as he pulled a leather bladder from the saddle pack. "Here, have some water."

Trading the jerky for a leather canteen of warm water, Issaria pulled the cork and drank greedily. "Mythos be damned, how much did I drink?"

"More than I thought you had." He winced. "You remember last night though, right?"

The evening in Belxac flashed through her mind. She wished she didn't remember, but the night was there in her memories with all its luck and loss. The idea of leaving their friends behind sat sour in her stomach alongside the dregs of last night's ale. But she knew that's not what had his voice pitched in concern and guilt the morning after.

"Do you mean to ask if I remember your atrocious attempt at dancing, our enemy finding us, or the fact that you finally kissed me?" She asked, turning a coy smile upon him.

Issaria felt the air whoosh out of him as he leaned down and pressed his mouth against the shaved part of her hair. "Finally kissed you? First, you think I'm heroic, and now I find out you've been waiting for me to kiss you?"

"That's not what I said!" She protested weakly.

He grinned. "Isn't it though?"

"Not at all." But she *had* wanted him to kiss her when they danced in the Hanged Hare, and before on the ship when he'd awoken and said she looked dangerous. She wanted to want him and *finally*... finally she was done feeling guilty about it. Finally, it had nothing to do with Calix. Finally had everything to do with Issaria letting go of her guilt over Elon's death and allowing herself the possibility of happiness in a world that was growing increasingly more dangerous each day.

"You were snoring," Calix said, interrupting her melancholy thoughts.

"Nuh-uh! I do not snore."

"You do. It was cute."

"I doubt that. If it's even true because I do *not* snore."

"Yeah, cute like a bear in hibernation. Or an avalanche."

"An avalanche!" She exclaimed and whirled to face him. The momentum set her stomach roiling. Issaria managed to lean over the side of the horse as the queasy contents of her stomach sloshed onto the trodden path beneath the horse's hooves.

"At least it wasn't on me," he said with a grimace. "Feeling better?"

She wiped her mouth on the back of her hand and turned away from Calix, stomach still queasy and more than a little embarrassed. "I think I need to stop moving. Just for a little bit."

Calix pointed one blackened hand in front of them, indicating the roofline and smoking chimney that had become visible beyond the crest of the hill. "Should be a farm or homestead over the next hill. We can probably stop there and rest for a little, as long as we aren't imposing."

Issaria clutched the leather flask to her chest. "I hope they have cool water," she grumbled, knowing she'd spewed the last of their water onto the road behind them.

"Most farms this far from a township will have a well or pump to draw it from the—"

He stopped mid-sentence as the stench reached them on a mild breeze. She'd scented it enough now to know it for what it was. Offal and the metallic tang of blood tainted her tongue and set her teeth on edge.

Death.

The pair exchanged wary looks before Calix nudged the horse into a trot, urging them toward the perfume of decay.

Despite the foreboding reek of blood on the wind, their horse seemed eager to reach the farm and whinnied as a wooden cabin surrounded by golden tufts of grass came into view. Pale woodsmoke swirled lazily from the chimney like steam from a teacup, but no one came to greet them. The Ascalith's red sand mired the little cabin like an unforgiving tide, threatening to swallow the farm in due time. A pen beside the cabin housed a barrel of water beside an open window and a piebald goat that bleated and chased them along the fence as their horse brought itself to the gate of a pasture where another brown horse grazed on yellow grass, unperturbed by their arrival.

Calix slipped from the saddle and helped her down, hands lingering on her waist as she leaned against him. "You okay?"

Face pressed into his broad chest, Issaria nodded. "Just…perfect."

He chuckled and kissed the top of her head. "I saw a water barrel near the house. Fill the canteen while I see if anyone's home?" he asked in a hopeful voice as he let their horse into the gated pasture.

She cast cautious eyes across the yard toward the dilapidated barn that stood sentry next to the horse's paddock. Swallowing her nausea as the remnants of her hangover, Issaria stepped over the short fence and patted the horned head of the prancing goat as she made for the barrel of water.

Sinking the leather skin under the surface, she watched as the bubbles billowed out of the canteen as it flooded with water. It wasn't cool by any means, but it was relatively clean. Only a shimmering layer of red sand clouded the surface. Around the corner of the cabin, she heard Calix knock three times. Issaria peered in the open window, looking over a sink and wooden table in a small but cozy kitchen. A clay cup sat on the table. The fire in the hearth was barely smoldering embers, though a stack of firewood sat nearby, ready to fuel the fire once more.

Calix knocked again, the sound echoing through the empty space. No one stirred to answer him.

"I don't think anyone's home," he announced as he joined her by the goat's paddock.

"I have a bad feeling about this place," she admitted as she pulled the canteen from the water and replaced the cork.

"Me too," Calix confessed. "We should keep moving."

Issaria held up the solitary canteen, dripping from the barrel. "This won't be enough for both of us. Maybe there's some supplies in the barn?"

"Good idea. We can leave some Metals and hope that whoever lives here isn't too upset we borrowed their stuff."

Issaria smirked. "We're quite good at borrowing things, aren't we?"

"At least we're going to leave compensation this time," he mused as the pair started toward the barn. "I would have loved to see the look on—" Calix threw out an arm, stopping Issaria in her tracks. "Wait here. There's…something in there," he cautioned as he peered into the structure.

Damp leather canteen clutched to her chest, Issaria stayed rooted where she stood as Calix approached the barn. Cinders accumulated in his open palm, ready to summon his fire mana at the slightest threat. As he crossed through the beam of crimson sunset that slanted across the barn's threshold, Calix pulled the collar of his tunic up over his nose and mouth and disappeared into the murky gloom of the derelict stable.

When he started coughing, the sound bordering on a wretched gag that would have rivaled her upheaval on horseback earlier, Issaria took a tentative step forward and called out, "Are you okay?" He emerged a moment later, eyes shrouded with loss, and shook his head. "What is it?"

"Nothing you need to set your eyes on." Calix tucked her underneath his arm and steered them back toward the cabin. "There's nothing in there for supplies," he added as she looked back over her shoulder. "And they won't be missing anything if we take it."

"Calix, what did you see?" Issaria asked again as he opened the front door to the cabin and let them into the abandoned homestead. It hadn't been locked. "How do you know they won't come home?" She was as afraid of the answer as asking, but his stricken expression told her more than she wanted to know. Something far worse than ordinary death had been here.

Calix began rifling through the sparse cabinets, taking anything that may have aided their journey. A pouch of hard cheese. A dark loaf of bread, the heel missing. Out the window, Issaria had a view of the barn that housed whatever horror he refused to let her see. The stench of decay seemed to stretch acrid hands across the distance and choke her with its phantom grip. "It was him, wasn't it? The Khaosson? He was here."

In another cabinet, Calix found two more canteens. Leaning over the sink, he submerged them both into the water barrel outside the window. "If it was him, he's no enemy we want to cross now. Not when we're this unprepared for what he can do."

When they returned outside Issaria opened the goat's paddock, though the spotted creature didn't know what to do with the freedom. "He can't stay penned up here. He's got no water. He'll die," she explained when Calix arched a curious eyebrow at her.

Out in the pasture, their stolen stallion had settled beside the other brown mare and was grazing contentedly in the glow of perpetual sunset. It suddenly made sense to Issaria why the horse had been so eager to head west with them. This farm was familiar to him, and it had been ruined by the man who'd stolen him first. A heavy sigh escaped her at the thought. Another home ruined by her unseen enemy.

"We should let the other horse go free as well. Maybe they'll both make their way back to town," Calix offered as he opened the gate to their enclosure and headed toward their mount. "I'm sorry, buddy. But your journey isn't over yet."

After filling the saddle pack with their looted supplies, Calix led their horse from the pen and left the gate wide behind him. Across the yard, the piebald goat bleated balefully from outside his pen.

"Will they be okay?" Issaria asked as Calix hoisted her back into the saddle and climbed up behind her.

"I'm not sure. If they stay here, probably not. But this one knew the way home better than I did, so I'm sure the other horse knows the path to Belxac as well," he replied, having come to the same conclusion about their stolen steed as she had. "I do know that we shouldn't linger, not here, or anywhere." With a gentle tug on the reins and a nudge with the heel of his boot, their horse turned from the forsaken homestead and continued west.

As they left the farm behind, Issaria bowed her head. "May you find peace in the Cosmos," she murmured in quiet gratitude and prayers to their departed patrons.

PART IV
FRAGILE REMAINS

3 2

SHURA

Shura arrived in Pallis to lay in wait for Princess Issaria to arrive with her pitiable prince with a whole day to spare. His new mode of transportation, the rolling wave of sand the size of a horse he'd ridden across the desert coast, was exceptionally fast and allowed him to travel in a direct route toward his destination, even crossing channels of water with ease. The longer he maintained the wave, the more he felt the pull of Terran mana within him like he was bleeding himself to power his transport. Though draining to maintain for long periods, Shura imagined that with a little extra effort and perhaps some verbal tweaking, he could use this same *cantus* on a variety of terrains.

After the hostility in Belxac, and still being very much alone, Shura extinguished his Terran mana well before arriving in the township.

Pallis stood sentry at the mouth of the Straights of Nazair and was the last city claimed by King Akintunde in his crusade to expand Hinhallow's territory. Previously an Aresian port, this stucco-square grid of buildings bore the skeletal frame of creeping vines across eaves and balconies. Once this port boasted a flowering laurel crowning every rooftop and arching bridge, but the Eventide had burned the delicate blooms away. Now it looked as though hideous hands threatened to drag the town into the sand.

Despite the general aura of desiccation that emitted from the town, it seemed as though the people were in decent enough spirits. Triangular banners in every color draped between buildings, and colorful chalk paint had painted a brilliant mosaic on the street beneath his feet.

Striding into town with his hands in the pockets of his trousers, the first thing Shura did was locate a decent inn. The Sleeping Lily stood on a street corner across from a tailor and bakery that scented the street with sugared cinnamon. The cozy bed and breakfast was painted a soft honey yellow that reminded Shura of a gentle morning sun that hadn't been seen in years, but as he approached, he realized the color had been badly bleached in the sun and odd splotches of bright yellow spotted the rough surface of the building like too-thick cake frosting.

After checking in for the night and requesting a bath be drawn in his room, Shura immediately headed across the way to visit the tailor. Desperately tired of wearing the borrowed clothes from a man he murdered, Shura selected new black breeches that buttoned up the side and a red Hallowvanian-style tunic with a high, stiff collar and sleeves that rolled back above his elbow. A new hooded black cloak completed his ensemble and he paid the clerk before exiting onto the street.

"What? They're not coming anymore?" A young woman whined as she passed, arm in arm with a taller woman. "But the children put up all these decorations!"

New clothes tucked into a brown paper bag under his arm, Shura stepped behind them and followed at a short distance, listening intently to the couple's conversation.

"I didn't say that. I just heard they're not going to arrive on time," replied the taller woman. "Councillors said that it's probably the Terran magic that's got them held up in Tanzer."

"They're still going to come then? The children wanted to put on their play for them."

The tall girl shrugged as she opened a shop door and let her partner enter before her. "Who knows? I bet they've got a lot to deal with," she said as she followed inside the shop.

Shura didn't need to guess who they were sorry to be missing.

He returned to the Sleeping Lily and washed in the steaming bath, turning the water murky with grime in moments. Rid of red sand at last, Shura dried and donned his new wardrobe. Thundering down the dark wooden stairs of the Sleeping Lily, Shura left the inn without checking out.

Pallis was a waste of time.

Tanzer would not be.

TANZER WAS A WOODED LITTLE HAMLET NESTLED BETWEEN THE ZATLAN Woods and the Wildrine Mountains. Comprised mostly of log cabins with mossy roofs that sprouted meager vegetation, he spied barefoot children on the rooftops, frowning as they pulled up stringy yellow carrots and needle-thin parsnips, pale as slivers of forgotten moonlight. Skinny hides of squirrels were stretched over fires, and chunks of skewered meat charred on open flames. Strung laundry snapped in the forest breeze, and women with babies on their backs bent over bloody blades as they cleaned whatever lucky kill had been brought home.

This town, far north of the Timeline, suffered in the blistering heat of the Day and was not as bountiful as beautiful and jovial twilight-straddled Belxac, or even as plentiful as port town Pallis. Shura was a little surprised to find this sad little town on the itinerary for a royal caravan, but this town was once a beacon for hunters and travelers. With nothing to hunt and travel this far from a city becoming increasingly dangerous, Tanzer had been nearly forgotten between the trees.

Perhaps the loss of Terran magic had delayed their procession more than the officials in Pallis had known or said, or perhaps the royal caravan had abandoned their pilgrimage altogether, but Shura knew without speaking to a soul that his prey was not to be found within these walls.

There was no bed and breakfast with a charming moniker and pretty hostess here. Shura located a nameless tavern with an open post-and-lintel threshold that revealed a table-crowded room with a generous length of bar along the far wall. Outside, log tables with stump-cleaved benches encircled a stone fire pit were crowded with day drunks.

At the bartop, Shura inquired about a room.

"No inn." The barkeep, a dark, mustachioed man with large hands said. "Can rent you the attic space upstairs," he added with a sniff toward a rickety staircase behind the bar. "No washroom though," he cautioned as Shura eyed the staircase.

"I'll take my chances camping," Shura replied with a wink as he laid Metals on the wooden bartop. "How about an ale then, friend?"

Shura had his mug in hand and was searching for a space to sit among the locals to discern where his lost niece could be when he heard the plea echo against the trees. Heads turned toward the forest path that wound through the small town as a barrage of hoofbeats accompanied a desperate cry, "Help!"

Two soldiers wearing Ballentine crimson rode in on wide-eyed horses that stamped as their riders drew them up short and nearly leaped from their saddles. One cried out as his foot caught in the stirrup and he hopped in place to free himself, "Please! We need healers!"

"The royal caravan," the other explained, "We've got some very sick people. We need a healer immediately."

No one rushed to attend them, and the soldiers spun about with expectant looks on their faces. Shura hid a smirk in his drink.

"We're all sick, buddy," replied one bearded man from by the tavern's fire. "We ain't got a healer."

"Every township has a healer—" The first soldier started to explain as if the royal decree meant anything this far from the crown's purview.

"Well, we don't," another townsman, thin as gristle and bent with age, interjected brusquely from where they'd been haggling with a neighbor about eggs.

"Ours died when the Terran magic went," said the neighbor with a basket of small speckled eggs. "Took her last breath with it on its way back to the Cosmos."

The recent loss struck them both silent as they exchanged wary glances, but to Shura, this tale was becoming familiar. A side effect he hadn't anticipated, but relished all the same. What better way to impart his divine right to rule than to be the only magician remaining with magic?

A united Ellorhys would kneel at his feet.

Shura finished his ale and found himself crossing the town square. As he neared, he observed that their horse's flanks foamed with sweat. They'd ridden hard to get here quickly.

Quietly they whispered to each other in panic. "No healer? Then…"

"The princess isn't going to make it," the other confirmed the unspoken statement.

"Sounds like a lot of people might not make it. What are we going to do now?"

"You said you were looking for a healer?" Shura interjected.

The soldiers spun about. "Are you a healer?"

"Not officially, but I might be able to help if you'll let me try," he said vaguely, letting their hope fill in the blanks on what he wasn't saying.

"Yes, please," he exclaimed, relief sagging his shoulders as Shura removed the weight of failure from them. "Princess Shairi is in great danger."

The Aresian princess? Not his niece? What care has he for—Shura almost abandoned his tired charade there, but then the second soldier said, "There are others, too. Soldiers and handmaidens. Prince Calix requested as many healers as we could bring. There's so many who just…"

They didn't have the words for what had happened, but Shura nodded knowingly. "The godsplague has returned. I've heard."

"Have you a horse?" Shura shook his head and the soldier nodded as if he'd known. "We'll have to walk back, then."

"Horses probably need it," replied his companion as he patted his horse's neck.

Shura looked between them expectantly. "What are we waiting for? Time is of the essence!"

Reins in hand, the soldiers led their steeds from the village with Shura following behind.

33

ELON

Elon could hear wind chimes. Shells and glass balanced along a length of pale driftwood. Simple objects given rebirth by the sea sang sweet notes in a salted breeze. It should have been soothing, a peaceful memory stirred deep within, but Elon knew before he opened his eyes that something was intrinsically wrong. He could feel it.

Maybe it was the pressure in the air or the way his tongue felt bloated and dry in his mouth like a beached whale. His body felt so distant from his now-racing mind. But he knew he'd been asleep far too long.

At first, he thought he might be paralyzed. His limbs did feel… heavy. It took him several moments to want to even attempt to wiggle his big toe.

But it did move, first on his left, then his right. Elon tested his body, joint by joint, muscle by muscle, bending and rolling until he turned his head from side to side. Relief shot through him, as did the audible sigh that escaped his parched lips.

He opened his eyes and found sheer valances of fabric canopied like clouds from a pale blue shiplap ceiling. There was another to his left, and right—Elon realized as he struggled to sit up on his elbows that he was in a medical wing somewhere—an open ward with scores of beds, each with its own canopy. A few had their silks drawn, providing privacy for the patient, he assumed.

A healer dressed in pale blue robes ducked out of one of the partitioned bedsides, carrying a bowl of pink water and blood-stained bandages. Tired eyes swallowed by bruise-dark circles told Elon that she had been working too long without rest. She startled a little as her dazed middle-space gaze focused on Elon and realized he was awake.

"Good evening! It is good to see you up and about. You…you'll be wanting water." She looked from her full hands to his empty bedside and seemed exasperated. "I'll be right back with some water for you, sir."

Elon tried to thank her as she bustled away toward a sanitary station against the ward's far wall, but his throat felt like crushed parchment as he coughed instead.

When she returned to his side, he guzzled the water she gave him and then extended his cup for more. Thirst satiated, Elon felt his resolve buckle as he asked, "Where are the people I came to the city with? The wounded and refugees from Espera?"

The healer dropped her gaze to the floor. "Many are still unconscious. The Terran magicians—" She paused, looking into his emerald eyes with undisguised pity. Her mouth dipped into a frown for only a moment as she said the words that hollowed out whatever remained inside his soul. "Their magic has been stolen from them. Many elders are dead, and those who remain seem to wish whatever stole their mana stole their life as well."

That was what was wrong with him. He could feel it now, put a name to the wrongness inside him. He was *empty*. Not just weak from injury, but lacking altogether.

Was this how Issaria felt before they knew of Aurelia? Or had her ignorance of what was missing truly been the bliss that allowed her to be as joyful as she had been?

The thought of her as weak sat sour in his stomach alongside the last shreds of his usefulness.

"Sir, you look pale. Please, lay back down," the healer urged as fatigue washed over him and Elon allowed the healer to guide him back down to his pillow with gentle hands and kind words. "I'm sorry, sir. I knew as soon as I marked your eyes that you'd been a Terran. I detest telling those who wake of the new horrors in the realm. Nothing like taking the wind out of someone's sails just as they've made it through the storm."

"The group I came in with," Elon tried again as the healer fluffed his pillow and pulled his blanket back up. "Not all of them were Terran. Do you know where the rest of the wounded are?"

Her brow creased in worry. "I don't, but if there's someone in particular you seek, I can make inquiries among the healers."

Elon closed his eyes, feeling more tired than he had his whole life. There were so many he wanted to check on, but a few stood out among the refugees. Safaia was Terran like him, and likely close by if they were brought in together. The boy and his mother as well. He'd go bed to bed seeking them out himself.

But the only one who wouldn't be, who'd be alone when she woke up in a strange city with no memory of how she got there. "Maiyra Cardinalè," Elon said. "She's a storm magician with long, scarlet hair and eyes like warm honey. She had a head injury."

The healer's lips quirked up into a coy smirk as he opened his eyes to ensure she'd heard his request. "Scarlet hair and eyes like warm honey, eh?"

"What? Is that not a sufficient description? Her hair is not just red, it is scarlet, like a sunset."

"Nothing at all," the healer said with a teasing smile as she shook her head and rose from his bedside. "I'll see if I can find your girlfriend."

"She's not my girlfriend!" Elon protested, but the healer had already left his bedside, a knowing smirk on her otherwise weary face.

He was too weary to argue the point further. Physically, he knew he was fine.

But the loss of his magic left him with wounds unseen.

Without his magic, without Espera, and without Issaria, Elon wasn't sure what he had left. Darkness swirled at the edges of his thoughts. As it had been after he'd been orphaned as a boy, his place in the world was unsettled. Unlike when he was a boy with only the skills of a stable boy, Elon was sure was his value as a swordsman. With war now a certainty, perhaps he could be a mercenary. A rogue warrior for hire.

He still had to warn King Fraxinus of what happened in Espera, of the horrors that were coming for them at the hands of the Khaosson. But right now, loss weighed heavy on him, bone-deep as he came to terms with the newest tombstone in his mind. For right now, all he wanted to do was close his eyes and accept defeat. When he woke again, maybe something would be different.

Maybe this would only be a nightmare.

Nightmares were worse, Elon resolved as he pulled himself from a fitful sleep plagued by ghosts to the press of a cool washcloth against his forehead. Disoriented, Elon focused tired eyes on a familiar face.

"Maiyra!" He exclaimed as he shot upright and seized her hand. Scanning her over, he noted she looked well, healthy, and whole, despite having been comatose for several days. Her scarlet hair was pulled back in a ribbon that looked almost diminutive to the fierce woman he'd come to know, but her cheeks were bright and rosy, and he found he was truly relieved to learn she was not only alive but well enough to be there when *he* woke.

"Thank the Cosmos you're okay! I was so worried about you after Espera…I'm so glad you're—" But for all Elon's relief and joy in seeing her before him, there was a deep sorrow in her face that he understood without a word. "You *are* okay, right?"

Maiyra didn't reply. Instead, she withdrew her hand from Elon's took up a small leather-bound notebook from the bedside table, and began to write with a narrow black quill. After a moment, she pushed the notebook toward him, urging him to read.

I can't hear. They say they could have healed me when it happened, but it's been so long since the rupture that there's nothing they can do.

Elon's heart skipped a beat as he read the missive. His eyes flashed back to hers and he knew his face betrayed the pity he felt for her, the grief and guilt that haunted him. "Oh, Maiyra. That's… I'm so sorry. I should have never let—"

Mayra's brow furrowed in frustration and she thrust the quill point back into the notebook, underlining the first line again and again.

I can't hear.

Elon took the quill from her and wrote back: ***I'm sorry. I feel responsible for your injury, and also for taking so long to get you to a healer. If I'd have been faster, there's a chance you would have been okay. This is my fault.***

Maiyra's lower lip wobbled as she read his reply, but she took no time in scratching out a hasty reply.

It's not your fault, Elon. I knew it would cost me when I pushed the kid out of the way. I made that choice, not you. My loss is not your guilt to bear, so don't look at me like that.

Elon glanced between the note and Maiyra, arms crossed with a scowl on her face as she sat beside his bed. He held back a little smirk at the tone of her message. He could almost hear her sass as she scolded him.

Then you should rest assured knowing I'm too busy wallowing to spare any pity for you, Maiyra.

He'd meant it to tease her, distract her from her obvious misery, but her mouth dipped into a frown. Maiyra didn't even look at him as she scrawled a lengthy response and thrust the notebook back at him.

I'm sorry, Elon. I heard about the Terran magic. It's terrifying and I can't even begin to imagine how horrible it must feel to be severed from something so intrinsic to existence. Safaia still hasn't woken up and I feel terrible that I'm a little glad for that small boon. Some people aren't taking the news well if they manage to survive the taking at all. I'm scared for her when she does awaken.

I know you're thinking I can spare some sympathy for myself, and you're right, about what happened to me. To say I am bitter is an understatement. I am angry at the situation, of course. But if I'm being honest I'm angry with myself. If I had known the sonic burst that monstrosity unleashed would cost me the use of my most valued sense...I would not have taken the risk and those people would most certainly have died.

Zephyrus has seen fit to punish me for my self-importance, a sacrifice of my own in lieu of the blood he would have shed should I not have interfered. My mana is still there and I should be grateful that I can feel it trapped within me, but it feels so distant. I don't understand it anymore. They say I should be able to relearn my skill as a Whisperer, but I don't know how I can think about rehabilitating my talent when I can barely tolerate the newfound silence of my existence.

Sorry, this new way of talking is all too time-consuming.

When Maiyra passed the notebook back to him she emphasized the last line with her finger before offering him a shrug and the ghost of an apologetic smile. This was taking a lot out of her.

Elon took a moment to absorb her words and then wrote back: **You may think it's not my fault, but I led us into Espera. I thought us above the law of the Cosmos just because our actions were righteous. If anyone has insulted the Mythos and earned their ire, it would be me and my hubris.**

Writing is, Elon's quill hovered over the page as he contemplated the word for unflinchingly sharing one's thoughts as they leave your pen before finishing with, **more intimate. But if this is how you feel comfortable talking, I am only so glad to share in your words knowing they take so much effort.**

And then an idea struck Elon. Maiyra's affliction with her magic was something he wasn't sure he could help, but he *could* help her learn to communicate with the world faster than writing.

Maiyra wasn't unique in being deaf, and there were methods. When Elon was a child, he had known a deaf boy in the village of Larkham. The boy had been born that way and a natural lack of hearing was nothing to be healed, as it was the will of the Cosmos. But his family managed to speak to him all the same. They'd used their hands to convey words into gestures and quick movements of their fingers. Elon wasn't sure if this hand language was something he could learn, but even if they had to create their own language, he resolved to see Maiyra through this storm.

If there were an easier method of speaking, would that be helpful?

Maiyra's amber gaze went wide and tore from the notebook to meet Elon's hopeful stare. She nodded eagerly and he gestured for her to pass the notebook back to him. She did so quickly and he wrote quickly, holding up the page so she could read from a distance as he explained.

There is a hand language we can learn to speak to each other...

34

CALIX

They stopped to make camp in the western foothills of the Rilaan Mountains. Grass grew in golden tussocks that shifted silver in the breeze. Bordering the red sands of the Ascalith like a shimmering snake, the Myrgos river bumbled a winding path through the hills and emptied out somewhere further to the west, a mere trickle of the torrent it had once been. Calix planned to follow it as far as they could before cutting North into the desert itself.

For now, though, they needed to rest. The stallion they'd stolen from Shura in Belxac had brought them quite a distance since they left the farm behind, but they hadn't slept properly since their last day aboard the *Siren's Song*. Especially after the horror they'd discovered on that forsaken farmhouse. Even if Issaria had slept off her hangover in the saddle, she had spent the last length of their journey complaining of how stiff her legs were. Begrudgingly Calix withheld that he was also feeling saddlesore when he selected their campsite, a little expanse of glade that nestled against a bend of the river.

As Calix flattened out a circle of grass for them to sleep on, Issaria saw to their horse by the river's edge. They'd have to forego a fire, but the temperature was mild enough that he thought they'd be more than fine. He laid out the horse blanket atop the grass to make a more comfortable place to rest.

Leaving the horse by the river to drink and eat tender shoots that still grew in the shallows, Issaria snaked a trail through the tall grass, skimming the tops of the stalks with gloved hands.

Between the river and their camp, she stopped.

"What is it?"

"The closer we get to the Vera Caelum, the more I can feel it." She brought a hand to her chest as she stared out over the sea of golden grass, and across the ocean of red sand beyond. "I don't know how I didn't notice it before, it seems so obvious now. There's like…a pull in my heart. It's drawing me there."

The evening air seemed to have taken on a rosy hue like spun sugar, and as Calix looked upon her, he was certain he knew the feeling.

"We'll set out into the desert tomorrow," he said for the sake of having something to say. She seemed so far away and he wasn't sure how to bring her back. How to keep Issaria *here*.

Turning from the next league of their quest, Issaria joined him in the small hollow of grass he'd created for them. As he pulled their supplies from the saddle bags and began to divide up some rations for the evening, she settled beside him and stretched out her legs before laying back against the horse blanket with a sigh.

"A Metal for your thoughts?"

Issaria rolled onto her side and propped herself up on her elbow. "I'm just wondering what will happen when we reach the Vera Caelum. What will happen after…whatever happens there."

"You mean what will Aurelia do once she's regained her strength?"

Issaria flopped back on the blanket and slung her bandaged forearm over her eyes with another heavy sigh. "I can feel her, Calix. I could hear her before, but now… now I can feel her beneath my skin."

"I never did thank you for…" he held up his ravaged hand between them. There were no words for what she'd done. Stopped the *fervent* from claiming him. Raif had called it a miracle, but Calix saw it for what it was.

A sacrifice.

For a moment, Issaria stared up at him, and that pull she'd spoken of tugged in his chest. He was certain something was lingering on her lips that she was considering, but then she waved her gloved and bandaged hand dismissively.

"Don't thank me, I didn't do anything. Though from the sound of it, Aurelia would be thrilled to have your gratitude. Maybe more. She's *very* fond of you. She wasn't a fan of how you dismissed her." She made to turn away and he snagged her hand again, threading his blackened fingers through hers.

"That's not true, Issaria." He captured her face with his hand, and gently turned her toward him until he was able to lay her back on the blanket. Brushing stray curls from her face, he traced the line of her jaw beneath the black lace eyepatch with his blackened fingers and said, "I would have died. We both know what you did for me."

He took her hand in his and slowly, one finger at a time, Calix pulled the black glove off and tossed it aside before shucking the other in a similar fashion. "What it cost you."

Her exposed fingertips betrayed Aurelia's presence, iridescent and shimmering in the crimson glow of the Timeline. Gently, he unwound the linen bandages she'd wrapped from palm to elbow. Free from bindings, the sacrifice was clear. Her hands, all the way up to the delicate crook of her elbow emitted a soft, silvery-white glow. Shimmering and radiant with iridescent light until it faded at her elbow like a shimmering glove of moonlight.

A hollow gasp escaped her at the sight. He wondered if this was the first time she'd looked at her hands. When the *sanuignis fervent* began to consume his hands as a boy, Calix could barely stand to look at them and took to wearing gloves himself.

"Each time I call her, let her take me…she's going to remain. Bit by bit until there's none of me and all of her."

"I won't let that happen." Eyes burning bright, he pressed her fingertips to his lips. "You're caught in the tide of fate, this destiny that is—" He couldn't bring himself to speak of endings when he was determined to make a beginning out of this for them both.

Calix lifted their hands. Pressed palm to palm, the contrast was striking against a blood-red sky. Charred, star-damned black against stunning, celestial white.

"Inescapable," she murmured, drawing his heated gaze back to her to find she was already looking at him, her eye searching the lines of his face for something unspoken.

"That's how I feel about *you.*" He propped himself up on his elbow and looked down at her as he brought her hand to his chest. Beneath her palm, he was sure she could feel the frantic gallop of his heartbeat. "It's inescapable. Aurelia may have stopped the *fervent* from consuming me but I still burn, Issa." Calix leaned down. His crow-black hair brushed across her nose as he breathed his words like a prayer against the upturned column of her throat, "For you, I burn hotter than any star."

His mouth brushed against the scar on her collarbone and a ragged sigh escaped her. With hesitant hands, she brought him back to her, one in his hair, the other drifting down to his chest. "Then burn with me, Calix. Burn with me while I am still me to burn."

His mouth crashed against hers as if he meant to swallow her words before they could tempt fate. Calix shifted his weight on top of her, half pulled by wandering hands as she forced him to shed his shirt. Fumbling fingers worked to loose her corset as they inhaled each other's kiss as though this act would be the last act they would ever make together.

Calix pulled her corset strings until it fell away beneath her. Her skin was soft as flower petals beneath his fingers as he pushed her blouse up over her head. He took his time peeling her grey breeches from her lithe legs, leaving teasing kisses and scrapes of teeth behind her knees and upon the curve of her hip as he lay her bare before him. Raven curls hair spread beneath her like a black halo. Issaria shivered in the crimson twilight as he brushed a charred finger across the curve of her breast, down to the full swell of her hip.

Calix lingered on his knees, breathless at the sight of her. Gloved in nothing but starlight, his voice was honey-thick as he said, "You're stunning, Issa."

Her gaze traveled down his bare chest. Breath hitched in her throat as her gaze caught on the full moon scar above his hipbone and the indent that dipped beneath his too-tight trousers before her eye flicked up to meet his lustful stare. "I like it better when you think I'm dangerous," she whispered, bruised lips curving into a coy smirk he couldn't help but return.

"You are the most dangerous woman I know. The way you hold my heart? There's nothing I wouldn't sacrifice for you."

She was a goddess. *His* goddess.

And he would worship her properly.

He bent to trail reverent kisses from below her ear to the scar on her collarbone, to the peak of her breast, and down until her thighs framed his face. He swept the pad of his tongue up her center and her hips jerked against him. She tasted of sweet summer melon, crisp and bright against his tongue.

With one hand, he alternated between palming her breasts and pinching her nipples. Unexpectedly, her hand joined his, mimicking his motions until she was gasping for breath. He smirked as he continued to lick and tease her. "Oh, *Calix,*" she sighed out in a heady whisper as he slid a finger up inside her, coaxing her pleasure as she rocked against his hand.

"There you go," he praised. "That's a good girl."

"Please don't stop."

"And deny myself the blissful expression on your face? Never." He slipped in a second finger and his smirk turned feral as she moaned, her hands tangling in his hair as his tongue painted strokes across her bud.

She came apart in ragged breaths, fists clenched into the horse blanket beneath her. Calix gave her a smirk as she peeked down at him tonguing her through the final throes. "I want you, Calix," she whispered. One hand caught him beneath his chin and pulled him up to meet her in a tangle of tongues and a rush of discarded clothing.

"Are you sure about this?" he asked, seizing the back of her knees and pulling her towards him across the blanket. "I don't have any…"

"It's okay. I am. Protected that is. Aunt Cate would have none of that," she murmured almost thankfully as she met his gaze. "I've been protected until I'm twenty-one," she said more confidently. Issaria's eyes reflected his image as she nodded and said, "I love you, Calix. I want you to know that. I love you, and I want you. Now."

The declaration untethered any restraint he had left. Calix dropped his head beside hers, lips brushing against the column of her throat. Her name left his lips as a prayer, more devout than he'd ever been as he aligned himself with her slick center and claimed her.

Issaria's nails scored his shoulders as she gasped and arched into him. She wrapped her arms around his neck and drew him close, where could bury his face in her hair. He could drown in the heady scent of her, dark and floral despite how travel-worn they were.

Apologies tumbled from his lips as he stilled above her, giving her time to adjust to the feel of him. It took a moment, tears budding at the corner of her eyes as she clenched them shut against the sting of their union. She lifted her hips to meet his and he pushed deeper. Legs curled around him, and Issaria encouraged him with the gentle rock of her hips in time with his. Calix growled against the shell of her ear as he worked her body to accommodate him. Gently, slowly at first, but when her breath quickened and Issaria gasped, "More. Calix, please," he seized her and lifted her into his lap until she was riding his cock with her head tipped back and her nipples peaked with friction. Calix found his rhythm in this new position and reveled in the erotic sounds he could coax from her wicked mouth as he clutched her against him.

Issaria's head fell back as she moaned his name at the sky. The sound of her pleasure laced with his name was like a summons from the Cosmos as she writhed against him, caught in the carnal euphoria. All the soft curves of her body molded against the hard planes of his muscles as they moved together. With one hand tangled in her wild curls and the other pressed against the small of her back, Calix held them together where their bodies met in a sea of rolling hips that had him moaning his bliss alongside her.

Tension strung Issaria's body like a bow, and Calix met her climax with powerful thrusts that left her trembling as she shattered astride him. Only when he was certain she was satisfied, wrung out and boneless did he chase her over that precipice, head kicked back and riding out his pleasure.

After, they lay naked together under the scarlet sky, hidden from the world and all its pressures by the hollow of grass he'd created for them. "I've been in love with you Issaria. Probably since the day I met you," Calix said as she nestled against him, breathless and sweaty.

He felt her smile against his chest as she pressed her face into his chest and replied with a confident, "I know."

Calix listened to her breathing slow and even out before he pressed a kiss to the soft fuzz of Issaria's shorn scalp.

"I will tear the Cosmos apart if she tries to take you from me," he vowed.

"Is that a promise, Prince of Fire?" she asked, but the voice was all wrong. Though familiar, it was no longer Issaria's.

ISSARIA

"Or maybe it's a threat?" Aurelia asked as she pressed the line of her naked form against him.

The shift happened so swiftly, Issaria felt as though she'd only fallen asleep, blessedly content in her lover's arms when suddenly she was…trapped within herself, peering out from behind her own eye, yet not in control of her own body. Darkness surrounded her. Solid beneath her folded knees, but nothingness crushed down upon her as Issaria raised a fist against the window of her soul. A frustrated scream mounted in her chest, but when she opened her mouth to release the cry, oblivion swallowed the sound before it could become more than a gasp.

Beyond the cage of her mind, the scene before her continued to unfold.

"What are *you* doing here?" Calix exclaimed. Startled by the change, he shoved Aurelia away from him, and Issaria grinned at his repulsion, feeling a strange sort of reassurance bubbling in her stomach. "What have you done with Issaria?"

Calix only had eyes for her. Aurelia, *the* Aurelia, Mythos of Light, was inconsequential to him. An interloper that had infringed on their time together.

Aurelia languished, leaning back to prop herself up on her elbows, unfazed by Calix's rejection or even her nudity. "Me? Why, I've been here all along." Shifting her weight beneath her, she pointed to Issaria's blinded left eye. "I told you I'd be watching."

Calix visibly shivered at the thought as he turned to gather his clothing and hers. "Watching was all you were supposed to do until we reached the Vera Caelum," he shot back as he flung Issaria's clothes at Aurelia. "You said you'd give us until—"

Aurelia watched with marked interest as the muscles in Calix's back and shoulders flexed while he dressed himself. Inside herself, Issaria seethed as the Mythos' gaze lingered on his blackened hands, the full moon scar marring his abdomen. Aurelia made no moves to follow his lead, instead brushing aside Issaria's blouse and pants. "What I said was then. Before Baelfor was struck down and the balance was further eroded. This is now, and circumstances have changed, as have the terms of our agreement."

"Baelfor?" Calix sounded alarmed as he pulled his shirt over his head and turned to see Aurelia still lounging in the nude. Issaria could feel the coy smile on Aurelia's face despite the snarl contorting her lips. Calix rose to his feet and focused his attention on their stolen horse, still milling about in the shallows of the river, as he jammed his boots back on. "Is he…is Baelfor dead? Is that what happened to the Terran magic?"

"I've been wondering," Aurelia began, ignoring Calix's question about the Terran Mythos as she trailed her shimmering fingers between her breasts and down the firm line of her stomach, "if this is a wise use of the time you have been allotted. It seems to me that you're wasting precious seconds with base acts such as dancing, frivolity, and fornication when my enemies are slaughtering our kin and stealing magic from magicians like a thief steals jewels in the night." Aurelia felt a surge of satisfaction as Calix sucked in a breath when at last she swirled her fingers through his seed, seeping down her inner thigh. "Reminds me of old times." Smirking, she whispered up at him through heavy eyelashes the color of snow, "You even fuck like him."

Calix disregarded Aurelia's sexual taunts, but Issaria couldn't help but pick up on the words she'd chosen. Though she loathed to think it, it wasn't like Aurelia to lie. "We're going where you want us to! Cosmos above, we don't even know if it exists let alone *where* it exists. We're doing the best we can with what resources we have available!" Calix objected, sounding more like a politician than he'd ever before, only this time his opponent was not some stuffy councilman with a priority for lining his own pockets, his opponent was an obstinate Mythos, unaccustomed to being disagreed with or disobeyed.

"Why, you're merely *lucky* that I was still too weak to signify when we encountered the vermin the other night. One more day and I would have recovered enough mana that he would have known me, known *her*, like the day knows the night regardless of how much strength I have recuperated. He would have slaughtered you all because I was too weak to stand against him. What then, little prince?"

"What more do you want from us? I swear to you, I am doing all I can to honor my vows, to you *and* to Issaria. I swore to you I would help her get to the Vera Caelum, and I am. I am going there, now, with her. What more do you want from me?"

"Want? I have no wants, Prince of the First Flame. I have only needs. I *need* you to stay the execution of our brethren! I told you to bring me to the spring, and I will return balance to Ellorhys. It will be increasingly difficult to restore balance when we're now without one of the elemental pillars. The loss of Terran magic, the loss of Baelfor, is *your* doing."

"No." Calix shook his head as if he could deny whatever truth Aurelia professed. "We didn't even know Baelfor had fallen until now. We thought it another Godsplague."

"It is a Godsplague. Magic was given, and so too shall it be taken away. It was never meant to be coveted by only one of you. One of *us*, yes. One of you? Your fragile forms would be destroyed. Only one other could stand to carry that much power, and that means we are running out of time."

"We had nothing to do with Baelfor," Calix insisted.

"You have *everything* to do with Baelfor. Have you forgotten, sweet

Prince, that it was Baelfor's rebirth that brought you and your *darling* Issaria together in his wood?"

Behind Issaria, a memory lit the darkened hollow of her mind like a flickering flame. She turned and watched a silent memory of herself striding defiantly across the forest toward her would-be-assassin without an ounce of fear to tell him he knew nothing of her life, even as he revealed horrific truths to her.

"I forget nothing, Aurelia." Calix's contempt tugged Issaria's attention back to the present and she put quiet memories behind her. The sanctum of her mind once again pitched into swallowing darkness as Issaria watched on from within, helpless to interfere.

"Your inaction has led us here, to this precipice."

"Inaction?" Calix asked, affronted by the accusation. "You must be joking. We've been traveling as fast as we are able."

"It is not fast enough, not now that the balance erodes more completely. Time is our enemy. Chronos wishes nothing more than to unravel the loom and begin anew, but where I would make a quick death of this world, the Time Mythos will take immense pleasure in the misery of a slow demise. Anything to wound Dovenia the way she shattered him when she took Essos as her partner instead. He wishes for Khaos to devour you all and he will force me to confront what is left of my sister."

Issaria sucked in a harrowing breath. She'd thought only Aurelia had designs on razing Ellorhys to create a new world, but if they had earned the ire of Ethereal Mythos as well, they were well and truly up against the end of everything. If their creators wished to erase them, what hope did Ellorhys have? Was all of this futile when they could be eliminated with the wave of a divine hand?

"What would you have us do?"

Aurelia pushed herself up to her knees and arched an eyebrow at the way Calix's eyes flickered down her body. "I will summon an envoy to guide you the rest of the way. Aimless wandering will only hinder our mutual goals," she said as she cupped her hands before her as if to welcome rain.

Instead of rain, her hands—Issaria's star-stained hands— shimmered like fresh snow in the moonlight. Mist curled out of her palms weaving like a ribbon into the shape of a small songbird that looked like it were carved out of wind. It chirruped and bounced in her hands as if it were alive.

Calix's mouth twisted into a scowl as he watched her work her mana. Mana that, Issaria noted, she could not feel in her own body. Not locked away as she was, tighter than a banished memory, and the thought of never knowing the kiss of magic beneath her fingertips saddened her in a way she had not been in moons.

"We have no mutual goals," Calix assured her.

Aurelia smirked as she brought the small bird to her lips. "You say that now, but you will change your mind," she said before dropping her voice and whispering to the creature she'd summoned, "Fly fast, little breeze, and find your true master. Bring him here."

The bird sang its agreement and launched itself at the sky, disappearing into a gust of wind. Aurelia and Issaria both watched the little bird go, far after it had vanished into the scarlet sky, but only Issaria could feel Calix's eyes on her like molten embers. He'd not taken his eyes off her for more than a moment since she'd shifted as if he didn't trust Aurelia to linger despite having Issaria's skin.

"Are we through here? I'd like Issaria back now if you please," he asked in a mild tone as he leveled a glare at her that shot down Issaria's spine like lightning.

She'd never seen that look on his face before. It was a promise of his fury. Contempt. Involuntarily, her attention flicked to the prince's hands fisted at his side. Cinders shimmered through the air and flames licked his wrists, and Issaria felt Aurelia tremble.

No one had ever looked at Aurelia like that before, either. Hatred, yes. But disgust? Issaria could feel the discomfort curling through her body like a shot of cold venom.

"If you like," Aurelia replied cooly, snubbing him with a turn of cheek. "Besides, I'll see you soon enough, Prince of Fire."

She winked and suddenly Issaria was aware of the deficit in her field of vision again. Her consciousness seemed to fill her body like water fills an amphora. Warmth returned to her limbs like a fire being rekindled from embers, and she glanced down just in time to see the last vestiges of shimmering white hair seep away into her midnight curls where it draped over her shoulder.

"Issaria?" Calix asked, tentative as he crouched before her where she knelt on the horse blanket.

"It's me. I'm back."

"Are you okay? Did she do anything to you?" Calix's concern tumbled from his lips as he inspected her for injury, warm hands trailing across her flesh as though he could sense if something was harming her.

"I'm fine. I was..." She couldn't find the words. Awake but not present. Watching, but not seen or heard. A shadow of herself. A ghost within herself. She'd been trapped. Physically she was unharmed....But Issaria knew she was anything but fine. "I'm fine."

Blackened fingertips skimmed the soft shorn hair of her hair before hooking underneath her jaw and pulling her forward to meet her mouth with his. She sighed into him, relieved to be grounded once more. Calix's kiss could chase dark thoughts from her mind like sunshine banished cloudy skies.

"I'm not," he whispered as he pulled back, his forehead resting squarely against hers. "Every time I see her I'm terrified I'll never see you again. It's hard to get answers from her when all I can think is...is this it? Is this the last time I see you?"

"Oh, Calix."

Calix drew her into his embrace and she curled against him, burying her face into his chest and inhaling the warm, rich smell of him. Leather and embers. "I won't lose you, Issa," he said against the crown of her head. "She can't just take you."

"I could hear you," Issaria murmured. "I could see you too," she added with a small smile. "You scared her a little. I could feel it."

And then it hit her. "That bitch," Issaria hissed under her breath.

"What?" he asked as he pulled back, distress scrawled across his features. "What is it?"

"She could see with *both* my eyes."

Calix pursed his lips, fighting a smile that threatened to break across his face.

"It's not funny, Calix!" Issaria protested as she squirmed to escape his grasp.

Calix released her with a chuckle and said, "She also refused to dress," as he plucked Issaria's discarded clothes from the rumpled blanket and offered them to her piece by piece. "We should get ready to meet this envoy of hers." He cast a slow, lustful gaze at her before adding with a suggestive quirk of his eyebrows, "Though I do prefer this outfit. Even over the red dress."

Issaria snatched her blouse from him and pulled it over her head before retrieving her undergarments. "I'd rather not invite the endless sea of sand into my nethers, thank you very much," she said as she dressed, keenly aware that Calix observed her every move with smoldering yellow eyes. "I can feel your gaze on me," she said when her back was turned and she was stepping into her pants.

"You make it rather difficult to look away, love," he said as he stood to help her lace her corset. Calix planted a kiss on her shoulder as he tied a final lop-sided bow at the base of her spine.

"I'm going to check on the horse," Issaria said as she stepped away from him and into the tall golden grasses surrounding them.

"I'll gather our supplies," Calix replied as she strode toward their steed in the shallows.

Issaria was nearly to the stream's edge when the horizon darkened with a wave of thunderheads. She murmured more to the horse than to herself, "Looks like a storm is coming, pony. We'll have to hope this envoy doesn't lead us straight into it."

Distant thunder shook the land as lightning strikes danced across rolling red dunes in white-hot flashes that clapped through the sky.

"I don't like how fast that storm is approaching," Calix called from behind her. "It's not natural."

Issaria glanced up from where she stood stroking their steed's mane and spied a long, white coil snaking through the sky as if it were riding the bulging crest of the storm clouds. Like a sidewinder in the sand, a scaled beast churned through the sky toward them with preternatural speed. Lightning sparked in its maw and crackled across the twilight as it cried out in a thunderous roar.

Spooked by the approaching beast, the horse flattened its ears and whinnied as he backed away from the encroaching maelstrom and the long, white creature overtaking the horizon as it headed directly toward them.

Calix dashed out to the stream, horse blanket folded over his arm and saddle pack slung over one shoulder. "Think that's our guide?" he asked as he caught the horse's reins in an attempt to steady the nervous creature.

"I think if it's not, we might be in a bit of trouble."

The storm came across the Ascalith like a demon from the depths of the Cosmos, swallowing the desert in a hurricane of wind and showers of lightning like rain. Fat bolts sent red sand into the air with every cataclysmic strike. Smaller arcs of electricity sizzled the air until it popped with explosive bangs. Bucking and thrashing, the horse yanked his reins free from Calix's grasp and bolted, splashing up the stream the way they'd come.

"We need to get back!" Calix cried as the storm seemed unlikely to stop, even as they stood ankle-deep in the river. He snatched Issaria up by the waist and leaped back until he was sure his boots stood firmly on bent stalks of grass and solid earth beneath that.

When it was upon them, wind whipping their hair and clothes, nearly cowering before the beast and its storm, the creature let out another lightning-spangled roar at the red sky overhead before settling on the far side of the stream. Its massive body draped across nearby dunes like an unfurled ribbon. Malevolent winds died down and the storm evaporated from the sky as if it had been no more than a mirage.

Issaria noted that the beast wasn't scaled, but pearlescent with feathers in every shade of moonlight. A mane like a great cat surrounded its face in a white, fuzzy bloom, and two bone-pale antlers crowned its tufted head like storm spires. Electricity crackled off of their body and their face resembled an owl with a predatory beak that crackled with electrical discharge. Ringed with fine feathers were two large, intelligent aqua eyes with black pupils that glinted like chips of obsidian.

Even from across the stream, Issaria could see herself and Calix reflected in the darkness of the creature's gaze.

"Zephyrus?" Issaria asked, taking a tentative step forward.

Beside her Calix whispered reverently, "I've seen you before, haven't I?"

Many paths forged by the Cosmos often lead to the same destination, Prince of Fire. The beast cocked its head to the side in an inquisitive motion that reminded Issaria of the palace hounds in Espera. *I am the one you call Zephyrus, Bringer of Storms, Reaper of Souls. Lord of the Skies.* He bobbed his head in acquiescence, seeming to accept the monikers as his own. *I have come to guide you to the Vera Caelum, little star.*

Issaria barked out a laugh at the Storm Mythos. "Star?"

Perhaps not in this moment, but you carry within you the light of the stars themselves. Once, long ago when Ellorhys was new, we were born of the same magic. Conceived among the threads of fate and shaped by the hands of Ethereals to house the gifts of their power, and so you must be again. Let's not dawdle, little star, or the seed burning inside you will swallow you whole.

"How do you expect us to get there now?" Issaria asked as she folded her arms across her chest. "You scared off our horse."

The inquisitive tilt of Zephyrus' head returned with all the perplexity of having been asked a question to which the answer was obvious. *I shall carry you both, of course. Time is short and you must drink of the Vera Caelum. Even now, your body decays.* Zephyrus extended their head in a distant gesture to her unbound hands. *It cannot contain her much longer, and if it fails before the Yielding, we will surely be lost to the one who calls himself Khaosson.*

"Is he really my blood? He's actually an Imperial, mortal like me?" Issaria asked as she made to cross the stream to meet the owl-faced creature when Calix's hand captured her wrist and interjected, "I fear your lightning may cause a problem for our frail bodies, as you've deigned to point out."

Zephyrus swiveled his horned head around to examine the length of his shimmering body, still crackling with arcs of electricity. He considered himself for a moment, then gave a savage shake of his massive head. Electricity exploded off of him in an array of sparks that dissipated into the air like scattered stars.

Without the hum and sizzling pops of electricity to fill the air, their corner of Ellorhys, where shifting red sands met the careless sway of golden stalks of grass against the curve of a silver stream seemed too quiet.

Better? With a heavy sigh, Zephyrus swung his head back toward them, an irritated spark flickering in the endless aqua of his discerning gaze. *The sooner we rid your flesh of its frailty, the better. Why anyone would give up their divinity to become a pitiful creature of bone and blood is beyond my comprehension.*

Calix steadied Issaria as they crossed the stream. Weak currents swirled around their boots as they wobbled across the uneven bottom. Together, they scrambled up the opposite shore, dislodging plumes of red sand as they climbed to meet Zephyrus.

Issaria approached the Mythos, hand extended as if to pet the beast. "Thank you for coming this far. It is a great honor to meet you. Greater still to be able to fly with you."

Zephyrus lowered his head toward the sand. *Grasp my mane, straddle my neck, and for Cosmos' sake, don't let go.*

Situated behind his horns, each with fist fulls of silver hair as fine as dandelion silk, Issaria, and Calix swallowed terrified screams as the great Storm Mythos struck skyward. Zephyrus gyrated through the air with great lurching movements that reminded Issaria of the gait of a galloping horse. Soon, the crimson smear of the Timeline was a red smudge across the landscape behind them.

In every direction, there was only blue sky and red sand.

3 6

SHAIRI

Shairi wanted to go home. Not to Hinhallow. That had never really been her home. Just a place she lived as she tried to achieve an impossible dream. Shairi wanted to go back to Ares.

She could barely remember the Alcazar, the palace that rose from the hilltops like it had been born of the trees and earth. If she were to walk the halls, cross bridges, and scale the spiral staircases, she'd surely become lost within the maze of towers and passages.

Even if she could return, she already knew that the only thing that awaited her was more death and misery. Last she'd seen her younger brother, Micah, he'd been but a baby and had not yet claimed magic for his own. That had been more than a decade ago. Now he would be a young man in his own right. Perhaps preparing to inherit Ares now that her father was likely dead. She prayed to the Cosmos that he would be spared the misery of losing his mana before he'd even mastered it, but she knew in her heart that Terran magic ran thick in Chrysanthos blood. Unlike the other royals in Ellorhys who'd strengthened their lines through marriage to other elementals, the Chrysanthos royals almost exclusively married other Terran magicians. Shairi's prospective marriage to Calix, a prince of fire, would

273

have been a first. Micah developing an affinity for another element would have been improbable, if not impossible.

She was still impossibly weak. And blind. The cocoon of fog that enveloped her vision had only thickened as time trudged onward. Breathing became difficult. Quick and shallow breaths turned to hacking coughs that filled her mouth with the metallic taste of blood. She knew Zephyrus was coming for her, and soon. She only hoped that once he'd reaped his bounty from her, her companions could carry on with their task.

Maybe they'd be kind enough to bring her body home.

She knew they were only rooted to this spot, stuck somewhere in the Zatlan Woods, because of how frail she was. With the loss of her sight, her sense of hearing had heightened. Shairi had heard soldiers from their retinue talking about their procession and how officials would begin to worry when they hadn't arrived at their destination.

No healers had arrived, but Shairi knew it had been a slim hope anyway. With Terran magic gone, only water magicians would have healing magic, and the limitations of water without Terran supplement would only go so far. Proper healing was done in tandem. This far from the capitol they would be lucky to find any healers, let alone one capable of the magic that would be required to reverse the poisons infecting her organs.

Shairi had sunk deep into her melancholia when she heard the screams from outside her tent.

Eiren was the first voice she recognized in the cacophony of commotion that assaulted her heightened hearing. "Cylise, no! We have to get Shairi out of here! C'mon Ciz, Asmy. We can carry her between us."

The distinct sing of alloy swords clashing pierced the forest alongside bellowing war cries from soldiers in their retinue. A haunting cackle echoed off the trees, seeming to surround the encampment. It sounded like laughing wolves, hungry for whomever they could bring down.

Hiccuping sobs accompanied the sound of her tent opening and a herd of footsteps entering the small enclosure.

"Shairi! Princess, we have to get you out of here." Eiren's panic was palatable.

"Is Zak—" Shairi started, but was unable to even ask. Of course, he'd be out there, facing down whatever had come for them. "What's happening?"

"He's here," Vixenya gasped as she tore into the tent. "He's here for me. For us," she choked out.

"Who's here?"

"He's got Terran magic."

The statement sucked away what little air she'd had in her lungs. Someone had Terran magic?

"Who's got Terran magic?" Shairi tried again to get information, but she could feel bodies surrounding her. "Where's Zak?"

"There's no time, Princess!"

The skirmish was growing closer. Shairi could feel the ground trembling beneath them. Trees groaned as though they were being torn from the ground. Dying moans of men were silenced all too quickly, and Shairi could only imagine the devastation that had come down upon their entourage.

The scream of agony that followed had Shairi's heart twisted as if she'd been struck.

"Stay away from her!" Zak's warning felt less like a threat and more like a plea.

"I'll do no such thing," a cruel voice as sharp as glaciers replied from nearby.

Too near.

Eiren's grip on Shairi's arm tightened. She felt them standing between her and certain death, and for the first time since she lost her magic, Shairi realized she *didn't* want to die.

But more so, she didn't want *them* to die for her.

"Eiren, please…"

"Shh, princess, we'll protect you."

The girls gasped as the tent was breached. The sound of canvas rustling sounded so ominous when before it had provided a welcome distraction from her self-loathing.

"So this is where you've been hiding, Issa—Who are you? You're not my niece."

"No. I'm not. And you'll *never* get your hands on her," Vixenya hissed, her hatred laced with shards of ice that even Shairi could hear.

"We'll see about that."

Shairi recognized the shimmer of Terran magic, so close and yet so out of reach. The familiar magic seemed so foreign as it was wielded against them.

"Xenya!" An alarmed chorus of the concubine's name erupted from the assembled women.

Horrified screams filled the tent as a thick spray of viscous liquid splattered across them. Shairi felt it spray across her exposed flesh and heard the sickening thud that followed.

Shairi didn't need eyes to know what had happened. She recognized the metallic scent of blood, and the sound of a body dropping to the ground.

Sobs shook through the women who'd surrounded her. Eiren's grip had only tightened.

"And who is this poor soul?"

"She's no concern of yours, *witch*," Cizabet spat from somewhere near Shairi's feet. "Just another magician suffering when you *stole* our magic!"

"Silence yourself before I do it for you," said the cold voice. "Do you even know who I am?"

"It doesn't matter who you are," Eiren replied with venom in her voice. Shairi felt her eyes well with stinging tears. "You'll not have her."

"And why would I want someone so tainted? Look at her." He laughed, clearly at her expense. "I am the Khaosson. Last born son of Obsidia. I am the Imperial Emperor, uniting the kingdoms at last. What use would I have for such a foul woman?"

A spark of memory surfaced in Shairi's mind.

A Starfall Festival many years ago, when she still lived in Ares, among her people. With her family. A wagon with peeling yellow paint had brought a self-proclaimed oracle to their celebration.

Intrigued by the prospect of her future, a young Shairi had sat before a hideously misshapen woman with stringy silver hair that had reminded her younger self of spider silk.

The oracle had proclaimed that one day Shairi would wed a dark prince. The heir to all of Ellorhys.

"You want me," Shairi croaked.

"Princess, no!" Eiren's surprise betrayed her position and Shairi felt her hand withdraw, heard the clap as she covered her mouth.

"Princess?" The title had piqued the dark heir's interest. "What could have befouled a princess so deeply that without your magic it would turn on you so vehemently?"

"Poison."

A silence as thick as the blood that surely stained the ground between them filled the air. "I'm listening, *Princess*."

"Shairi, don't!" Cizabet hissed.

"Silence, woman! This is your last warning, or I will take your head like I took the fraud's."

The truth of what had become of Vixenya nearly extinguished the courage in her heart, but Shairi knew this would be her last stand if her ploy did not work. Her body would rot among the corpses of her friends if she did not do something.

"Leave them be and you can have me. I am Shairi Crysanthos, only daughter of King Fraxinus, and the princess of Ares." Her voice was stronger than she felt. She'd yet to lift a limb, but knew tears streamed from her blinded eyes as she laid herself on the line. "And before I lost my connection to my mana…my talent was for poisons. I was immune, and a great asset to the Ballentine throne."

"And what use would I have for a poisoner who has lost her magic? For one who is so near to death, I wouldn't even bother killing you myself?"

"If what you say is true, that you have stolen the Terran magic somehow, then surely you who is all-powerful can restore my talents to me."

At that, the Khaosson laughed. Uproarious laughter filled the tent and nearly shamed her to silence but Shairi plowed on, knowing her time in this world was short. Her lungs clenched like fists. Zephyrus was near, and only this man's power could stave off the reaper now.

"And if you heal me, restore my magic, then you will have found a partner in your quest to unite the continents." At her claim, the Khaosson ceased to find humor in her offer. "I was told as a girl that my destiny was to wed the heir to all of Ellorhys. I believe that the oracle was speaking of you, Khaosson." Shairi took a shuddering breath and steeled herself for her offer. "I will help you. I will *join* you. But only if you leave my companions be."

He seemed to consider her words. She imagined this nameless, faceless man considering her from where he stood, the body of Vixenya between them. Covered in blood splatter and creeping fungus that choked the life from her with each passing moment. She would not be a tempting conquest. Not as she was now. But if he could use his stolen power to return her to her glory...she could use her place beside him to turn him from total annihilation.

Shairi had heard what happened to Ellorhys. She would *not* allow that fate to befall Ares. Nor Hinhallow.

"And why would I let your companions go free when it would be much more satisfying to kill them where they stand, little spider?"

"Because if you leave them alive, they will not only speak of your mercy, something that will help your reputation with the people once you've united Ellorhys, but they are the *perfect* messengers to bring word of your might to the Kings of—" A wet and rasping cough cut her off and shook her body as she hacked and wheezed.

She was running out of time, and this man, this *demon* was her only hope.

A weight settled on the edge of her cot.

"If we are to be wed, then you shall call me by the name my mother bestowed upon me." Silk met the corner of her lips, cleaning away the blood that had bubbled from within her like swamp mire. "Only you may call me Shura, Princess Shairi."

3 7

SHURA

Shura gazed down on the wretched woman before him. Her body was ravaged. Plagued by the loss of Terran magic, unlike anything he'd seen before. Even the desiccated corpse of the farmer's wife had been less distressing than gazing upon the inky spores and fungus that bloomed from her flesh like it were rotten wood.

"And why would I want someone so tainted? Look at her." He laughed, sneering down at her. "I am the Khaosson. Last born son of Obsidia. I am the Imperial Emperor, uniting the kingdoms at last. What use would I have for such a foul woman?"

And yet…there was something about her.

Perhaps it was the way these women had crowded her like a human barrier as if it could keep him from his quarry. These people had valued her safety above their own, and there was something to that.

"You want me," the wretch croaked.

"Princess, no!" The woman beside the invalid clasped her hand over her mouth, too little too late to stop the title from slipping past her lips.

"Princess?" While he was certain this was not his niece, it was a

279

curious thing to find the Aresian Princess in such a distressing state. "What could have befouled a princess so deeply that without your magic it would turn on you so vehemently?"

"Poison."

A thick silence permeated the tent as Shura realized the ramifications of that one, whispered word.

He was well aware of many—too many—suspicious illnesses and even deaths that had occurred within the walls of the White Palace over the last several years, and a pattern began to form. This princess was quite formidable if he was to believe she had been responsible for even half of the incidents his spies reported. "I'm listening, *Princess.*"

"Shairi, don't!" Another wench hissed.

Unwilling to allow anything to distract from this new acquisition, Shura snapped. "Silence, woman! This is your last warning, or I will take your head like I took the fraud's."

With more strength than he would have imagined she had, the princess stated, "Leave them be and you can have me. I am Shairi Crysanthos, only daughter of King Fraxinus, and the princess of Ares." Her voice wavered and Shura spied the shimmer of tears rolling from milky pale eyes that stared unblinking at the canvas above her. "And before I lost my connection to my mana…my talent was for poisons. I was immune, and a great asset to the Ballentine throne."

Shura grinned ruthlessly at the admission. He must have this one. With him, this power would be feared and coveted, not hidden away. Among his court, this jewel would shine. Risa Amorelle was an abomination among water magicians, and with him, she had found a home. Timbrel, may his soul find peace in the Cosmos, had only been capable of a magnitude of power that leveled forests and towns alike with his quakes. And his Commander, Phelix Stormgren, could rip the air from the lungs of ten thousand men without breaking a sweat. His command of Storm magic was devastating in a way few appreciated.

But Shura couldn't fold so easily. "And what use would I have for a poisoner who has lost her magic? For one who is so near to death, I wouldn't even bother killing you myself?" He taunted.

"If what you say is true, that you have stolen the Terran magic somehow, then surely you who is all-powerful can restore my talents to me."

Shura couldn't stop the unbridled laughter that erupted from his gut. He hadn't even considered that was within the realm of his newfound powers, and yet he was certain he could now that she'd declared it.

"And if you heal me, restore my magic, then you will have found a partner in your quest to unite the continents."

Mirth choked out of him and he focused steely eyes on the frail princess. She was more green than flesh-colored, and toadstools and lichen covered her like a forest floor being carpeted in ghostly white fungi. Her offer was more than acceptable, but she continued as if she were compelled to share her motivations with him before she ran out of time. "I was told as a girl that my destiny was to wed the heir to all of Ellorhys. I believe that the oracle was speaking of you, Khaosson."

A thrill shot down his spine at the way his chosen name sounded on her lips, spoken in earnest.

Princess Shairi took a shuddering breath that sounded like a death rattle. "I will help you. I will *join* you. But only if you leave my companions be."

It seemed a simple, compassionate request.

Shura narrowed his gaze, examining the princess as if he could detect deceit through her desperation.

He was unsure how far news of his conquests had traveled, how long this caravan had been traveling. If she knew of his siege on Espera this could be an attempt to gain leverage through emotional manipulation. It was a gamble, to assume he was capable of feeling deeply enough to even be influenced in such a primal way, but Shura imagined that Shairi had a lifetime of practice in Hallovanian courts to refine her flatteries and falsities on individuals in positions of power. The webs of intrigue she must have weaved to attain her goals suggested she was as adept at reading her marks as she was at delivering exactly what they wanted from her. Formidable indeed.

Or perhaps more simply, and more urgently, she merely wished to save her own life and would promise her soul to oblivion if she thought it would grant her a miracle.

"And why would I let your companions go free when it would be much more satisfying to kill them where they stand, little spider?"

"Because if you leave them alive, they will not only speak of your mercy, something that will help your reputation with the people once you've united Ellorhys, but they are the *perfect* messengers to bring word of your might to the Kings of—" A wet and rasping cough cut her off and shook her body as she hacked and wheezed.

Shura perched nimbly on the edge of her cot and took a torn scrap of silk from a pile prepped for the princess' wounds. "If we are to be wed, then you shall call me by the name my mother bestowed upon me." Gently, more tenderly than he thought himself capable of, he dabbed the corner of her paper-thin lips where black blood had dribbled down her chin. As he allowed his power to seep from him and into her in a haze of emerald light, he said in a whisper only meant for her ears, "Only you may call me Shura, Princess Shairi."

3 8

ISSARIA

Coming upon the Vera Caelum was startling. The crisp line of red and blue, desert and sky, seemed to encircle them like a snake eating its tail, and then suddenly a speck on the horizon grew into something more as they raced through the sky with each rhythmic pulse of Zephyrus' mighty body. Great plateaus of red earth rose like monoliths from the dunes. A snarled grove of grey trees stood petrified in the shadowed valley beneath the pillars of earth.

It was nothing like the verdant valley she had once seen in a vision. There were no shimmering rivers threaded through a lush green valley. No lagoons to provide refuge in this forgotten oasis in the red sand sea.

"This isn't right!" Issaria shouted over the wind to be heard. "This is supposed to be a jungle!"

"It's the curse!" Calix cried. "All the forests north of the Timeline have withered."

The Eventide has destroyed much, this is true, Zephyrus said, his voice crisp and clear in their minds as if they were still standing by the river. *But the damage to these fragile remains goes beyond the curse of the forsaken one.*

283

The new moniker her aunt had earned amongst the Mythos sent a chill down Issaria's spine. Without thinking, she settled back against Calix's chest, drawing comfort from his warmth.

Zephyrus struck for the tallest plateau, coiling his long feathered body like a cyclone as he shot skyward, propelling them up the side of the mesa at terrifying speeds that had them flattened behind Zephyrus' antlers and clutching desperately at whatever silver fur or feathers could be found. Blessedly, the storm Mythos did not seem to mind, rather he appeared to delight in their terror and flew faster as they neared the top of the mesa.

Zephyrus launched himself like a whale from below the plateau's rim and breached the cloudless sky above. Bright sunlight scorched the mesa top in a shimmering haze that made it hard to decipher exactly what was atop the plateau. The storm Mythos looped and circled, his long body following behind his massive head and haunches like a snake's body would follow its head before undulating in place, keeping them aloft for an aerial view of the once-sacred oasis.

All at once, Issaria remembered the concept of gravity as she gazed upon the wreckage of the Vera Caelum.

The sky-bound island that housed the fabled Temple of Life lay scattered in rubble across the mesa. Precious artifacts glinted among the ruins like hidden treasures. She'd seen a version of this place while trapped in a poison-fueled fever dream, but this was a living nightmare. Shriveled tumbleweeds caught against shattered pillars of moonstone, disembodied statue heads, faces long since lost to the erosion of time. Even here, sand from the Ascalith so far below had coated everything in a fine layer of red.

"What happened here?"

This planet has been in decay since long before your time, Zephyrus said, regret saturating his words. *When she was alive, your star-sister committed dark atrocities for her mortal mate, Erebus. A love built on deception and ambition, Obsidia fell prey to the greed of mortals. She must have known the consequences of her actions, but even still Obsidia gifted her lover the darkest part of her magic as proof of her eternal love and devotion to him, despite his frail mortality.*

Our magic was not meant for mortals, Zephyrus cautioned. It was meant to be housed in the flesh of the Cosmos. As even you know, each time you use it, it will erode your body. Despite the risk, you are blessed little star, for you have been gifted the sanguinem descendia, *chosen through the bloodline to be the vessel for your divine ancestor's return. On your eighteenth orbit when the moon and stars aligned and maturity is at its most malleable, the Saros Curse shattered the lock upon your soul-bonded ancestor. Aurelia was woken from her hibernation, and you have heeded the call of the Cosmos. Now you have journeyed to the Vera Caelum for the Yielding, and you will return her to Ellorhys!*

Issaria froze. The way Zephyrus said that…implied that she was supposed to be excited about this arcane ritual, perhaps even *grateful* for the opportunity to be a vessel for the potential annihilator of their world. Behind her Calix tensed, perhaps also reading the inflection in the storm titan's voice. He slid an arm around Issaria's middle, a protective hand splayed against her stomach.

Erebus was not so lucky as you to be descendia. His mortal flesh was consumed by the magic, and dark as it was, it devoured more than just his body. It took his mind, his morality. To keep him from becoming truly immortal—a Khaos Mythos of his own making—you brought Vera Caelum to the ground.

Issaria sucked in a breath. "You mean *I* did this?"

"No," Calix denied it immediately. "Not you. Aurelia." His voice held a bitter accusation in it as he drew a definitive distinction between the two.

Zephyrus did not seem to signify the divergence of Aurelia of old and Issaria of now. To the Mythos, they were one and the same, and he did not trouble himself with her woes.

You were wise to destroy it. The temple, though borne into the sky by cosmic magic, was never required by the Mythos to access the Vera Caelum. Erebus was not of the Cosmos. He was an interloper and thus never knew the temple and its infamous fountain of starlight was merely a facade, a gilded reward for the dedication of the acolytes who wished to serve the Mythos. He came looking for the Vera Caelum and climbed the acolyte's staircase to find nothing but ruins atop the plateaus. In his fury and anguish, he lapped at the ground like a starved dog, hoping to absorb some fragment of power, but your foresight saw that he never licked a single molecule of divinity.

"That desperate for power?" Calix asked.

Power he had, a token of devotion from his queen. It was control that he craved. He cursed you, Aurelia, and vowed he would find a way to ensure he could return to power even if he had to search to the very edges of the realm.

"Does that mean, if Erebus never found it, that the fountain's source is still around here?" Calix exclaimed. "Where? Do we have to dig it up?"

Zephyrus did not race through the sky as he had before. This time, he was as languid as a summer river as he meandered further upward. *It is here. Where it has always been. Where we have always been, even after our bodies were destroyed, our souls have been waiting for you.*

Far above the plateau, where the wreckage was no more than smudges and shapes, the real Vera Caelum appeared in the air. Unseen from below and flat as a mirror's surface was a thin *line* in the sky. No more than a finger's breadth tall, the wide surface opened up to a gaping tear in the fabric of the universe, all jagged edges and full of star clouds that pulsed with luminescent color.

Ringed with ornate columns towered over the cosmic reservoir so that they seemed to hold up the very sky itself, the Vera Caelum, the fountain of life, was humbling and overwhelming to behold. The sheer magnitude of it, made Issaria feel like her mind was playing tricks on her. They stared into the depths of the Cosmos, peering into some vast distant space where stars and magic were simultaneous and the fates of even the tiniest creatures were woven into conception. Nebula clouds in incomprehensible colors swirled beneath the still surface of the Vera Caelum in a multicolor maelstrom that seemed impossible all contained within a celestial sea that couldn't be seen from the world below.

Equally placed around the jagged tear were four massive thrones, each grown and formed from a different Elementia. Issaria imagined that the throne which was dim and dark with cracked Terramond crystals as dull as if they'd been ignited from within, had belonged to the fallen Baelfor. Red and orange Solarium glittered like embers in the sunlight. The throne was jagged and sharp like spears of sunlight. Blue Aquathyst looked more like ice than a gem, an elegant, high-backed throne ornately carved of glacial crystal when compared to the raw nature of the other seats around it. The shimmering yellows and opaque whites of the Zephyrite crystals on the far side of the stellar sea beckoned to the Storm Magi.

Zephyrus coiled himself like a snake and lowered his head toward the rift.

Issaria cast a wary eye at the empty space that it seemed the beast wanted her to fall into. "Where are we to stand?"

Oh, how your mortal eyes fail you. You are of the very stars themselves. Nothing does not bend to your will. It's quite solid if you believe it to be, little star. Taking the Mythos at his word, Issaria slid off of his feathery body with ease and dropped down to find her footing solidly, as promised, on the shore of the celestial pool. She marveled for a moment at how she did not plummet to her death but then turned her focus instead to the miracle of this place concealed beyond the clouds in a castle of light and radiance.

Just as Calix was about to follow, the lightning beast reeled back and admitted, *Maybe not for you, flame-blessed prince. You should take your throne, long has it imbued your fire, and so shall it aid you in bestowing your favor upon Aurelia's chosen.*

"Throne? What are you riddling about now?" Calix questioned.

"Zephyrus, what do you mean by that?" Issaria asked, realizing only as she turned to see the Mythos launch himself into the sky once more that Zephyrus had taken Calix from her and left her alone on a distant shore.

Come now, Prince, you must know the truth of your fire by now, the storm Mythos alluded as he glided toward the solarium throne. *You mean to tell me you came all this way and you don't even know why you're here?*

"I'm here for Issaria," Calix stated. "I promised Aurelia that I would ally with the princess when I met her, and I would help her reach the Vera Caelum."

You never once stopped to wonder why, of all the people across Ellorhys, you became tasked with her delivery? Zephyrus asked incredulously as he stretched out his talons and found purchase along the parapet that formed the faceted arm of the crimson crystal throne.

Across the Cosmos-filled sea, Calix and Issaria exchanged confused glances before Calix provided an answer from his seat atop the storm Mythos' head. "I admit it was a strange request at first, having been strangers but after meeting Issaria, I...suppose I began to believe that I was chosen to guide her because I love her. If she was fated to this life, with this curse of being a blood descendant, and I was destined to join her quest to reach this sacred ground, then I surmise I was always fated to love her as well. Can the Cosmos will the hearts of their pawns, or was that at least a choice of our own?"

Calix's banter with the owl-faced sky serpent suddenly felt sharp as a dagger against her heart. Was he insinuating that he'd only fallen for her because it was fated that they do? That...wasn't possible, was it? But what Zephyrus was suggesting as he landed atop Tarlix's empty throne, *that* felt impossible too.

It's sweet that he believes that, don't you think Zephyrus? Issaria started as a feminine voice taunted, echoing across the silence from everywhere and nowhere at once. *But the little princess is already figuring it out, isn't she?*

39

ISSARIA

Zephyrus barked a bolt of lightning at the sky in challenge. *Do not mock their ignorance, Naia. They are not yet whole, and the prince may never be. I know not the confines of his consciousness, only that his power burns bright within him. Now join us for the Yielding, or go await your doom, hunted down and harpooned like a whale for a mere handful of ambergris.*

Only because I value the loss of the decades we have spent waiting, not *because you command me.* The moisture in the air glowed azure blue and pulled through the air like sapphire gems. Threads of water coalesced into a humanoid shape with a long, serpentine tail that bore a fringe of translucent fin like the train of a gown. As she materialized, she moved toward the high-backed throne of carved Aquathyst. A frill of ivory-colored fins encircled her neck like a ruffled collar, and long-tiered fins grew where ears should have been. Luminescent hair like the glittering tentacles of a jellyfish wafted about her in lazy clouds as if she were underwater.

Adorned in waves of translucent water like the many silken layers of a dress, sea foam bubbled around her ankles as she turned to take her seat and her lithe, aquatic form seemed to glitter like she'd been encrusted in gems. Scales shimmered along her skin with a shifting pattern like a jungle cat, and Issaria was forced to acknowledge that the water deity was more fish than human, in the same way, Zephyrus was more beast than man. ***Without Baelfor, we are now gathered. Hurry this along, wouldn't you?***

A crown of coral glistened with pearls from within the cloud of her ribbon-like hair as Naia settled into her high-backed throne with a scaled porpoise tail curled around her ankles. Large eyes as black and knowing as the deepest depths of the ocean emitted a faint blue glow as she peered down the end of her nose at Issaria who stood her ground on the opposite shore.

Naia smirked, feral face pulling into feline cunning. ***You are a clever one, aren't you? You've nearly worked it out, but not quite. You're scared. Afraid to admit what you suspect, afraid of the truth. Again. There's no room for fear here, girl. It will only allow her more control.***

"Issaria? What does she mean by that?" Calix turned nearly backward to see her from his perch behind Zephyrus's antler. "These mythos all speak with twisted tongues," he cursed.

Issaria froze under the glacial gaze of the water Mythos and her warning. Calix being divine did seem impossible as he came from a long line of favored but relatively normal fire magicians. His lineage had never shown signs of being exceptional in anything but conquest, but she'd learned that nothing was impossible when it came to the whims and wishes of the Cosmos. They were working outside the laws that governed magicians and were dealing with the will and impulse of the Mythos, the very children of the Cosmos. If anything were denied them, they simply *reshaped* the universe to attain their desires.

As a child, she'd been afraid, unwilling to ask the truth of what evils her aunt could truly have been capable of and her willful ignorance had kept her prisoner for years.

Issaria refused to be compliant to her fear again. Naia was right. She couldn't risk it, not here when her strength of will mattered most. She steeled her spine and resolved she would not hide from her fate like a lost lamb.

She refused to look at Calix, not afraid of the truth, but afraid she'd lose her nerve if she did, and locked her broken gaze upon the water Mythos, glowing blue with aquatic magic.

"What you insinuate isn't possible. And if it were, she would have told me," Issaria insisted, thinking that if nothing else, Aurelia would have enjoyed needling her for the past few weeks with the knowledge that not even her heart had the freedom to decide its fate. Her mind was a dark spiral of tangled threads, of destinies woven within each other like a huntsman's snare set to catch prey centuries later. "I would have known if he was what you say. I would have…"

Would you though, oh sweet, broken one? I think not, Naia simpered before turning her attention toward Calix as he navigated the coiled length of Zephyrus's body toward the seat of the throne. ***And you. Surely you cannot be so pompous as to believe yourself chosen solely because you wear a crown.***

"You mean to tell me there's more to our alliance?" He grunted as he leaped from one coil of massive Mythos body to another, making his way down to the crystal seat. "I wasn't a pawn of convenience?"

A pawn of convenience? I grow tired of your ignorance, boy. Quickly regain yourself and recall what it is she means to you. What you mean to yourself, Zephyrus echoed as he unspooled himself like a ribbon as Calix slid down Zephyrus' feathered body.

The Mythos swiveled his head to meet Issaria's eye across the Vera Caelum. *Watch as he rises with the strength and fire of the First Flame of Ellorhys.*

Issaria reached out a hand as if she could stop time from across the rift, but all she could do was watch as Calix found his footing on the seat of the massive throne. The moment Calix was clear of the Mythos, Zephyrus was airborne, winging toward his colossal chair.

Alone atop the seat of the solarium monolith, Calix cried out as the throne flared with the light of a thousand suns.

"Calix!" Issaria screamed until her throat was raw. She splashed into the shallows of the Vera Caelum. Starlight sloshed up her boots, staining her pants like molten silver. The viscous liquid sucked at her like quicksand, holding her in place despite her desperation to free Calix from the tangled web of their past.

Caught in the brilliant aura, Calix was incandescent with fire. It burned within him, through him, and because of him. As his golden eyes filled with crimson light that cut his face in terrifying shadows, Issaria imagined her terror for Calix mirrored his fear when he watched Aurelia take over her body. It was terrifying to be forced to do nothing but watch as Calix was ravaged by divine radiance. Issaria knew from firsthand experience that nothing the Mythos influenced remained the same, and that frightened her more than she realized.

"Calix, please! You have to come back to me!" she wrenched her gaze away and leveled an insidious glare at the water Mythos. "Is he truly reborn of the Mythos? All this time?"

Naia's smile grew, revealing thousands of needle-like teeth behind her pleasing human smile, her predatory nature revealed behind deceptive lips. *You already know the truth of him. You only wish to ease the pain by hearing it spoken as fact so you cannot question it. So be it, I inflict upon you this small mercy. Your prince once stood among us as a Mythos. He was the mighty fire elemental summoned from the center of our galaxy for one purpose: to tend and sustain the Covenant.*

She shook her head, disappointed. *But as soon as Tarlix cast his eyes upon the Queen of Starlight, there was no other purpose for him but her. Eons he'd spent toiling to keep the Gemharte ablaze were abandoned in moments. In accordance with her duties, Aurelia had already sworn a union with a nobleman from a powerful family already favored by Tarlix himself. It mattered not. The two entertained a lengthy affair, and after Obsidia destroyed Aurelia, Tarlix cast himself out of his divine body and sought to be reborn again alongside his lover when they had the freedom to choose each other above all others.*

"Is this true, Zephyrus?" Issaria asked, judging the storm Mythos to be a bit callous, but not one to exaggerate or torment.

Coiled around his crystal throne like a constricting snake encircles prey, Zephyrus seemed remiss to confirm. After a long moment, he huffed, clicking his beak in irritation as lighting crackled between his horns. *Naia enjoys instigating, but in this case, her tale is true,* Zephyrus confessed. *We have not seen our Elemental brother since Aurelia fell to Obsidia and Erebus's tyranny. But the Cosmos have shown favor for balance.*

Tarlix's wish was fulfilled, and you have both arrived at the divined moment when Ellorhys needs you most. We're already at a disadvantage with Baelfor's loss, but we three can still imbue you with much of our power.

Issaria felt as though she could barely breathe, caught beneath an avalanche of fate. Tarlix, Mythos of the sun, keeper of the first flame, and guardian of the Covenant, chose a mortal life with Aurelia instead of the immortal obligation of his element. To take such a suicidal leap of faith, Issaria reasoned, Tarlix *must* have known Aurelia had bound her soul to her bloodline, had known she'd return in a mortal vessel.

Aurelia must have confided in him her suspicions of Obsidia's impending betrayal and thus shared the possibilities of bloodline magic. Despite Aurelia's famed relationship with the mortal king of fire, Issaria was inclined to believe Aurelia was more entwined with the flame Mythos than history alluded to.

Across the Vera Caelum, Calix gasped as his body was surrendered to him. Still aglow like a sword still lucent from the forge, his gaze settled on Issaria with the weight of knowledge smoldering behind familiar golden eyes.

40

ISSARIA

I ssaria was trapped in the intensity of his stare.

Maybe it was because she knew now, with certainty what he truly was, but she found it a wonder she didn't recognize the intensity of his mana for what it was immediately upon meeting him. Aurelia may not have shared knowledge of Calix's soul resonating with her secret lover with her, but as Issaria felt the aura of raw power that enveloped him in his own gravitational orbit, drawing her eye like a moth to flame, it *did* feel familiar.

It wasn't as vast as Aurelia's power, unending and influential as the Cosmos themselves, but Calix's aura had always commanded *much* more than the average magician's maximum exertion, and the prince was essentially projecting a neutral baseline as he stood atop the solarium throne, expression caught between pity and betrayal.

"Issaria, it doesn't change anything for me," he said. "His memories of her are not the same as my love for you. This isn't the same as being him, there *is* distinction. You know that better than anyone. You're not Aurelia anymore than I am Tarlix. Just because I recall *his* previous life does not mean that we are the same." His distress was well disguised, but she could see it in the embers of his gaze, even across the Vera Caelum. "This doesn't have to change anything."

294

But is that true, little princess? Naia taunted, teasing unwanted fears from the recesses of her mind. ***Can you ever really know for sure which of them is influencing his heart?*** She challenged.

Zephyrus roiled his body around from where he'd settled on his throne and snapped his beak at the water Mythos beside him. *Cease your incessant manipulations, Naia. Your games are wearisome even for me. Leave them be. This is of no matter to us as long as the little star drinks.* He swiveled his focus back to Issaria and added with insistence, *Soon. Time does not pass the same here as it does in the mortal realm.*

Issaria tried to ignore the banter of the Mythos, but Naia's words churned in her stomach like a stormy sea. Focusing on this when she had bigger woes at hand was foolish. She had to make a choice.

But she'd never been free to choose.

"It changes things for me," Issaria admitted, guilt coloring her words with regret. "I'm sorry, Calix, but it's true. I *am* Aurelia. You've known she and I were the same since the moment we met. If you were fated to love me, it was only because fate saw fit to reveal my true self to you before you were even aware of the significance. Even if you were not aware, Tarlix's soul resides in you. He recognized his beloved within me long before you even knew Aurelia was of importance beyond being who she was. He very well could have sweetened your disposition toward me enough to stay your hand and save me instead of killing me."

"Issaria, that's absurd. I wouldn't have killed you because —"

"Because you promised Aurelia you'd befriend me. Ally with me and protect me. You said so yourself. Consider that she did so in self-preservation, knowing that if she appealed to Tarlix, to *you*, that I would be spared."

"What are you insinuating?"

"Only that I must free you from this endless subjugation to a destiny we did not have a chance to choose for ourselves. If you are not Tarlix, then you will honor your promise to me and find a way to bring me back. And if you are…"

"Issaria, whatever you're thinking, don't," Calix pleaded. "What you're offering, that's not even a choice. Of course, I'm going to bring you back. I swore I'd defy the Cosmos if they tried to take you from me. I meant every word, Issaria."

"It is, actually. A choice. You say there's distinction between Aurelia and me, but there isn't. Not anymore, and certainly not after I drink this," she said, gesturing widely to the roiling rift of stars between them. "She's always been inside me, watching and waiting, and speaking of vengeance and balance restored. If there is a distinction between you and Tarlix, I do not know the depths of it. If Tarlix rules your heart, then I am surely lost as Tarlix will relish having his lover back in his embrace, and won't mind I've been cast off like a shadow in the sunlight."

"No! There has to be another way."

Cosmos above, *she* didn't want to do this. Hearing him plead against fate was a torture cultivated specifically for her soft heart.

But there was no other way. This was how the Cosmos worked, and unlike her divine ancestors, Issaria was the first truly mortal one of them all. She did not make and remake the laws of the Cosmos, she only bent to their will.

She simply had no choice. Not when it came to this moment. This was the path the Cosmos had laid out for her.

Just like Calix had never had a choice when it came to loving her. The reality of their relationship soured her soul more than she wanted it to. Calix didn't love her by choice. It was some... cosmic imperative that warped his brain as soon as they encountered each other. The thought sent her reeling like a planet off-axis.

Breaking her focus away from Calix's fiery gaze, Issaria turned to Zephyrus, the only Mythos she felt she could trust after Naia's clear intent be as vexing as possible, and asked, sounding much braver than she felt, "What must I do?"

Zephyrus' turquoise gaze held hers in question before he dipped his owl-faced head in acquiescence. "First you will drink, and then, when your mortal body has been fortified by the Cosmos, we remaining three will yield our power to you."

We three... Issaria considered his words as she considered Baelfor's broken throne. It looked a ruinous state compared the the gleaming, reflective surfaces of the other three. "And what of Baelfor? What of the Terran magic?"

Baelfor is lost to us now.

"And there's no… reviving him?" she asked, her focus flickering between Zephyrus and Calix.

No. He is no more, may his soul find peace in the Cosmos. An equally devastating loss, his magic has been eradicated alongside him.

"Is that what's happening down there?" Calix asked, gesturing beneath the thrones, balanced impossibly in the center of the sky to the expanse of Ellorhys below them. "Is that why the people have lost the Terran magic?"

Solemnly, Zephyrus nodded, his turquoise eyes hooded with grief. *What is freely given remains pure, tethered to the primal source, and flowing ever free. What is taken by force is forsaken, lost to all, and hoarded by one.*

Issaria looked to Naia, who'd been indifferent on the matter since her mental ministrations.

Are you finished wasting time now, little princess? The water Mythos simpered, looking equally bored and pleased with herself.

"Yes, all right. I am ready as I'll ever be."

"Issaria!" Calix called, grappling for a moment before there were no more. "I meant every word. I will tear the Cosmos apart if they try to keep you from me. Not her, Issaria. You." His yellow eyes were focused, intent on imparting his last vow to her.

Holding his fiery gaze, she lifted her chin and commanded, "If I lose myself, you bring me back," before tearing her concentration away from him and toward the sea of stars staining her boots.

"Remember that you're dangerous, Issa," Calix growled from where he stood upon the edge of the solarium throne, resigned to her choice. "Don't just let her win."

Issaria would not look at Calix as she knelt in the shallows and dipped cupped hands into the Vera Caelum, pooling silver starlight in her palms. She gave herself a moment to examine the liquid, unable to fathom how stars had been trapped within her grasp like rain.

It felt like holding nothing and everything in the well of her hands. She couldn't imagine such a small amount of liquid to hold weight but her hands trembled as she fought to hold the silver aether. Metallic in appearance, it rolled around her hands and spilled back into the Vera Caelum with the consistency of warm honey.

Issaria knew she was on a precipice. She knew drinking this would allow Aurelia the strength to stabilize herself within Issaria's form. But what did that mean for Issaria herself? Was she just going to… evaporate? Would she be trapped in that dark place she'd seen when Aurelia commandeered her body in the meadow? Would she be reduced to merely watching a world she was no longer a part of?

And ultimately, she thought about what would happen if things went horribly wrong. Would she be strong enough to free herself from a true Imperial's power? She felt as though she were slogging against the undertow of destiny, and now she was finally here, facing it down only to find she was unsure she had the reserves for the final battle. And without that conviction, she knew she would fail to stand against Aurelia. There might not be an awakening for her, even if Calix tried to bring her back.

Without allowing that thought to settle on her mind for more than a moment, Issaria tipped her hands toward the sky and opened her mouth to the nectar of the cosmos.

Issaria's eyes began to glow a brilliant, effervescent white as soon as silver passed her lips, but her vision was not of the Vera Caelum, of Calix watching her with fear and worry etched in his features, or of the Mythos observing her with curiosity.

The vision that clouded her eyes was of the peaceful pond deep within her soul. She'd been there so many times before, tempted by the desire to wield mana for herself. The eerie silence that embraced her felt more familiar than sunshine to her moon-bound soul. As it always had in this sacred chamber of her soul, Aurelia's assurances washed over her mind like gentle ocean waves.

Sweet descendia, sleep now. Be at peace and know that when you wake, the balance of our world will be restored, and you shall know the peace of your ancestors.

Aurelia's reflection shimmered to the surface of the pond, one hand held to the fragile barrier between them. She did look a startling amount like Issaria herself. From the cut of her jaw to the pout of her lips, and even the shape and depth of the vivid violet hue of her eyes. Nearly twins in every aspect except for her white hair, it was like looking in a mirror.

That's because I am *you,* Aurelia insisted. *You are me. We are one. You know this truth even if it terrifies you. But you do what you must because that is our burden. So sleep, sweet girl. Sleep and let me handle things from here.*

So weary from their journey, tired of the burden of her lineage, of fates beyond her control, the promise was tempting. Issaria's willpower slipped, only for a moment, but it was enough for Aurelia to take hold. A moment of acceptance, of willingness to surrender, and Issaria tumbled forward into the pond.

The moment she fell through the reflection of Aurelia, Issaria felt as though she were being torn apart by shards of glass. Cold as ice, the splinters that sliced through her left ribbons of blood in her wake, red clouding the pond as she crashed through the barriers between them and sank deeper and deeper into rhapsodic oblivion.

41

CALIX

Issaria's eyes fogged over with radiance and her hands dropped into her lap. She looked almost to be kneeling in prayer or lost in pensive meditation.

"What now?" Calix asked of the other Mythos when her hair had fallen in curtains around her face.

We wait, Zephyrus replied.

"For what, exactly?"

For that, Naia said, lifting a translucent-webbed hand to indicate Issaria. She rose out of the Vera Caelum, body slack as if a thread had been tied to her heart and some Ethereal above were simply pulling her into the sky. Silver dripped from her, falling stars with long tails pulled like taffy behind fat drops of incandescent starlight.

As she ascended through the air, she began to flicker like a spark inside her was struggling to catch fire.

"You have to fight, Issaria!" Calix shouted across the rift to her, one hand extended like he could send forth his fire to help ignite her own. He wasn't sure if she could hear him in her trance, but perhaps she could feel him there, trying to imbue her with his strength.

As if encouraged by his determination to give Issaria his power, cinders began to spiral out of his palm, flowing in a steady stream toward her.

"What's happening?" All his instincts were telling him to pull his hand away, but the river of crimson sparks that poured toward her and vanished into her heart didn't hurt. It didn't even seem as though it weakened him, only that he could feel the pull of magic from him like a magma flow, steady but unrelenting.

You've begun the yielding, Prince. I had assumed I would have had to explain how to imbue her with your mana, but I see you remember how the ritual is performed.

Calix wondered if that was true, if Tarlix within him knew what had to be done and in turn guided Calix's thoughts and deeds toward Tarlix's goals. He'd only wished to lend her his strength, to have her feel his desire for Issaria, the one and only Issaria, to return to herself.

Faster and faster the embers swirled out of his scorched palm. Calix's arm began to tremble as cinders pulled sparks and flame erupted from within him, as he urged more and more fire magic toward Issaria. Like fire stoked in a hearth, Issaria's feeble flicker of flame within her kindled against the heat of Calix's fire. The infusion of power pooled in her body and Issaria began to glow sparkling with opalescent light.

"She needs more!" Calix shouted over the roar of the inferno.

Across the Vera Caelum from him, Naia scooted to the edge of her throne. She held out her hand, palm toward Issaria's floating silhouette, and cerulean water magic bubbled up from her hand like snowflakes coalescing in the air. Sifting toward Issaria, orbs of water merged, a cascading river surged forth from Naia's hand and caught in a vortex that funneled into Issaria like a whirlpool. Naia's power flooded into Issaria, her radiance flared and a glimmer splintered into a dazzling shift of iridescent spears of light.

Beside Naia, Zephyrus had coiled his powerful length atop the seat of his throne and leveled himself with Issaria. Unlike the human and human-like appearance of Calix and Naia, Zephyrus was confined to a beast's body. The storm Mythos closed his eyes and a breath later a projection pulled from his feathered body like strands of spun sugar that glowed with amber light.

A long hooked nose like a beak defined his features. Hidden beneath a long, feathery beard was a narrow, discerning face that shifted with motion like a vague sketch that had never committed to becoming a proper portrait. A spire of antlers protruded from either side of his head, and the vague impression of feathers grew from where human ears would be. The only trait that remained true between the beast Zephyrus and the astral being before them was his piercing turquoise eyes that crackled with spiraling storms.

Formed of the wind and sky, robed in dark storm clouds, Zephyrus lifted one hand toward Issaria. White-hot filament surged out of his extended palm and arced across the sky toward Issaria with a booming clap of thunder. Lighting struck her heart like an arrow and storm magic crackled as it charged into her heart in staggering bolts.

Calix felt the limit of his strength approaching just as his fire began to sputter. Moments later, his fire extinguished itself in a puff of white smoke. Magic spent and duty fulfilled, Calix shook a tremor from his hands as he watched Naia's magic evaporate in a pale shimmer of frost. She leaned back in her throne, gulping breaths like a fish out of water.

Some part of him noted that the water Mythos had overexerted herself in the ritual. Despite her malicious provocations and teasings, she was not as powerful as she alluded to being. Maybe wiser than he was, having retained her infinite wisdom through the ages, but certainly not more powerful. Not when he barely felt a tingle now that he'd had a moment to recuperate.

Sage-like Zephyrus was the last of them to siphon off his magic to Issaria. Power popped and sizzled as storm pressures gave out and the voltage fizzled out of his outstretched palm with a flurry of sparks.

Finished with his astral body, Zephyrus' luminescent form dissipated like a snuffed candle and woke once again in his feathered beast body. Eyes bright and self-regained, Zephyrus gouged his talons into the arm of his throne, drawing deep trenches in the opaque yellow crystal.

Surrounded by an aura of prismatic radiance, Issaria lay suspended like a corpse. Slack arms dangled beneath her, head tipped back. Her hair undulated around her in an inky cloud, and then, as if gravity remembered that her body was mortal, the iridescent spears of light that dazzled the sky winked out. As if time had slowed down, Calix watched in horror as she tipped backward and fell headfirst toward the Vera Caelum.

Calix didn't think.

He *moved.*

Issaria plummeted through the air like a meteor, her clothes incinerating as she plunged toward the nebulous spring of stars.

Focus fixed, he launched himself from Tarlix's throne and splashed down into the shallows of the Vera Caelum.

As if the fall could steal the color from Issaria, the moonless black of her hair stripped away leaving locks of moonbeam white streaming wildly around her as she dropped.

Liquid starlight soaked his boots and pants as he splashed forward, drawing on the dregs of his power to propel himself forward like a firestorm. Too swift for the syrupy consistency of the fountain to bog him down, Calix raced across the Vera Caelum, which he realized was no deeper than mid-thigh, despite containing the vastness of the Cosmos within its borders.

There was no choice when it came to Issaria, but she was wrong. It wasn't because of pasts or fates.

He didn't care if he had the entire Cosmos braided into his skeleton, Calix would *always* choose her.

Not Aurelia, but Issaria. Sweet, stubborn, clever, unexpected Issa.

Despite her speed, Issaria was deceptively light as she landed in Calix's outstretched arms. He clutched her petite body against his chest, grip tight enough to bruise before her momentum seemed to catch up with her and he stumbled on unsteady legs. He sloshed back through the Vera Caelum until he collapsed to his knees in the shallows and cradled her head in his lap. Calix shed his shirt and took care to dress Issaria in it, even though the shirt drowned her in fabric.

Calix's mind raced as he looked down at Issaria, cupping her face as he had when they lay together in the meadow. Even asleep she was radiant, but she no longer looked entirely like herself, and marking the subtle changes made anxiety bloom in his stomach. The shape of her face was still the same, the curve of her cheek and the bow of her lips. But her wild tangle of black curls had gone white as moonbeams and just as straight. The place she had sheared to scalp had grown back as if it had never been. Even her skin had taken on a faint glow like her flesh was paper thin and the starlight inside her could barely contain her light.

"Is she supposed to be out like this?" Calix asked, stealing panicked glances between the remaining two Mythos and the prone woman in his lap. "Can you do anything? Either of you? Please, I'll do anything you ask."

As tempting of an offer as that is, Prince of Fire, Naia replied, her voice heavy with regret, *But the rest is up to the little princess. She's got more spine than I would have thought, but her fear taints her heart.* The water Mythos looked away and sighed. *I thought her an admirable adversary, but if she allows Aurelia to surface, I was mistaken about the mettle of her spirit.*

Zephyrus ruffled his feathers and static sparked along his long body as he turned toward Naia, turquoise eyes narrowed in accusation. *If she falters, it will be because of your instigating, oh turbulent one. You eroded her fortitude with unnecessary doubts the way the sea harries at the shore.*

If that's all it took then she was weaker than I thought. Naia dove off her aquathyst throne, scales shimmering in the sunlight, and seemed to swim through the sky like a porpoise, propelled by her powerful tail. *My tithe is paid, Zephyrus. I've left my beast form adrift for too long. The hearts of magicians are devious in these dark times. I should return to myself least I end up like Baelfor and all my magic is stolen from the realm too.*

She turned over on her back, fins flaring around her like wings, and spared a pointed look at Calix. *That means **her** magic would be claimed as well, and she would be significantly weakened. Take caution, Prince. Should you meet your end, you'll forfeit the power you imbued her with. Freely given and **tethered to the source,*** she echoed Zephyrus' earlier words but put a hard emphasis on the bondage between the elemental blessings.

We should all be more cautious, now that we're being hunted. Baelfor's end was no accident, and if we are not wary, we each could meet the same end. Our enemy is powerful, stronger now that he has learned the taste of Godsblood. He will come for us all.

Always so dark and stormy, Zeph, Naia goaded. The storm Mythos huffed a wind that ruffled her fins and set her jellyfish tendril hair in tangles. ***I'll remain vigilant because I advised caution first, not because you fear the Khaosson.***

You are free to go, Naia. I know how the sky unnerves you.

Without another word or parting glance, Naia dove through the sky and dissolved into a haze of blue glow streaming toward the Norvenello Ocean.

I will remain until she wakes and we know with whom we are dealing with, the storm Mythos announced as he slithered around his throne to have a better view of them. *I feel...As the first of the Mythos, I should have reprimanded Naia sooner. If the little star does not return to you, I fear it will be as much my shame as Naia's.*

Calix did not want to even consider that Issaria would not come back. She was fierce, and strong, and... A heaving sigh echoed up his spine as he bowed over her. He laced his blackened fingers with Issaria's celestial white and pressed the back of her hand to his lips. "Issaria, please," he begged in a hoarse whisper.

"Come back to me, Issa. I promised I would fight for you. But you have to fight for me too, okay? Right now. Right now, you have to want to come back to me," he urged.

Calix tilted her chin up with his thumb and forefinger and pressed a gentle kiss to her lips, sealing his promise to her. "Nothing can keep you from me. I swear I will find a way to bring you back, Issa." He pulled back and tears stung his eyes as he stroked a thumb along the line of her jaw.

Abruptly, she sucked in a gasping breath, her spine arching to comply with her lungs as she as she gulped for air. Eyes clenched, Issaria shot forward nearly knocking his nose with the crown of her head as she flew upright. The Vera Caelum splattered like silver freckles across her face as she floundered on her hands and knees.

Calix crawled toward her, his tentative hands found hers beneath the surface and he guided her upright out of the viscous sea so they were kneeling face to face. He cupped the left side of her face, beneath her blind eye, and whispered, "It's okay, Issaria. You're okay. You did it, and I am so proud of you." His heart calmed as she pressed her cheek into the palm of his hand, finding comfort in the gesture like always. "And now a fragment of my fire will protect you always."

A soft smile curved her lips, and he almost sighed in relief.

Her violet eyes opened and Calix reeled backward, releasing her like she'd cut him to the bone.

That wasn't Issaria.

After a moment of wide eyes admiring the sky, peering curiously at her hands, and fingering the silky ribbons of white hair that cascaded around her bare shoulders, she met Calix's concerned gaze and said, *"Finally."*

EPILOGUE

AURELIA

The first thing she noticed when she opened her eyes was the colors.

How vivid and radiant the world was. Vibrant, ever-shifting sky, never the same moment to moment, let alone day to day. Stars sewn like gemstones across velvet dark sky. Night kept like a hush and darkness that gave way to a gilded sunrise. Each day would be marked by languid swaths of blue, fat white clouds pierced through with spears of yellow sunlight.

It was what she loved so dearly about this world that they had created, why she had wanted to be a part of it and not just another being with all the power to reshape and manipulate with a whim.

Each moment was a singular masterpiece, unique unto itself, like every soul within the realm.

And now the sky, part of their beautiful creation, had shattered into itself. Divided across day and night, fixed in time and space. Unbalanced and so wrong it made her sick to behold it.

So much had changed from that moment, eons ago, to the moment she opened Issaria's eyes and saw her broken, beautiful world. But her awe and wonder at the creation that was Ellorhys remained constant. It was truly a masterpiece of creation.

"Finally," she said and was surprised enough to hear Issaria's voice speak her thoughts aloud—wait.

Not Issaria's voice. *Her* voice.

Her *own* voice. She did not speak with the soft words of the meek and mild princess, but with the regal command of one who knows the universe is subservient to her will.

The second thing she took note of, was the anxious face wavering in and out of focus before her. Concern marred his striking features, creased his brow, and darkened golden eyes at her awakening. Despite being the vessel bound to Tarlix's power and having recovered his memories of his past life as well, the prince was disappointed.

"You're not needed here, Aurelia," he whispered, rage edging his tone with darkness and a promise of violence. "Give Issaria back."

"I don't think I will," she replied. She raked appreciative eyes over his sculpted core and muscled arms and a wicked smile curved her lips. Closing the distance between them, she crawled through the silver. He jerked back and her grin turned wolfish, knowing exactly how to tip his fiery spirit over the edge. She so *loved* seeing his control fray.

She couldn't wait to see it snap. "In fact, I think I mean to keep this form for quite some time. Issaria is sleeping deeply, and grateful for the chance to do so."

"You're lying," he accused in a hiss.

"You only wish I were. She was *so* tired, you know. Exhausted by all the constant pressures thrust upon her, the decisions made for her, the unending loss of it all. It only took a moment, but some part of her said *yes*." She held his gaze, imparting the sad truth of her words to him.

"To allow me through, she would have had to accept my proposal to take her place, " she confessed. "The magic is binding through blood and time, true. But despite what my *descendia* believes, it was a choice to surrender to me. That was something I discovered when I traded for her eye. She must accept me. She had to have been willing, if only for a moment."

The prince's face fell, and his disdain melted into panic. "She's there though, watching, right?" He asked, ire lost in the desperate tone of his voice. "Issaria said the last time you switched with her that she could see and hear me."

She shrugged, uninterested in where her *sanguinem descendia* had gone off to. "This is not like, last time." She cupped her hands, still sparkling and stained to the elbow with the residue of cosmic power, into the Vera Caelum and drew out a small puddle of stars. As she spoke, she let the silver drip through her fingers and back into the spring. "Issaria drank the Cosmos. You Mythos have given me access to your powers. I am whole again in every aspect except that this body, the flesh and blood of it, is hers."

Aurelia could taste mortality on her tongue. Sour with a hint of metal, like blood and citrus. This body was certainly not hers. It decayed. Crept closer and closer to Zephyrus' sweet oblivion with every breath she drew. From the scar on her collarbone to the magic staining her skin like starlight, this body was Issaria's. It may have been fortified by the Vera Caelum to withstand all the primordial magic an Imperial could hope to wield, but this body was still capable of expiring, and the thought unsettled the born-again Mythos more than she wanted to admit.

"But now her body is mine," Aurelia declared as she pushed herself to her feet and began walking toward the edge of the Vera Caelum. As she traced her hands along the curves of her new form, star-stained hands caught on the dark fabric of Calix's borrowed shirt and pulled wrinkles taut around her body until the prince's eye was caught on the hem of his shirt. She smirked, recognizing the heaviness of desire in a man's gaze. "And there's nothing you can do about it, though from the look of it, a little more time spent in my company and you won't be so quick to want me gone."

Guilty and caught, his yellow eyes flashed back to hers as his face flushed. "You may look like her, but it is her heart that I cherish above all else. You will *never* be Issaria."

Zephyrus snapped his beak at Aurelia, cutting off her retort as his antlers were wreathed in bands of angry lightning. *It is as I feared, Prince. Your little star has been eclipsed.* He hung his heavy head in regret as electricity churned down the storm Mythos' body in golden waves.

"Is what she claims true? Is there nothing I can do?" Calix asked, his head snapping to the sky-beast as if he'd forgotten he lingered.

I do not know if that is true. The old language was vague on the parameters of the Saros Curse, only specifying that it took eighteen years to take hold once a viable descendia *was born.* The storm Mythos launched himself off of his throne and spiraled his body about until he was near the edge of the Vera Caelum.

But I do know with certainty that eclipses do not last forever. Even this false Evernight shall come to an end. He gestured with his antlers in the direction of the Timeline before he swiveled his keen turquoise eyes in Aurelia's direction. *But so too shall you, Aurelia, I think. You were always too brash for your own good, and your shortsightedness where Cosmic power is concerned is what got us into this mess in the first place. I can see time tempered inside a mortal vessel has not alleviated you of your impatience.*

"Zephyrus," Aurelia pouted. "Have I fallen out of favor all because the girl did not wake?"

They'd never been adversaries before, but Aurelia could scent the storm brewing in the air and felt a heady drop in air pressure that commanded her fragile body to run. But she never *could* walk away from a true challenge. Lifting one hand to her left side, where she had traded her vessel's sight for a window to the world, she stared down the storm Mythos. "I could tell you had taken a liking to her, my *descendia,* so I can't help but feel a little jilted. I thought you would be glad of my return like Baelfor was. We are *old* friends, after all."

Zephyrus clicked his beak sharply and a low growl rumbled in his throat. As if in response to his ire, menacing spirals of dark clouds began to bloom in the air around him, summoned by his dour mood. *We may be of the Cosmos, but we are not friends. I warned you that your blood magic was an abomination to the Cosmos,* he rebuked and lightning cracked off of his horns and into the thunderheads roiling around him.

Aurelia refused to acknowledge what the silver reaper had to say about her being corporeal, incarnate again. She'd not escaped him. She'd only delayed her crossing. Irritated herself, she turned away from the beast, dismissing him with her back as she started for the distant edge of the celestial rift in the sky.

Zephyrus turned back to the prince. *Do not lose hope, Calix. Tarlix did not use the same curse on himself as Aurelia used to bind herself to her bloodline. Tarlix did not have a bloodline, only magicians he had blessed with his fire magic, so you are correct when you feel that it is different. He was exact where the Saros Curse was not. May that thought bring you some measure of peace.* He cast sad eyes toward Aurelia who was nearly at the edge of the pool. *I hope you are able to recover your Issaria. May we meet again, in this life or the next.* Zephyrus tore away as if he could not bear to stay. He churned through the sky until he was lost within his gathering storm.

Across the Vera Caelum, she felt Calix's yellow eyes pivot to her, his irritation palatable in the space between them. "What are you doing?"

"Walking," Aurelia replied without changing course. She left ripples in her wake, silver crescents that orbited her like the icy rings of distant planets. "We should probably get accustomed to it without Zephyrus to ferry us."

She reached the edge of the breach in the sky and peered over the side. It was a long way down, and there was nothing but red sand for some distance. A thin line of blue highlighted the coast near the horizon, catching sunlight like the blade of a sword, and beyond that, the crimson stain of twilight heralded the Timeline.

This body would not be infinite the way she had been in the past. She thought of the rest mortals required, of the sustenance needed to traverse the continent. It would be wise to find civilization again, if only for the convenience of her body's needs.

She wondered if she would be able to wield her newfound mana as she had in her past life. Once it would have been simple for her to make short work of this journey by opening a Wanderer's Mirror, but Aurelia thought better of using her magic for the first time on portal magic when the slightest misstep could have disastrous results that left her spliced in half.

She might be impulsive, but she wasn't stupid, though it irked her to think that Zephyrus' words had any effect on her. Aurelia decided she would test the limits of her power later, for now, she would take it slow, which was a very practical and well-conceived decision, she noted despite herself.

"Aurelia." Calix was behind her, still rooted to the spot where he'd last hoped for her *descendia* to awaken instead of her. "Where are you going?"

As if whisking herself across the continent wasn't problematic when it was just her, she also had the baleful prince to consider. Aurelia doubted he would let her out of his sight. Not when his precious Issaria was asleep in her heart of hearts.

"Where are you taking her?" Calix asked, finally sloshing through the Vera Caelum after her.

Over her shoulder, Aurelia quirked a devious grin at the forlorn prince as he neared. "I'm going home. Aren't you coming with me?"

THANK YOU FOR READING!

IF YOU ENJOYED SON OF SHATTERED SOULS,
PLEASE CONSIDER LEAVING A REVIEW
ON GOODREADS & AMAZON

✦ ✳ ✦

CROWN OF SHATTERED STARS
BOOK THREE OF THE SHATTERED TRILOGY
COMING SOON

ACKNOWLEDGMENTS

Immediately and above all else, I want to thank my readers for sticking with me. It's been a long journey since *Daughter of Shattered Skies* was published in 2021, and knowing that you're here with me now means the world. All the messages, comments, and DMs kept me moving toward the completion of SoSS when I thought the world might swallow me whole. I owe a great deal of motivation to the many kind souls who continued to ask me for more. From the bottom of my heart, thank you for simply being a reader. Just by sharing my stories with you, my dreams are coming true, and that's magic in and of itself to me.

To my father, who always encouraged me to follow my dreams. In addition to teaching me my most valuable skill, reading, you taught me to fall with my hands out. These last few years were some of the roughest, and there were times when I felt like I was falling at warp speed. But thanks to you and your endless love and support, when I finally hit bottom, I was able to get back up again. Thank you for always being in my corner, for listening to me talk even when you have no idea what I'm talking about, and for being my Dad. I love you!

Laura, my bestie from what feels like the dawn of time, thank you for inspiring me to stay creative through the years. You've been with me through it all, from elementary school to the existential dread of adulthood that envelops us today. And still, our friendship remains true. Without you by my side all these years, I would have turned into a very different person. I can't imagine not having those sleepover weekends where we marathoned entire anime series, brawled in Tekken tournaments, and spent WAY too much time on the internet.

Today, when I want to chat through the first spark of a story, you're the person I turn to. You always understand exactly what elements I'm pulling from, and your contributions to Ellorhys abound throughout the narrative. So thank you…to your mom for keeping the pantry open all these years—LOL. Just kidding ;) Thank you for being my best friend through the years, and for keeping me grounded…or at the very least tethered to Earth when my head was in the clouds.

To my booksta-fam, the internet acquaintances turned intrinsic part of my existence, I would not be in this position, able to pen the Acknowledgements of my second book, without all your consistent and *persistent* encouragement. Amber, Charlee, Kat, Mariya, and Marie-Lynn. From the moment I mentioned that I "dabbled in writing," you've all been so supportive of my goal to publish. From sharing and recommending, to being excited about my snails-pace progress, you've all kept the hype going and ensured I stayed excited about my work. But more than that, over the years you've all become irreplaceable friends. It's funny that one can find their tribe on an app, but connecting with all of you has made me understand the "found family" trope more than ever. I love you all and I'm so blessed to have you in my world, even digitally.

Reese, I know you're reading that last paragraph and internally screaming, "But what about me?! Am I not an internet-friend-turned-permanent-fixture?!" I hope you can hear me cackling through space and time. You are the real MVP, hype-woman, and all-around BEST non-official bookish assistant ever. So I thought you deserved your own thank you. I cannot even begin to fathom where I would be (besides lying on the floor staring at the ceiling) without you. The countless texts, the hundreds of miles traveled, the deep-dive brainstorms, and we can't forget the death-defying adventures! Thank you for being the other half of my brain, and for being your beautiful self. You've easily become one of my best friends and it is insane that the iNtErNeT brought us together! Cheers to 4 years of us, and to forever more! I cannot wait to have you on my squad for Imaginarium again!

Lexie, my talented cover artist without whom I would be completely lost, I am forever grateful for the time and effort you've put into creating these one-of-a-kind covers for the Shattered Trilogy. You're truly a visionary, and the way you bring my scatterbrained ideas to life in such stunning arrangements is mind-blowing. Your vision for this cover blew my mind and I am SO glad you went off-script. Cover Queen earns her crown time and time again! Thank you so much for everything, and I'll see you again for Book 3! (And maybe another project in between, but you didn't hear that from me!)

And finally, I want to extend a heartfelt thank you to everyone who helped spread the word of The Shattered Trilogy. To my brand new street team, InkDrinkers, you've now been exposed to the insanity that is my brain, and I consider you my prisoners to torture first and foremost before bringing my particular brand of chaos to the world beyond. I cannot thank you enough for being excited about my stories. I look forward to many years together!

It truly feels surreal to wake up every day and know that while I go to my mundane office job, I'm also living this amazing moonlit life as an indie author. I wouldn't be able to do this without each and every reader who has picked up DoSS and/or SoSS, so my final thank you is again to my readers. You made my dreams come true!

See you again for Book 3: Crown of Shattered Stars!

ABOUT THE AUTHOR

Sara DeLaVergne is an independent fantasy author with an MFA in creative writing from Western Colorado University, and a BFA from Franklin Pierce University. She has been passionate about storytelling from a young age, and attributes her visual writing style to spawn from a youth spent consuming manga and anime, playing and replaying RPGs for the "perfect" ending, and endless summer days reading any book she could get her hands on.

When she is not writing Sara enjoys playing video games, collecting and creating custom book-themed Funko Pops, and sniffing book-inspired candles in a totally non-addictive kind of way. She lives in New Hampshire with her adorable dog, Hammy.

Daughter of Shattered Skies, the first installment of The Shattered Trilogy, was released in 2021, and was praised as an unexpected favorite among fantasy readers.

You can learn more about Sara and The Shattered Trilogy by following on Instagram, TikTok, and by visiting silverquillsara-books.com

www.ingramcontent.com/pod-product-compliance
Lightning Source LLC
Chambersburg PA
CBHW022017310726

48972CB00006B/1698